The Agency
Dysfunctional Bloodline

by

Lynn Y. Moon

Bloomington, IN authorHOUSE® Milton Keynes, UK

AuthorHouse™
1663 Liberty Drive, Suite 200
Bloomington, IN 47403
www.authorhouse.com
Phone: 1-800-839-8640

AuthorHouse™ *UK Ltd.*
500 Avebury Boulevard
Central Milton Keynes, MK9 2BE
www.authorhouse.co.uk
Phone: 08001974150

© 2007 Lynn Y. Moon. All rights reserved.

No part of this book may be reproduced, stored in a retrieval system, or transmitted by any means without the written permission of the author.

First published by AuthorHouse 4/9/2007

ISBN: 978-1-4343-0274-8 (sc)
ISBN: 978-1-4343-0275-5 (hc)

Library of Congress Control Number: 200790257

Printed in the United States of America
Bloomington, Indiana

This book is printed on acid-free paper.

*This book is dedicated to my second cousin,
Linda Catherine Terry, who was dedicated to finding the
missing pieces of our family's heritage.
Linda... you will forever be greatly missed.*

Part 1

Professor Damara Van Brunt was discussing the correlation between inflation and unemployment to her first year economic students when the cell phone sang loudly from her belt. The melody of *YMCA* echoed off the classroom walls, which amused the students and brought smiles to their faces, for this time, it would be the professor who was in trouble for not turning off her cell phone during class time, not one of them. Annoyed more at herself than at the caller, Damara glanced down to see who it could possibly be.

Probably a student who couldn't make a lecture today, she thought to herself.

Never before had she left her cell phone on during a class; it just wasn't like her. Now frustrated and embarrassed, she grinned a half-smile at her students, but Damara's heart skipped a beat when she noticed the familiar area code... *406*, but the number itself she did not recognize. The caller, however, could only be either her mother or younger brother, but they would never call during class time, not unless it was a true emergency.

"Excuse me while I take this call," she said, pushing the send button and walking out into the hallway. As the door closed behind her, she spoke softly, "Professor Van Brunt."

"Damara?" A deep voice echoed from the small phone. "Damara!"

"Parker? What's wrong?" As her anxiety rose, Damara's stomach tightened and her thoughts flashed instantly to her mother.

"Damara..." Parker cried again. "Mom... Mom..."

"Mom what?" Damara demanded louder this time. Her students heard her shouts and immediately stopped joking about her call. Now they were concerned for their favorite teacher and fidgeted nervously in their seats not knowing what they should do.

"Damara..." Parker, her younger brother sputtered out between tears. "It's mom, sis. She's...she's..."

"She's what, Parker?" Damara was about to cry herself, but needed to hold herself together. Her mind raced wildly with horrible crazy thoughts.

"Mom's... I had to call an ambulance. Mom's in the hospital. Mom's... Mom's..."

"Mom's what?" Damara hollered again.

"She's hurt really badly... blood was everywhere... what do I do, Damara? What do I do?"

"Blood? Parker, get a hold of yourself." In order to get a straight answer from her hysterical brother, Damara asked as calmly as she could, "What happened? What do you mean by blood?"

"I don't know," he sobbed. "I found her... at home... on the floor." Parker was grief-stricken, his crying now uncontrollable.

"Parker, where are you?" she asked.

He cleared his throat and tried to speak without crying. "I'm at the hospital. I'm on a payphone... I forgot my cell."

"Hold on a minute, Parker. Don't hang up," Damara ordered her frightened brother, as she entered her classroom. Every eye was focused upon her; every face had a saddened expression. Damara felt warm sympathy emanating from each of her students and so she smiled.

"What is it, Professor?" A young female undergraduate asked from the front row.

"I'm sorry. It's a family emergency. I need to cancel class," she announced through tear-soaked eyes. With her voice cracking, she spoke slowly. "I'll e-mail you and let you know about the rest of this week. I'm sorry."

No problem... Don't worry about us... Don't be sorry echoed from her students as they gathered their belongings. Each student patted her shoulder gently or gave her a yearning smile as they left. Damara nodded or smiled back, but spoke no words. With the last of her students gone, she closed the door to focus her attention on her panic-stricken brother.

"Parker. Now, slowly tell me what happened," she said with her heart racing and fear ripping through her inner spirit.

The Agency

"As I said, sis, I came home and found her... on the floor... in her bathroom. I couldn't wake her." He started to cry again and it was difficult for him to get the words out. "Blood was everywhere!" Now he was screaming uncontrollably.

She wanted to reach out her strength and love to her younger brother, but they were so far apart - she in North Carolina, he in Montana.

"I'll come home right away, Parker. I'll get a flight out tonight," Damara stated, as she tried to think of what could possibly have happened to their mother.

Damara had just returned from a visit to their home in Montana where the three of them celebrated their mother's fortieth birthday on August 22, which was exactly one month earlier. This would be the new schedule since Damara accepted the position of professor at Duke University in North Carolina a year ago. Damara glanced up at the calendar on the wall confirming that it was now the fourth week of September.

"Wait, sis, here comes the doctor. Maybe there's finally some good news," her brother said, as he held the phone to his chest.

Damara could hear the doctor's voice but couldn't make out what he was saying. His words were muffled, but she knew immediately it wasn't good when she heard her brother's shrieks of agony.

"Oh, my God... No!" he screamed repeatedly. "No, no, no!"

Damara didn't need to hear anymore. She didn't need anyone to tell her that her mother had just passed away. The sounds of her brother's screams from the other end of the line were confirmation enough. Tears filled her eyes, but with the pungent adrenaline running rapid through her veins, she was unable to cry. Her heart was pounding and her stomach was in knots, but there were no cries of agony to be released. Only small tears rolled slowly down her cheeks. Damara had to go home. She had to get home to her little brother in Montana as soon as possible.

* * * * *

The flight was expensive, twice the normal fare, but Damara felt lucky just to find an adjunct professor to take her classes under such short notice. At least her students would be taken care of... *If nothing else,* Damara thought to herself. She loved teaching; it was all she knew. Her mother had been a professor of economics at the University of Montana. Damara loved that old school that had been around since 1893 and in her life for as long as she could remember. Many of the original buildings are still used today, and Damara always made it a special point to walk the old halls whenever she was home for a visit. Now those old walls would have a new meaning, and without her mother, her life would forever be changed.

It was late when the plane taxied from the runway and headed for the terminal. She had made this trip many times before over the last several years. After graduating two years early from the University of Montana with a masters in economics, Damara felt privileged and honored to land a full-time professorship so quickly at Duke University where she could begin work on her doctorate. With monies inherited from her father's legacy, she was able to buy a small house in Durham, North Carolina. It was a four-bedroom on a small but beautifully wooded lot. Working in her yard soon became Damara's favorite hobby. Warm memories filled her heart now as she walked mentally through her house. Remembering... every painting... every creak... every shadow... every sound. How wonderful it was to have her own home, her own job, and her own money. She was finally independent and had started her new life. Everything seemed wonderful - a beautiful house, wonderful students, and weeks off during the summer to visit her family in Montana, but as Montana invaded her thoughts, the pain of losing her mother returned. Only darker images filled her mind and heart now.

Damara faded into her sad dreams as she slowly retrieved her luggage from the conveyer, still not wanting to believe where she was or why. During the short taxi ride to the house, tears burned her eyes. A harsh painful reality hit her as she stood in the yard on West Alderson Street. Everything looked normal and calm, just as it should be. Even her lazy old black cat sat on the porch rail anticipating her return. The lights were on in the living room, and the crickets sang to one another in the wet grass. Damara took in a deep breath and walked up the few steps to the front porch. The sounds of her footfalls on the worn wood gave her heart the longing to hug her mother. Tears welled in her eyes as she realized that gone were the warm hugs and long talks of encouragement.

The Agency

The door creaked as it swung open. Housie, her black cat, rubbed his body against her legs and meowed. Stepping across that threshold now would only mean defeat, and she would have to accept her mother's death. Damara's legs wouldn't move. The cat continued to weave between her legs and meow. After another deep breath, Damara found the courage to enter the house. The intricately carved wooden panels greeted her with the wonderful aroma that all old wood possessed. Her feet moved slowly across the Victorian rugs that her mother had adored, and she dropped her suitcase along the wall. Housie followed her into the living room where the old furniture sat exactly as it had for the last twenty years. All was quiet except for the ticking of the old grandfather clock and Housie's cries for attention. Damara reached down and picked up her huge cat. She hugged him, petted his head as he purred loudly, and closed his eyes.

"Are you hungry, ol' Housie? Did you miss your momma?" Damara asked, no longer having the strength to hold back the tears.

As she cried, Damara filled Housie's bowl in the kitchen with fresh dried cat food. Parker entered the bright yellow room with a heavily sunken face.

"Hey," he murmured.

"Hey," Damara replied, wiping her nose with the back of her hand.

They hugged each other and then they cried together, for they were all alone now. There were only the two of them left. They couldn't really remember their father; he had died when Damara was about five and Parker only one. Although Damara remembered little things, like being held in a strong grip or hugging a tall leg, Parker, of course, had no memory at all. There were no other family members that they were aware of. Their mother had told them from the start that their grandparents had died many years before they were born, and both she and their father were their parents' only children. That meant no aunts or uncles and no hidden cousins.

* * * * *

The sound of the doorbell woke Damara from her disturbed sleep. She glanced around her bedroom and the pain immediately returned.

She just couldn't accept that her mother was gone forever. After all, wasn't a mother supposed to last a lifetime? Her lifetime!

Knowing that it did no good just lying in bed, Damara was reaching for her robe when she heard Parker hollering for her from downstairs.

"Coming!" she yelled back, sliding on her puffy white slippers.

As she descended the stairs, Damara could hear voices, but it wasn't until she was standing under the rounded wooden frame that bordered the stair's entrance that she realized a policeman was standing in the middle of their living room.

"Parker?" Damara asked. "What is it now?"

"Hi, Damara," the uniformed police officer said in a low and somber voice.

It wasn't until after he spoke that Damara recognized him. It was Ted, their long-time neighbor from next door. Damara had gone to school with Ted, all the way until she entered college. Every day they had caught the bus together, come rain or come shine. A warm memory flooded back to when they were very young and she had fallen from one of his trees. Ted carried her home, panicking, just knowing she was dead. Damara had broken her arm, but otherwise was just fine. That fleeting moment sealed their friendship forever, but today Ted didn't look like Ted. He looked older, much older.

"Ted?" Damara asked slowly, knowing she probably wouldn't want to hear whatever it was he was about to say. "What are you doing here?"

With his heart breaking, Ted only stared into Damara's eyes.

"It's strange," she said sarcastically. "But when a loved one dies, everyone feels it necessary to apologize, as though they had something to do with it." The stairs creaked as Damara took the steps slowly, as though walking into her own demise. "Flowers and cards never take away the pain... they only bring an agonizing realization to an otherwise horrible situation that people would rather forget."

Ted looked as though he wanted to be anywhere but here. His eyes were wide and his face pale. "Damara, I'm sorry to come over like this," he started slowly, which only meant to Damara that what he had to say wasn't good. "Can we sit?"

Damara hesitated for a brief moment, but then added, "Sure, why not? I'll make us some coffee."

"No, Damara," Ted demanded, "come here and sit with me. You, too, Parker."

Now Damara was sure it was bad news and tears once again rolled from her cheeks. He took their hands into his and stared into his lap. After several long deep breaths, Ted spoke.

"I just came from downtown," he said, as he took in another deep breath, "...from the morgue."

"And?" Damara asked between tears and sniffles.

"The coroner signed the death certificate this morning..." Ted paused, but before continuing, he stared directly into Damara's eyes. "Your mother... she was murdered, Damara. It wasn't a natural death."

Damara could not believe what she was hearing. Who would want to kill her mother? Everyone loved her mother, everyone! This was something Damara never would have believed she would have to face. Bozeman was a small peaceful college town. The only problems ever experienced were drunken college students who tried to bungee jump off the Spring Creek Bridge. The bridge wasn't very high, and therefore broken bones were common at the local hospital, but murder... in Bozeman?

"What?" Parker asked, almost in a daze.

Damara stood and headed for the kitchen. "I need some coffee... you want some, Ted?" Damara wondered how hard it would be to simply lie down and die. It would surely be easier than accepting what Ted was trying to tell her. "Ted... I still don't know how my mother died. I got in so late last night that Parker and I only had a few minutes together before I retired for the night."

Ted humbly followed her into the kitchen as Parker fell quietly into his private thoughts on the couch.

"I can only tell you what I know, Damara, and it isn't very much," Ted said, leaning against the kitchen door.

"There isn't much to tell?" Parker hollered from the couch. "I found her unconscious in her bathroom!"

Ted dreaded being the person to have to tell them exactly how their mother had died. They should be hearing this from a medical person, not him, but at the moment, he was all they had.

"At first, the doctors thought she had hemorrhaged," he began. "There was a great deal of blood loss and the hospital couldn't control the bleeding. Your mother bled to death in the emergency room. I'm so sorry, Damara. She never regained consciousness."

"Don't be sorry, Ted. You didn't do anything... but murder?" Damara watched as the coffee dripped into the empty pot. She didn't want to look at Ted; she just wanted everything to go back to the way it was supposed to be. The dripping of the water mimicked the emptiness Damara was feeling.

I should be lecturing in my class right now, Damara thought to herself. *This just can't be happening.*

"Damara, you really should talk to the coroner yourself, she has all the facts." Ted's heart was breaking now. He loved Damara's mother and would miss her terribly. She was the only person who ever really understood him. After Damara left to teach at Duke University, he would sit on the porch swing and talk with Nadia for hours. He loved Damara, but never had the guts to tell her how he felt, so he would tell her mother instead. Nadia, being the wonderful person she was, would simply smile and try to reassure him that one day, if they were really meant to be together, they would find their way to each other. Now Ted's heart was trying to reach out to Damara, but his mind didn't have the courage to approach her and tell her he was there for her.

"Would you drive me?" Damara cried, trying to pour a cup of coffee with shaking hands.

This was more than he could stand. Ted reached out and pulled her in close. Damara grabbed on tightly and cried into his chest. The aroma of her hair gave him a warm wonderful sensation as he pressed his cheek against her head. Ted both cradled and hugged her. It felt incredible having her in his tight embrace.

"I'm here for you, Damara, I'll help you get through this," he whispered.

"I need you right now, Ted," Damara cried.

"I know, my old friend... I know."

Damara cried in Ted's arms as he waited. He had all the patience in the world when it came to Damara. She didn't need to be rushed, not now, and her mother would wait patiently for her arrival.

* * * * *

Damara insisted that Parker remain home while Ted drove her downtown to talk with the coroner. It was only a short trip, but she didn't have the strength or the courage to go alone, and Parker had been through enough already. She knew that Father Hurley was planning on coming by the house early so Parker wouldn't be alone for long anyway. This was something she had to get over with as quickly as possible - this was something she had to do by herself.

Sitting in Ted's police car brought back fond memories of college. Before she was allowed to have her own vehicle, Damara had to prove to her mother that she was serious about her studies. Therefore, for her freshman year, Ted would escort her to and from in order to prevent her any embarrassment of having to ride with her mother. Ted had been lucky, he was hired onto the police force directly after high school graduation; and it probably didn't hurt having a father who was the chief of police either. Although Damara and Ted never officially dated, they were still very good friends. Lots of quality time was spent at movies, skiing, or white water rafting. There was one special day they went ballooning together. Damara just knew that the balloon would deflate and they would come crashing down. He laughed at her throughout the entire short trip, and she'd claim later that she'd never forgive him.

Damara glanced over at Ted and realized for the first time that he was actually quite handsome; dark brown hair, clean-shaven, and the darkest brown eyes she had ever seen. He was tall and well built. Damara wondered why she had never noticed that before. Ted glanced back at her and smiled, which made her look quickly out the passenger's window.

"You'll be just fine, Damara Louise Van Brunt. You are a strong and wise woman."

As the words reached Damara's ears, her mind agreed, but her heart was protesting. How would she be fine without her mother there to back her up? Impossible... simply impossible for her to continue without her mother. It wasn't until Ted opened her car door that she realized they had parked. Now was the time for Damara to confront all her worst fears and accept her mother's death. How? Her mother was so young... only forty years old; it just wasn't the right time.

"Come on, Damara. I'll be by your side the whole time," Ted said, taking her arm as she tried to stand.

Her legs were like rubber and didn't want to hold her weight, and her hands were trembling. Sweat dripped from her as if she had just emerged from a hot shower.

"I can't do this," she cried, looking hopelessly into his eyes.

"Yes, you can, Damara. I know you and you won't be satisfied until you hear it for yourself as to what really happened." Ted held on tightly to Damara's arm as they walked the short distance to the door.

Ted had a pass, which allowed them to bypass the main entrance. With his free hand, he slid his card and the door clicked. It was the loudest unwelcoming sound Damara had ever heard, a sound she knew she would never forget.

The corridor smelled of strong formaldehyde and other unpleasant odors. It made her sick to her stomach just having to come here, but now that awful smell too? The whole situation was just becoming too much for Damara.

"I can't, Ted," she cried out. "I'm going to be sick."

"Here, keep this close to your nose," Ted said, handing her a small bottle.

"Oh. Yuck. What is this... ammonia?" she asked.

"Yeah, good old-fashioned smelling salts, but it'll keep your head and thoughts straight."

Walking down the pristine corridor to discuss her mother's sudden death, Damara just couldn't grasp where she was or what she was doing. It was just a horrible dream and she would wake up at any moment. She kept telling herself that she would wake up and find herself in her own bed, in her own house in Durham, North Carolina, but she wasn't waking up; instead, she was still walking down the silent pristine corridor with Ted at her side. Up ahead, Damara saw the word CORONER across a glass windowed door. The realization of the entire ghastly situation suddenly hit her and her soul caught fire as the heat rippled throughout her body.

Coroner, the last stop before setting off to places unknown for the both of us, Mom, Damara thought to herself. *Make me strong, Mommy... please help me get through this.*

Ted slowly opened the door and motioned for her to go first. It was a huge bright room with many stainless steel tables on wheels. There were a few bodies covered with sheets and Damara wondered if one of them was her mother. The stench was much stronger now and her legs started to give, but Ted held her steady.

"Hang in there, ol' girl," he whispered fondly.

The Agency

Hang in there, ol' girl... that was what he used to say all through her college years. Every time the stress got too much for Damara and she wanted to say to *"hell with it,"* Ted would come to her rescue. It was Ted who supported her during the long hours of studying and missing out on the fun with her friends. *Hang in there, ol' girl...*

"Ms. Van Brunt." A woman in a white lab coat approached cautiously with her hand reaching out in gesture. "I'm Dr. Patricia Worthington. I'm so sorry for your family's loss. Your mother was my professor for all my econ classes. I don't believe I would be here today if it wasn't for her. We all loved and respected her very much."

Damara shook the woman's hand and smiled , although it was forced. She nodded her head slightly and added, "I understand that everyone enjoyed her classes very much."

They stood silently for a few brief moments in remembrance before sitting at a nearby table.

"What exactly can I do for you, Ms. Van Brunt," Patricia asked.

"Please call me Damara..."

"Why yes, thank you, Damara. Just ask me anything. I'll try to answer any questions or concerns you may have."

Damara silently organized her thoughts. She had so many questions, but didn't want to bother anyone with them. One question kept rolling repeatedly in Damara's mind. "Well, there is one thing that's been nagging me since Ted showed up. Why do you believe my mother was murdered?" Damara asked, blinking away the tears.

Patricia reached behind her and grabbed a box of tissues. "Here, you'll need this. Believe me when I say I understand how hard this is for you. I've seen it all. Things I never thought I would ever see, I would find right before my eyes. However, what I have to tell you about your mother chilled me beyond anything I had ever experienced before. It will be very painful to hear, but I believe it's important that you know and fully understand the truth."

Damara was shocked as to how candid the woman was speaking, but also appreciated the openness as well. The last thing Damara wanted now was sympathy from the person who had desecrated her mother's corpse. She only wanted answers – honest and quick.

"Continue," Damara said, trying desperately to hold back her emotions until after they had left the building.

"As you already know, your mother was rushed to the emergency room by ambulance. We understand that your brother had found her unconscious on her bathroom floor. She had lost a great deal of blood, but when the doctors at the hospital examined her, there were no signs of any puncture wounds. It was determined that the bleeding had come from her vagina. The doctors therefore concluded that she had hemorrhaged from her womb... which can be caused by various factors in a woman your mother's age. It wasn't until I was able to fully examine her that I was able to determine the exact cause of death."

Patricia's eyes fell away from Damara before she continued. "When your mother arrived, I thought I would find a cyst, perhaps cancerous, that would explain the large amount of blood. Your mother was young, so a miscarriage also could easily have explained the severe bleeding. However, I was able to rule that one out. What I did find stunned me more than anything I've ever experienced."

The doctor stood to pace the floor. Her voice had suddenly changed – became deeper... more concerned, but her attitude was more professional, more flat and unemotional.

"The hospital didn't take x-rays, Damara, everything happened so fast. Their only concern was to keep her blood pressure up – to keep her alive. She had lost so much blood and was crashing on the table in front of them. When I opened your mother's abdomen..."

"Yes?" Damara nudged.

Now the stern professionalism was gone and a deep caring individual was speaking and choosing her words carefully. "Damara, you mother had been badly beaten... actually... kicked, many times, in the lower abdomen. She had been kicked so violently that at first I had thought that perhaps the severe blows had ruptured her uterus, and therefore she bled to death. There are impressions of the killer's boot on her body." Patricia paused to watch Damara's reaction that now seemed frozen in place. "You see... we have many large blood vessels it that area, and if they should rupture, for any reason... Anyway, that wasn't the case with your mother. Everything was still intact, broken bones and badly bruised of course, but there was no rupture of the uterine wall. I therefore removed her uterus for closer examination and found several puncture wounds at the bottom, a large tear..."

"Bottom? Bottom of what?" Damara asked in horror.

"The bottom of her uterus," Patricia said, her eyes now wide and showing the full force of her deep fear. "A crazy maniac used some kind of a long thin instrument to puncture your mother's uterus! I've never seen any..."

"Wait a minute," Damara declared, interrupting the doctor in mid-sentence. "Someone did what?"

Damara was staring blankly at the floor trying desperately to comprehend what the doctor was saying, for the horror of what was being described was beyond anyone's comprehension. No one individual would ever do anything like that to her mother. She was loved by all her students and highly respected by all the faculty and staff.

The doctor's face was white and now seemed shallower. Her hands were trembling and she kept shaking her head as if to say, *No, this can't be happening.* Using her fingers to push her hair away from her face, Patricia took a deep breath and spoke very slowly. "Some person, or persons, took a sharp thin instrument and perforated your mother's uterus with it. And... not just once, but many times. From what I could tell, there are about thirty to forty puncture wounds."

The room became deathly silent. Ted reached over and took Damara's hand into his. She looked up at him with swollen red eyes. Her lip was quivering and tears fell down her cheeks. The terror in Damara's face sent chills through Ted's body and suddenly the realization of what the doctor had said hit him too. Not only had Damara's mother been murdered, but Professor Van Brunt had been sadistically tortured.

Without looking up, Ted asked his question so softly that the doctor almost didn't hear him. "Did she feel anything?"

"No, absolutely not," Patricia immediately replied.

"How do you know?" Damara shrieked so loudly that Ted jumped back in his seat.

"There's more that I haven't told you." Patricia paused for a few brief seconds, as though structuring her thoughts. "I thought the same thing, Ted. The first thought that ran through my mind was how in the hell was this woman able to withstand the pain? It had to have been unbearable. No one would have remained still for this to happen. So either several people held her down, or... she was drugged."

"Was she?" Damara cried out, now sobbing uncontrollably into her hands.

"Yes. At first, nothing was registering, but I remembered reading an article about date rape drugs that were popular back in the late nineties. They were highly illegal. We don't see as much of them anymore here, mostly you find them in the inner cities." Patricia sighed and grabbed a tissue to wipe her nose. She rubbed her eyes with the palm of her hands then rubbed the back of her neck. After pacing the floor for a couple of seconds, she continued. "After what seemed like forever, I finally found a match. It was flunitrazepam, a benzodiazepine. It's a very potent tranquilizer similar in nature to valium, but many times stronger. The drug produces a sedative effect, amnesia, muscle relaxation, and a slowing of psychomotor responses. Your mother was completely sedated several hours after ingesting it. Physicians in the United States never commonly used the drug, so I couldn't find it in the *Physician's Desk Reference* database. I had to search the listing of illegal drugs before I had a match."

Damara stood and walked across the room and paused near a small table. Her mind was racing and nothing was making any sense. Ingesting it? *Ingesting it? What? How?* Damara turned abruptly toward Ted and glared at him. "Tell me what you found when you got to my mother's house?" she demanded of him. "You never explained what you found."

Ted now looked as though he had done something terribly wrong. He wasn't sure how to answer her questions. What does he tell her, how much *could* he tell her? As Ted glanced over at the doctor, panic rose from within. He honestly didn't know what to say, he wasn't the one who went to the house.

"Damara, I can tell you..." Patricia started, which made Ted sigh with relief. "Part of my duties is to visit the crime scene. Professor Van Brunt let the murderer in, there was no sign of a struggle or forced entry. We did find two mugs in the dish drainer that had been washed and dried, so there was no residue of the drug on the mugs themselves, but I did find small minute traces on the dishtowel, which told me that the killer simply rinsed out the mugs then dried them with the towel. My theory is simple. Someone visited your mother and she served tea and cookies. The package of lemon cookies had been left out on the kitchen counter along with the plate she had served them on. Somehow, the killer was able to distract your mother long enough to put the drug into her drink. Then when she was out…"

Once again, the room became silent. How do you comprehend the brutality of what happened? How do you accept it? The questions were endless and the answers just didn't exist.

"What else are you not telling me?" Damara asked, not sure if she wanted to hear the answer or not.

Patricia took in a deep breath and explained slowly. "When the uterus is punctured or torn, there's a risk to nearby organs such as the bowel and bladder. In extreme cases, other physical complications can occur such as infection. We do not believe your mother died immediately. We believe she must have come to and realized that something was wrong. We're not sure exactly where in the house the procedure was performed, but your mother was found passed out in her bathroom. Excessive bleeding didn't occur immediately. I believe there were several hours between the procedure and your mother's collapse."

"Procedure!" Damara screamed. "How can you call it a procedure?"

"Damara…" Ted said, reaching for her.

"I'd call it more of a slaughter!" Damara cried.

"I agree," Patricia answered. "And I know this is painful, but I feel it's important that you fully understand what happened."

"Why? Why should I *understand?*" Damara was close to losing her mind. Someone had tried to rip her mother's insides out while she was still alive and Damara *had* to understand.

"Because maybe you could help us find the killer. We believe it was someone she knew," Patricia tried to explain.

"So how long after she came to do you think she collapsed?" Ted asked.

"Not long. With the amount of drugs in her system, she was out several hours. Those hours allowed an infection to set in and get into her blood. I found traces of a blood thinner in her system too. I believe that had been injected after she was out. That helps to explain the excessive bleeding a few hours later. In her weakened condition…" Patricia couldn't finish her sentence.

Ted decided to try to add some facts to Patricia's story. "When we interviewed your brother, he said your mother was asleep on the couch when he returned home around six in the afternoon. Not wanting to wake her, Parker went to his room and changed his clothes. He said he left about seven to meet some friends for dinner. He returned home around eleven and she had already gone off to bed or at least she was in her bed. When he checked in on her, she appeared to be sleeping. It wasn't until the next morning that Parker found her in her bathroom on the floor."

"What? Why didn't she go to the hospital?" Damara cried.

Patricia answered, "We're not sure. I've concluded that she must have come to on the couch and was disoriented. The infection was already running ramped throughout her body. She would have felt achy, feverous. I found traces of over the counter Acetaminophen in her system. Maybe she thought she was coming down with something and simply went to bed. It would be a few hours before she felt any cramping."

"Cramping?" Now Damara was near panic. Did this mean her mother was in pain before she died?

Patricia seemed to know where Damara was going with her thoughts so added, "She probably felt some cramping in her abdomen and therefore headed for the bathroom. It was there that hemorrhaging started... we found no blood in her bed. The combination of the infection and the punctures must have weakened her uterus enough so that when she stood, the pressure was more than the organ could handle. It gave way and severe bleeding occurred. If Parker had known, perhaps something could have been done, but there was no way Parker could have known anything was out of place, and I'm sure that's what's bothering him. The emergency room doctor told me that he kept saying *if only he had gotten to her sooner*, but he would have had to have been there in order to get her medical help in time. Trust me, Damara; there was really nothing Parker could have done that would have made any difference. With all the drugs that were in her system at the time, she probably never realized what was happening to her."

Damara was stunned, trying hard to comprehend what she had just heard. Someone had brutalized her mother, but who, why? "Who'd do such a thing?" Damara cried, wiping away her tears.

"That is what we keep asking ourselves," Ted answered. "She never failed anyone. Your mother would go out of her way to help people. We checked the college records; no student ever received anything less than a 'B' from her. They all deserved the grades she gave, it was just the extra time she spent with each student that made the difference."

"Your mother would read to them personally if it helped," Patricia added.

"We don't believe it was a student and there's no sign of forced entry. Whoever it was, she voluntarily opened the door and let them in. Whoever it was also knew the exact time she would be home alone," Ted added with a sad look of apprehension.

Damara thought for a few seconds before responding. "You mean the killer knew when Parker would be out?"

"That's what we believe," Ted answered.

"So... she was being stalked?" Damara cried out with her tears flowing stronger.

Ted didn't want Damara jumping to any wrong conclusions and quickly added, "We're not sure."

Patricia wanted to stop the growing tension and spoke up quickly. "Damara, would you like to say goodbye to your mother?" When there was no reply she added, "Damara, she looks fine, just a little pale."

Damara reluctantly agreed. Patricia unhurriedly led her to a covered gurney in the back of the room. As the doctor slowly pulled the sheet back, Damara grabbed her hands and shook her head *no*.

"Please... let me?" Damara asked. Patricia backed away slowly in respect.

Damara looked down at the covered body. "Oh, Mommy," Damara cried. "What's happened to you?"

Damara's shaking hands slowly reached out and drew back the sheet. Her mother's face was a light whitish-blue and her eyes were shut. Tears dripped from Damara's cheeks and fell gently onto her mother's face.

"Oh, Mommy," Damara whispered. "I love you so."

Ted's eyes reddened as his tears began to fall. He pulled out his handkerchief and wiped his eyes. The only connection he had to Damara had been cut. Why? Why would anyone do this to such a wonderful person?

Damara bent down and gently laid her head on her mother. As a little girl, she had slept many nights lying on her mother's chest, but as she grew older and heavier, only Damara's head would rest on her mother's chest as they slept. Sleep would come quickly as her mother gently stroked her hair. There was such comfort, such love, but now she would never feel her mother's loving touch again. She would not experience the gentle rising and lowering of her chest or the rhythmic beating of her heart. All was still... silent... cold.

"Oh, Mommy," she whispered between tears. "I'll miss you so."

Damara cried for what seemed like forever with her head resting tenderly on her mother's chest, just as if she was a little girl again. Ted stood by patiently waiting – there was no reason to rush. Patricia watched with sadness rippling throughout her body and soul. If it hadn't been for Professor Van Brunt, she knew she would not be where she was today. Now there would be many students who would miss out on a wonderful teacher's ability to bring out their best. Patricia turned away and cried. Ted blew his nose and Damara continued to whisper loving words through her tears to her mother.

* * * * *

Carrie shook her head with absolute cynicism as she darted for her car. *Imbeciles*, she said to herself. *Total idiots!*

"I work with complete imbeciles," she yelled out as loud as she could.

The three men's jaws dropped as they heard her expressions echoing through the bright clear sky. One of them took special exception to her comment and screamed back, "You're no fucking picnic either, Ms. Clarke!"

As she clicked the remote for the car's lock, Carrie flipped them the bird never once giving them the satisfaction of a glance back, but she continued to shake her head in total disbelief.

It's about time this damn case was over, she said to herself.

Carrie had to curb her anger with these three bumbling fools Jeff had stuck her with, and he would definitely hear about it when she got back to Oklahoma. She grabbed her cell phone and clicked the speed dial. As soon as she heard the familiar *hello* from the other end, Carrie yelled into the receiver. "Arrg!" she screamed. "I don't know how you ever did it, Maddie. I'm ready to kill some of these idiots I get stuck with."

"I guess I was lucky. I always worked alone," Maddie sniggered and laughed.

"Yeah, well... I sometimes think it would be easier to bump off these *so-called* partners rather than complete an assignment with them." Carrie was at her wit's end. For months, she had stayed on her assigned tail and at the last moment, her three imbecile partners almost blew their whole case. "I just don't know, Maddie."

"Well, tell Jeff you'd rather work alone from now on. It's just that..." Maddie's words stopped before she said what they both knew she was about to say... *making one's self a whore for their government wasn't always what it's cracked up to be.*

"I know, Mad. Sometimes when I read through those training manuals you wrote, I just can't fathom having some of the assignments you did," Carrie responded quickly.

"I sometimes laugh or cry when I look back on my career. Funny what life does to us and we're not even aware of it until it's all over."

"I know exactly what you mean. I find it hard to believe how much my life has changed over the last year or so. Well, at least The Agency is keeping you busy writing those training manuals under an assumed name. I'm just damn glad I'm heading home now," Carrie sighed.

"Thank God you got through this one safe. I was so worried about you," Maddie added.

"Thanks for caring, I'm glad, too... oh, hold on, I have another call coming in." Carrie switched to the other line and was happily surprised by someone she had not heard from in months. "Maddie, I hate to do this but can I call you back? An old friend is on the other line and I haven't talked to her in so long."

"No problem, Carrie. I'll be here about another hour then Nate and I have to go to the airport to pick up the grandbabies."

"How's the newest little Toby doing?" Carrie laughed.

"Growing like a weed and he looks just like his daddy. I can't wait to see them all. Toby is staying home an extra week, but Marleena and the kids are flying in today. Call me when you get a chance."

"I sure will. Take care and give everyone a hug for me. Bye..." Carrie smiled to herself as she clicked the call over. "Hello... Damara? My stars, I can't believe it's you. How are you? It's been a while, ol' girl."

Damara couldn't hold back the sobs any longer. Simply hearing her old college roommate's voice was all it took. Carrie had been the sister Damara had always wanted, and they bonded the first day they met.

"Damara, is everything all right?" Carrie was about to pull onto the highway, but decided against it. She pulled over to the side of the road, turned off the engine, and sat silently listening to her old friend's cry of agony.

"Damara, slow down, what's happened?" Carrie asked again.

"Carrie, I need you now more than ever. I don't know who else to turn to."

"I'm here, Damara, I'm here." Carrie was almost in tears herself knowing her friend was in such distress.

"I need you, Carrie," Damara wept into the phone. "My mother... my mom..."

"What about your mom?" Now fear was rising in Carrie. Damara's mother had been her mother away from home for three years. She loved Nadia, and to this day, continued to share sporadic e-mails with her. Only rarely would she hear from Damara, or vice-versa. Each was busy with their own hectic schedules and time simply passes all too quickly.

"My mom... she was... she was murdered, Carrie. Murdered!" Damara shrieked out the words still not wanting to believe it to be true.

"My God," was all Carrie could get out. "My God."

"Carrie, I need you now. I can't go through this alone." Damara was almost hysterical.

"I'm on my way." Carrie was crying now, too. She was not only feeling for her old friend's deep loss, but also for her own. They cried together that day... one in Bozeman, Montana, the other in San Francisco, California.

* * * * *

His legs and back ached terribly. The muscles were very sore. He glanced around the small diner just off Interstate 29 and smiled to himself. Another success and he was making good time while on the road too.

"More coffee, sir?" the waitress asked, holding the pot before him.

"Oui," he replied, handing her his cup. "Merci, Madame."

"Canadian?" she asked. "What province? I'd love to go there someday, but I just don't have the time. I'll bet it's just..."

Now he was getting agitated. Who did she think she was anyway, disturbing his peaceful thoughts? Without saying a word, he stared at her and shrugged his shoulders.

"Sorry, I guess you don't know much English," she sighed, filling his cup.

As she walked away, he admired her curvy frame and frisky bounce. Oh, he understood every word she had said. It was just that Americans were so damn interfering, so nosy. They just had to know everything about everyone, otherwise they remained suspicious of what you were doing and why. He glanced at his watch and noted that he should be home in a day or two. He rubbed his right leg and wished he had some aspirin. The pain seemed to be getting worse.

Now all he had to do was find the other one to complete his task. It bothered him dreadfully that he couldn't have accomplished both on the same day. It would only have been befitting since they came in together, that they went out together. But then again, he really didn't expect they would be living in the same state, let alone the same town. If only he could find the other one. He shook his head and knew he had his research cut out for him. Time was running out, and he had to find the other one soon or else it would be too late. The blood is filthy and he had to sanitize it... purify it... completely disinfect it before it strikes again.

He threw a few coins onto the table and wiped his mouth with the paper napkin. As he left, he nodded to the waitress who smiled. Damn, his leg hurt. He limped as he left the diner.

* * * * *

"Dr. Lewis? Carrie is on the line for you, sir." Connie's voice echoed through Jeff's office stirring him from his thoughts. It had been a year since Maddie's retirement, or death as everyone called it. He was reminiscing over an old photo of a young Maddie hugging a little Toby on a sandy beach – somewhere. They looked so happy and content. He missed them both very much, and wondered if he would ever see them again. Toby never did fully forgive him, and Maddie, well... one can't really communicate with a dead person now could they? He shared e-mails with her surname writer, but she was just an employee. No special words could be shared between them. Not anymore.

"Dr. Lewis? Are you there?" Connie's voice echoed again.

"I'm sorry, Connie, yes... I'll take it."

He sat the small frame back on the credenza and turned toward the phone. Carrie was due back in the office later today to debrief him, so why was she calling?

"Carrie, hope everything's all right."

"Jeff... can't go into a lot right now, but it's urgent I have some time off." She was on her cell phone, which meant she wasn't at home.

"How much time exactly?" Jeff asked.

"I'm not sure. It's a family emergency."

"Is it serious? I hope not."

"It's a long story, sir. Once I reach my destination, I'll call and explain everything. I'll also give you a full debriefing about the case at the same time. But... can I ask a big favor?"

"Why, of course, Carrie. What is it?"

With a deep breath, Carrie said, "Would you please not assign me with those idiots ever again? They were awful."

"I know, I heard about everything, Carrie. Another agent you were not aware of gave me the full story. After I hear your side, I'll have a long talk with your ex-partners. They violated just about every regulation The Agency has in place to protect our agents and our agency. Where are you headed to anyway?" Dr. Lewis was concerned. It just wasn't like Carrie to run off like this.

"Montana, it's where I went to college. I'll call you when I arrive."

Carrie sounded stressed.

"Okay, let me know if there is anything we can do to help," Lewis added.

"I will and... thanks, Jeff," Carrie replied.

"Anytime, oh, have you spoken to your old friend lately?" he asked nonchalantly.

"As of a matter of fact... yes. Just a few minutes ago. She's fine and is expecting her family for a short visit." Carrie knew that Lewis missed Maddie greatly. They called her Carrie's old friend just in case someone was listening. She also knew that he had no contact with her or Toby; it was just better that way.

"Good, good. You take care now, Carrie, and we'll talk later." Lewis' voice lowered as his thoughts drifted back to Maddie and Toby.

"Okay, bye."

The line was now silent.

Part 2

As the rental car idled in the driveway on West Alderson Street, Carrie noticed how empty the big old house seemed. Just knowing that Nadia was not there made the place seem colder somehow - just not right. Carrie continued to sit and watch as squirrels busily searched for food for their nests. It was almost October and the air was cool and crisp. The leaves were swirling under the trees as the brisk fall air swarmed wildly through the yard as in protest of the coming winter. The wooden fence that protected the backyard was in need of some fresh paint, and the hanging potted plants had long since dried and died. Fond memories of long warm evenings sitting on the porch swing and talking to Nadia flooded through Carrie's mind. Tears formed in her eyes and she just couldn't bring herself to accept that Nadia was gone forever.

"She was so young," Carrie said through her tears. "Why? Why did she have to die?"

Banging from her car window startled her, but Parker's warm smile from the passenger's window was a welcomed sight. He was yelling for her to unlock the door. As he jumped into the car, Parker couldn't grab hold of Carrie fast enough. He cried in her arms as she tried to reassure him that everything would be all right, but Carrie was asking herself if everything would be fine. Something was bothering her and she wasn't sure exactly what it was...

"Carrie!" Damara yelled from the front porch. "Carrie!"

Carrie and Parker ran up the steps and all three embraced. They all cried together. Cried for their own loss and for each other's loss. Cried for the words of wisdom they would no longer hear. Cried for the love and warmth they would miss. Cried because it felt good to let their emotions out. Cried because there just wasn't anything else to do.

After what seemed like forever, Damara dried her eyes with the back of her hand and stepped back. "Let me get a good look at you," Damara said, staring at Carrie. "I like your hair that way."

"Thanks," Carrie laughed nervously. "It's tailored around my face like I wanted, but still long enough to pull it back when I need to."

They stood silently staring at each other, rubbing each other's arms or caressing each other's faces in their hands. It felt damn good knowing they were together again.

"Well, let's not stand out here in the cold like a bunch of dummies. Parker, can you grab her luggage, please?" Damara asked.

"Sure," Parker answered, taking Carrie's keys from her hand.

As they entered the huge old house, Carrie exclaimed, "Wow, the house hasn't changed at all."

"Mom never did like change, ya know," Damara replied.

"Mom..." Carrie whispered. "I'm really going to miss her."

"I know, we all will. You know that she loved you as a daughter, Carrie," Damara added.

"And I loved her as a mother." Carrie smiled back.

"I fixed us some lunch. We're probably not hungry, but we've got to eat," Damara said, heading for the kitchen.

Carrie tossed her jacket on the back of a chair as she did all through college and headed for the dining room; it was the only way into the kitchen aside from the back door. The old house was huge. It was built in the late 1800s and was loaded with delicately carved wooden trim and paneling. Carrie never knew the type of wood that had been used, but it emitted a soothing aroma that one never forgets. It instantly pulled Carrie back many years; to a time that was full of happiness and love. She had spent many years living in this house with Damara and her family. Although they didn't room together as freshmen, they both decided it would save Carrie lots of money to move in with Nadia and Parker. Not only did Nadia enjoy that her daughter remained home, but also enjoyed having Carrie as a houseguest, a second daughter. Carrie soon grew to love Nadia as a mother. She respected her as a teacher, of course, but also developed a deep love for her as her own. Parker, four years younger than Damara, was of course a major pain at that time. He was only sixteen when Carrie met him. He would play all the usual tricks whenever he could, frogs in their toilet, worms in their beds, and harmless spiders in their sock drawers, but he eventually matured which made the last few years at college rather uneventful.

"I can't believe how nothing has changed," Carrie stated again, as she entered the kitchen. "Wow, a new stove?"

"Yeah, the old one finally had to be laid to rest," Damara said, as she sat the tuna fish salad on the table.

"This looks great," Carrie said, taking a seat and a sip of her iced tea at the same time. "It's really great to be home."

Damara looked down at Carrie with a tear rolling down her cheek. "I'm glad you're home, too. You are as much my mother's daughter as I am."

The tears began again as Parker entered puffing from carrying the heavy luggage. "What do you have in those things!" he exclaimed through panting breaths.

The girls laughed as they saw how red in the face he was from struggling with the bulky suitcases, which was a welcomed relief from all the tears. The meal was used for talking about old times and filling up the gaps of their lost friendship. The questions... the whys... could wait. The coroner would tell Carrie everything she needed to know when she visited her tomorrow. Her two surrogate siblings had been through enough pain and torture, they didn't need to be spending their precious time answering questions that they probably didn't have the answers to anyway. Tomorrow would be soon enough for Carrie to begin gathering all the information she would need to start her investigation into Nadia's death.

* * * * *

The day passed quickly and dinner soon came and went too. As the wood blazed in the fireplace and pleasantly warmed the downstairs, Carrie stood contently in her warm pj's and bathrobe in front of the fire.

"That hot bath felt wonderful," she said. "It was just what I needed."

"I'll bet," Damara added, picking up another picture from the box.

"What have you got?" Carrie asked, plopping down next to Damara on the floor.

"They were dropped off right after Mom died. Have no idea who they're from. Oh, her funeral is the day after tomorrow, did I tell you? The funeral home arranged everything. I didn't have to do a thing, which is good."

"That makes things simple," Carrie said, picking up an old picture of some lady. "Wolf! Boy, people were ugly a long time ago. You don't know where these came from?"

"Nope... some of these pictures are wild." Damara laughed. "And, I don't even know who these people are."

"You must have thousands of old photos here," Carrie surmised.

"I've got more boxes over there," Damara pointed out to her.

As Carrie crawled toward the other boxes, she asked, "I thought you didn't have any relatives?"

"I don't. I mean... Mom and Dad... well, they didn't have any brothers or sisters, and their aunts and uncles never had any kids either, so that ruled out cousins for her and for us. I'm afraid that Parker and I are it. We are all that's left of our family," Damara answered, still searching through the box.

"Then who are all these people?"

"I have no idea," Damara said, now interested in a photo of a little girl.

Carrie ripped open a box, none of which was small. The boxes were all the size of a medium storage container. The box that Damara was shuffling through was filled with loose pictures of people that varied in ages and eras. The box in front of Carrie was more organized. There were several smaller boxes inside, each labeled with a specific year. Some of the boxes dated back prior to the 1800s.

"Hmm," Carrie moaned. "More photos, but these are a little more organized, not just piled on top of each other like yours." Carrie started to laugh and smiled as she picked up several pictures. "I see dead people."

Damara had to laugh. "You are sick!"

"Let's see what's in the last box," Carrie said, still giggling. "Sorry, that was kind of crude."

As Carrie ripped off the tape and pulled back the top, she gasped.

"What is it?" Damara asked, crawling over to her.

"There's a large envelope in here with your name on it. It says it's from your mom." Carrie was holding a large manila envelope in her hand staring at Damara.

Damara stopped crawling and glared at Carrie. "You open it," she said quickly.

"It's yours. I shouldn't open it," Carrie replied, shoving the envelope toward Damara.

"I can't. Please, you open it." Damara's eyes were now tearing again.

Carrie held the envelope in her hand and stared at it. She turned it over several times before reading the handwritten words.

To my darling daughter Damara
With all my love and protection
Your mother, Nadia
September 19, 1985

"Damara, this was written on the day you were born. Have you ever seen it before?" Carrie asked.

"No, never," Damara answered with a look of complete surprise. "Open it, hurry!"

"Okay, but what a strange note, *All my love and protection*. What is *protection* supposed to mean?" Carrie ran her finger under the lip of the envelope and dumped the contents onto the floor. They were now looking at a smaller sealed envelope, some pictures, and a five-page document that was stapled in the upper left-hand corner. "Here." Carrie handed the smaller envelope to Damara.

Carrie examined the five-page document while Damara opened the small envelope. After a few seconds, Damara whispered, "Oh, my God."

"What?" Carrie asked.

"This note, it's a warning from my mother."

"A warning? What kind of a warning? Read it out loud, please," Carrie urged.

Damara slowly read the letter to Carrie with trembling hands.

September 19, 1985

My Dearest Little Damara,

If you are reading this right after my 40th birthday, then the curse is real and I am gone. My mother, your grandmother also died on her 40th birthday and it doesn't stop there. For her mother, my grandmother, died on her 40th birthday too. I wanted to warn you about the curse that has threatened our family's eldest daughter for generations in order to hopefully spare you from this awful fate. Be careful, my little one. And most of all, be safe.

I never wanted you to live in fear, so I will not mention this unless it comes to pass then you will receive this small note. Stop the curse, Damara, before it stops you. Your father and I love you very much. Be strong, my little one, for both of us.

And if by chance you have any brothers or sisters, protect them and care for them in my absence.

All my love, Mother

They stared at each other not believing what they had just heard. What was Nadia talking about? What family curse?

"Your family had... *has* a curse? You never told me about any curse!" Carrie whined.

"You? I never knew about a curse! What's the paper you're holding?" Damara asked, trying to look into Carrie's hands. Now she was angry and excited, both emotions running simultaneously throughout her veins.

Carrie smiled; it was as if she sensed Damara's feelings. "I believe it's a handwritten family tree."

"Really? Whose?" Damara asked, stunned. "Parker and I don't have a family."

Carrie sighed. "Well, according to this you do. Let's go to the kitchen table and I'll try to draw it out." Carrie grabbed the small document and the old pictures and headed for the kitchen.

Settled in at the kitchen table, Carrie laid several pieces of blank paper in front of her. She studied the handwritten account of Damara's family and chewed on the end of the pencil for a few moments thinking of how to approach this delicate subject. It had been very painful for both Damara and Parker believing they were the last of their family. Now, she was about to expose a lie that had been their mother's legacy, a deep dark secret that only Nadia could explain, but she was gone, quiet for all eternity and for what purpose the secret has, no one will ever know.

"Okay, let's start with you, Damara. I'll put you down first and then Parker right beneath you. Now, you were born in 1985 and Parker…"

"Nineteen eighty-nine," Damara said with her interest perked.

Carrie glanced back at the stapled sheets then continued. "Now, your mother was Nadia Louise Kundick, and your father was… Thomas Parker Van Brunt. Hmm… Mom born in 1969 and Dad born in 1955. Your dad was a lot older than your mom, I never knew that."

"I never really paid it any attention before. This stuff is interesting, keep going," Damara urged.

"What's interesting?" Parker's voice blared from the kitchen door startling the girls.

"Come see what we found," Damara said, gesturing her brother to join them. "Carrie is doing a family tree for us. See, here is you and here is me." Damara pointed to their names.

"And here is your mom and dad," Carrie added, feeling comfort in knowing that at least their minds were on something else instead of on their recent tragedy and loss.

"Hmm… well, I'm hungry," Parker stated, not really interested in what the girls were doing.

"Make a sandwich," Damara snapped, staring at Carrie's paper. "Eat some cereal or something, I'm busy. Go on, Carrie."

"Fine! I'll just fend for myself, anyone else want anything?" Parker asked.

"No!" the girls barked in unison.

"Now this is interesting…" Carrie said, ignoring Parker and his growling stomach.

"What?" Damara almost screamed.

"You have some half-siblings," Carrie said. "Look, your dad was married once before to a Helen McMillan. Says here she died at the age of twenty-three from complications in childbirth. Therefore, your dad and she had... um... three kids. Haden, born in 1975, Fauna, born in 1977, and Yanka, born in 1979," Carrie said while scribbling it down on the sheet. It was all emerging before Damara's eyes. The tree with little boxes was growing larger as Carrie continued. Since her mother never spoke of any relatives from either side of her family, Damara found it very fascinating.

"Go on, Carrie, go on," Damara urged, sounding like a child.

"I'm going, I'm going," Carrie whined. "Hmm, looks like Helen died in 1979 and he married your mom in 1984, that's about five years later. Oh, here's a little note... it says your mom was his babysitter... if I do the math... wow, your mom was fifteen when they married. Your mom was fifteen and your dad was... twenty-nine. Over fourteen years apart!"

Damara was looking at the pictures and reading the names on the back as Carrie was talking. "Here's their wedding picture. She looks much older than fifteen here, and he doesn't look all that bad for twenty-nine either. Actually, they make a good-looking couple," Damara said, handing the picture to Carrie. "Mom used to tell me all the time how much in love they were, but she never mentioned that he had been married before or that he had other kids. That would make them our half-sisters and brother, Parker!"

"Interesting," Parker mumbled with a huge bite of a peanut butter sandwich in his mouth, and a large glass of milk in his hand.

"Let's go over this way on the tree. I have nothing more on your dad, except that his parents were Thomas David Van Brunt, born... 1931 and Helen Eileen McArther, born... 1933. No death dates," Carrie said, scribbling.

"I wonder if they're still alive," Damara said.

"Possibly. He'd be about seventy-eight, and your grandmother would be about seventy-six. That's not all that old these days. They could be alive," Carrie added.

"Grandparents! But Mom said all our grandparents were dead," Parker interjected, almost choking on his food.

"Well, don't fall off your seats, wait until I tell you this one," Carrie exclaimed.

Damara and Parker stared at each other silently. Their family history was a complete mystery to them. For some unknown reason, their mother never discussed their heritage. As far as they were aware, they were all that was left.

"On your mom's side, her dad is... oops, was... Peter Kundick, born 1945 and died in 1982, three years before you were born, Damara," Carrie calculated.

Damara shook her head. "I never knew that!"

Carrie continued. "Your mom's mom was Maria Lee LeBoisne, born 1949 and died in 1989."

"Her fortieth birthday," Damara whispered with saddened eyes.

"So?" Parker asked.

Carrie ignored them and continued to explain. "Your mom, Nadia Louise, was born September 22, 1969 at 10:45 A.M. but... it goes on to say that her sister, Nidra Louise, was born September 22, 1969 at 10:53 A.M." Carrie grinned. "Twins! Your mom was... is a twin!"

Both Parker and Damara's jaws almost hit the table at the same time. Their expression shocked Carrie into complete silence. All sat speechless staring at each other. Tears pooled in Damara's eyes. As she blinked, each tear rolled slowly down her cheek. Parker placed his sandwich back on the plate and took a large gulp of milk. He wiped his mouth then his forehead with his napkin and closed his eyes.

"You didn't know your mother was a twin, did you," Carrie said softly.

"No, we didn't," Damara replied in almost a whisper. "What else is on that paper?"

"Oh... um," Carrie continued, but her stomach was now feeling queasy. It never occurred to her that they would know absolutely nothing about their family's heritage. "It just says that your mom's grandparents were Byron and Bella LeBoisne, and that they both died in 1973. Nothing else except that they lived in Falcon Lake, Manitoba, Canada."

"Canada?" Damara asked, as she rose from the table.

"Where are you going?" Parker asked.

Damara didn't answer, but left the kitchen muttering the word *Canada* repeatedly.

"I think she just lost it," Parker exclaimed.

"Shock," Carrie said, staring after Damara. She turned her attention to Parker. "I can't believe neither of you knew anything about this. That alone is amazing."

"Our mother always told us that we were all that's left of our family from both sides. We never thought she would have a reason to lie to us." Parker's face deepened as he spoke.

Damara returned with a large book in her hands. It was an Atlas of the world. She had creased the pages of Canada searching for Falcon Lake.

"Here it is," she said, pointing to a spot on the map.

All three studied the large picture of the world map. Falcon Lake was just above Minnesota.

"About a two- to three-day drive," Carrie surmised, studying the map. "We could easily make it in two days if we hurried."

Damara glanced up at Carrie with a worried expression. "Are you suggesting that we drive to Falcon Lake?"

"How else do you expect to get there?" Carrie asked, still studying the map.

"No, I mean why go there?" Damara added, still in shock.

Carrie chuckled. "How else do you expect to uncover anything? There is obviously a reason why your mother never mentioned your family to you. And... we now know that she was murdered. With the note she left in your box, there must be some connection."

"What note?" Parker asked with a puzzled look.

"This one." Damara reached across the table and pulled the note in close to her heart. She passed it to Parker who read the message then frowned.

"What the hell is this supposed to mean?" he demanded with an angry gaze.

"That's what we'd like to know," Carrie replied to him.

"I don't know if I want to go to Canada," Damara said to no one in particular. She turned and stared out the kitchen window. The leaves were falling and the squirrels and birds had already retreated to their nests for the coming winter months that would soon be upon them, but Damara already felt helplessly submerged in a cold and hostile environment that frightened her beyond comprehension.

"I don't think you have a choice," Carrie surmised. "Obviously your mother knew she was next. And after her... *you*. I'm sure this warning was to get you moving. Not hiding."

"But Canada! What does Canada have to do with this?" Parker asked with the girls ignoring him as usual.

Tears fell from Damara's eyes. Her heart ached and her mind was asking more questions than she had answers. Aside from Carrie, she had no one to turn to... to ask questions to...

"Let's sleep on it. We don't have to decide right now," Carrie suggested to her two dear sibling-friends. "How about I take you out to dinner tomorrow? My treat. We'll run away from everyone and everything!"

"Fine with me," Parker agreed, tossing their mother's note on the table, believing once again that his two sisters had totally lost it; and that was only *if* they ever had it to begin with. "Well, if you leave for Canada in the next few days, would you mind going shopping first? I don't want to starve while you're gone." Parker was serious, but the girls just laughed.

Damara grabbed the note and again pressed it close to her heart. She looked directly at Carrie and said, "I'm afraid."

Carrie smiled and nodded her head before speaking. "Me too! However, I won't let anything happen to you or Parker. I'll do everything I can to figure this out." Carrie then shrugged her shoulders. "I'm going to bed; I suggest you do the same, Damara."

The stairs creaked as Carrie headed to her familiar and comforting room. Damara and Parker stood silently in the kitchen absorbed in their own private thoughts. Damara was thinking about her mother and Parker was now wondering about a father he never knew.

Parker was the first to break the silence. "So, do you want to tell me what this is all about?"

* * * * *

They would have preferred that the funeral remained low-key, but the turnout of mourners was overwhelming. Many more people came to pay their last respects than anyone could have imagined. Almost every student Nadia had ever taught was now standing in the cool September breeze with tears in their eyes. Without a cloud in sight, the priest finished his reading of the Rite of Committal and then led the mourners in a silent prayer. A lone violinist softly played Nadia's favorite song, *Will You Walk With Me, Jesus*. Many eyes were fixed on Parker and Damara while others were either closed or staring blankly at the darkened soil. Damara couldn't cry anymore, her feelings were now numb and her tears had long since dried up. Parker's eyes were swollen, red, and wet; Carrie continuously wiped her nose with her handkerchief. The three held hands and stared at the casket with vacant eyes. The flowers that were sent by the university and mourners were absolutely beautiful. There were so many flowers, in fact too many. Instead of a fall day, the area resembled a cool spring day when the flowers first bloom. The air had a wonderful floral aroma that filled the senses with a feeling of newness, an awaking, an arrival. The recently fallen leaves from the nearby trees danced to the tune of the violinist as the wind darted through the foliage as in remembrance of Nadia.

As the last few notes were played, the priest looked toward the heavens and spoke softly. "Amen."

Each mourner sundered solemnly toward Damara, Carrie, and Parker, each giving their condolences as they nodded with a frown or a forced smile. It had been a long week and everyone was ready for it to be over, and to start remembering Nadia in his or her own way. When the last of the attendees paid their respects to the family, Carrie was surprised as she looked deeply into the face of Maddie Edwards.

"I can honestly say I know how you are feeling. I couldn't let you go through this alone," Maddie said with a small grin.

Carrie wrapped her arms around Maddie and cried into her shoulder. Parker and Damara didn't know this woman, but realized that she was there to support Carrie. After a long embrace, Maddie slowly pulled away from Carrie, kissed her cheek softly, then left quietly with the other grievers. They all stood silently watching as Maddie approached a taxi then waved goodbye. Carrie had been so stunned that it was impossible for her to have spoken any words, for Carrie understood the danger Maddie had put herself in just to be there for her.

Parker whispered that perhaps they should return to the solitude of their home, which instantly pulled Carrie from her thoughts.

"What about the gathering in the church? People will be looking for us," Damara added.

"Tough, isn't it," Parker said. "It wasn't their mother that died!"

Carrie was grateful that neither of them asked her any questions about Maddie. They all agreed that going straight home would be best for each of them. First, Carrie wanted to say her goodbyes to Nadia alone. Damara fully understood. She already had her opportunity to be alone with her mother back at the coroner's office.

Damara affectionately kissed the top of the casket and said, "I will miss you so, Mommy. Sleep in peace."

Carrie and Parker wiped their eyes and watched as Nadia's daughter said her final words to her mother. Parker, as any man would, only touched the casket lightly and grinned. He nodded his head accepting his mother's death as a part of life.

Damara and Parker headed toward the car, as Carrie spoke softly to Nadia. "I will miss you terribly and I do promise to protect Damara and Parker. I will get to the bottom of this, Nadia, I promise." Carrie kissed the casket and rested her head near the flowers.

The wind swept through her hair and the sound of rustling leaves felt soothing. As she closed her eyes to remember Nadia as she was many years ago, a strong cold wind suddenly swirled around Carrie that almost made her lose her balance. She jerked upright and looked around, half-expecting to see Nadia standing right before her eyes, but no one seemed to have noticed the sudden drop in temperature, except Carrie. The flowers had fallen from the casket to the green carpet below. Carrie knew she could not have imagined it. As she carefully replaced the flowers back on the casket, Carrie addressed her surrogate mother one last time.

"Are you trying to tell me something, Nadia?" she asked softly, almost at a whisper.

When she didn't hear or *feel* a reply, Carrie hesitated a few more seconds before turning and heading for the car where Damara and Parker waited patiently, but Carrie could not shrug the strong sensation that Nadia was trying to tell her something. Therefore, her short walk to the car was continuously interrupted as she glanced back over her shoulder at the now silent and tranquil gravesite.

* * * * *

Heat was emanating from the floor of the old car, but he was still very cold. Chills ran rapid all through his body. His aching leg was beyond consoling now, and the throbbing pain was almost more than he could deal with. Chills continued to send waves of prickling pain throughout his small fragile frame. From his head to his toes, every inch of his skin was on fire. He knew better than to have tried to hop that fence, especially at his age, but he simply had to get a better look. It was critical that he find the right person. Any mistakes would have been devastating. There was no need to take an innocent life; it was the bad blood he was after. Once the bad blood was gone, then the pain he felt every day of his life would also be gone forever. That he was sure of.

The ride up the dirt road to the house took longer than he had expected. Snow had come very early this year. Only a light dusting was on the ground, but still made the drive slow and treacherous. As he made his way through the small mountain town, anger rose from deep within. When his parents first settled here, not much was around, only a few mountain dwellers here and there. Their humble general store was enough to keep their small family and the local community stocked with basic supplies, but when his father died, the small store died too. He had family in another province – yes, but they never really understood him. Besides, they were all strangers to him anyway. The last time he saw them up close and personal was probably over twenty years ago. He hadn't thought of them in a long, long time, and now wondered why they suddenly were so vivid in his mind.

The vacationers or tourists some called them, were arriving in large numbers, and would make traffic ridiculous for weeks upon weeks. It used to be so quiet and peaceful here, but people began buying up the land and building lodges and campgrounds on the once virgin soil. Others found that tourists would buy anything, so they cleaned up the old shops and brought in their own merchandise – homemade quilts, clothes, and other items. Vacationers were now walking the streets peering into the old shops or bragging about their recent finds.

The Agency

They also filled up the local restaurants and diners so that it was almost impossible to get a decent meal without having to wait in long crowded lines. And... this ridiculous pace would continue until January when the real winter set it. Then there would be a few months of tranquil peace and quiet before the spring and summer crowds appeared.

"Imbeciles," he shouted aloud. "Vi rentrer chez soi!"

The old house was only a few more miles. His father had built it years ago for his stepmother, the *new* bride, whom he had hated with a vengeance, but his father adored. The day of her funeral, he danced around her grave in ecstasy after everyone else had left. The ground was pure and would cleanse the blood – do all the work for him. It felt elating, invigorating, and released him from the pain – even if only for a little while. The freedom didn't last long though, for as soon as he returned home and saw *her* face, it all came flooding back.

With a high-pitched squeal, the car braked to a stop in front of the double garage that he had built about fifteen years ago. He sat for a few minutes staring at the small square windows that needed new paint. Cobwebs lined the inside of each frame. Although used only for storage now, the garage added symmetry to the otherwise bleak landscape. When his stepmother was alive, so were the gardens. Roses grew almost as high as the trees, and her flowers were so beautiful that no painting would dare compete.

His childhood had been a good one. Although losing his mother at a very young age, he had been spoiled with all the comforts his father could provide. The house his father built was huge, three stories with an attic and a basement. There were over eight bedrooms on the second floor and another five on the third. Rooms on the first included a modern kitchen for the late forties, library, conservatory, living room, dining room, music room, small bathroom, and a smoking room. Wrap around porches hugged both the first and second floors. Every hallway and door was framed in a circular arch. Rich dark mahogany lined the stairs and entryway. Each room on the first floor was paneled from the center down in intricately hand-carved mahogany sculptures. In today's world, a house such as this would cost a fortune to build, but in 1949, it only cost his father a little more than a hundred and fifty thousand dollars to begin, and then only another twenty thousand to finish his grand spectacle of a house.

Then to top it off, when the house was finally finished in 1951, the crazy fool paid another small fortune to furnish it! The money spent had always amazed him, and to this day, he still could not understand why the fool spent all that money for a house tucked so far into the mountain forest, that unless you, a person, were deliberately looking for it, it would not be found. No... this elaborate display of wealth was constructed only for the benefit of his dear departed stepmother. They had planned to have many children together, but for some strange reason, once his little half-sister was born, his stepmother never conceived another child, so the many rooms that awaited the pitter-patter of little feet remained silent and still. It was only when his half-sister married and brought her husband home with all his kids that the house became too noisy and unbearable. He hated those years when they all lived together, as one supposedly happy family.

After his stepmother's death, his father grieved himself into a grave right next to hers only three short months later. Of course, he only inherited part of the wealth. His half-sister remained in the home in Falcon Lake with her husband until her death sixteen years later. *And we mustn't forget her darling little girls, now should we?* He laughed to himself.

"Damn leg," he said with his deep French accent as he tried to stand. The air was crisp and cold, but it felt good to be home.

The large foliage seemed to have grown even larger since his return. Huge white spruce trees taller than the house swayed in the wind. Several balsam poplars and white birch had long ago overtaken the rest of the yard. Forget about the gardens, they had long since been left to fend for themselves. Various vines finally grew far enough up the side of the huge brick house that they now crept slowly onto the slate roof, as if testing the material for strength or something else.

The front door creaked as usual, and the stained glass rattled in the frame when he shoved the door shut. No reason to lock the doors or windows, no one could ever find the place, and if they did, no one would dare enter. The local ghost stories were enough to keep even the bravest away. The only company he ever received was from the local sheriff to see if he was still alive. It seemed as though everyone was just waiting for his death, too!

The Agency

He glanced around the living room and everything was as he had left it. Limping toward the kitchen, the pain intensified and he had to grab onto the doorframe to steady himself. On the shelf were bottles of pain medication and antibiotics. He grabbed both, a couple bottles of beer from the refrigerator, and headed back for the sofa. With the remote, he found the national news and settled himself down for the night. He plopped a couple of pain pills and several of the antibiotics into his mouth and rinsed them down with the beer.

He glanced around the room and realized that even after everyone had either died or left, all the original pictures remained. Over the huge mahogany mantel of the rock fireplace was the large ostentatious wedding portrait of his dear father and his lovely young bride – the stepmother, his mother. Then there were the smaller black and white or color framed pictures of his darling little sister and her darling little girls that were plastered all over the place. The piano was covered with them. The sight of them suddenly made him completely aware of his surroundings. Then he wondered to himself why he had never thrown the damn things out?

Family, who needs them? he thought to himself, as he nestled deeper into the cushions of the sofa. *Tomorrow, they go.* As he pulled a blanket over him, he realized that all the original furniture remained in the house, too. This was a strange sensation he had never felt before. What was it? Is this what someone felt when they were truly home? As sleep engulfed him, he continued to laugh and amaze himself with his thoughts. Soon, very soon, he had to finish his job. *If only he knew where in the hell she was!*

* * * * *

September had finished out its days and it was now October's turn to run havoc on the land. Stores were already filled with Halloween candy and decorations, and Carrie could not help wondering if this month would be any better than the last. Her mental stress level was higher than ever, and Carrie needed a break from the every day struggles of life, but one thing she did know for sure was that October was definitely going to be a much cooler month than September had been. She now wondered if the clothes she had brought with her would be warm enough.

She glanced around the small attic room and wondered why she was so worried about the stupid weather and her clothing. If all else failed, a nearby store would yield her all necessary apparel she would need for the coming weeks. Over the last several days, she had succeeded in turning the small room in the attic into a semi-war room with many notes, family tree charts, and pictures of Nadia's ancestral history. These small treasures were either clinging to the wall with a small strip of tape, or poked precariously onto an existing nail. The stark empty walls were, without a doubt, not empty any longer.

A recent picture of Nadia that had been taped to the wall stared blankly into Carrie's eyes. The eyes ejected an evil foreboding that sliced through Carrie's heart and ran riotously throughout her body, finally ending in uncontrollable trembling hands.

The voice of Patricia Worthington, the coroner, rang vividly in her mind. *It's the most hideous case I've ever had the un-pleasure to investigate. Agent Clarke... Nadia had been brutally attacked... while sedated for Christ's sake! What kind of wild maniac... why? For what purpose?*

Carrie took a few steps back and tried to shake Patricia's voice from her thoughts. Suddenly the walls of the attic blasted her many years into the past when she was working with Thomas, Maddie's son. She could see his face clearly as her tears stung her eyes. The need to reach out to Maddie was stronger than ever. Carrie sat solemnly down at her computer and stared into the blank screen. How does one start such an e-mail? With her mind racing wildly through feelings of isolation and dread, Carrie placed her fingers on the keyboard and sighed. Her brain just wouldn't cooperate with her fingers. Dear Mad was all she could type. Dear Mad...

The jingle of *YMCA* echoed from her phone and startled her. Instead of grabbing the phone, it flew across the room from her hand landing squarely on its side.

"Damn!" Carrie screeched, jumping from the chair to chase the phone that was now twirling wilding.

"Hello?" Carrie panted into the phone.

"Hi, sweetheart. How's everything and where are you... exactly." It was Devon Arvol and it was wonderful hearing his rough deep voice. His call could not have come at a better time.

"Devon! Are you finished yet?" Carrie quickly asked, holding back the tears. "Are you home?"

"Just got off the plane, sweetheart. I'm on my way home now. I guess I really lucked out; we finished early. Now where are you?" he asked again.

"Oh, sorry. I'm in Montana and…"

"Montana, what in the name of Sam Hill are you doing in Montana?" he asked, more surprised than angry. For it was impossible for Devon to be angry with Carrie. His love for her was deep and his devotion was everlasting and strong.

Carrie and Devon were to meet at home in Renovo, Pennsylvania after his assignment. Then they were to rendezvous with friends onboard a twenty-foot sailboat for a romantic weekend of sailing around the eastern seaboard.

Carrie had spotted her house during an assignment for The Agency. Since the case was moving slowly, she had some time on her hands and decided to take a drive. When she found Renovo, her heart fell in love. It's a small town on the west side of the Susquehanna River. At the time, Carrie was staying at a town nearby, North Bend, but when she saw the house on Spruce Street, it was instant magic and she had to have it. The house had to be over a hundred years old. The old structure reminded Carrie of a sweet gingerbread house she had seen in a bakery once. It was in bad shape, but she didn't care. *Tender loving care was what it needed,* but when Devon saw it, he was horrified. Dollar signs ran through his mind and he knew it would take thousands to fix it up just to be livable. However, in the end, Devon lost and Carrie won. She would have a house that was the find of a lifetime, and Devon would forever be searching out good plumbers and carpenters for the constant repairs that the house would need.

"It's a long story, sweetie, but I'll try to make it short. Do you remember my surrogate mom I've told you about? Anyway, she's my friend's mom who took care of me while I was in college. Devon… she was murdered!" Carrie squealed.

"Murdered? Carrie, what have you gotten yourself into this time?" Devon asked, now with concern showing in his voice.

Carrie sighed then continued to try to explain. "Well, if you'd let me talk and not interrupt me, maybe I can get a few words out."

"Sorry," Devon quickly added.

"Anyway, I'm here at the house with Damara and Parker." Carrie proceeded to explain as much as she knew as to what had happened and what she was hoping to accomplish for her friends.

It had been several months since Carrie and Devon had been together and Devon was anxious to see her. "Do you want me to come up and help?"

"That would be wonderful, Devon, but I think you'd probably do me more good at The Agency than here. Don't you think?" she stated and asked at the same time.

"Well, like I said, we finished early. The Agency really isn't expecting me back for another two or three weeks. How about I come up and we spend a few days together, then when I get back, I'll do some research for you. What do you think?" Devon was fishing.

Carrie thought for a moment. She wondered if it would bother Damara if her boyfriend suddenly showed up. "Maybe not. It's not that I don't want to see or be with you. I really do miss you, Devon. It's just that I don't know how Damara would take it, with her mother just passing and all."

Devon knew how Carrie was, and sometimes she would put other people's needs before her own... and once Carrie's mind was made up, it was best not to try to change it.

"Okay, sweetheart, I'll wait. Besides Lewis will probably want a full report right away, but if there's anything you need..."

"I know," Carrie said, finishing his sentence for him. "Just call. I love and miss you. Will you call me in a few days?"

"I love and miss you too. And yes, I will call you. Be safe, my love." Devon ended the call and Carrie felt even more lost. She and Devon had been dating seriously for about a year, but with their hectic schedules, the time they shared together had been sparse.

She sighed then remembered the unfinished e-mail to Maddie. It started - *Dear Mad...*

* * * * *

It was late when Damara stood on the top step glancing around at Carrie's handiwork. Her eyes were red and swollen. It was obvious she was having a difficult time accepting that her mother was never coming home again. Carrie stopped what she was doing and smiled at Damara from across the room.

"Wow," Damara said. "You've been busy."

"Yeah... but it appears you've been busy too. Can't stop crying, huh?" It hurt Carrie to see her friend in such pain, but sometimes it was just best to allow a person to mourn in his or her own way. There really wasn't a thing Carrie could say or do that would lessen Damara's agony.

Damara sighed and wiped her eyes with the back of her hand. She smiled briefly then examined the papers Carrie had either taped or hooked to the wall.

"What's all this?" Damara asked.

"It's you... your family," Carrie said, turning to examine her work that was splattered across the walls. "I'm not sure if any of this will help to explain your mother's death, but for right now, it's all we've got to go on. And, it's interesting."

As her eyes ran down the pages, it wasn't until Damara saw her mother's name that she froze in time and place. Carrie realized the intense silence and stood quietly next to her friend.

"Something caught your interest?" Carrie asked.

"Yeah... my mom."

Carrie knew the best way to solve a mystery was to allow people to have space and feel free to talk. Not specifically to Carrie, but to any ear that would be close by. Sometimes, people knew things they didn't realize. Carrie had learned over the years that the only way to get it out of them was to give people time to search through their sleeping past memories. She placed her arm around Damara and rested her head on her dear friend's shoulder.

"It really hurts now," Carrie whispered. "I know, but over time, the pain will diminish. I promise."

"I know, it's just so very hard," Damara added, wiping her nose with the sleeve of her pajamas. "I want my mommy back and I can't have her." Damara was now crying again.

Carrie sighed realizing she had to change the mood that was engulfing them both in longing and despair, before they both lost it. "You are a mess, girlfriend. But I still love you." Carrie gently shoved Damara with her shoulder and Damara playfully pushed back. It didn't take long before they were both laughing and giggling while studying the charts and pictures.

"Want to tell me what all this means?" Damara asked.

"Sure. It all starts over here." Carrie headed to the other side of the attic and pointed to a sheet of paper that had been pushed onto an existing nail that had been in the attic probably since it was built. "I found several things on the Internet about your family, believe it or not. There's a website where people upload information about their family trees and other cool stuff. I subscribed to it for a year; it wasn't too expensive, but let me read to you what I've found so far. Ready?"

"You didn't have to do that!" Damara protested.

Carrie sighed and replied, "I know, but I wanted to. Again, ready?"

"Ready!" Damara declared, plopping down on an old torn couch that had been pushed into a dark and dusty corner. Dust rose all around her and Damara laughed as she waved her hands to clear the air.

"Okay," Carrie sighed, shaking her head at her dear silly friend. "Here goes nothing. I received this little tidbit of information from a Lucy Winchester. She must be some kind of a distant relative to you. Anyway, your common ancestor with Lucy, a person that connects you two by bloodline, is a Byron LeBoisne. I'll explain more about him in a second. When I found Byron's name on Lucy's family tree that was on the web, I immediately sent her an e-mail. She's loaded with your family's history and sent me some great stuff. It seems she's done a lot of research into your family's limb of the tree."

"Why? What would it be to her?" Damara asked.

Carrie sighed. "Duh... common ancestor? Relative? Hello! You two share a family tree, but live on different branches and tracing info about family heritage is a hobby to a lot of people. Some are even obsessed about it. They spend lots of money and time. Any trail available, they jump right onto it. Anyway, she was excited to hear from me because she was stuck and couldn't go much further on that limb and was anxious to hear about what I knew or know." Carrie shook her hair from her eyes and continued. "Anyway, back to this first. And... quit pushing me off the track, will ya?" Carrie winked then spoke softly as Damara bit her lip as in protest. "It seems you two share a grandfather, that is, if you go back far enough. She doesn't know about you or Parker personally because she ended your family's branch with Byron and Belle, your great-great grandparents. Anyway, you're related because Byron is her great-great-great grandfather."

Damara looked lost so Carrie decided it was probably best to just read the information as she had received it and try to explain everything later as Damara asked questions.

"I'll just read what I have, okay? Then if you're still confused, I'll draw a picture."

"Okay," Damara said, sneezing from the dust.

"Sinclair and Shannelle LeBoisne migrated to Canada from France sometime during 1865."

"Who are they?" Damara asked.

"Would you please just let me read the stuff, then ask your questions?" Carrie rolled her eyes and huffed a little before continuing. "Now, as I was saying... Sinclair and Shannelle LeBoisne migrated to Canada from France sometime during 1865. Rumor has it that they may have been either brother and sister or at least first cousins."

"Yuck!" Damara shrieked.

"Damara! Please. Let me read *all* of it first. Where was I? Oh... they had two boys, Mortimer and Sinjon. Sinclair owned a general store and Shannelle was a seamstress. That means she made clothes."

"I know that much," Damara sighed.

"Sorry," Carrie smiled. "Both of their boys were a little off, but it showed more in their children than in themselves. Mortimer grew to become a carriage driver and Sinjon went into farming. Both of their wives died in childbirth and neither remarried. Now this is where it gets very interesting, Damara. See if you can catch the connection. Byron and Bella were first cousins, and were about twenty-eight years apart. When they married..."

"Married!" Damara interrupted, but Carrie ignored her.

"...Mortimer was Byron's father and Sinjon was Bella's father. Bella was sixteen and Byron was forty-four. It created quite a scandal throughout the town of Montgomery, Quebec. Everyone scorned them so Byron and Bella moved to Falcon Lake, Manitoba, Canada." Carrie glanced up at Damara and smirked. "It gets even better."

"Terrific, can't wait. And this is *my* heritage?" Damara stated, not sure if she wanted to dig up the rest of the old bones or not.

"Ready? Bella became pregnant by Byron and when his first wife, Sheila Aaron, found out in January of 1949, she killed herself on their wedding anniversary the following month, February 22, 1949!" Carrie paused to watch for a reaction, but Damara was staring into the darkness as if in a deep thought, so Carrie continued to read. "The only child Byron and Bella took with them was Aaron, Byron's youngest son from his first marriage to Sheila. He would have been a widow now and free to marry whomever he wanted, whenever he wanted. Aaron was seven at that time, but Byron's older children from Sheila didn't want to have anything else to do with him after their mother's suicide. It seems they blamed him for their mother's death, but little Aaron was too young to realize what was going on. Strange that the last child from his first marriage was named Aaron – Sheila's maiden name. Byron's older children remained in Quebec with their maternal grandmother – that would have been Sheila's mom. Byron and Bella created a new life together in Falcon Lake where they eventually opened a general store. They only had one child together, a Maria Lee LeBoisne who was born shortly after they arrived in Falcon Lake."

"Maria LeBoisne. My God, Carrie, she was…"

"Your grandmother, I know," Carrie finished Damara's sentence for her.

As Damara stared into nothing, she asked, "Is there more?"

"Yes, and this is too cool. Since Byron and Bella couldn't legally marry in Quebec because of their family relationship, they supposedly married on the way to Falcon Lake where they were not known by anyone, but nobody can find any record of their marriage. Family rumor has it that they never really married at all. Just pretended they were."

"Wow, too wild. Anymore?" Damara asked urgently. "And what year would that have been?"

"Uh, let me look." Carrie ran through some papers until she found what she wanted. "Nineteen… uh, forty-nine. That was when Sheila killed herself and Bella was about four months pregnant."

"Anything else?"

"Not really, that's where Lucy stops on your side of the family," Carrie explained.

"So, how exactly am I related to this Lucy person?" Damara asked.

"Her grandfather is Lewis John LeBoisne. He's one of Byron's children from his first marriage that remained in Quebec with his grandmother."

"Do you think he's alive?" Damara asked, trying to put it all together.

"He could be... Lucy doesn't have a death date next to his name. There's a good chance he could still be living," Carrie surmised. "He would be your great-uncle."

"This is a lot of information to digest. But what did she mean when she said something about the cousin's marriage showed in their children's children?" Damara asked.

"I e-mailed her back and asked that same question. We must think alike. Scary!" They both giggled. "She replied that Fragile X runs in your family and she traced it back to Byron. Seems she has a daughter that has it. That's what got her interested in her family tree. She wanted to see where it came from. She said that the more research she conducted, the more she was led to believe that both Sinclair and Shannelle had been carriers of Fragile X, and that the gene had skipped their generation. It didn't appear in the two boys, but appeared in Byron and Bella," Carrie stated, as she glanced through a different stack of papers for more information on the subject of Fragile X.

Damara was now horrified. No wonder her mother didn't want to talk about her family. If all of this was true, it was definitely something a person wouldn't go around sharing with other people. "So, what's Fragile X?"

"Here it is," Carrie said, as she began to read from a printout from a website. "I'll read it to you. Fragile X is a hereditary/genetic condition. It includes Fragile X syndrome... FXS, the most common cause of genetically-inherited mental impairment ranging from subtle learning disabilities and normal IQ, to severe cognitive or intellectual challenges such as autism or "autistic-like" behavior. Symptoms include unique physical characteristics, behavioral deficits, delays in speech, um... language development. Fragile X also includes Fragile X-associated tremor ataxia syndrome... FXTAS. A balance, tremor, or memory condition that affects the older male carriers. When I found this information on the Internet, I remembered that Lucy had said in her e-mail that in her research, she concluded that Byron and Bella did have some problems, but they were subtle and it didn't really manifest until later in their lives. Therefore, I e-mailed Lucy back again and asked her why she felt they had this FX thing, and she said that it was noted in the family history that later in life Byron had severe problems with his balance and couldn't walk without assistance. Byron was sixty-eight when he died, so he really wasn't a young man, but not really old either. She also said that Bella had had memory problems since birth and was slow, which she surmised as either a slight mental retardation or autism. On the bright side, they were a good-looking couple, just had some health and mental problems." Carrie tried to add a little flair into this otherwise dismal news.

Carrie handed a couple of pictures to Damara who immediately darted for the lamp. The room was rather dim, and Damara wanted, no needed, to see the faces of her past. As she studied the pictures, her face became void of emotion. It was hard for Carrie to read her mind or determine her thoughts.

"Well?" Carrie asked cautiously and added, "You're actually lucky because someone wrote names and dates on the back of all the pictures that were in the box I went through. So, once we have all the names of your family members, alive or dead, it will be easy to put a face with the name. Some people are not that lucky. Most do not write who's who on the back of photos, which is a real loss because after a few generations, people tend to forget."

Damara sighed and shook her head. "This is really something, isn't it? Damn, first my mom, now I find out I'm the result of inbreeding from my great-great relatives. This Byron dude does sort of look like Parker and I can see some of me in Bella, but interbreeding, twice on the same branch? Wow, this is a lot to digest. Makes me feel a little dirty inside."

"It's not your fault," Carrie interjected. "You weren't there, they were. And believe it or not, incest only increases the risk of birth defects by a few percentage points. You have nothing to worry about. Since Fragile X ran in your family to begin with, the birth of Byron and Bella just gave the disease a higher probability of occurring. I find it interesting that Maria was perfectly normal. She had had a double dose of the bad genes... remember that her grandfathers were also her uncles. I wonder how they explained that one to her. She probably never met them, and they probably never told her the truth about her family's history. Would you? I wouldn't. There are a lot worse genetic abnormalities out there. I'd say your family was quite lucky actually. And, interbreeding does not create monsters."

"Thanks, that really makes me feel better. Let's not tell any of this to Parker just yet, he'd freak."

Carrie laughed. "Yes, he would freak. How about a snack, then we can get a few hours of sleep. Tomorrow, I'll tell you more."

"There's more?" Damara asked nervously, not really sure she wanted to hear anymore.

"Yes, there's a little more, but nothing really terrible. I've already told you the freaky stuff. No more surprises." Carrie smiled as they descended the dark quiet stairs together. They were two old friends heading off to unexplored territories together, bonded by a mutual friendship that swept way beyond the boundaries of normality, but skimmed the edges of an idiosyncrasy that would soon submerge them both and would test the strength of the thread that connected them.

* * * * *

Devon paced the room slapping his fist as he walked. Each of his steps hit the floor with a precise statement of need. He was worried. It wasn't like Carrie to just run off and not tell anyone where she was going or why. Carrie had explained to him when they first started to date about her college days and how she found her surrogate family that she loved so much even to this day, but that wasn't what was on his mind now. No... he wasn't jealous – though it would have been nice to have her here waiting for his return. No... what troubled Devon now was the grisly murder. Why would a college professor be murdered in a small town where she was so loved and cherished?

The newspaper articles about Professor Van Brunt were spread out on the kitchen table that had been downloaded from The Agency's computer yesterday. Any news from around the world was instantly at an agent's fingertips. With just a few keystrokes, any newspaper, from anywhere, could be displayed on his computer screen. Devon had printed every article from the Bozeman Daily Chronicle since the date the professor had been taken to the hospital. He also had the coroner's and police report pulled and printed. There were a few other stories about the professor from former students that had been placed on various private websites that Devon had stumbled across during his searches for the name Professor Van Brunt.

The kitchen table was now the resting spot for the printed material about Van Brunt's life and death. A few colors from the flowered tablecloth were only slightly noticeable through the scattered sheets. As his eyes scanned the pages for any flicker of enlightenment, a small red rose flashed from between the words that instantly threw Devon back into a time where he had objected adamantly to the horrible, ugly tablecloth that Carrie was proudly beaming about purchasing.

"This thing looks like something my grandmother would have bought!" he stated sternly. "It's the ugliest thing I've ever seen. You're not *really* going to use it are you?"

"I know, isn't it wonderful!" Carrie beamed with a huge smile, as she quickly tore open the clear plastic and pulled out the ghastly material. She unfolded the colorful cloth with delicate tender care. Her hands gently rubbed the glittering fabric, which was sprayed randomly with bright red, yellow, and orange roses of various sizes and shapes that tried desperately to jump off the stark white background. Carrie was obsessed and excited with her recently purchased treasure. This was the find of a lifetime, and if wasn't snatched and bought immediately when first discovered, it would have been lost forever.

Devon loved Carrie with all his heart, but she did lean toward the strange and unusual. The home they shared was filled with the strange and unusual. And because of his deep love for this woman, Devon could now accept his strange and unusual life. On normal early mornings, the flowers seemed to mock him, tempting him to grab the cloth and shove it deep into the closest trash bin. He hated the tablecloth more than any other item Carrie had brought into their relationship. He only tolerated the stupid thing because to Carrie, the cloth was a find of the century. Perhaps it reminded her of some cherished moment in her childhood – but with love comes no explanation. This tablecloth would just have to torture him until the colors faded and the threads wore bare from years of tumbling through the wash cycle.

Now it felt like a single red rose was trying to get his attention. It was as if all the other flowers had left and only that one small red rose remained begging him to understand. He wasn't sure what it was, but the color of the rose seemed redder than before. It now resembled the color of blood. Not the healthy blood that pumps through our veins, but the damaged blood that remains behind after a brutal and morbid murder. Why the color was different after an attack, Devon never could figure out. Perhaps it was because the victim had been breathing so heavily while still alive that the blood changed color somehow with all that extra oxygen… or maybe the color changes from the sudden rush of fear hormones. Whatever the reason didn't matter now, what did matter was that Carrie was in serious trouble, and he had to get to her – fast. How he knew she was in trouble, Devon didn't know… osmosis… mind transfer? The knowledge was somehow being transmitted through that dreadful ghastly flower. That stupid hideous tablecloth was trying to reach out to Devon, to get Devon to go help Carrie!

With that sudden revelation, Devon grabbed for his car keys and the papers on the table. He needed answers and the only place they would be was back at The Agency. The Agency that was thousands of miles away.

Thinking back on his conversation with Carrie, Devon wanted to kick himself. Now that he had time to think about it, promising to remain here probably wasn't such a great idea.

Part 3

"What smells so good?" Carrie yawned, as she entered the kitchen.

Damara was setting plates on the kitchen table and smiled as her dear sister-friend entered the room wearing her baggy pink bunny pajamas. "I ran out and grabbed us some breakfast. It's piping hot! There is this great little diner not too far from here. I didn't want to wake you or Parker, so I thought I would surprise you two."

"Where's Parker?"

"Don't worry, once he smells the food, he'll be down." Damara smiled.

Damara was correct; it only took Parker another three minutes to bounce into the kitchen and plop himself at the table. "Good morning!" he declared. "Wow, where are my sunglasses? Carrie you're blinding me."

"Very funny! Everyone is so chirpy today. What's up?" Carrie asked, yawning and stretching.

"Nothing," Damara said. "Maybe it's just the healing process. Going through all the emotions one-by-one."

"Maybe," Parker added. "By the way, where did you sleep last night, Damara?"

Damara's smile left her face as she glanced out the window with folded arms. "In mom's bed."

"Oh," Parker said, filling his plate with food. "I've got an early class this morning. What are you two going to do?" Parker never noticed the subtle change in his sister, but Carrie picked up on it immediately.

"Oh, nothing much," Carrie answered, gently pulling Damara away from the window.

"Um, yeah, nothing much," Damara said, passing the fried potatoes to Carrie.

With a mouthful of food, Parker asked, "Found any good ghosts in our closet, Carrie?"

The girls exchanged a quick glance before Carrie spoke. "A few."

"You'll have to tell me about them later," he said, gulping his orange juice. "I'd love to hear about all the sex and betrayal that is buried deep in our past! I'll bet we're loaded with good stuff."

"Why do you say that?" Damara asked nonchalantly.

"Why else would Mom have hidden us from her relatives?" he answered. "We seem pretty normal, I guess her family wasn't."

The girls exchanged another quick glance then began eating. Throughout the rest of meal, the only sound was the clink of forks on the plates or the muffled thud of cups returning to the table.

* * * * *

"Excuse me, Dr. Lewis. Devon is here to see you, sir," Marsha buzzed into Lewis' office.

Marsha had held her position here at The Agency for almost forty years now. She started right out of high school, and although Marsha was a great employee, she just didn't have the hindsight or intuition that Connie did. Both women were devoted to Dr. Lewis, but when it came to asking for help on puzzles, Lewis always turned to Connie. When it came to detailed work, Lewis turned to Marsha.

"Thank you, Marsha, you can let him in," Lewis answered then rose to greet his visitor.

Jeff and Devon had an unspoken understanding. After meeting over a year ago, Lewis knew that Devon and Carrie would become some of his greatest agents. When they had met, Jeff was still mourning over his loss of Maddie and Toby. Whereas Carrie was a more hyperactive individual who finds joy in everything, Maddie was more reserved and determined, but he now loved both women as his own and felt grateful that Carrie and Maddie remained in contact with each other. Jeff could not count the number of times he wanted to either pick up the phone and call Maddie or suddenly show up at her front door. However, for her own safety, Lewis knew he could never see or speak to her again. As far as anyone knew, Maddie

Edwards was dead. Although Maddie wrote papers for The Agency under an assumed name, all evidence of Maddie's involvement with The Agency had been erased. Therefore, the unspoken understanding between Devon and Jeff would be left alone for now. Jeff blaming himself, and Devon blaming The Agency for failing Maddie after everything she had done for her country.

"Devon," Jeff stated earnestly with his hand outstretched. "It's so good to see you again!"

Devon approached Jeff and grabbed his hand. Lewis immediately pulled, or tried to pull Devon into a hug. Devon was a large man, over six feet tall, weighing in at over two hundred and seventy pounds. He wasn't fat by any means, just big. Devon gave his Native American heritage all the credit for his large stature. His mother was from the Lakota Tribe of the Great Sioux Nation... a pureblood and beautiful. His father, Devon had surmised since he had never met him, was probably a little bit of everything. Just a plain white man, perhaps Irish because of his last name. The strange combination of genes created a man who was - huge... but gentle - intelligent... but wise, and who had an intuition and curiosity that was surpassed by no one except perhaps little Carrie Clarke.

Devon embraced Lewis then stood back to face him head-on. "I'm worried about Carrie."

"You've always jumped straight to the point haven't you, Devon," Lewis said. "Want something to drink?" Lewis asked, heading for the small kitchenette on the far wall of his office behind his desk.

"No thanks," he answered. "I want to find out what is going on and help Carrie. Something doesn't smell right here. I'm worried, sir."

Jeff sighed and took a seat on one of his couches with a drink in hand. "Please sit."

Devon sat down but wasn't happy. He wanted answers - now - fast. "Please, sir..."

"Devon, you know that The Agency will do everything it can to help Carrie. If you would like to make that your next assignment, you're more than welcome to. However, we do need to tie what we do back to the safety of our citizens. That is our mission."

"I understand, sir, but isn't any murder a risk to our citizens?" Devon snapped.

"But that is what the local police are for. Not us. Since you just returned from a long assignment, you do have thirty days of leave coming your way. Why don't you use that time to help Carrie? You'll never know what you'll come up with, and if it turns out to be a serial killer or something, well, then we could probably become involved somehow."

"Thank you, sir," Devon stated. "That was all I wanted to hear."

He rose to leave but Lewis quickly added, "Excellent work on your last assignment, by the way. Very impressive."

"Thank you, sir, but there is no need to praise me for having to kill. That is an aspect of this job I would rather forget, sir."

"I completely understand, Devon. I feel the same way. Sometimes I ponder the whys, but then when I look back on it all, for some strange reason everything seems to make sense. Our country has a powerful government that stands a close watch over its citizens. It is our job to watch over that ruling power... we must remember that a government is just made up of people. People who can become corrupt from either greed or power. People, Devon, are just people and they do make mistakes. It's the mistakes that are made on purpose... now those are the most dangerous; the most devastating."

Devon turned slowly to stare at Lewis. His eyes were filled with an abhorrence Lewis had never seen before. "Excuse me!" he coughed out.

"Devon, let me tell you something personal. I miss Maddie and Toby something terrible. They were a big part of my life. They were not just a part of my job. I loved her as a daughter and Toby as a grandson. I will never see or hear from either of them again. That is because of this place. What happened happened." Lewis then walked toward his large windows to stare into the sunlit sky. "I must admit though, that there have been times during my career that I had second thoughts. And... I still do, but, Devon, if you want to know *why* we do what we do, I have an old case you may want to read over. It started almost ten years ago. Children were being kidnapped in large numbers."

"I remember that, sir. Was probably in the early to mid-nineties right?" Devon added. "Alien abduction or something like that?"

"Something like that, yeah... aliens?" Lewis chuckled and lowered his head. "But the aliens *were* of this world! In time, it doesn't really matter after a while does it? Anyway, with the return of those children, which was one of my first cases here at The Agency, a completely new perspective on this place emerged before my eyes. Although we never saved all the children because a few did perish, we were able to return over five hundred ranging in age from only a few weeks to as old as thirteen."

"I had no idea it was that many, sir!"

Lewis turned to his window and placed his hands on the darkened glass. He leaned his forehead between them in thought. "As I was saying, one little boy we had brought back to this Agency was declared dead five years earlier. For over five years, this little boy went through hell on earth because we had said he had died. Starting at the age of five until we found him at age ten, he was used and tortured by these... aliens, as you call them. He had witnessed things and experienced things that not even Hollywood could imagine. The boy is still here in counseling, his parents at his side the whole time. He's almost twenty now, but in many ways he is still just a child. Better, he's much better mind you." Lewis faced Devon to study his face, but continued to talk. "Danny wants to start college so perhaps life does go on, but his life will be forever tarnished." Tears rolled down Lewis' cheeks. "You see, Devon, if The Agency had not declared the boy dead, we probably would have found him sooner. I wasn't in charge when Danny first disappeared, Greghardt was. I'm not placing blame, don't get me wrong, but I have learned from that case and I'm still learning."

Devon was touched by Lewis' frankness and display of emotion. He took a few steps toward Lewis and said, "And what have you learned, sir?"

"I learned that life is precious, Devon. That memories, good or bad, make us who we are. And if I can ever ensure that no one suffers from the dirty hands of people in our country or government again, then I will die doing so!"

"Are you saying we have corrupt people in our government today, Dr. Lewis?" Devon mused.

"Corrupt is a nice word, Devon. Those with dirty hands do not deserve a title. Only their early death can justify their existence." Jeff raised his head and took in a deep breath.

"That is quite a heavy statement, sir. I do understand where you are coming from. For me, however... it's just hard, sir. After being raised to believe that there is good in everyone, in everything... to have to accept that some people only have bad blood running through their veins is a reality I didn't want to have to accept. I have accepted it, sir. That is why I can do my job. But I don't have to like it." Devon left quietly leaving the door ajar while Dr. Lewis was left to dwell in his good or bad memories... alone.

* * * * *

Damara bounced up the stairs anxious, but dreading to hear what else Carrie could tell her about her family's past. Once over the shock of the incest, she found the information interesting and intriguing. Carrie was right, after all, she wasn't around when all of it was going on, so it wasn't her fault. Nothing to be ashamed of, it simply was. Carrie was busy at the computer when Damara hit the landing.

"Hey." Damara smiled greeting Carrie with a hot cup of coffee.

"Thanks, was just going to go get some myself," Carrie replied.

Damara glanced around the room which now seemed different somehow. After having time to digest all the information last night, Damara wasn't afraid of it anymore and that surprised her. With eyes searching for something, she walked slowly around the attic looking for it.

"What are ya thinking?" Carrie asked, eyes still on the small laptop computer screen.

"Well, my mom was a twin, right?" Damara paused to look into Carrie's eyes, and then said softly, "So where is she?"

"My thoughts exactly," Carrie said quickly. "I've been able to trace her steps only so far though. It seems that the girls left Canada at different times. One went west; the other east." Carrie smiled as her surrogate sister continued to scan through the information that clung to the walls. "I guess your mom liked it here and stayed. I'm not sure how far her sister, your aunt, got before she settled down. I'm also not sure if her sister ever came out this way or not before heading east. We only have one correspondence from her that was dated 1989 and mailed from a small city in Ohio. It simply said that she was fine and not to worry about her. You have to remember that with women, it's very easy to change our names... you know... marriage? I've got someone working on tracking her down right now and I'm hoping to hear something soon."

"So what other surprises do you have for me?" Damara asked bravely.

"Nothing much really. I was able to match some pictures with some names, so I can tell you who's who for most of your relatives. Are you ready to meet your family?" Carrie asked.

* * * * *

"Do we have an address of where they lived or a picture of their home?" Damara asked, shifting through the pictures, amazed that she had never seen any of them before.

"There's this one," Carrie answered, handing her a black and white photo of a huge house. "This one could be it, it says LeBoisne home and is dated 1955. If you look on the porch, that is your grandmother on the tricycle and Bella, her mom, sitting next to her. That may be Byron on the stairs and Aaron on the top porch, but it doesn't say, I'm only speculating because of the other pictures. Only Maria and Bella's names are on the back of this one with the date of 1954."

"Any way to find out for sure?" Damara asked, studying the picture with intense interest.

Carrie shrugged her shoulders and said, "Couple of ways actually. I could send them to my work and have them analyzed, or if we ever find any of your relatives, perhaps they could tell us more."

Damara continued to study the picture. "They must have had money. That house is huge." She placed the magnifying glass over the picture and adjusted the light. "But why such a big house? They only had two kids."

"People were weird back then. They may have had their reasons," Carrie answered, as her cell phone sang the *YMCA* song again. "I've got to change this ringer, it's getting old. Hello?"

As Carrie talked into the cell phone, Damara continued to look through the pictures. There was one of a young boy about seven or eight that immediately caught her eye. His hair was long and straggly. He wore shabby clothes that were very dirty. "Hmm," she said, as she turned the photo over. On the back, the scribbling of a name and date was faded but could still be read. *Byron – 1951 – LeBoisne House.*

"Carrie, look at this," Damara declared.

"What?" Carrie asked, tossing her cell phone onto the table.

"Who's this?" Damara asked. "Maybe it's mislabeled or something."

"Yes... there's a lot of pictures of Aaron in here."

"Yeah, but look at his eyes. He's very angry with whoever is taking the photo," Damara surmised.

"He looks angry in every picture," Carrie sneered with a soft sigh, then added, "That was my office. They've located your aunt."

* * * * *

"Honey, I'm going to be late tonight. Do you have any plans?" Bob asked, trying to straighten his tie.

Louise sighed and smiled at her husband, he never could get his tie right. "Here, let me help you," she said, taking over for him. As he lifted his chin his eyes rolled down to meet hers. "Nope, no plans. Just a hot bath and a few hours of complete nothingness."

"What about Paulie?" he asked.

"Auntie Mae's for the night! I'm all alone," she smiled. "And I can't wait to get you out of here," she tugged on his tie and he coughed.

"All right, I'm out of here," he laughed. "No need to choke me with my own tie. I'll call you if I'm going to be real late. You should feel lucky that we live so close to my sister."

"I do." Louise kissed him thinking about how lucky she was just to have him. They had been married for almost fifteen years, and never during any of that time had they ever argued. He spoiled her to the point of almost ruining her. Anything she desired, Louise received. They met during Louise's first year at college and remained best friends and lovers ever since they married during her senior year. Paulie was born a few years later. He weighed in at six pounds, seven ounces, but he sure didn't weigh that anymore. At twelve, Paulie was already racing to be larger than his father was.

Louise loved being a wife and mother, but she also loved her career. After college, she attended law school and was quickly accepted by the most prestigious law firm in New York. After never losing a case, it wasn't long before she felt she needed to have more in her life besides money. After all, her husband was dripping with it. He had been born with a silver spoon in his mouth. So, with tears and many voices trying desperately to change her mind, Louise soon became the youngest district attorney New York ever had the privilege to know. Then only a few short years later, she was talked into running and won the race for senator. Everything happened so fast, she never had any time to think about what was happening. One day a wife and mother, the next a senator racing between home and Washington, DC to fix her country's problems while forgetting her own.

The woman staring at her from the mirror looked tired and worn out. Suddenly, her thoughts ran to her sister whom she hadn't thought about for many years. From her own lips, Louise had been an only child and her parents had long since passed. With her story being only a partial lie... what could be the harm? Now, instead of herself, Louise saw her sister staring back at her, and a strong feeling of doom stabbed at the pit of her stomach.

"What is it, Nadia?" Louise asked the reflection. "What are you trying to tell me?"

Louise wanted to panic, to run, but her mind kept telling her that everything was fine. *If anything had happened to Nadia, I would have been notified.* She told herself.

As she ran her bath water, a harsh thought ripped through her soul and terror beyond terror chilled her inner core. She froze in place, afraid to look back into the mirror, but the urge to see Nadia was now stronger than ever. Louise quickly turned around and stared at the large eyes staring back at her.

"Nadia!" Louise yelled. "No one knows. No one knows how to contact me!"

The shaking started in her hands and then escalated into her arms and body. This was a cold fear, a deadening fear. A fear that was more like a hot and sticky humid day – she was dripping from it, drowning in it. Louise slumped down onto the toilet seat and wept.

"Nadia. My God, Nadia!" Louise screamed and screamed, repeatedly. For some unexplainable reason, Nidra Louise knew that her twin sister was gone. How she knew, she did not know, but she knew when it had happened – September 22, 2009. "Our fortieth birthday,"

Louise whispered and sobbed into her hands. "And... I'm going to be next," she predicted to herself and her soul. Now Nidra was afraid... very afraid.

* * * * *

"A senator? How? How could she be a senator?" Damara asked, chasing Carrie down the stairs. "I've never seen her on TV."

"Name me some senators," Carrie replied, almost running now. "Name one; picture one in your head right now."

Damara stopped in the middle of the landing almost losing her balance. Faces and names flashed through her mind, but no matter how hard she tried, she could not name even one senator or congressman. "I guess you're right."

"I'm always right," Carrie yelled back, darting into the kitchen.

Hurried footsteps echoed around the house as the girls dashed through the rooms. Housie slept quietly basking in the warm filtered light that hit the back of a huge stuffed chair every morning, but the girls never noticed him; they were too absorbed in their own thoughts - their own world to notice anything else. Regrettably, even the silver-handled cane that was leaning against the huge overstuffed chair was also overlooked.

* * * * *

The phone rang unexpectedly and sent spine-chilling waves of terror through the woman standing despondently at the kitchen window. The small house in White Planes, New York was no longer her safe haven, for now she realized that it would only shield her from so much. Instinctively, without thought, Louise knew who the caller was and what they would ask of her before she answered. The idea of ignoring the unwavering and determined ringing crossed her mind for only a brief second, but if she didn't answer the questions now, she would have to eventually. There would just be no way of hiding from the truth any longer. Nidra Louise Kundick would soon be introduced to the world, but with half her soul now dead, Nidra would forever be only part of what she once was... now she was a grieving and lonely old woman. Earlier, Louise was somewhat optimistic that the morning would bring enlightenment to the frazzled emotional roller coaster of the previous night. Now with the screaming phone demanding her attention, Nidra knew her life would forever be changed.

Sitting her coffee cup on the counter, Nidra serenely picked up the phone. "Hello," she murmured into the receiver. It took almost as much courage to say a five-letter word than it did many years ago to step boldly onboard a train to set off for a faraway unknown destination. Her sister and niece were in tears only a few feet away, Nidra's hand reaching out as far as she safely dared with her sister frantically reaching back, but never again would those two hands meet.

Carrie was both excited and apprehensive about the call. Not too sure what to say first, her natural instincts took over for her. She didn't have to think about what to say, it just came out. "This is FBI Agent Carrie Clarke; I'm trying to reach Senator Bangle. I was given this number."

Nidra was slightly taken aback. She was sure that either her niece Damara or nephew Parker would be calling, or even that nasty lawyer, but not the FBI. Perhaps she was mistaken and… "Yes, this is Senator Bangle," Louise replied, a little less apprehensive.

"Thank you, Senator, please hold for the caller. Thank you, ma'am." Carrie gently handed the phone to Damara who had tears streaking down her face.

Damara nodded and lowered her eyes as she spoke. "Aunt Nidra?" Damara's weak voice broke through the phone.

When those two fearless words hit her ear, Nidra began to cry. When Damara heard the sobs from the other end, she, too, cried. It took a brief moment for both women to regain their composure. Damara spoke first. "Aunt Nidra, I don't remember you… I was too young. I'm sorry, but I have some terrible news to tell you…"

"My sister has passed. I already know," Nidra replied softly, almost apologizing.

"How did you know? Who told you?" Damara asked with a sudden alertness that awoke Carrie from her thoughts.

Nidra cleared her throat; she needed to speak softly, gently because this was Nadia's little girl she was speaking to, not some stranger. Her niece that she had not seen in almost twenty years. Parker was only a baby when she had stepped onto that train, but Damara was four and had cried so hard when Nidra told her she was leaving that Nidra's heart broke and began to bleed. The scar that eventually covered the deep wound never allowed her to forget that little round face with the big round eyes that were filled with tears as the train pulled away. Her small tiny hand waving, not saying goodbye, but saying – I'm sorry because I won't ever remember you. That was the last time Nidra Louise ever saw her family.

Nidra took in a deep breath and let it out slowly. "Damara, my sweet little Damara. But I do remember you, and Auntie is so sorry for leaving you so many years ago." The tears were flowing faster and stronger now. The waves of sobs were out of her control.

"How did you know, Aunt Nidra?" Damara asked again, a little more demanding this time.

"I... I... I just knew. Last night, I..." Nidra could hardly talk.

"She came to say goodbye didn't she?" Damara wept.

"Yes, I believe she did."

They continued their conversation for quite some time, but never once spoke about the family curse or Nadia's death. They only spoke about their accomplishments and failures during the last twenty years, no explanation of why Nidra had left or why they never had contact with each other. They simply began where they had left off. Carrie left the room allowing Damara some private family time. Something Damara had barely experienced during her brief life. Healing was such a strange process. No two people ever heal in the same way. Although scars eventually camouflage the wounds, each scar looked and felt different to each person who owned it.

After a twenty-minute conversation with her aunt, Damara found Carrie in the backyard studying the old fence. The fence was a mixture of wood and wire. It was very old and was probably erected when the house was built. Damara approached Carrie with a new inner feeling of hope. If felt wonderful knowing that she wasn't alone – that her and Parker *did*, in fact, have living relatives was comforting.

"Hey," Damara said, dragging her feet through the fallen leaves. "What are you looking at?"

"There's dried blood on this wire and a small piece of torn cloth. Could be from someone's clothes," Carrie had decided.

Damara reached out to pull the fabric off the fence but Carrie grabbed her hand. "No, don't touch it! I'll come back and get it when I have a plastic bag and some gloves."

"Why?" Damara asked.

"Could be evidence. I don't want it contaminated," Carrie said, taking Damara by the arm to head back to the house. "Now how did your meeting go?" Carrie asked with a brisk bounce in her step.

Damara's eyes lit up for the first time since Carrie had arrived. "Oh, wonderful! She sounds so much like my mom, but different somehow. She said they are... were identical, but now she has highlights in her hair. She wants us to visit her. Me, Parker, and you!"

Carrie sighed. "We need to talk, Damara. Your mother was she *is* no longer."

"Why can't you see that everything is going to be fine now?" Damara started to cry again, as Carrie escorted her to an old wooden bench. The lit eyes now dulled from pain – again.

"I hate to ruin your private party, Damara, but you are still in danger. This person – the murderer – I'll bet he's looking for your aunt as we speak. *We* must warn her. Not Parker. He should stay here and continue his classes. He doesn't need to get involved, not right now. He's been through enough. He should be safe here. It's obvious the murderer was not after you or Parker, otherwise you two would be dead by now."

"No... I can't," Damara cried. "I want this nightmare to be over. I'm tired of it all. Why can't things just go back to the way they were? And what about me! Haven't I been through enough already, too?" Damara cried into her hands.

Carrie squatted before Damara and cusped her face in the palms of her hands. When both girls' eyes met, Carrie spoke tenderly and lovingly. "Damara, we can *never* go back. We can only go forward. What was... is gone. You couldn't save your mother, but you have a chance to save your aunt." Carrie smiled. "And I will help you. I will be by your side every minute. I promise!"

Damara cried a few more tears never taking her eyes away from Carrie. "You're right, I know you are, but it's so hard, Carrie. I'm so scared. Nothing is making any sense right now. Everything is so mixed up. So wrong!"

Both women remained in the yard under the leafless tree talking about how life changes and there was no way to stop it. Although some things can be controlled, life makes us take the path it wants us to take, and sometimes we just don't have any say in the matter.

* * * * *

The doorbell rang and Carrie dried her hands with the dishcloth. She left the kitchen and headed to the front door to find out who was invading their quiet world. Damara had gone to take a nap while Carrie prepared dinner. It was a little after four in the afternoon, but Carrie was ready for anything. Her training had been by some of the best at The Agency. Lessons learned from other agents were a constant subject of interest to her. Whatever mistakes other agents had made, Carrie was always hoping to avoid. Her gun was safely tucked behind her under the band of her sweatpants. With all that had been happening recently, nothing was ruled out. As Carrie pulled the curtain aside that hung on the glass door, she saw a man in a gray suit standing rigidly on the porch. He was examining the dead hanging plants. He didn't look at all familiar, so Carrie prepared herself for the worst.

With her right hand tightly gripped around the small pistol, Carrie slowly opened the door with her free left hand. She placed her foot next to the door to prevent a forced entry. The man smiled and tugged on his tie. He was carrying a tan leather briefcase, his hair was short, and his demeanor reminded Carrie of an acute introvert. He cleared his throat several times, as he held out his business card for her to take.

"Excuse me. Let me introduce myself. I'm Calloway Arrington, with Arrington, Arrington, and Arrington law firm." It looked as though he was forcing a smile from his gritty snarling face. "Are you Professor Van Brunt? Damara Van Brunt? Daughter of the late Professor Nadia Louise Van Brunt?" he asked so softly that it was difficult to make out each word clearly.

"And who wants to know?" Carrie asked with such a stern force of authority and protectiveness that it made the man jump. He took a large step back from the front door. Now he looked confused and cowardly. No one ever confronted him like this before. His job was always easy and uneventful. When he finally found the courage to speak, he was stuttering and his eyes were looking at everything except Carrie.

The Agency

"Again, ma'am," Arrington sputtered. "I... I... m... m... must sp... sp... speak to Ms. Va... Va..."

Carrie sighed and released the grip on her pistol. The only person this man was a danger to was himself. "Oh, come in before you lose all your nerve."

Without speaking another word, Arrington entered and headed straight for the couch. He sat rigidly and placed his briefcase firmly on his lap with his hands clasped on top.

"I'll get Ms... Ms... Van Brunt for you," Carrie mocked at the timid little creature.

Damara had fallen asleep and Carrie hated to wake her, but as both girls descended the stairs together, Carrie noticed that the man hadn't moved a muscle since he had sat down. "Watch this one," Carrie joked. "It may take a while for him to say what he needs to say."

Damara rolled her eyes and sighed. They took seats opposite Mr. Arrington and Damara spoke first. "Hi, I'm Damara Van Brunt. You wanted to see me?"

"Yes, ma'am." He handed Damara one of his cards, but with the distance between them, she had to stand to reach it. "I was your mother's attorney," he added quickly.

"Oh, I didn't know my mom had an attorney," Damara said, glancing over at Carrie who shrugged her shoulders.

Arrington didn't smile or frown as he continued his small speech he had practiced many times before he left the office. Ignoring her surprise, he said, "Your mother has been a client of our law firm for many years. Oh, good," he added, noticing the pictures scattered on the rug by the fireplace. "I see you received the boxes I sent."

The faces on both Damara and Carrie turned to sudden delight. "So *you* sent those boxes to me," Damara exclaimed. "I was wondering where they came from."

"Yes, ma'am. It was directed that you receive the boxes immediately after your mother's death."

"Weird," Damara whispered.

"Not really, we get this type of request all the time. Some people don't want things passed on until after they've gone on. We simply respect our clients' wishes. Anyway, the reason I am here is to discuss your mother's finances. It seems..."

Damara interrupted the man in the middle of his sentence. "Did she have a lot of bills that Parker and I are responsible for?"

"On the contrary, Ms. Van Brunt. Your mother was quite financially stable. You and Mr. Van Brunt have inherited a small fortune I'm pleased to announce."

He spoke without changing his facial expressions, which immediately raised Carrie's flag of concern. Carrie also wondered if this was the man's typical behavior. If so, then he would make a very boring partner. She wondered what he did during his spare time.

"Mr. Van Brunt?" Damara asked.

"Parker... your brother! Hello, are we all together or what?" Carrie mocked, shaking her head.

"Oh, sorry." Damara grinned with embarrassment. She wasn't used to hearing Parker referred to as Mr. Van Brunt. "So exactly how much of a fortune are we talking about?" she asked.

Clicks from the briefcase startled Damara and Carrie smiled as her friend squirmed in her seat. The lawyer pulled out a few slips of paper and thumbed quickly through them. "Let me see. To date, you and your brother are worth about fifteen million dollars... together!" He quickly added, "Give or take a few thousands, of course. There's also an allotment for Ms. Clarke, which totals about two point three million dollars spread out over a few years. It's all spelled out in her will."

"What?" Damara almost screamed. The timid lawyer became even more ridged as his eyes widened.

"Wow, Damara. I never knew Mom had money!" Carrie stated in amazement.

"Neither did I." Damara was now in complete shock.

The small group sat silently for a few minutes as Damara thought about her mother and her life. "What happens now?" Damara asked.

"Well, I'm done here for today, but we will need you and Mr. Van Brunt to come to the office and sign a few documents, and Ms. Clarke too. You are Ms. Clarke?" Carrie nodded. "Oh, and you and your brother only own one quarter of the estate in Canada. Her sister owns the other quarter and their uncle owns the rest." Once again, his facial expression never changed.

"Uncle... *estate!*" Damara yelled, but then quickly lowered her voice. "And... yes, this is Carrie... I mean Ms. Clarke."

The Agency

"Yes, he would be your great-uncle and I have all the information on the estate at the office. Well, nice to meet you Ms. Clarke," Arrington added and Carrie nodded back. "My law group will be happy to continue to represent you three if you wish. We can discuss it further when you come to my office. You can call my secretary and make an appointment. The sooner the better." He stood to leave but Carrie quickly asked about Nidra.

"Do you know where Nidra is?" she asked.

"No, I'm sorry but my firm is not handling that account. Well, it was very nice meeting you both. I look forward to meeting Mr. Van Brunt soon. Thank you for your time."

"Thank you," Carrie said, almost pushing the man out the front door. "You can rest assured that we *will* call and make an appointment very soon."

After the door was shut and locked, Housie meowed from the top of the overstuffed lounge chair. It was now close to five and he was hungry, but Damara was in a dream state and not thinking about dinner. Carrie couldn't stop giggling. A whirlwind of emotions was rising up in Damara. She didn't know whether to be mad or happy with her mother.

"What?" Carrie asked, smiling.

"I don't know. I just can't believe this. My mom never said a thing about the money." Damara was still in shock.

"Actually, if you think about it, your mom never told you a thing about anything. And you and Parker never went without. I mean, you weren't spoiled by any means. But you definitely didn't go without either," Carrie interjected.

Damara had a faraway look in her eyes. "It's almost as though she was hiding us all here. With all that money, she and Nidra could have lived together anywhere. They could have hired bodyguards or something." The look in Damara's eyes alarmed Carrie. Where was she going with these assumptions? "And where did all that money come from. General storeowners didn't make that much back then."

"Damara!" Carrie stated sternly. "You cannot second-guess your mother. There are a lot of unanswered question here… yes. But it'll take us some time to sort everything out. You must remember that you did not walk in *her* shoes. She's gone so we can't ask her, but I'm sure everything she did was to protect you and Parker. From what, I don't know. She obviously wanted to give you both a chance for a safe and happy life."

The room became disturbingly silent. When their eyes finally did meet, Damara's began to tear. Stress from the unknown and the realization that her life had been a complete deception was a horrible truth she did not want to believe. Betrayal... that was what she felt. Her own mother had been unfaithful to her by not telling her the truth about her legacy.

"No, Carrie. This just isn't right!" Damara yelled. "Oh, I'll call that stupid lawyer's office all right, and we will go see them, but then we go to New York. What answers I didn't get from Mom I will definitely get from my aunt!"

Carrie sighed and knew it was time to call Dr. Lewis for guidance. She felt she was way in over her head and that their lives would be in jeopardy if things were not handled delicately.

* * * * *

It had been hours since he had clicked onto the Internet. No matter what website he visited, there was nothing about Nidra anywhere. His back was aching now, and his leg was still throbbing. He swallowed a few more antibiotics and a couple of pain pills. At least the swelling had gone down a little and his fever was gone.

"Where in the hell is she?" he yelled at the empty silent room.

He thought about his twin nieces and frowned. His damn sister had to make his work hard for him by having two. No! She couldn't have just one, not Maria. No, that bitch had to double his work – but also... double his pleasure! He was also angry with himself for not ransacking Nadia's house before he left to see if there were any letters from Nidra that would yield an address, but with that stupid kid, Parker, due home any minute, it was important for him to hurry and leave the residence. It took longer than he had expected for the sedative to kick in. Usually a person was out in about fifteen minutes, but Nadia lasted for almost an hour before she fell asleep. She drank her damn tea so slowly and all she wanted to do was talk about old times. Why she had been so happy to see him was beyond his comprehension.

Part 4

Mark J. Lumer was both excited and apprehensive. He simply could not believe his recent good luck. The exact day of his retirement from the Army's Space and Missile Defense Command, he ran into his old friend, Allen Greghardt. Greghardt asked if he had any plans for the future, which, of course, was a major *no* and… if he was interested in a *real* job. What exactly did he mean by *real* job? So with his curiosity aroused plus the great salary and benefit package that was offered, Mark said yes before he realized the words were coming out of his mouth. Now he was working at The Agency's headquarters in Oklahoma City, Oklahoma reviewing cases in a stark and bare office.

During his career with the Army, Gail, his wife, was content to remain at their home in Springfield, Virginia, which is near Washington, DC. The separation greatly bothered both of them, but it was always necessary for Mark's job. Mark was the Director of Contracts and spent the majority of his time traveling far away from home. He had an office at the Pentagon, an office in Huntsville, Alabama, and an office wherever the government wished at that particular time. Then there was the office he toted around in his briefcase that seemed to follow him everywhere. His family suffered many frightening times throughout his twenty-five year career where he would suddenly find himself in hostile territory. During the US invasion of Iraq many years ago, Lumer was sent overseas to ensure the troops had the required supplies and services they needed. The day after leaving Iraq, the office he had occupied was destroyed by a suicide bomber. If he had stayed even one more day, the world would have been less one Mr. Mark J. Lumer.

Wow, Mark mouthed, as he read over the case file. "Where do I start?" he said aloud to no one.

"I'm constantly asking myself that same question," a voice came from behind.

The unexpected sound startled Lumer who instinctively jumped up from his chair. He thought he was all alone. He remembered closing the door before he took his seat and began flipping through the papers in the large folder. As he turned to respond to the uninvited intruder, Mark instantly smiled when he recognized the warm and familiar face. "Allen! So nice to see you."

"Same to you, my old friend." Greghardt took several steps toward Mark and they shook hands, both gripping each other's elbows with their free hands. "Now tell me, how are you settling in?"

The two had met many years ago during a meeting at the Pentagon. Lumer had been assigned to a highly secret project for the Army. He had been told that Greghardt was running the show and that he would be receiving his directions directly from him. Although he was never sure exactly who Greghardt was working for, Mark found Greghardt easy to please and they soon became very close friends and confidants. Mark also found it interesting that Greghardt had followed his career so closely behind his back. Why would anyone be so interested in his boring job? All he was responsible for was making sure that the government had all the necessary supplies and services it needed. His days were filled with the constant harassment of dealing with contractors who felt they were not being paid enough or by his employees complaining that the contractors were complaining too much. Nothing difficult, it just required someone with a lot of patience and understanding. In addition, by the time Lumer had retired, all his patience and understanding were about gone. Working on the outside was much less stressful and the pay was more than he ever expected to make.

The only thing that continued to bother Mark was that if he was actually working for a temporary agency, how did Greghardt get involved in such a highly classified government project? That was neither here nor there anymore. Who cared? Not him, he wasn't a government employee any longer. As long as his retirement checks kept coming, Mark was happy. Anyway, anything that was really important would sooner or later end up on the major news channels. After all, when the government needed to find out about anything Top Secret, the easiest way was to simply turn on the television or search the web.

"I'm settling in just fine," Mark happily responded. "Just fine."

"Good, good, and you are being treated well? Yes?" Greghardt smiled, already knowing the answer.

"Oh, without a doubt," Mark added quickly. "This place is absolutely amazing. I would have quit my old job years ago if I had known about The Agency."

Greghardt chuckled and replied, "Not many people do know about us." The two stood silently for a few moments before Allen added, "Mark, I'm sure that you have realized by now that this company isn't exactly as it appears on the outside." Greghardt's eyes studied Lumer closely as he spoke. "I need to reassign you to another case, that is, if you don't mind."

"Oh?" Mark asked. "Mind, no, not at all."

"Good, I have set up a briefing at ten this morning in room 814. I believe your in-depth knowledge about the government's people is just what we need." Greghardt's smile left his face and his stance became rigid.

Mark smiled at his friend and said, "Allen, I've noticed the wealth and depth of money this building holds. The individuals and the outreach this company has at its disposal is absolutely amazing. And... I do realize that this... company..." Mark smiled, "*is* a little more than just placing temporary employees around the countryside. I'm not completely stupid. I do see and hear things."

Greghardt smiled. "Well, they have medication for that. Seeing and hearing things now are we?"

They both laughed.

"That is why I hired you, Mark. We need good sharp people like you," Greghardt added.

The two gazed at each other with a calm silence and mutual understanding. Friendship can sometimes be stronger than love if both are working toward the same goal. Mark nodded as he left his case file behind on the desk in the stark and empty office. For some strange reason, Mark knew that he had been brought here for other reasons than to simply write-up lessons-learned from old solved cases from years past.

* * * * *

Louise stared into her husband's eyes with two horrendous emotions tugging at her heart – dread and fear. She saw something that she had never seen before – was it disappointment or revulsion? Throughout their marriage, not once had she ever thought that it would come to this. Her life was a simple one. It was what she had wanted it to be. Now, after telling her husband the truth about her past, Louise knew she had made a terrible mistake. She now realized that she had treated her life as a rest stop on a continuing journey through time. Why didn't she know that her husband *was* her life? And... now, for the first time, she knew that she had been very wrong. Their marriage had never been temporary, but that was exactly how she had treated it. It now dawned on her that they were not two individuals, but one entity... experiencing life's joys and sorrows together. It was a union... a merging of two souls into one. Two partials never to become a whole unless joined with the other.

She reached out to him with her shaking hand. He hesitated for less than a second before he grabbed hold. Immediately, Louise could feel Bob's forgiveness and love. Her heart ached for him; she knew she had hurt him deeply.

"I'm so sorry, Bob. I should have told you everything from the start." She paused and lowered her eyes. Bob remained silent. "It's strange how easy it is to camouflage our fears and weaknesses. I honestly believed that my past would never come back to haunt me. What hurts more than anything else is that I abandoned my sister when she needed me the most. I was so damn afraid of that stupid family curse that I never saw what was really important." Tears rolled from her eyes. As her husband began to form a word, she cried out. "I'll never see my Nadia alive again!"

As Louise sobbed into her hands, Bob waited at his wife's side and embraced her tightly. It wasn't important for him to speak any words. All she needed now was to be held, to be loved, and if possible, to be understood.

* * * * *

The plane landed gently without any bounce. Carrie sighed and released her tight grip on Damara's arm.

"Ouch!" Damara teased, as she rubbed her sore arm. "You really do hate to fly don't you?"

The Agency

"No, I just made it up!" Carrie snapped back. "It scares me to death. I absolutely hate it!"

"Well, you're alive and we're down on the ground so relax." Damara shook her head and began to gather her belongings. It had been a long flight, a little less than five hours, but to Carrie it had been an eternity.

As the seatbelt light dimmed and the *ding* echoed throughout the plane, the captain's friendly voice stated, "For those of you like me... welcome home. To others, welcome to Washington, DC. We hope your flight with North-Central Airlines was a comfortable and pleasant experience. Please remember us again the next time you need to fly. You can always count on North-Central Airlines to get you to your destination safely and without delay. Thank you again for flying North-Central."

The door to the plane opened and the aisle was quickly filled with anxious people ready to depart. Carrie backed into the crowded aisle using her butt as a crowbar to part the way. A rather thin, but tall man objected harshly with a verbal slanderous attack as Carrie squeezed between him and another man. Ignoring him, she simply took her time pulling her bags from her seat and stood firm in place as Damara stepped in front of her to exit. Instead of following Damara, Carrie abruptly turned and stared angrily into the rude man's eyes. His face was unemotional, but if looks could kill... hers would have.

"I just love people like you because you are the best kind of birth control. Did you know that? Because if I felt I would ever have a child that was as rude and crude as you, I'd have to destroy it!" Carrie looked at the man without blinking an eye. Immediately, he turned his head away but she continued. "Unless you are attacking from the back, you have no guts do you!" She paused a few second then added, "Sorry folks back there, but I simply can't allow anyone to be as rude to me as this man was and get away with it. It's cowards like this that I wish would trip walking off the plane so they'd know how painful it is to hurt!" Carrie waved with a large bright smile to the people in the back and walked eagerly down the empty aisle that stretched out before her.

The clapping and gleeful chattering of the other passengers who had long ago tired of this rude man's attitude over the long flight cheered from the back of the plane. And... to Carrie's pleasure, the man was so disturbed by her words and actions that he actually stumbled exiting the plane. To her displeasure, he was able to steady himself before falling to the floor. The other passengers, however, who had yet to depart, laughed and toyed with him as they headed toward the terminal.

* * * * *

Devon smiled as the short stout man walked timidly into his office. He stood to allow the stranger to introduce himself. Devon had a way of intimidating strangers even before he spoke. Over six feet tall and weighing almost three-hundred pounds, Devon's stature would frighten even the most muscular of individuals. There was not an ounce of fat on Devon, no. His weight was due to his bulging muscles that resulted from not only his heritage, but from his daily workout rituals. When he wore a suit and tie, he resembled more of an out of place gorilla than a person. His muscles pulled and tugged at the fabric and caused the suit to fit rather awkwardly. That is why today Devon was dressed in his usual attire: blue jeans and a loose-fitting pullover shirt.

Mark's eyes were wide with anticipation and his smile was meek. Devon wasn't sure what was going through this man's mind. He was tired of people being afraid of him. At times, it did come in handy, but at times like this, it was just annoying. When Mark raised his hand, he spoke with energy and strength, which shocked Devon.

"Wow, this place is just full of surprises around every corner now isn't it?" Mark exclaimed.

Devon shook Lumer's hand gently, but Mark clasped on with a strong and firm grip which surprised him. He spoke fast which made Mark smile. "Good day to you, Mr. Lumer and welcome to The Agency." Devon released his grip and took a step back. He had to regain the control in this meeting, so quickly added, "Allen holds you with the highest of regards. I am very glad you're here." Devon had to chuckle. This little man was in no way intimidated by his large physique as he had first thought. In fact, the man was actually quite confident and comfortable.

Lumer stepped back and studied Devon up one side then down the other. It felt strange to Devon to have someone examine him with such interest. As he stood quietly awaiting perhaps a cynical reply, Mark smiled instead and said, "Sioux?"

Now Devon was speechless. He hadn't expected the conversation to take this path at all. "Why yes, thank you," Devon replied rather reluctantly. No one had ever been able to guess his heritage before. "How did you know? Allen?"

"No, not at all," Mark answered. "Hobby. I study different cultures and races. I'm Jewish by birth. My grandparents died in the Holocaust. And… since I'm standing before you, it is obvious that my parents avoided such a fate."

Devon laughed. This man was just what he had ordered. What he needed now was not only someone who had brains, but someone who possessed an inner light, a natural curiosity along with a good sense of humor.

"Please have a seat, Mr. Lumer," Devon said, pulling a chair from the corner.

"Mark, please," Lumer responded. He pulled another chair out from the wall in order to sit directly in front of Devon. If he had come any closer, their knees would be touching. "And thank you for welcoming me to my new position." Mark looked around Devon's office and added, "Whatever that may be."

Devon continued to laugh; he really did like this person. "I know exactly how you feel. Confused? We all are. Overwhelmed? All the time. However, what we have to work on should be most interesting. How about lunch and I'll fill you in."

"Sounds good to me." Mark instantly liked Devon too and felt relaxed and safe in his presence. This was indeed going to be a great adventure… not just a job.

* * * * *

It took forever to finally get the keys to the rental car, but with their luggage safely locked in the trunk, the two were anxious to get as far away from the airport as possible. Carrie was tired and her body was urging her to languish in a hot shower. The plane ride had been long and frustrating, and that rude man didn't help matters any either. They were not scheduled to meet with Nidra until tomorrow morning, which would give them some time to settle down and get a bite to eat. It seemed like it took forever, but within an hour of landing, the two were standing in the elevator of the hotel awaiting the ping of the fourth floor.

"I'm nervous. I don't think I want to go through with this," Damara said, not wanting to look at Carrie.

Carrie sighed and ignored Damara's comment. She watched the numbers change from two to three, then three to four. After a short ding, the doors opened and both girls exited pulling their luggage behind them. Carrie was happy this wasn't a real business trip; otherwise she would have had many more bags. Since this was a leisure trip, she only needed one nice outfit. Otherwise, an extra pair of blue jeans worked just fine.

"Are you ignoring me?" Damara asked.

"Yep," Carrie answered, inserting the card into their door.

"Why? I said I was scared," Damara said again.

"No, you didn't," Carrie replied, pushing the door open, pulling her luggage behind her. "Now where is that light switch?"

Damara took a deep breath and said, "Yes, I did!"

"No, you didn't," Carrie snapped back. "You said you were nervous. Get over it! Now where is the phone? Do you want to go get something or have it brought up?"

"Brought up," Damara answered, emptying her suitcase and placing the toiletries on the bathroom sink. "I wish you would be a little more understanding," she yelled from the other room.

"I am… yes; I would like to place two orders for room 423…" Carrie gave her menu choice then handed the phone to Damara as she took a seat on the opposite bed. As Damara placed her order, Carrie decided to use the bathroom. She could now hear Damara talking to what sounded like her brother. She was giving him the room number and describing their flight.

When Carrie pulled the covers from the bed, Damara started to cry. Carrie shook her head and sighed. "Sweetie, it will be all right. Don't worry about it."

"It's not that. I'm just wondering if I can handle looking into my aunt's eyes. I mean if she looks like Mom, I'm going to…"

"Twins can look alike, but usually their personalities are different. Everything will be fine." Carrie was tossing her tennis shoes across the

The Agency

room and puffing up her pillows when she added, "If it would help, I have a few tranquilizers in my bag. They'd calm you down enough so you can sleep."

"That's probably not such a bad idea. There's no way I can sleep tonight on my own. Parker said all's fine at home and to have fun. I'm not sure how he feels about having an aunt that looks like Mom." Damara wiped her nose with her sleeve.

Carrie handed her a glass of water, a pill, and a box of tissues. "Take this, dinner won't be up for a few minutes so why don't you go take a shower. You'll be ready to sleep once you've eaten then I can take a nice long, hot bath."

"Okay," Damara said, swallowing the pill. "Thanks for everything, Carrie. I do love you."

"I know, and I love you, too. Now go take your shower. I'm going to call Devon and check in."

Damara smiled at her surrogate sister and added, "You're lucky you have that guy, ya know."

"Yeah, I know," Carrie answered with love and devotion.

Damara took a shower and Carrie called Devon, both knowing that tomorrow would be full of more tears and heartbreaks. For some strange reason, even time doesn't heal everything.

* * * * *

Gail combed her hair and examined her face in the mirror. *Not too bad for being over fifty,* she moaned to herself. Her cheeks only sagged slightly from the years of gravity's continuous pull and the rings under her eyes were still small enough to be covered up by makeup. The memory of years past flooded her thoughts and she was reminded of the days when her hair was left long and straight. It was only thirty years ago or so, but seemed like another lifetime. She glanced silently around the room worried about what she had gotten herself into. This was the first time she had accompanied her husband, Mark, on his travels, but The Agency had insisted, there was simply no way to back out. It was explained that even the spouses were briefed on The Agency's rules.

Glancing at her watch, she knew that Mark would be a couple of more hours before he returned for dinner. "Oh well," she said to herself. Her briefing wasn't scheduled until 9:00 A.M. tomorrow, which gave her lots of time to walk and explore the halls of this huge complex. She grabbed her purse, turned off the light in the bathroom, and exited into the brightly lit hallway. There were many people coming and going, much more than she would have expected for this time of day. As she thought about the busy people hurrying along the hall, Gail noticed a slender sandy-haired woman in her late fifties or early sixties standing quietly waiting for the elevator.

Perhaps a friend? Gail asked herself.

"Hi," Gail said to the sad-looking woman.

The woman glanced over at Gail, but then quickly looked away as she spoke. "Hello."

"Do you work here?" Gail asked, eager to make a new friend.

The woman kept her eyes fixated on the elevator, which Gail thought was rather unusual. "No, my husband does."

"Same here. We're in room 515. What room are you in?" Gail was determined to break the ice with this woman.

"Five twenty-five," she answered meekly.

The elevator had arrived and both women entered. Gail hit the button for the first floor then asked the woman, "What floor?"

"Oh, um, the fourth please." The woman kept her eyes focused on the doors.

Now Gail was curious about her, she looked very upset. "Are you all right?" Gail asked with honest concern.

"Yes. I'm sorry. I just have many things on my mind," she answered.

"My name is Gail."

"Brandy," the woman answered.

"Nice to meet you, Brandy." Instead of receiving a reply, the woman wept tears and had a look of despair and hopelessness.

"Oh my, is there anything I can help you with?" Gail quickly added, now feeling responsible for the woman's state of mind. Before Gail received an answer though, the elevator doors sprang open and the woman quickly escaped to the protection of the fourth floor's empty hallway.

Gail sighed as the doors slowly closed. "This trip should be interesting," she said sadly to her reflection on the doors.

* * * * *

Mark sat quietly as he studied each face... each person's body language. He had discovered that if one simply studied another person carefully, a lot could be learned about that person, even before he or she ever spoke. He was not receiving anything at this meeting. Every individual sat rigidly upright, their hands clasped and rested on the table, their eyes focused forward, and their faces void of any emotion. Every person sitting at that table resembled more of a mannequin than a live human did. It was eerie and just plan unnatural. People just didn't do that.

Maybe they're really not people at all. Maybe they're robots... or worse – zombies! Mark chuckled as the thought ran through his mind.

Each man was wearing a plain black suit with a starched white shirt and a thin black tie. The women wore the same, minus the tie. Their attire reminded Mark of an old movie, *Men in Black,* from years past. Now he was thrown in the middle of a strange scene that sent chills up and down his spine. As he shivered from the sensation, the prickly hairs on his arms stood straight up as if warning him of the impending danger.

Mark jumped from his chair as a hand clasped firmly on his shoulder from behind. "Enjoying yourself?" Greghardt asked, taking the seat next to him.

With a sigh of relief, but from what Mark wasn't sure, he answered. "Oh, mounds!"

"The meeting will begin shortly. Devon will be describing the case and what your duties will be," Greghardt added.

"We discussed it a little at lunch today," Mark said. "But only the history of events up 'til now."

"Good, good, that means you'll be prepared to start right away," Lewis interjected, taking the seat opposite Mark and Greghardt across the table.

"Yes, most definitely," Mark answered. "Now, would either of you tell me where you found these," Mark said, looking around at the mannequins, "people from?"

Several agents turned their heads to look at Mark, but then quickly reposed themselves. Greghardt laughed and Lewis looked quizzically at Allen.

"Well, we do look long and hard for our agents, Mark. We are very picky as to who we hire. After all, we did hire you, ya know," Greghardt laughed.

"Thanks," Mark smirked back.

The other agents took the hint, softened their posture, and began to talk softly to the person sitting next to them, but the room became ghostly silent when Devon entered with Dr. Loomsbury trailing behind with his arms full of papers.

Greghardt leaned over to Mark and whispered softly. "Loomsbury is only sixteen and he possesses four PhDs, one's in molecular physics, another's in solar-neutrino physics, and the third is in nuclear chemistry with a minor in neuro-bio-electronics. He's currently working on his fifth PhD in forensic anthropology. That'll give him extraordinary knowledge in the application of skeletal analysis as applicable to criminal cases... especially murders."

Mark suddenly felt the need to sit as rigidly as the other men and women around the table. It was strange the effect this place had on a person.

"Gentlemen, if I could have your attention, please," Devon Arvol said loudly in front of the podium. Loomsbury stood quietly next to him still holding the massive stack of papers.

All eyes turned toward Devon Arvol and the good doctor. Even Mark had a hard time ignoring the impressive strong personality that was being demonstrated before him. This was definitely not the same man he had lunch with a few hours before, this was a determined and serious man who was not going to let anything thwart him from his established goals. Even Lewis and Greghardt, Mark noticed, were giving their full attention to Arvol.

"Thank you," Devon started. "Dr. Loomsbury, you can distribute the handouts now." Devon waved his hand once across the room, which was the signal for the doctor.

As the papers were being distributed, Arvol continued. "It has come to our attention that Senator Bangle's life is in danger. Your next assignment is fully detailed on the papers you have in your hands. I cannot stress the importance of this mission. Not only must we ensure the senator survives, but that the general public *does not* become aware of this situation. I do hope I am making myself quite clear."

All heads nodded as one.

"Good, now let's proceed…"

* * * * *

"Rain," Louise sighed softly to her husband and son who sat stunned at the early morning breakfast table. Her hands were tenderly balancing an empty coffee cup as her eyes stared blankly into nothingness. They were not sure what she had wanted this early in the morning, nor was she talking about anything other than the rain.

The only thought that was running through the senator's mind was how noticeable the raindrops were on the windowpanes. Each drop glittered as it slid slowly down to the wooden sill. Louise blinked her eyes and studied each drop one by one. They seemed to be reflecting scenes from her past, but how could that be? No, that wasn't what it was, it was lives starting and ending, that's what it was, most definitely. It was various lives from her past, starting as a huge round drop, and slowly losing its life as it ran down the window only to become absorbed by all the other drops as they too died. Just as her family had lived and died. She watched as each slowly faded into her deep memory to be buried along with all of her other life experiences. None being anymore important than another, but that was wrong; her family's memory should have been kept alive.

"Where are their pictures, Bob?" Nidra cried. "I don't have any damn pictures. I have to get some pictures!" She was breathing erratically, taking in deep, short breaths almost at the same time. "I can't believe I don't have any pictures. Stupid little pictures!" Nidra yelled out.

"Honey? What is it?" Bob asked affectionately, not sure if he should reach out to her or not. This was her battle, not his. This was her doing; this was her fate.

Both husband and son studied the woman that sat before them as she blinked back the tears that were threatening to explode.

"See the little raindrop, on the windowsill," Louise sang softly, staring at the darkened window. The morning light wouldn't be out for at least another hour. It was too early. Way too early for this, but Nidra didn't sleep at all last night. Instead, she walked her house, looking for pictures of her past, never finding even one.

"What?" Bob asked, now concerned over his wife's mental state. "What is it, baby?"

Setting the empty cup on the table, Louise answered her husband. "That's a song my mother used to sing to my sister and me when we were little." As she sang the song again, tears fell from Louise's eyes.

See the little raindrops on the windowsill,
You can see them dancing if you hold real still.
Sparkling little raindrops with their faces bright,
You can hear them singing when you sleep at night.
When you close your eyes, raindrops dance inside,
They will sing for you, they will see you through.
Darling little raindrops help the flowers grow,
They are here to help us, more than you can know.

As she reached the last few words, her sobs took control of her small body and she collapsed onto the table. The sudden rush of happy memories of her childhood was simply more than she could handle. The faces of her father and mother were too vivid. Louise was longing for her old bedroom and the sister who slept at her side for over fifteen years. That was until Nadia's marriage to Tom when she was fifteen and a half. Although their mother was livid, she understood the heart and how short life could be. Maria cried on that wedding day, but to her surprise, instead of moving away, Nadia and Tom moved into her mother's house, but the joy would only last a short four years. Because on her fortieth birthday, their mother died suddenly and they were left alone to ponder their family's legacy and whether there was any truth in the old family stories told by their mother.

Louise raised her head and tried to sniff back the tears. "My name is Nidra Louise Kundick," she sobbed. "My middle name, Louise, I shared with my twin sister. Her name is... was Nadia Louise Kundick." She tried hard to control the crying, but it was impossible. Her eyes were swollen and red, her lips quivered, and it was necessary to use the back of her hand to wipe the continuous drip from her nose.

Louise's family was too much in shock to hand her anything that could help at that particular moment. This was the first time she had spoken so candidly about her life that neither wanted to stop her.

"But now my sister is gone... I'll never get to hold her or look into her eyes. We'll never share our thoughts again." The tears were flowing down Nidra's face. The pain in her heart was growing and overtaking her. "I used to feel what she felt... I would dream what she dreamt. We shared everything... but because I was too afraid to... to accept our past... our fate, I left her when she needed me the most. Oh God! I left her alone with those two little babies, all alone..."

Nidra laid her head on her folded arms and cried. Her husband didn't know what to do but her son cried with her. He approached his mother and rested his hands on her shoulder. His tears dripped slowly, where hers could not be turned off.

"I want my mother... I want my father back. And most of all... I... I want my sister! Please God, I want my sister back!"

* * * * *

After reading about his assignment, Mark sat quietly; he couldn't speak. The shock was too much. He read the pages repeatedly, but each time they read the same. His bizarre behavior, however, did not go unnoticed.

"What is it, dear friend?" Allen asked from behind.

Jumping up, Mark turned to stare at his dear old friend. "I'm going to spy on people? I'm no... I'm to be a private detective?" he asked.

Greghardt laughed as he spoke. "No, no, no, not at all. You and Gail are just going on a vacation, that's all. Just a long vacation."

"To DC!" Mark exclaimed. "We *live* in DC. Won't that be a little obvious."

"That is correct; we know you live in Springfield, which is only a short distance from DC. It's perfect, don't you see?" Greghardt patted Mark's shoulder. "Well, I guess you don't actually. Let me explain, dear friend. You are retired. No one knows where you are working, correct?"

"Yes," Mark answered honestly. It was prohibited for most agents to tell others about The Agency. It was only the immediate family who knew and they, too, were briefed on the confidentiality that was necessary to protect The Agency's interest as well as all Americans.

"Good, good," Allen added. "So while in DC you do as the other patrons do, and when necessary, you simply go to other places. You and the misses are just traveling around. Living the easy life. It's perfect." He smiled.

Lumer had his concerns. Something was nagging at him and he wasn't sure what it was, but he knew that this wasn't a good thing.

"Don't worry, my friend. Everything will be fine. Believe me; The Agency will not let you down. You'll be provided with everything you'll ever need. You simply report on everything, every little detail. You leave nothing out. Nothing." Greghardt looked sternly at his worried friend. "This place is great, as long as you're great to it. So all is well, all is just fine."

"Any problems here?" Lewis asked.

"Nope. All's fine here, Jeff," Greghardt said with his hand still on Mark's shoulder.

* * * * *

Gail was never so happy to see her husband before. "Mark, you're back!"

"Anything wrong?" he asked, tossing his notebook on the table.

"No, it's just that this place gives me the creeps. There are some strange people here," she added.

"Oh, like who?" he asked, changing into his sweats.

Gail sat on the small couch and smiled at her husband. "Well, I thought I would walk around, get to know the place a little. Just like our sponsor said I should."

"And?" Mark asked.

"And, when I did, I met this woman who looked like she was going to start crying at any minute."

"I see. Did you get a name?"

"Yes, she said her name was Brandy. Why?" Now Gail was sure he knew something and perhaps she should too.

"Brandy?" Mark almost shouted. "Not Brandy Davison?"

The Agency

"Well, I didn't get her last name but how many Brandy's could there be around here?" she asked, perturbed. Gail felt her husband was trying to second-guess her.

Mark sat in front of the laptop computer and began to type. "Let's see if the system actually works."

"What?" Gail asked, now anxious to see what he was doing.

"Well, I have access to the central databases now, and I should be able to get a list of everyone who was here today."

"Really?"

"Yes, really." Mark glanced up at Gail and smiled. He loved her more than he loved himself. At times, it was hard for him to believe that he had ever found her. They met at college and he instantly fell in love with her when he saw her. It was love at first sight, and he loved her now just as much as then, if not more.

"What?" she asked when she noticed that he was staring at her.

"Nothing." He smiled. "Let's see, well, you did meet Brandy Davison. What an honor. There was only one Brandy here today." After clicking a few more keys, Brandy's face appeared smiling and looking happy.

"That's the women all right, but she wasn't smiling when I saw her. She was very sad," Gail surmised. "Do you know what's wrong?"

Mark shook his head and clicked a few more keys. "Ah, yes, I see the problem."

"Well, will you tell me?" Gail demanded.

"After I run a few miles in the gym," Mark answered, kissing his wife on the cheek. He was smiling as he closed the door behind him.

Gail sighed and shook her head. "Mark, I just don't know sometimes!" she yelled at the empty room.

* * * * *

Carrie and Damara sat in the now quiet and peaceful car. The keys were in Carrie's hand and no longer in the ignition. Neither wanted to move from their safe sanctuary and enter the unknown world that awaited them only a few steps away. It was a few minutes before ten in the morning. Birds were eagerly searching the wet grass for any type of food they could scrounge up. It was a beautiful crisp fall day. The trees were almost bare of their leaves now ready for the coming cold winter months. The sidewalks were barely noticeable now covered with all the fallen foliage. The cool air had a wonderful fresh aroma, almost as if introducing a new beginning. It was as though nature had a way of cleansing itself from all the evil of the previous hot summer days now past. The house in the distance was not at all elegant, just a simple home sheltered in the branches of several large old elm trees.

"Well, we can't exactly sit here all day now can we?" Damara asked. Although her heart wanted her to move, her legs refused to obey. The last few weeks were hard to accept. Losing a mother was never easy, especially when the mother was so young and healthy. Walking into the coroner's office was hard enough, but walking up that sidewalk meant admitting that her family was anything but normal. Her life, anything but surreal.

Carrie sighed and opened her door. Without answering the question, she opened Damara's door, then waited. Carrie knew that this was hard for her surrogate sister and she didn't want to rush her. Damara had to do this on her own.

With all her strength, Damara left her safe haven of the car and stood on the sidewalk staring at the house. Her heart was pounding so hard that Damara tried to feel her pulse in her neck.

"Trying to give yourself a stroke?" Carrie asked with a smile.

Damara looked quizzically at Carrie. "Huh?"

"You're pushing on your neck so hard you're probably cutting off the circulation to your brain!" Carrie reached over and pulled Damara's hand from her throat. "Come on. Let's go before you need a stress test or something. Just follow me, you'll be fine."

As the girls started up the sidewalk to the steps of the house, a woman resembling Damara's mother came running from the white, glass-framed door. Her arms were stretched out as far in front of her as she could get them. The pain in her eyes was real. Tears fell from her cheeks and Carrie was worried that if she lost her footing now, this poor woman would probably break her neck on impact with the sidewalk.

"Damara!" the woman screamed. "Damara, my baby."

Instinctively, Damara ran toward the screeching woman. "Aunt Nidra!"

The two women collided in a tight embrace... crying... screaming. Behind them stood Carrie in complete shock. In front of them stood a boy and a man. Both looked as surprised as Carrie did. After all the doubt, all the fear, the two women acted as though they had been together their whole life or that they had been waiting for this moment their whole life.

Carrie shook her head and decided to get the luggage from the trunk while they continued to hug and cry. "This is nuts!" Carrie said, as the trunk sprang open.

"Here, let me help you." Bob smiled at Carrie from the sidewalk. She hadn't noticed that he had moved. That made her feel slightly uncomfortable. Being an agent, she was supposed to know everything that was going on in her environment. Carrie missed the fact that he had started walking toward her and she never noticed it.

"Hi, I'm Bob, Louise's husband," he added with his hand out.

"I'm sorry," Carrie added quickly, trying to shake the thought from her mind. "I'm Carrie. Nice to finally meet you."

They smiled as their hands clasped together.

"I'm glad you made it without any trouble," Bob said.

"Thanks," Carrie said.

Her computer bag hung from her shoulder and she had a couple of small boxes in her hands. Bob smiled as he watched the two hugging and crying women.

As Carrie passed them, she winked at Damara who looked longingly at Carrie. Damara's lips formed the words, *Thank you*, and Carrie lipped the words, *You're welcome*. For some strange reason, Carrie just wasn't ready to look back at a face that resembled a woman whom she had loved so much. It was one thing having to bury a loved one, but quite another to look into their eyes again. Instead of stopping to say hello, Carrie followed Bob into the house where she was introduced to Paulie, a younger looking Parker.

"Wow!" Carrie exclaimed, as she shook Paulie's hand. "You look just like your cousin Parker."

"Really? Do you have any pictures? I've never seen a picture of him," Paulie eagerly asked.

"Well, actually I do. I'll tell you what. Let me get these bags settled in a room and I'll dig them out for you. Okay? I'm sure your mother and cousin have a lot to talk about and we can visit."

"Cool!" Paulie yelped. "This is great."

"I'd like to see those pictures, too," Bob quickly added.

"Of course," Carrie answered.

"Did you bring any pictures of the other family members?" Bob really wanted to see what Nidra's family looked like.

Carrie paused then asked. "Nidra... I mean Louise doesn't have any pictures?"

"None that we know of," Bob said.

"Strange. Yes, I brought many pictures and I plan to leave them here. They are copies for Nidra... I mean Louise." Carrie was embarrassed that she kept calling Louise by the wrong name.

They smiled at each other. It was an awkward moment, but also somehow rewarding.

* * * * *

Mark sat on the couch in their room and stared at the floor. It was disconcerting for him to be tasked with spying, which could not possibly be his expertise. How and why was it suddenly his responsibility to follow someone so closely? With *his* luck, he would be arrested for being a Peeping Tom!

"What is it?" Gail asked.

"Nothing," he replied.

"Mark," Gail added quickly. "How many years have we been married? I believe I know you a little more than you think I do. I can always tell when something is bothering you. Now talk."

Mark glanced up at his wife and smiled. He reached out for her hand and she lovingly took his. His devotion for her was deep and undying. As she took a seat next to him, he began to explain his new assignment. It would be affecting her too because Gail just had to *tag* along beside him during his travels. After all, wouldn't it look a little odd for a retired husband to travel and leave his wife at home?

* * * * *

Nidra didn't want to loosen her grip on Damara. Never again did she want to have to experience the dreadful feeling of loss and despair that she had experienced twenty years before. She was afraid that if she let go now, then all of this would have been nothing but a wonderful dream, that in reality, Damara would be grieving alone thousands of miles away.

Damara felt warm and safe, it was as if she was finally home. All her worries and fears would now be taken care of for her. No longer would she feel lost and alone. Never again would she have to solve or handle problems that were too much, too difficult. Damara would forever have her family's support with her Aunt Nidra, Uncle Bob, and cousin Paulie at her side.

A light breeze swept softly around the hugging women as they loosened their grip on each other. Slowly they extended their arms until their eyes met. With their hearts racing, Damara cried as she stared into her mother's eyes, and Nidra wept as she stared into the face of a young Nadia. They both used the backs of their hands to wipe away the tears. Damara's nervous giggle broke the ice and Nidra was soon laughing with her. They laughed and cried at the same time. Laughed for the joy of finding each other again, but cried because of the mutual loss they shared.

As Nidra wiped away the tears, she spoke softly. "My God, if you don't look like your mother. I almost feel like I'm twenty-something again standing next to my sister. It's amazing."

"Amazing indeed!" Damara exclaimed. "I'm... I'm looking at my mother with highlights and shorter hair. You two must be identical. Same eyes, nose, mouth, even the same little wrinkles under your eyes. I... I..." Damara couldn't finish her sentence.

"I guess we are both a little shocked, sweetie. If we had been together while you were growing up, we would look different somehow. It could be the way we hold our head or hands, but the years apart have hidden those little things. Now we only see what everyone else in the world sees." Nidra smiled at her beautiful niece and the tears fell again.

"Yes, I suppose you're right. Just never thought of it that way before." Damara sighed and smiled back before finishing her thoughts. "But I can't tell you how wonderful it is to see you, Aunt Nidra, to be next to you. I had forgotten everything, but when you came running for me, all my memories came flooding back. I even remember when you climbed onboard that train. I was... how old?"

Nidra grinned and said, "About four or five. You were so sweet and I loved you so much. Did you know it took all I had just to board that stupid train? Sometimes I wished I had stayed. I missed you guys so much after I left. I regret it mostly when I think of your mother."

"Yes," Damara said, lowering her head. "My mother. She never spoke of you, never."

"It was a promise we made together. It was our only way of protecting each other. We were hoping the curse wouldn't find us both if we weren't together," Nidra added.

"Well, it sort of worked." Damara looked up into Nidra's eyes. "You're still alive."

"For now," Nidra said, taking Damara by the arm and walking toward the house.

* * * * *

"Agent Laurel speaking, how may I help you?"

"Yes, Agent Laurel, this is Agent Kragger in Central Intelligence. We've received a tip off that one your senators may be in danger."

"And does this senator have a name?" Laurel asked sarcastically.

"Senator Bangel, Senator Louise Bangel of New York," Kragger answered professionally.

"I see," Laurel replied. "Exactly how is she in danger?"

"We received a report stating that a relative of hers was murdered and she's next," Laurel answered.

"I see," Laurel said. "And... your point is?"

"We need you to send an agent over to keep an eye on her," Kragger answered.

"Right," Laurel replied. "And who did you say you were again?"

"Agent Kragger from Central Intelligence. You're the closest field office to Senator Bangel's home. Therefore, it falls under your jurisdiction."

"Like we have nothing better to do than sit in front of a senator's house and wait for some killer to show up. Now who was murdered again?"

"A relative of hers," Kragger answered.

"Does this relative have a name?" Laurel asked.

The Agency

"I'm sorry, but I'm not at liberty to say," Kragger replied.

"Well then, I'm not at liberty to respond!" Laurel stated, slamming the phone back on the receiver.

"Who was that?" another agent asked from across the room.

"A crank caller. Damn, like we have nothing better to do than talk to stupid people." Laurel turned back to his computer screen. He took a sip of his coffee, then moved the curser to select the five of diamonds and placed it on top of the six of spades.

* * * * *

Mark and Gail were glad to be home. Gail instinctively headed for the kitchen to determine what she needed to pick up from the store. As she wrote out her grocery list, Mark stood at the kitchen door and laughed.

"What's so funny?" she asked with a quizzical look on her face.

"You," Mark replied laughing. "We're leaving again, we're not staying."

"Not even for the night?" Gail asked, concerned and tired.

Mark shook his head. "That's correct. Not even for the night. We leave for New York as soon as we're ready."

"But I'm not ready. I need to do laundry and repack our clothes!" she protested.

"Sorry, honey, but that's the new job. We have to be in New York by tonight if at all possible. We are to fly out on the redeye a little after eleven. We should arrive in New York by midnight or so."

"Then why did we take all this time to come home? Why didn't we just stay at the airport?" Gail demanded.

"Because we're flying out of Dullas not Regan, and… I would like to take a shower in my own home. I'm sweaty from the long flight. All right?" Mark replied, as he unbuttoned his shirt.

"Fine, I'll have one of the girls do our laundry while we're gone, and I'll pack what little clean clothes we have left." Gail dropped the pen onto the table and marched upstairs.

"You don't have to get upset!" Mark hollered.

Gail stopped midway up the stairs and yelled back, "After several weeks in Oklahoma and a six-hour flight on a plane, I'll act any way I want. I'll be ready to go in about an hour. You'd better hurry up or I'm leaving you behind. We have a case to solve!"

Mark laughed and his love for her warmed him. Gail was a practical woman and had always taken life one day at a time, but now she was motivated by a new goal and Mark had never seen her more happy. Perhaps this job was a great move for the both of them after all.

* * * * *

Lewis read the FBI memo and chuckled to himself. He had been with The Agency for over ten years and it seemed that nothing would ever change... especially in his view anyway. Lewis arched his back and stretched. His eyes were sore and he rubbed them with the palm of his hands. As he rested his elbows on his desk, the pressure against his eyes was soothing. He yawned and arched his back again not taking the pressure from his eyes. His legs ached. In fact, his whole body was tender and weary.

"What's up?" a familiar voice said from his kitchenette.

"Make me one, too, Allen." Lewis had recognized the voice at once as Allen Greghardt, his boss and mentor.

"We have a problem with the FBI, they just won't follow orders." Lewis continued to put pressure on his eyes.

Greghardt set the glass of bourbon and ice next to Lewis and took a few steps back. "And your point is? After all, isn't that normal for our FBI? You wouldn't want them to earn their living now would you?" Greghardt chuckled and Lewis sighed.

"I guess not." Lewis stopped rubbing his eyes and reached for his drink. After a long gulp, the alcohol soon relaxed him a little. "Allen?" he asked, as he stood to stretch out his legs. "Why is it that people tend to want to not believe the truth? I mean, say your child is kidnapped. If someone called you at work, your first reaction would probably be, *you're kidding*, or *right*. We tend to not believe the truth even when it's staring us in the face."

"I guess it's just our nature to always want or to demand that our lives are perfect; that nothing evil could ever happen to us. I believe it's called... denial, my dear friend and co-worker." Greghardt smiled and raised his glass to the heavens.

"Yeah, toast to our human nature. Now I'll have to take another route to get the FBI involved. I'll have to call in Harry Davison."

Greghardt had to laugh. "You really don't like that guy do you, Jeff?"

"No, I'm sorry to say I do not. He refuses to accept any responsibility for his son. Especially now that his son has killed himself." Lewis was peering out of his large window that spread the full length of his office – floor to ceiling, wall to wall.

The outside scene was beautiful. The fall colors were in full galore with various shades of red, gold, yellow, and brown decorating the landscape. Even the horizon didn't disappoint him by proudly spraying its blue, red, and orange clouds across the afternoon sky. As he admired God's artwork, he wondered how anything in life could ever go wrong.

"Where did we fail Danny, Allen? Where did we go wrong?" Lewis asked with a tear ready to fall from his eye.

"I don't know," Greghardt answered. "But we did everything we could to save him. You know that. It was probably more than the child could handle after being a prisoner of the Columbian sex traders for all those tender years. Those evil, sick people. I guess when he finally reached adulthood he just couldn't go on living with the memories that haunted him day in and day out."

"How's Brandy handling his death?"

Greghardt had to make himself another drink. He had such high hopes of saving the boy. As he poured himself more bourbon, he reluctantly answered Lewis' question. "Not good."

"Perhaps another case would be just the right therapy for Harry now," Lewis surmised, still staring at the heavenly painting before him.

"Perhaps," Greghardt agreed. "But what about Brandy?"

* * * * *

The fireplace was crackling as the logs breathed in the flames that danced around them. The warm aroma welcomed Damara and Carrie into the family room with a sense of security and love. Damara took in a deep breath and let it out slowly. As she walked toward the warm glow, she stretched out her arms and yawned.

"Long trip, huh?" the voice from the couch asked.

"Oh my! You scared me, Uncle Bob. I didn't see you there," Damara replied with a startled expression, warming up next to the fire. "I love a real fire, don't you?"

"Yes, I do," he replied.

"Me, too," Carrie added, standing next to Damara.

The three stood uncomfortably for the next several minutes until Paulie ran into the room.

"Carrie, can I see the pictures now?" he asked anxiously.

"Yes, please," Nidra's voice echoed from the other room. She was carrying a tray with mugs and cookies. "Hot cocoa! Now about those pictures, Carrie. I'd love to see what you brought."

"Okay," Carrie answered, looking over at Damara who smiled and nodded her head.

As Carrie left to retrieve the mysterious photographs, the others took sips from their hot mugs.

"So, how do you enjoy teaching?" Bob asked Damara.

"I love it," she replied.

"Your mother loved teaching too," Nidra added. "We used to play school when we were little and she was always the teacher, I was always the student."

Damara smiled. "My mother was a great teacher. Everyone loved her."

Bob nodded his head, but didn't say a word. He didn't have to, Carrie had returned with the box. As Carrie took a seat next to the coffee table, the others gathered around her, anxious to see what she had brought.

"Now, we know who some of these people are, but not all of them. We were hoping you could help us, Nidra," Carrie said, glancing over at Damara to make sure she was handling this without getting upset.

"Oh please, call me Aunt Nidra. I know how close you were to my sister, and I'd like you to be that close to me, too."

"Okay, Aunt Nidra," Carrie said, as she pulled out a photo. "Now, before I hand this to you, we have a question."

"Okay," Nidra answered.

"What happened to Haden, Fauna, and Yanka?" Carrie asked.

The Agency

Nidra smiled, this was an easy question. She was afraid they would have many personal and embarrassing questions for her. "Oh, they stayed in Canada with their grandparents, the Van Brunt's. When Nadia decided to leave Falcon Lake, Mary refused to let her take them with her. She demanded that Thomas' children from his first marriage remain behind with them. Nadia didn't object. Nadia and Tom married in 1984 and he died in 89, so she only had his kids for about three and a half years. Oh, it was hard for her to give them up. After all, she really did love them, but Nadia also knew it would be easier on her if she only had the two to take care of."

"How well did you know my half-sisters and brother?" Damara giggled.

"Pretty good. I was around for about five years when Nadia played mom to his kids. They called me auntie, just like you did, Damara."

"Auntie... I sort of remember that, Auntie," Damara whispered.

"I'm sure a lot more will come back as we continue to share memories," Nidra said, reaching her hand out to Damara.

Damara rose from the lounge chair and sat next to her aunt. She placed her head on her shoulder as Nidra hugged and kissed her forehead.

Everyone was silent for a few seconds before Paulie spoke up. "Well, can I see some pictures now?" he asked.

Carrie laughed and nodded her head. "Okay, but first..."

"Not another first!" Paulie interrupted.

"This one will be quick, I promise." Carrie winked at him. "How much do you know about your family history, Aunt Nidra?"

"Not much. I know my grandparents' names. Why?"

"Well, I've uncovered some interesting facts and I don't want to shock you," Carrie replied.

"Oh? Like what?" Nidra asked, now with her interest peaked.

"It's not all good, Aunt Nidra," Damara added.

"Okay, let's have it," Nidra urged.

"What about Paulie?" Damara interjected.

"What about Paulie?" Nidra said. "Family history is family history. What was... was. We're not responsible for what our relatives did. Is it that bad?"

"How old are you again Paulie?" Carrie asked.

Paulie sighed. "Twelve and that's old enough."

"Okay, have it your way." Carrie pulled out the folded sketch paper and laid it on the table. "Let me read what I received from a family historian first. I've been e-mailing a distant cousin of yours. Her name is Lucy Winchester. Let me read what she wrote and then we can discuss it." Carrie glanced around the room but no one spoke a word. She decided this was her cue to start.

Carrie read slowly so everyone could grasp what she was saying. "Sinclair and Shannelle LeBoisne migrated to Canada from France sometime..." she paused, but when no one interrupted her, she continued. "Rumor has it..." As she finished her sentence, *"When they married..."* Nidra gasped, her eyes opened wide with horror.

"Do you want me to continue," Carrie asked respectfully.

Nidra nodded slowly.

"...Mortimer was Byron's father..."

The room was too quiet. Carrie studied each face as she read and wasn't sure what they were thinking, but she continued reading all the way to the end; then sat quietly, watching.

"Can I see that?" Nidra asked.

"Sure, this is your copy anyway," Carrie said, handing the paper to Nidra.

"Is any of this substantiated with backup documentation?" Bob asked, glancing over his wife's shoulder at the paper.

"Yes, by the family historian. I have her contact information for you. It's on the last sheet there in your hands." Carrie awaited for their response.

"This is too cool," Paulie spoke up. "Real dead skeletons in our closets."

"Paulie, please!" Nidra snapped at her son.

Paulie sighed. "But Mom... this is way too cool!"

Bob cleared his throat, which was a sign for his son to back off; Paulie did so immediately.

"Fine!" Paulie barked out and frowned at his parents. Carrie elbowed him and he smiled at her.

"So... my mom's parents were first cousins," Nidra said, studying the paperwork. "How interesting. I remember Uncle Aaron. He was weird."

The Agency

"Oh, how?" Damara asked.

"Just weird," Nidra added quickly. "But I do remember he hated my mother with a passion. She was his half-sister and they fought constantly. They were about four or five years apart, so I always figured it had to do with sibling rivalry and never paid it much attention... well, let's see those pictures."

"Oh, okay. Now this first one has LeBoisne Home written on it and dated... 1955." Carrie handed the picture to Nidra who studied it.

She nodded her head as she spoke. "Yes, this is the house. It was beautiful; that's how I remember it anyway. I remember this picture. I used to look at these when I was little and my mother would tell me about them. That's my Grandmother Bella sitting on the porch and my mother on the tricycle. That's my Uncle Aaron on the upper porch or at least I think it is. Yes, it has to be... who else could it be anyway? My mother had told me that my father was the one who took the picture."

"Then who's that man?" Carrie asked, pointing to the person on the porch.

"Oh, that's Aaron's grandfather from his mother's side. He'd come out every summer to pick him up and take him back with him for a visit. He'd stay the whole summer with them. Then when he was about, oh, thirteen, fourteen, or so, the visits suddenly stopped." Nidra smiled as she studied the black and white photo.

"Oh, why was that?" Carrie asked, her inquisitive mind now taking control.

Nidra shrugged her shoulders and answered, "Not sure. Never asked. Sometimes when kids get older they seem to have better things to do than visit relatives."

"Perhaps you're right," Damara added. "That house is beautiful."

"Nadia and I loved playing in that old house." Nidra sighed. "But that was many years ago. So what else do you have?"

Carrie made some notes in her journal before pulling out the next photo.

"This one's of a group of children. We have no idea who's who." Carrie handed the photo to Nidra who smiled.

"Oh my," she said with her face lighting up. "Isn't this one wonderful?"

"Who are they?" Damara asked.

"Well," Nidra answered, laying the picture on the coffee table. As she leaned over, Nidra pointed to each child. "That's Candice and there's Sarah... um, Lewis, Thomas, Aaron, and Jacob. And that's my mother... Maria. These are all the kids my great-grandparents had. I remember my mother talking about that one summer. It was the only time they ever visited their old home in Quebec that I know of. She said they all had a wonderful time, but for some reason they never went back. I believe she was about ten at the time. I don't think she saw any of them ever again."

"So," Carrie said, calculating the dates. "It would have been about 1959 or 1960."

"I guess, I don't have the dates in front me," Nidra answered.

Again, Carrie made notes in her journal then pulled another picture from the box. "We assume these kids are Damara and Parker's half-sisters and brother," Carrie explained, handing the picture to Nidra.

"Yep, that's right. There's Haden and the girls, Yanka and Fauna. You resemble Fauna, Damara," Nidra said smiling. "This is fun. What's next?"

"This one," Carrie replied, handing her a picture of two couples.

"Hmm, I have no idea who they are. I've never seen this one before." Nidra flipped the picture over and noticed the date of 1904 written in faded ink on the back. "Whoever it is, they're standing in front of a general store and that's probably snow on the ground."

"Well," Carrie surmised. "I thought it might be the LeBoisne brothers and their wives standing in front of their parents' store in Quebec."

"It very well could be. I'm not sure," Nidra replied, looking puzzled.

The remainder of the evening was spent going through old photos trying to figure out who was who. By the time they were finished, there were two piles of photos; Those that Nidra recognized, and those she didn't. What interested Carrie was that the piles were about equal in depth.

"Aunt Nidra, are your relatives in Canada still alive?" Carrie asked.

"I'm sure some of them are, why?" Nidra asked, studying Carrie's hand-drawn family tree again.

Carrie was placing the unknown pictures into an envelope as she spoke. "I thought it would be a good idea for Damara to go visit them. See if we could dig a little deeper into your family's curse."

Nidra looked up from the paper with horror in her eyes. "Why would you want to do that?"

"Because," Carrie said sternly. "Whoever killed your sister either had something to do with your mother's killing or someone is copying what happened to her. You also have to remember that your grandmother was also killed at that same age."

"We don't have any proof of my mother being killed or my grandmother..." Nidra protested.

"You can't disprove it either. Don't you think it's a little strange that all three died exactly on their fortieth birthday?" Carrie asked. "And I believe that whoever it was is probably coming after you next."

"Whoa there!" Bob spoke up, staring at Nidra. "You didn't tell me your sister was murdered."

"Murdered!" Paulie yelped. "Who was murdered? What sister? Mom?"

"Okay... okay..." Nidra tried to calm her family. "I didn't tell you because I knew you'd get upset."

"Upset!" Bob yelled. "You're damn right I'd get upset. If your life is in danger, don't you think I should know about it? Damn it, Nidra. What other secrets are you keeping from me?"

"Mom?" Paulie was close to tears now. "Is someone going to kill you?"

Carrie jumped up from the floor and tried to take over the conversation. "Look, I'm an FBI agent. One of the reasons for coming here was to make sure that nothing happened to Nidra."

"Well, what if you coming here has put her in danger? What if the murderer followed you here?" Bob asked sternly.

"Bob!" Nidra snapped. "I've had enough of this. Stop it at once. Now I know everyone is a little jumpy right now, but we have to calm down. Paulie, no one is going to kill me. Bob, no one followed them."

"Nidra is right, we have to calm down. But you also have to take this situation seriously, Nidra," Carrie added quickly. "We don't know who killed Nadia or why, and until we do, your life *is* in danger!"

"Okay... okay!" Nidra started to pace the room. "Let me think."

"Hon, I don't like this at all," Bob added.

"Well, I don't think you have anymore control over this than I do!" Nidra snapped. "So what in the hell do you want me to do?"

"I don't know," he replied with concern written all over his face. "I don't know."

Carrie stood back and tried to think. This was not going as she had hoped at all. Damara was close to tears and so was Paulie. Bob and Nidra were about to duke it out in their family room, and Carrie wasn't sure what to do next. This was not going according to her plan.

* * * * *

Mark sat across the street in the rental car studying the quiet house. He felt stupid and naked... totally exposed. He watched as Gail strolled nonchalantly down the sidewalk carrying a Wal-Mart plastic bag which held fake groceries.

"I sure hope there's a Wal-Mart store around here somewhere," he said, feeling ridiculous. He knew they couldn't stay here long before someone started asking questions. As the car's engine started, Gail gleamed at him from across the street. He pointed to the end of the block and slowly headed in that direction. Gail shrugged her shoulders and shook her head. As she passed the senator's house, she could hear someone yelling inside. This concerned her so she hurried her pace. When she finally reached the car, she told Mark about the loud voices.

"Okay, let's see what we can pick up." Mark grabbed his laptop from the backseat and snapped it onto the stand attached to the dashboard. After a few clicks, he had patched himself into the senator's house. Now they could hear the argument clearly.

"What in the world?" Gail asked in amazement. She had never seen such a thing before, not even in the movies.

Mark smiled an almost sinister grin and replied, "Oh, just another toy they gave me at work."

The Agency

Gail sighed, but was still amazed. Not only could they hear the whole conversation, but they could see into the room as well.

"I hope our house isn't bugged," Gail whispered.

"Who knows?" Mark replied. "Let's listen."

As the two sat quietly in the rental car, they soon learned the story of the senator's seedy heritage, and her scary legacy of the curse. Gail was horrified. She had no idea that the case her husband had been assigned to involved a US senator and a murder of a college professor. She had only read about how they were to track one of The Agency's agents and her friend on their travels and report any unusual activities.

"Well, I'd say this was rather unusual. Wouldn't you, Gail?" Mark asked.

As Gail sighed, she rolled her eyes. "I didn't pack enough for a trip to Canada!" she exclaimed.

Part 5

The phone rang several times and Nidra was about to hang up when a crusty old voice echoed in her ear. "Hello?" The crotchety response was unnerving and for some reason sent chills up her spine. Louise swiped at the back of her head as though something creepy was invading her space... but nothing was there, nothing but her neatly combed hair.

At first, she didn't say anything. Nidra Louise held the phone away from her and wondered if it was such a good idea to make this call. She quickly pushed that idea away. After all, this was her uncle on the other side of the line, not a stranger, an uncle she grew up with, one she argued with... an uncle she disliked.

"Uncle Aaron, its Nidra. Do you remember me?" she asked.

The darkened room seemed to get even darker. A cold mist now surrounded Nidra and she shivered. A shawl was draped over a nearby chair and as she pulled it over her shoulders, he answered her question.

"Oui, I remember you. How are you doing, ma petite familiar?" His deep French accent filled her heart with both the feeling of home and of doom.

A nervous laugh escaped her lips. "I'm not little anymore, Uncle Aaron. Not anymore."

"So why do you call?" he asked.

"I'm not sure if you heard or not, but Nadia passed away last month. I just found out recently myself." Now Nidra was feeling guilty for not calling him sooner. After all, he was their blood relative.

"No, no. I had not heard. Oh, what sadness, what loss. How are you doing?" His sincerity seemed genuine but also cold at the same time. For some strange reason, Nidra felt violated; she had to get off the phone and fast.

"I... I'm... I'm fine, Uncle. I'm just fine. The reason for the call is that I will be coming up to see the house. Damara wants to see it again..." she was ready to hang up.

"Damara, how old is she now?" he asked in a low deep voice. "When do you plan on coming?"

"She's in her twenties. Not real sure, in a week? Would that be all right with you?" Now her skin was tingling, as though a thousand little bugs were boring their way into her flesh.

"That would be fine," he replied.

"Well, I must go now, Uncle, goodbye," Nidra almost slammed the phone back onto the receiver. If felt good not to be holding the phone, but why? Now she was confused. Why was she suddenly feeling so warmed and repulsed by her uncle's voice at the same time? It was an emotion Nidra never wanted to experience again.

* * * * *

If there had been any neighbors, they would have heard his yells and screams. He had found her at last! With her phone number listed on the Caller ID, it wouldn't take much to get an address now. With bare feet and only a T-shirt, he limped through the house yelling and hollering, "The blood will now be cleansed!" This was better than he could ever have hoped for; luck was finally on his side. First, it was time to clean house. Everything had to be perfect for her arrival.

"What are you so happy about?" The voice from the hallway made him stop and smile.

* * * * *

"Parker? Hey, how's everything?" Damara was excited that Parker was home when she called. She missed him and was worried that he wasn't taking care of himself. This was the first time in his life he was truly alone.

"Hey to you, too. Everything is fine. I'm keeping busy. How was your flight?"

Damara filled him in on everything she could remember. She told him how much their aunt looks like their mother and how little Paulie is so cute and funny. The call lasted over forty-five minutes, but seemed like seconds.

"Yes, I'm feeding Housie and he's just great. The cat box is no fun; Mom used to keep it clean. Your cat stinks," he complained and laughed at the same time.

"No, he doesn't!" Damara protested, but it was wonderful just talking with him. "Well, I'm hanging up now. You take care and I love and miss you."

"Oh, before you go, where did you get the old cane from? It's pretty cool. Can I have it?"

"What cane?" Damara asked.

"There's an old cane by the front door. It has a silver handle in the shape of a dog or some other animal. It's pretty worn so it's hard to tell. I found it leaning against the green chair."

"Hmm, I don't remember any cane. Hold on a sec." Damara opened the bedroom door and hollered for Carrie who answered immediately. She was in the bathroom brushing her teeth.

With toothpaste dripping down her chin and still chewing on her brush, Carrie exited the bathroom. "What's up?" she asked, trying to hold the suds in her mouth.

"Parker found an old cane by the front door. Could it belong to the lawyer?" she asked.

"Doubt it," Carrie tried to answer, but her mouth was full. She put up a finger to say *wait a second* and ran into the bathroom to rinse out her mouth. On returning, Carrie smiled. "Sorry about that. No, I don't believe he had a cane. He was carrying that briefcase and that was all. I didn't see any cane."

Damara relayed the conversation to Parker and was about to hang up when Carrie grabbed the phone from her. "Parker, it's Carrie... hi, yeah, I'm fine. Look... okay, I will. Okay, tell Ted we said *hi* too... Parker. Shut up! Now listen. Tell Ted to take pictures of that cane and I want fingerprints. It may have been left by the killer... I don't care if you touched it, we have your prints to rule out... okay, okay, that's fine. Just call Ted when you can. And would you ask Ted to call my cell when he gets a chance? Yeah, the number's on the fridge. Okay, I love you, too. Okay, we will. Bye."

Damara gave Carrie a gaze that horrified them both. What if it belonged to the killer and the killer wanted it back!

"I'm going to send Devon an e-mail. I need to give him an update on what we're doing and where we're going. I don't want to leave the country and not have anyone know where we are," Carrie told Damara, as she pulled out her laptop.

"Good idea," Damara agreed, but she was now very worried about her little brother.

* * * * *

"Excuse me, sir," the young agent said to Lewis. "I know it's late, but I need to talk with you. It's about the Bangle case."

"I didn't know you were on that case, Chad," Lewis replied. "Come in, have a seat. Want a drink?"

"No, sir, just talk." Chad quickly took a seat on the sofa and opened his binder. His hands shook as he flipped the pages. He'd never been in Lewis' office before and felt nervous being in his presence. He'd just started working for The Agency as a researcher, but he had worked hard. He wanted to be a field agent more than anything else. First, he had to prove himself, and this just might do it for him.

"Okay... talk," Lewis said, taking a seat opposite him on the other sofa.

"Well, sir," Chad began. "It's my job to complete the files." The young man stopped talking and stared over at Lewis as though asking for approval to continue.

"Okay, I'm listening," Lewis urged.

"I noticed that Senator Bangle's file was connected with a Professor Van Brunt's file that Agent Clarke is working on. She had asked me to pull a few documents, but when I looked them over wondering why they were connected, I noticed that the women are related, and more, sir. They're identical twins."

"Go on." Lewis smiled.

"I read the coroner's report on Professor Van Brunt and re-read Agent Clarke's notes. I did a little digging, sir. What concerns me is that the twin's mother died on her fortieth birthday. I pulled the reports on Ms. Maria Lee Kundick and what I found was alarming, sir."

"Which was..." Lewis asked, leaning forward, now interested in what the man had to say.

"Sir, Professor Van Brunt bled to death from the... um, women's area, sir." The man blushed and Lewis had to smile. "Well, sir, the report on Ms. Kundick was the same; severe bleeding from the uterus. I went back another generation, sir, to March 12, 1973. Ms. Kundick's mother, Bella LeBoisne, died on her fortieth birthday from severe bleeding from the uterus."

"I see, and what have you conjectured from this information, Chad?" Lewis asked proudly to his new agent.

"Sir, I honestly believe we may have a serial killer on our hands, and not just any killer. We may have a family serial killer, which puts Agent Clarke and Senator Bangle in danger, sir."

"I agree with you completely. Very good work, very good. I assume you took it upon yourself to go this extra step for Agent Clarke?"

"Yes, sir, I did. In training, they told us that to ignore our inner feelings could be a fatal mistake, sir. I hope I did the right thing." Chad was both excited and apprehensive with Lewis' reaction.

"Yes, you did the right thing, Chad. Now, you need to get this report to Ms. Clarke immediately. Also, you need to discuss this with Agent Arvol." Lewis knew this kid was hungry and if he ignored his hunger now, it would never come back. "And, let Arvol know I've assigned you to the case, too."

Chad's whole face lit up brighter than the noon sun. "Wow, thank you, sir. I won't let you down."

As the young man ran from the room, Lewis had to chuckle. Chad reminded him of himself many years ago. "If only I could be that excited and full of energy these days," Lewis said to no one in particular.

* * * * *

Patricia had been confused ever since Professor Van Brunt left her office over a month ago. There was one small little bit of information that she had refused to share with Damara when she was here. Patricia had found a small metal tip lodged deep inside of the dead Professor's uterus, and she had no idea what in the world it was. After sending it off for analysis, the report came back stating that it was made from a special type of surgical steel, but that's not what confused her; what confused the doctor was the report. It stated that the metal contained minute traces of animal blood. It wasn't visible to the naked eye, but was wedged deep inside the old cracks of the steel tip.

"What would animal blood be doing on a surgical steel tip deep inside the professor?" Patricia asked this question repeatedly.

Even a large manufacturer of surgical instruments couldn't identify the steel tip. Her last hope was a local veterinarian she just called asking for help. He was now searching his catalogues to see if anyone in his profession would have a need for such a tool. Her cell phone rang, and her Caller ID displayed *Vet*.

"Please let him have some answers for me," Patricia asked the ceiling. "Doctor, do you have anything for me? I hope."

"Not really, Pat, it doesn't resemble anything we have, but it reminds me of my dentist visits. Did you try Dr. Duglass? Perhaps he could match it up."

Patricia was disappointed but understood. This was not going to be an easy hunt. She wasn't going to give up anytime soon.

* * * * *

"Trick or treat!"

Three little Batmans all wearing a different style outfit, a golden-haired princess, and a little Holly Hobbie with yellow braids held out their bags, anxious to grab and run.

"Thanks, lady," one of the little Batmans said before darting down the steps and across the lawn. Little Holly Hobbie grabbed the candy from Louise's tray and quickly ran down the stairs.

"What do you say?" a voice from the lawn yelled.

Holly Hobbie stopped running, turned, and yelled out, "Thank you!"

"You're welcome," Louise yelled back. She loved seeing all the little ones in their cute costumes.

Louise turned to set the candy back on the small table when a buzz and a hot flash singed her ear. As she reached up to brush away the bug, blood ran down her face and onto her shoulder. A vase in the living room exploded into pieces and scattered around the room. A small fragment of glass hit Bob on the arm and a small trickle of blood pooled on his skin.

"What the hell!" Bob yelled, jumping to his feet.

"Get down!" Carrie was already on it. Her instincts took over before she realized anything was happening. Her gun was ready and in her hand pointing to the ceiling as she clung to the wall next to the front door. "Everyone all right?" Carrie asked, demanding an answer. "Crawl into the living room and stay flat on the floor, *now!*"

Louise crawled to her husband who was already on the floor. Damara came running down the stairs with Paulie only a few steps behind.

"*Stop,* stay there!" Carrie ordered.

The two froze on the middle landing as if a motion picture had been paused. Carrie was now on her knees and inching her way out the front door. She had already turned off the porch light and the dark landscape with its ominous shades of hidden dangers lurked only feet in front of her.

"What the..." Carrie whispered, as she squatted behind the bushes in the senator's yard. "There's no way he could have gotten here that fast."

"Who are you talking to?" Damara asked from directly behind Carrie.

"Holy shit! I thought I told you to stay put." Carrie rolled her eyes and took a deep breath. "You scared the crap out of me!"

"Sorry," Damara said meekly. "What's going on?"

"I have no idea and you shouldn't be out here," Carrie answered, now peering over the bushes.

"Why not, it's only trick-or-treaters," Damara added. "And why are we whispering?"

"Trick-or-treaters don't usually carry guns; unless your aunt is giving out really crappy candy," Carrie snapped.

"Guns? What are you talking about?" Damara asked, ducking her head down further.

"Someone shot into your aunt's house and just missed her. It scraped her ear, that's what." Carrie's head poked up again as she scanned the yard for anyone moving.

The parents of the young monsters and angels had already grabbed their children and ran for cover. A few were now just regaining their nerve to move. She could tell they were not sure whether to stay put or try and make it to the safety of their homes.

"This is Agent Clarke of the FBI! Stay where you are. I need to determine if it is safe. *Do not move!*" Carrie sat on the damp dirt next to Damara and checked her belt for her phone. "Damn, it must be inside... Damara, I need you to crawl back into the house and call the police. Someone may have called already, but I'd feel better if I knew that they had actually been notified."

Damara sighed. Her hands were shaking and her legs felt weak. "I'll be right back." Damara had spoken as though she was simply running into the other room for something.

Carrie sat on the moist earth for a few more seconds before she poked her head up again to get a look. Nothing, all was silent except for some movement in a car across the street, but she brushed it off deciding it was probably a parent and child taking harbor from the gunshot.

Sirens wailed in the distance and Carrie sighed as three patrol cars screeched to a halt in front of the senator's house.

About damn time, she said to herself.

Two armed officers ran into the house and another one stood boldly in front of Carrie. His gun was pointing directly at her face.

"Put it away, Officer. I'm an agent of the FBI. My badge is in the house." Carrie glanced up at him. "If I was the bad guy, you would never have made it this far."

She handed the officer her gun; handle first. He reached down and helped her up. She smiled at him, but he didn't smile back.

"What took you so damn long?" she asked.

"We came as soon as we got the call then we were called off. It was about ten minutes later that the call came again. How long have you been here?" he asked.

"The call was called off? Yeah, right. I need to see how the senator is doing. Can you check out the yard, please?" Carrie asked with a slight hint of sarcasm. "And when you feel all is clear, you can come in and give me my gun back."

Louise was holding a cool cloth next to her ear and her family was sitting protectively around her. She smiled as Carrie entered the house.

"Thank you," Louise said. "I'm glad you were here."

"I am, too," Carrie answered. "Is this how all your Halloweens are? Gunfire and all that? I always thought New York was rather wild, but you live in the suburbs. What happened to happy families and apple pie?"

"This isn't normal for this neighborhood. I'm just glad you're here, Carrie," Bob answered for Louise.

"Senator Bangle," a young officer spoke gently but with authority. "We've checked out the house and yard. All's clear, ma'am. The Secret Service will be here in a few minutes. They'll be standing guard all night."

Carrie walked outside as the officer continued to talk with Louise and her husband. The young officer who had her gun approached from the driveway.

"Here you are, ma'am," he said with a smile.

"Thank you, and here's my badge." Carrie smiled back. "Find anything?"

"No, all's quiet. A few men will be here soon and will stay all night. You should have no more trouble."

"I hope you're right." As she spoke with the policeman, Carrie couldn't help but notice the movement in the car across the street.

"What is it?" he asked.

"Nothing, I'll check it out later. You said you covered the whole area, correct?"

"Yes, ma'am," he answered, jotting down notes in his small book.

"We should all be fine then. Thanks," Carrie said, still staring at the car across the street.

* * * * *

"What the hell was that?" Mark asked as someone or something bounced off the side of their car.

Whatever it was had jumped back up and ran down the street like a cat being chased by a vicious dog.

"I don't know," Gail answered, trying to see what was going on. "Maybe some kid?"

"No, something is wrong. The lights just went out on the front porch. I don't like this." Mark pulled out his cell phone and punched in 911. When the dispatch answered, he gave the senator's address and requested the assistance of the Secret Service.

"Someone's just come out. Look! They ducked behind those bushes," Gail said, pointing toward the house.

"Maybe I should get out and investigate," Mark suggested.

"You'll do no such thing!" Gail demanded. "I'm not going to be a widow now that you've retired. You're staying right here."

He looked over at her and frowned. "I wonder if James Bond had this much trouble?"

"If you looked like him and had his body, I'd probably let you go. But you're my old and frumpy husband, so you stay here."

Mark had to smile. There was no arguing with her. He knew she was right and it would be stupid to leave the safety of their car right now, but he felt he had to do something.

"Duck!" Gail whispered and with a forceful pull, yanked Mark's head down below the dashboard.

"Hey, I'm losing my hair fast enough; you don't have to help it!"

"Shh, quiet!" Gail demanded.

"What?" Mark asked.

"She's looking this way."

"Who?" Mark asked.

"Carrie! She's looking this way. I think she saw us."

"She has no idea we're here," Mark reminded his wife.

"No, she doesn't. So she would have no reason not to shoot us!" Gail sneered at her husband.

"I hadn't thought of that," he answered.

"I sure hope no one sees us," Gail murmured.

"Why?"

"Cuz they'd think we were doing the nasty," she whispered.

Mark glanced over at his wife, which kinked his neck. As he rubbed the muscle just below his ear, he asked, "The what?"

Gail rolled her eyes. "The nasty!"

"What is the nasty?" he laughed.

"Oh, Mark. You know… what girls do to guys as they drive around. I read about it in a magazine." Gail's face blushed pink and she quickly looked away.

He had to laugh. "The nasty, huh?"

The two remained hidden in the rental car long after the Secret Service had fallen asleep in their car. Once all had quieted down, Mark felt it was safe to start the engine and head back to the hotel. This was supposed to have been an easy case, but now he wasn't so sure and it didn't make him feel any better knowing that his wife was with him.

The Agency

It would be one thing to get himself killed, but completely another if anything ever happened to Gail.

* * * * *

"What do you mean you don't know," Carrie screamed into the phone. "Then find out, damn it. Somebody shot at the senator. If it had been any closer, we'd be going to another funeral!"

"Carrie, I have some agents looking into it," Lewis said, trying to calm her. "I am not taking this lightly."

"I don't like this, Lewis. I don't like this at all." Carrie knew her blood pressure was rising, but at this point, she didn't care. "Jeff... someone tried to kill the senator tonight..."

Lewis stopped her in mid-sentence. "Carrie, if someone was really trying to kill her, Louise would be dead now. Not alive with a bandage on her ear."

His statement worked. Carrie quieted down, just thinking. If someone wasn't trying to kill her, then what were they trying to do?

"Carrie?" Lewis asked.

Carrie didn't answer. Her mind was turning; she had to figure this one out.

"Carrie?" Lewis asked again. "What's wrong with you?"

"Okay... okay," she said into the phone. Carrie wasn't talking to Dr. Lewis. She was actually talking to herself. As Carrie paced the floor, she spoke aloud into the phone. "If someone shot at her, not wanting to kill... then they're just trying to scare her. But if it was an honest miss, then..."

"Carrie, why don't you take care of this one yourself? I'll talk to you in a few days."

She didn't answer; instead, Carrie continued verbally to surmise as to what was going on.

"I'll talk to you later!" Lewis yelled into the phone; then he hung up.

* * * * *

"I'm sorry, sir, the mission was a failure," the young man stated into the phone. "Yes, sir, I know. Sorry, sir... Yes, sir... Next time I won't miss."

The phone slammed down in the oval office. He then proceeded to pace across the blue and gold rug talking to himself. "Damn bumbling idiot."

"Who's a damn bumbling idiot?" Vivian Strickland asked, as she closed the door behind her.

"Madame President! You startled me," Stan said with his eyes now wide with dread.

"You didn't answer me," Vivian replied. "Who is a damn bumbling idiot?"

"Oh... um, no one," he stammered through his lie.

Vivian walked around her desk and sat in the large chair. She rested her elbows on top and leaned forward. "Stan, I may've been the president for only about a year, but I'm not stupid! And... I don't appreciate being lied to. I'll ask again. Who's the bumbling idiot?"

Stan was getting angry. How dare this woman put him on the spot like this? Just who in the hell did she think she was anyway? After all, he *was* the secretary of state, and he never gave her any reason to question him before. So what's the point? What was she after?

"I'm sorry, I was talking to myself. Don't you ever talk to yourself, Viv?" he asked, now wishing that when he talked to himself he didn't talk aloud.

"Sometimes," she smiled. "Now, who is it?"

Stan didn't answer, but he did stare deeply into Vivian's eyes.

"If you're trying to intimidate me, give it up. Been there, done that, got the T-shirt. So who are you talking about?" Vivian stood and walked around to the front of her desk. As she leaned back against it, she folded her arms across her chest and said, "Ya know, Stan, I've experienced things I never thought I would. And... I've learned, Stan. I've learned. You are mad at someone for not doing something you wanted or for doing it poorly. So, who is it? Who made you mad, Stan?"

"*No one!*" Stan yelled at her. "Why does it have to be anybody anyway?"

"What are you up to, Stan?" she asked, not reacting to his shouts. "What have you done?"

* * * * *

"Carrie, would you quit fidgeting? Now you're making me nervous," Damara stated, pulling the thin blanket up over her shoulder. "Why is it always so cold on planes anyway?"

"Don't know, but I have got to go." Carrie repositioned herself again for about the hundredth time.

"Then get up and go!" Damara demanded. "We still have about forty minutes before we land. They'll be announcing it any minute, so you better hurry."

Carrie tugged at her seatbelt. As the clasp loosened its grip, she stood and stretched. "I hate planes."

All was quiet except for the hum of the engines. The floor vibrated beneath her feet and the reflections of the passengers' faces in the windows gave Carrie a feeling of being entombed.

"I hate flying," she whispered, as she headed toward the back of the plane.

A man was heading up the aisle toward Carrie. He glanced away as she smiled at him. As he edged around her, she suddenly got the feeling that she knew this person, but she just couldn't place the face.

Strange, she said to herself, as she opened the bathroom door.

* * * * *

Mark plopped into his seat and fastened his seatbelt. Gail stirred gently in her sleep. Mark smiled at his peacefully slumbering wife.

She is too trusting, he thought to himself. Then he kicked himself. Why didn't he smile at Carrie? Now she'll be thinking about him. *What an idiot.*

* * * * *

Two dings echoed through the cabin. "Good evening. The stewardess will be by to pick up any last minute items you'd like to discard. If you'd please put your trays away and adjust your seat in its upright position, I'd really appreciate it. We have been cleared to land, folks, so it shouldn't be much longer. For those of you who'd been sleeping, I apologize for having to wake you, but after all, this isn't the Hotel Hilton now is it? For those of you who are visiting, I welcome you to Winnipeg. For all others, welcome home and thank you for flying Air Canada. We hope to see you again soon."

"Thank God." As the message was repeated in French, Carrie sighed and glanced at her watch. "We're just about on time. Maybe a couple of minutes early."

"What time is it?" Damara asked groggily.

"It's almost eleven." Carrie yawned.

As the girls adjusted their seats, a young man across the aisle smiled. "I take it you do not like to fly?" he asked with a strong French accent.

"Now that's an understatement." Damara smirked.

"Sorry, no I do not," Carrie grinned.

"Hmm, az long az ze number of landings equal ze number of takeoffs, you are fine." He laughed.

"Thanks," Carrie added, not sure if she liked that comparison or not. "So, is this your home?"

"Yez, it iz. I've lived here me whole life. What about you?"

"Oh, I'm from nowhere special. Just a generic American." Carrie looked into his dark blue eyes and felt a warm caring gaze coming back at her. "Actually, I'm from Colorado," she added with a smile.

"I zee, Colorado iz a beautiful place. I've been there many times."

"Stewardesses, please prepare for landing. Ladies and gentlemen, we will have you down in only a few minutes," the captain's voice echoed through the cabin again as he repeated his message in French.

"Well, you enjoy Canada. Okay?" he smiled.

"Yes, I will. Thank you."

He nodded then busied himself by gathering his belongings that were under the seat in front of him.

"A friend of yours?" Damara whispered.

Carrie grinned then prepared herself for landing.

* * * * *

"Are we there yet?" Gail asked, as Mark tapped her shoulder.

"Yes. We're landing," he said.

"What's wrong?"

Mark sighed. How in the world could she possibly know that he was bothered by something? All he did was tap her shoulder.

"Nothing."

"Right." Gail smirked.

"How do you know these things?" He shook his head. "All right, I had to walk past Carrie earlier. I'm sure she recognized me."

"Recognized you from where?" Gail asked. "She has no idea who you are."

"Maybe, but she will. Just give her time."

"You're paranoid." Gail laughed. "Perhaps I should be the one employed, not you."

"To coin a phrase, ha-ha... you're so funny," Mark replied, tugging on his seatbelt.

* * * * *

Greghardt stood solemnly next to the newly dug grave. The beating of his heart slowed as the wind chilled his soul. A feeling of helplessness overwhelmed him. Suddenly, Maddie Edwards was standing in front of him; judging him.

"It wasn't my fault, Mad. None of this was my fault."

"Can't you ever accept the responsibility for anything?" she asked.

A strong urge to run, to hide, was more than Allen could stand, but this wasn't the place or time to surrender to his inner urges. As he fell to his knees, tears stung his eyes.

"Maddie, my God, Maddie, what have I done?" he yelled as loud as he could. "My God, what have I done?"

Sobs stronger than crashing waves hit Greghardt. He sobbed into his hands and rocked back and forth on his knees.

"God, please forgive me," he prayed.

"And why would He?" Maddie asked. "How many lives have you helped to take from this world? What did you do to try to stop it anyway? Anything? Anything at all?"

"It's not my fault! It's out of my hands," he sobbed.

Maddie shook her head. "Nothing is out of anybody's hands unless they want it to be. You just don't want to get involved anymore. It's easier to look the other way, isn't it? Or are you just playing at being in charge?"

Allen raised his head to look into Maddie's face. What he saw amazed and frightened him. A strong and determined woman standing bold and strong challenging him to be more than what he was or ever could be. Everything The Agency had put her through would have destroyed him, but what she endured only made her stronger. How was this possible? He had to remind himself that he was supposedly talking to a dead woman, a woman who not only accepted her fate, but also accepted it honestly.

"How do you do it?" he asked between sobs.

"The same as every other woman in this ugly world of ours. We simply do."

As Maddie walked away from the broken man, Greghardt wished he had handled everything differently years ago. He had failed her when she needed him the most. He had turned his back on the one person who would never have turned her back on him.

Greghardt remained at Danny's gravesite late into the evening hours. For the first time in his life, he prayed. He prayed not only for Danny's soul, but also for his. A soul that needed more help than anyone could offer. He also made a deal with God that evening. A deal he would take to his grave, but would never break.

* * * * *

The mid-morning air was crisp and cold. Not a bitter cold, just a wet cold. The Fort Garry Hotel stood boldly silent behind Carrie as she pulled the fur collar of her jacket closer around her neck. She smiled to herself as she turned to admire the towering old hotel. It was a symbol of strength for this city. According to the pamphlet in her hand, the Grand Trunk Pacific Railway built The Fort Garry in 1911 when it completed the link between its east and west lines.

"Beautiful... absolutely beautiful... wish you were here," Carrie said into the cold breeze.

"Yes, it is," said a deep voice from behind.

Startled, Carrie turned to stare into a forlorn face of someone who had seen and been through it all.

"I'm sorry, I didn't think anyone was out here but me," she said, slightly embarrassed and confused.

Where did this man come from anyway? There was no one here when she descended the front steps. The beautiful landscape hid nothing. It was as if he simply appeared out of thin air.

"This is a beautiful hotel, is it not? This site chosen is one block from the railway station. Chateau style. Many railway hotels built across Canada before 1930 are chateau style." The old man smiled as he lit his hand-rolled cigarette. He offered one to Carrie, but she smiled and shook her head no.

"You like old buildings?" he asked.

"Oh, yes, very much. I've been told that I must have lived before because I can stand in front of old buildings for hours upon hours."

He smiled and winked at her. "Yes, I'm sure you can," he added between puffs.

"Well, I'll be missed for breakfast if I don't go in soon." Carrie nodded goodbye and headed for the steps, savoring every second.

"What room did you stay in last night?" he asked from behind with his thick French accent.

"Excuse me?" she asked, turning to stare at him.

"Room? What room?"

"Why?" Now Carrie wondered where this conversation was going.

He was short with graying temples and a thinning hairline. He wore a checkered vest and carried a matching cap. His wool slacks were long and covered his shoes. A long woolen overcoat protected him from the cold, and a scarf was nestled around his neck to protect him from the sharp breeze. His apparel definitely matched the era of the hotel, but for the current period they were living in, this old man's choice of clothes was way outdated. Carrie instantly liked him, for he did possess a strong eccentric disposition.

"This old place is full of ghosts. You said you lived before. Did you feel them?" he asked with a wink.

The worn-out old man now had Carrie's undivided attention, for this was a subject that definitely interested her. It actually wasn't until she felt Nadia's presence at the gravesite that she believed in ghosts. Carrie knew that Nadia had been there that day, but for what purpose she had no idea.

"Ghosts? Really?"

"Yes, ghosts. Mostly on the second floor."

She sighed. "We're on the fifth. Nothing happened. I slept like a log."

"Hmm, well, maybe next time you'll answer her?" he asked with a smile and puffed on his homemade cigarette.

"Maybe."

They both nodded their farewells and parted with one last quick look and a smile.

* * * * *

As she walked through the immense lobby, Carrie's steps echoed off the marble and dark sculptured wood, which gave her a warm sensation of contentment. The dining area was just ahead and she could see Damara and Louise at a table next to one of the large draped windows. They waved to her as she entered and Carrie waved back.

"Well, nice of you to finally join us," Damara said with a hint of sarcasm.

"Sorry, I was enjoying the fresh clean air for a few minutes." Carrie swayed her arms as she mocked her friends. "By the way... did you know this place is haunted?"

"No, I don't believe we did," Louise added, sipping on her coffee.

"Well, I guess that will be for another time since we're leaving today anyway," Carrie yawned. "I met a nice man out front this morning. He told me all about it... he even told me what room to stay in."

"Really?" Damara asked. "What's the number?"

"Number of what?" Carrie asked, taking a drink of her orange juice.

"Of the room?" Damara added.

"Oh, two something... we can ask the desk clerk," Carrie said while reading the menu.

Louise and Damara winked at each other before reading over their menus.

* * * * *

Arvol paced the floor. He had not heard back from Lumer in a couple of days nor had he heard from Carrie since she'd arrived in New York. Not being involved... or being involved at a distance wasn't something Arvol cherished. Was he even involved at all? As he stared out the window, Arvol suddenly felt very left out; almost pushed out. He grabbed the phone and hit the small numbers with such force that a couple of the buttons remained lit. No ring came

The Agency

from the other end. Arvol had broken the phone. The brightly colored tablecloth flashed across his mind. That damn ugly red rose still shining brighter than all the others did. His stomach hurt and his ears were ringing.

"Damn!" Arvol yelled. "Damn, damn, damn!"

"Sir?"

A young man stood nervously in front of Arvol with shaking hands. His eyes were wide and his smile tense.

"Sorry, didn't see you come in," Arvol replied.

"Yes, sir," the young man said. "I'm Chad, sir. Chad Bloodworth. I'm assigned to your case, sir."

"What case?" Arvol asked, looking angrily up at the nervous young man.

Now Chad didn't know what to say. "Sir, the uh... Senator Bangle... um, Carrie..."

"Yes, yes." Arvol suddenly remembered that since a senator was involved, it became an official case. If it was just one of their agents' lives in danger, no one seemed to care. It was as if the agents weren't as important as a senator. "I'm sorry. Come in, sit down."

The boy-man anxiously fumbled through his papers.

"Well?" Arvol asked. "I don't have all day."

"Yes, sir. Well you see, sir..."

"Cough it out, Chad." Arvol knew he was being overcritical of this new agent because of his concern over Carrie. He had to calm himself down and stop overreacting.

"Well, sir... I..."

"Yes, yes," Arvol urged.

"Sir, I've researched the shooting into the senator's house, sir. And..."

"Yes, yes."

"Well, sir, it wasn't Agent Davison, sir. We don't know who shot into the house, sir."

"Fuck!" As Arvol's large-fisted hand struck the table, his knuckle caught the side of the phone and sent it flying off the table. It crashed against the wall and broke into pieces.

"I'll get you a new phone, sir," Chad said, not knowing what to say or do.

"*No!* Not the phone, *Chad*. Schedule a meeting with Lewis immediately. Something else is going on here... and I don't like the smell of it."

* * * * *

Carrie handed the clerk her credit card and paid the bill, but before leaving, her curiosity had to be fed. "Ma'am," Carrie said, as she signed the receipt. "Is the second floor really haunted?"

The desk clerk smiled. "There are rumors to that effect. Who told you? Did you read it somewhere?"

"No, I met a man outside this morning and he told me."

"I saw you outside as I was coming in. You were alone. Out front, right between the hedges, right?"

Carrie handed the signed receipt back to the clerk and frowned. "There was a man with me."

"I'm sorry," the clerk said, as she examined the signature. "Ms. Clarke, I watched you. You walked outside, turned, and admired the building. Then it looked like you were talking to yourself. I thought you might have been on your cell phone. After a few minutes, you climbed the steps and entered the hotel. There was never anyone with you."

The skin on Carrie's back hurt as though a thousand needles were jabbed in at once. "Are you sure?" she asked. "You're just trying to scare me aren't you?"

"Yes... I mean, no... I mean, yes, I'm sure and no, I am not trying to scare you. I was gathering my things from my car. I watched you."

"Why? Why would you watch me?"

"Because I was wondering if you were all right. You kept turning around."

Carrie glanced around the room. It seemed that time had stopped. She turned back to the clerk and asked, "Is this hotel really haunted?"

"Yes, ma'am, it is. The second floor, room 202 especially."

"Thanks," Carrie replied and hurried off.

* * * * *

"Okay, Arvol, you called this meeting." Lewis drank his coffee as he jotted the date on the top of his paper.

The room was quiet. Too quiet. Arvol didn't move; he only stared at Lewis. Lewis raised his head and their eyes met. Neither stirred; neither spoke. Chad studied both of them with intent. His fear grew, as the room remained silent. For the longest time, no one moved as the gaze between the two men intensified. Chad now felt warm. The heat from these two men was making him sweat. Water, Chad needed water. As he reached for his glass, Arvol spoke.

"So, Jeff. Will we do this again? Or this time, will it be done right?" Arvol knew he was striking a nerve and that was exactly what he wanted to do.

Lewis' anger had awakened and he wanted to curse the day he hired this man. "Fuck you!" Lewis yelled out in defense.

Chad was caught off-guard by Lewis' explosive response and his hand knocked over his glass of water. The flow rolled to the other side of the table and began to drip on the floor, but no one was concerned over the mess. Chad sat glued to his seat as the two men stared at each other again.

"Want to kill off another? Let another one of yours down?" Arvol asked with no emotion other than force of stance and determination.

"Another what?" Chad whimpered softly.

Lewis wanted to kill this man. As his mind raced through his options, suddenly all his past mistakes flooded in to haunt him all at once. He could think of nothing else. Hundreds of children... Maddie... little Danny... Toby.

Instead of yelling, Jeff only whispered, "Fuck you, Arvol!"

The room became deathly quiet again. For several minutes, no words were spoken then Lewis said in a soft but broken tone, "Do what you have to do."

"Thank you, sir." Arvol immediately stood and motioned for Chad to follow.

Again, Lewis was left to deal with his haunting past... alone.

* * * * *

The excitement was almost more than he could handle. She was coming to him! He didn't have to go anywhere. She was coming home and eventually she would find her way to him. The house, the house would have to be cleaned. As he dialed the number, his feet danced to a silent tune. His housekeeper was surprised to hear from him. She had been ordered out and to never return over ten years ago.

"Fine, I'll come, but it will cost you!" she ordered.

All he did was laugh. Money was no object now; everything had to be perfect for this special reunion. Absolutely perfect!

Part 6

Vivian stood at the window and gazed out over the immaculate and pristine lawn. Faces of curious visitors faded in and out only a few short feet away. Faces of people that she was responsible for, who relied on her and her judgment to keep them safe. Alfred's voice, the man she had to replace only a year earlier, echoed through her mind; taunting her... challenging her. Why was he so prevalent in her thoughts at this particular moment? Something suddenly occurred to her that made the palms of her hands sweat.

"Damn, why am I so stupid?" she asked herself, as she pushed the buttons one at a time on her phone.

"Yes, ma'am?" the young voice replied from the other end.

The sweaty palms made her feel uneasy and tugged at her. It was always a sign of trouble to come. She wiped them down the sides of her slacks, but that never did any good. They would always remain just as wet as before she wiped them. As her hair fell into her eyes, Vivian used her damp hands to push her hair from her face. *At least they're good for something!* she said to herself.

"I need a copy of Stanley Copperline's resume, please. How difficult would that be to get for me, Sandy?"

"I'm printing it now as we speak, Madam President. I'll bring it right in," Sandy replied with her stern professional voice.

Vivian had to smile. No matter what she asked for from her aide, Sandy always treated it as a number one priority. Nothing was too small or insignificant. A quick knock at the door signaled that the resume was ready.

"Thank you, Sandy." Vivian smiled, walking toward her.

"Will there be anything else, ma'am?"

With a strong sigh, Vivian studied the resume. "No, Sandy, that will be all. Thank you."

Without a word, the door closed softly behind the young woman and Vivian walked toward the window to stand in the warm sunlight. As she scanned the words on the paper, her heart pounded. "Damn, why don't I scrutinize my people better before I appoint them?" Vivian asked herself. "Not again."

* * * * *

"Where's Carrie?" Louise asked. "She was at the front desk, but now she's nowhere in sight."

Damara glanced around the lobby; her aunt was right, Carrie was nowhere in sight.

"I'll go ask the desk clerk if she saw which way she went. You go check the car."

However, before Louise reached the door, Damara was hollering for her to come back. It wasn't long before they had left their luggage at the front desk and were running up the large circular staircase to the second floor.

"Why would she be up here?" Louise panted.

"Because, she thinks my mom's up here!" Damara shouted out, "Carrie?"

The two ran down the long hall, but there was no Carrie.

"Carrie! Where are you?" Damara yelled.

As the two women continued down the corridor, they turned a corner just in time to see Carrie enter a room.

"Carrie, stop!" Damara yelled.

"What do you mean she's looking for Nadia?" Louise asked, chasing after Damara.

Damara ignored her aunt. She was more worried about Carrie right now.

When she reached room 202, Damara hesitated, not sure why, but she hesitated.

"What?" Louise asked.

"Nothing, let's go," Damara said, as she turned the knob and pushed the door open.

Carrie was standing in the middle of the room with her back toward them... motionless.

"Carrie, are you all right?" Damara asked.

* * * * *

"Are you sure you can read a map?" Mark asked, trying to see where her fingers were pointing to on the paper.

Gail sighed. "Yes, I can read a map and keep your eyes on the road. Not me."

"Well, I don't want to get lost. It'll waste precious time."

"Precious time? They haven't even left the hotel yet. We're way ahead of them," Gail protested.

"Fine, but a couple of wrong turns and they'll get ahead of us. Now, which way?" Mark asked.

"Maybe I should direct you to a few wrong turns just to teach you a lesson," Gail snarled. "Now let's see... we head toward the city."

"But that sign back there said that the expressway's the other way!" Mark objected.

"Who's reading the map here, you or me? Now just drive in the direction I say, okay?" Gail sighed. There was nothing more she disliked than to argue on which way the right way was while they were traveling.

"Are you sure? Should I pull over and double-check?" he asked.

Gail gave him that gaze that told Mark that if he did pull over it would probably be the last thing he ever did. Mark cleared his throat and flipped on the blinker. As he eased the car onto Saint Mary's Road, Mark smiled uneasily at his wife, then immediately fixated his eyes on the road in front of him.

"Well..." she started, "now that we've established that I'm not a total idiot, we'll follow this road and then veer to the left onto Saint Anne's Road to Fermor Avenue."

Gail stared out the window admiring the view... and what a beautiful view. Mark was confused. What happened once they reached Fermor Avenue?

"All right, I surrender. Then where?"

"You're okay. Simply stay on that road."

"Excuse me?"

"Fermor turns into Highway 1, which runs right into Falcon Lake, silly," Gail said, smiling. She knew that she was getting on his nerves, but he deserved it right now.

Besides, there was an added value. She could now read her novel in peace and quiet; for the ride from there on out would be without much talk. Gail pulled out her paperback book and flipped to the middle. She took in a deep breath and let it out slowly. As she read the first sentence, she smiled. She was happy and she was in love.

* * * * *

"Jeff, I'm telling you that something just isn't right. I can feel it. I can smell it." Vivian was adamant in her assumptions. After being publicly humiliated by someone she had completely entrusted as a mentor throughout her career, she promised herself that never again would she let her guard down. Never again would she ever second-guess her inner intuition.

Jeff's stomach was now in knots and the walls were closing in on him faster than he could organize his thoughts. *Not again, Lord, please, not again.*

"Jeff!" Vivian hollered into the phone. "Are you even listening to me?"

Coughing to give himself more time to think, Lewis wished more than ever that Maddie were here to give him advice. He no longer had anyone to turn to... no one he could confide in.

"Yes, Viv, I'm here." Jeff's hands were shaking and his heart was pounding. His self-confidence had been broken. "I'm..."

"You're what?" Vivian asked, irritated with his obvious lack of concern.

"I'm... I'm thinking... what to do," he stumbled.

"Jeff, are you all right? What's wrong with you?"

"I... I..."

The memories were too much; the final pressure had cracked the last of his resilience. Something was wrong, terribly wrong. Lewis felt, no, Lewis knew that he had caused little Danny to take his life. It was because of him that so many children had suffered. It was because of him that Maddie was living in exile. Why was God torturing him so?

The Agency

It wasn't fair. He had such high hopes for this organization and it was he who could take it to the next level of existence. Now, Jeffery Lewis just wasn't so sure.

"Jeff?" Vivian asked softly. "What is it, what's wrong?"

Lewis couldn't hold it together any longer. The sobs of self-hate and doubt overwhelmed him. Jeffery Lewis cried with every ounce of fiber within his existence. "My God, Vivian, my God, what have I done?"

Vivian sat motionless, without words. She had called to ask Jeff for help, but it seemed that he needed her right now more than she needed him.

* * * * *

The Trans-Canada Highway was an experience Damara never wanted to forget. She was going home, but to a home she remembered very little about. It was great to be alone in the backseat, for it gave her time to think about her life, her mother's life, and everything that had happened to her over the last several weeks. What used to be normal to her was anything but normal now. Damara missed her mother terribly and wished that she were now at her side. She had thrived on her mother's pride for her; she had blossomed within the embrace of her mother's love; and she had learned from her mother's patience. Now Damara was concerned as to who her mentor would be for her future trials. As her mind and heart ached, her aunt spoke softly from the front seat.

"Damara, sweetie? We're almost there." Louise was watching Damara through the rearview mirror. "Honey? I can tell you're thinking about something."

As Nidra waited for her reaction, a tear fell from Damara's eye.

"Hey, ya know what, Damara? When you were little, you used to sit in my lap and tell me how I could live with you when I grew old. Do you remember that?"

Damara laughed and wiped away the tear. "Funny, but yes, I do. I was going to build a big house and have you and Mommy come live with me forever." Damara paused before continuing. "Wow, I hadn't thought about that for a long time. Strange how our priorities change, isn't it, Aunt Nidra?"

"Yes, it is."

It didn't take Damara long to realize what her aunt was trying to do. She was trying to help her to understand that change was an okay thing to happen. That in some strange bizarre way, everything would turn out fine in the end, but before Damara could complete her thoughts, Carrie whooped in excitement.

"Thank God we're getting off this road. My legs are dead and so is my butt!"

They all laughed as Nidra eased the SUV off the highway and onto South Shore Road. They had finally arrived at Falcon Lake.

* * * * *

"Where are we staying again?" Gail asked, enjoying the sights of Falcon Lake, Manitoba, Canada. "It is absolutely beautiful here."

"Yes, it is. We could move here," Mark suggested.

"Don't tempt me."

"Check the printout. There are directions on how to get there."

Gail pulled out the paper and gave Mark the rights and lefts. "This place sounds wonderful. Falcon Lake Resort Hotel. It should be great, just like a second honeymoon. I love the word resort."

"We'll see, we'll see." Mark laughed, as he drove into the parking lot of the Falcon Lake Resort Hotel.

"Well, at least you don't have to worry about running into Carrie. I'm sure they'll be staying at the house. Don't you think?"

Mark didn't reply, he just squinted up his eyes a little and got out of the car.

* * * * *

Patricia sat stunned and couldn't say a word. What in the world was the tip of an old taxidermy pick doing lodged inside the womb of a college professor? Not to mention that it still had minute traces of animal blood. What in the world was going on? The room began to spin and Patricia wasn't sure if she was going to be sick or pass out. Her heart started pounding and her ears were ringing. The room was growing dark and her mouth was dry.

"Dr.? Dr. Worthington, are you all right?" A voice, barely audible, echoed through Patricia's thoughts. "Dr.?"

The Agency

Someone was shaking her. She could feel their fingers squeeze her shoulder. Suddenly she could hold it back no longer. Patricia had to lose her lunch or else it was going to lose her.

* * * * *

The house was immaculate. Everything was in its place. The kitchen was stocked with food and supplies. Clean linen hugged the beds and hung from the racks in the bathrooms. Not a speck of dust anywhere. The house was clean and ready for its guests. Its special, wonderful guests. Actually, they weren't guests at all. They were finally coming home. After all those long years, they were coming home, coming home to him.

It was all he could do to keep himself from running down the hill to greet them. Everything was exactly as it had been when they left. Nothing had been moved or replaced. Yeah, he'd admit that some of the furniture was beginning to look a little scruffy and worn; but after all, the stuff was old.

He glanced at the clock on the wall and wanted to scream. It was time; they'd be here any minute! What should he do, what should he do? As he plopped down on the couch, his leg ached and he rubbed it. It never did heal right ever since he broke it as a child. As he pulled his pants leg up to look at the old scar, a car pulled into the yard. His mind went blank and he sat motionless. Aaron didn't know what to do. He could hear voices outside, anxious voices. Someone was calling his name. Calling for him, but Aaron couldn't move. He was too excited.

* * * * *

As the car pulled into the yard, Louise's heart skipped a beat and Damara sat quietly in the back. Carrie glanced at the two of them and shook her head.

"Fine, I'll get out then," Carrie said, as she reached for the car door handle.

"My God," Louise whispered. "I'm actually home."

"Yeah," Damara added between tears.

Carrie hopped from the car and admired the neatly trimmed yard. Winter roses grew all around, beautiful, large, and colorful. The house was huge and even more gorgeous than its pictures. The wraparound porches gave the house a sense of comfort and belonging. She immediately wanted to sit on the top porch and admire the view.

"Are you two just going to sit there?" Carrie asked, as she headed for the house.

Louise and Damara slowly exited the car. They held hands and smiled. It felt wonderful to be back. Even though Damara didn't remember much, it was a wonderful feeling to be home.

"Uncle Aaron!" Louise yelled. "Hello, Uncle Aaron. It's us… we're home."

The three stood on the porch and stretched their arms. The fresh air was full of wonderfully mixed aroma; the pine trees, the fall flowers, and the colorful brush.

"How could you ever leave this place?" Carrie asked. "My God, this is beautiful!"

Louise pulled out a key and tried it on the door.

"Don't you think the lock would have been changed by now?" Carrie asked.

The key fit. "It wasn't locked." Louise giggled, as she pushed the door open. "Uncle Aaron, are you in here?"

"Yes, I am, young lady," a deep French accent floated in from the other room. "Come here and let me see you."

The three walked under the large wooden-framed arch. The huge room was exactly as Louise had remembered it. Damara noticed the piano immediately in the corner with all the old family photos on top.

"Uncle Aaron!" Louise exclaimed, heading directly for him. "I need a big hug, Uncle."

"My goodness," he replied, hugging her back. "Let me stand up… and is this little Damara? Oh my, how you have changed." He gave her a quick hug too and smiled. "You look just like your mother. I was sorry to hear about our loss."

"Thank you, Uncle Aaron," Damara replied. "And this is my dear friend Carrie. Carrie, this is our Uncle Aaron."

"Nice to meet you, sir," Carrie answered, holding out her hand.

He shook her hand and smiled. Carrie wasn't sure if she liked this guy or not.

Damara had already reached the piano and all the pictures. "Aunt Nidra, who are all these people?"

The Agency

"Our family. Things haven't changed a bit, Uncle Aaron. How wonderful," Louise said, walking over to Damara.

"Well, I couldn't really change our family home now could I?" he asked, winking at Carrie.

Carrie smiled back and then looked around. The bottom of the stairs was visible through the arch from where she stood. The room beyond looked like a study. Louise had been right; this house was amazing.

"Would you like a tour?" he asked Carrie.

"Why, yes, I would love one," Carrie answered.

"We'll leave you two to your memories," he said, as he took Carrie by the arm. "This way, my dear."

Carrie felt weird and almost dirty. She didn't like this man, not one little bit.

* * * * *

Devon and Jeff stared into nothingness as though each was deep in thought. Chad sat quietly not wanting to rouse either of them. Greghardt was the first to speak.

"So, Viv," Greghardt said. "Tell us again why you think Stan is involved."

"What is it with you guys anyway?" Now she was getting angry. For some strange reason, men just didn't believe her and she always had to argue with them. "Because I know this guy. He was angry at someone for screwing something up and he wouldn't tell me who he was mad at or why."

"We ran a check on him and nothing came up," Lewis added.

"Well, run it again, damn it," she yelled. "Have him followed or tap his phone. I don't care what you do, but do something!"

Lewis' phone buzzed, it was Connie. "Sir, I have the information you wanted."

"Thank you, Connie. Would you bring it in, please," Lewis asked.

"Be right there."

Vivian stared in total disbelief at the men. "What information?" she asked.

"We tapped his phone," Lewis added. "And Connie is bringing in the results."

The door opened slowly and an older woman entered. "I think you will be interested in this," she said with a smile.

"Oh?" Greghardt asked, taking the papers from Connie.

As he read, Greghardt frowned.

"What?" Vivian asked, now worried that her earlier hunches were wrong. Feeling weary, the palms of her hands began to sweat. With nothing else to use, she wiped them against her jeans.

"Hmm," Greghardt said, looking over at Vivian. "Seems you were right, Madame President."

"Oh?" Lewis asked, reaching for the papers.

"Yes," Greghardt said, handing the papers to Lewis. "This Stan guy made several calls to a man in New York. Seems the calls involved a murder for hire. How much do you pay this guy anyway? He's paying this hit man over two million."

"What? He makes nowhere near that kind of money. And who does he want dead?" Vivian asked, now worried for her own safety.

"Not you," Lewis added. "Seems he's after Senator Bangle."

"Senator Bangle! I'll bet that's where those shots came from at Halloween," she surmised.

"I bet you're right. I need to call and warn Carrie," Lewis said, heading for his phone.

"I'm going to have him picked up for questioning," Greghardt added, pulling his cell phone from his jacket.

"This is nuts," Vivian whispered, as she walked toward the large windows.

The evening sky was beautiful and gave her a calming sensation. It was always a wonderful experience visiting The Agency headquarters in Oklahoma City. *I wonder if I could get away with moving my office here,* she asked herself, gazing out at the colorful sunset.

* * * * *

Gail and Mark sat comfortably at the diner content and satisfied sipping on their coffee.

"I'm stuffed," Mark said, rubbing his stomach. "I'll never move again."

Gail yawned and stretched out her arms. "Now what?" she asked. "We can't just sit here."

The Agency

"Well, I don't exactly know," he said, taking another sip of coffee.

As she shook her head in disbelief that her husband didn't have a plan, Gail noticed a small group entering the diner. "Psst..."

Mark raised his eyebrows and swallowed. "Huh?"

"Psst..." Gail whispered again, but this time jerked her head back over her shoulder.

Mark stared at her with confusion. As he squinted his eyes, he also shrugged his shoulders. "Huh?"

Gail sighed and leaned forward. "They're here," she whispered.

"Who's here?" he asked.

"Oh my, and you're the agent! Carrie, her cousin, and her aunt and uncle. Who else?" Gail glared at her husband. "Are you here on business or pleasure?"

"Business. I knew that. I was only kidding. Can't you take a joke?" he asked with a half-smile and half-frown.

"Mark, this is not the time to argue. Now go agent yourself," she demanded.

"Go agent myself?" he asked, scooting off the booth. "That's an interesting way of putting it."

As he headed toward the men's room, he mumbled to himself, "Go agent myself. Jeez, this *is* my assignment after all."

Carrie and her small group were sitting in the last booth near the restrooms. As Mark passed, Carrie nodded to him and said hi. He nodded back but hurried his step. Carrie studied his face just knowing that she recognized him from somewhere, but from where exactly she couldn't put her finger on it. Now she had another small mystery to figure out.

"Carrie, are you going to order?" Damara asked, nudging her a little.

"Oh, sorry," Carrie said to the waitress. "Yes, I'll have..." but she couldn't shake the man's face she just saw. This was going to drive her crazy until she placed him.

* * * * *

Chad stood patiently waiting for Arvol to exit the men's room. Voices echoed throughout the airport announcing the arrival and departure of various flights. Men and women hurried by carrying their luggage or pulling screaming children by the hand. The elderly were either pushed down the aisles in wheelchairs by tired sons or daughters or escorted by motor-cart driven by half-blind drivers, their faces frozen with terror as the wheels squealed from the sudden pressure of the brakes. Chad laughed to himself. He thought it was funny how he never noticed such things before.

"Ready?" Devon asked from behind.

Chad immediately adjusted his stance. "Yes, sir!"

"Cool it, Chad, we're not in the military," Devon added, shaking his head.

"Oh, yes, sir."

Chad followed Devon, not sure how he got himself into such a horrible situation. He just knew that at any minute this guy would blow his top and that would be the last anyone ever saw of poor little Chad.

"What are you doing? Keep up, will ya?" Devon demanded.

"Sorry, sir," Chad said, hurrying to keep up with him. "Our flight doesn't leave for another hour, sir, why the hurry?"

Devon stopped dead in his tracks. Chad stopped too knowing that he had finally said the wrong thing.

"Sorry. You're right. I'm just worried about her, very worried," Devon said, lowering his eyes. "I've never loved anyone as much as her and if anything ever happened I'd never forgive myself."

Suddenly, Chad felt closer to this man and his heart reached out to him. Perhaps he really wasn't as tough as he tried to portray. Perhaps it was just a façade.

"I know, sir," Chad said thinking hard and quickly added, "So let's rush, we wouldn't want to miss that flight now would we?"

As Chad hurried off, Devon smiled to himself. Perhaps this little guy wasn't such a pain in the ass after all. Perhaps he just might be of some help, and it was nice not to be alone.

* * * * *

The house exploded with such force that all the other houses on the block rocked back and forth on their foundations. Several of the nearby homes lost their windows as the shockwave bounced off their walls. Pictures of loved ones fell from their nails and crashed against the floor. Precious knick-knacks shattered in tiny pieces as expensive vases cracked then rocked on their bases. Those unlucky enough to be home at the time sat stunned with ringing ears. Sirens blared as the local police and fire department rushed to the scene. Two secret service men remained silent in their cars, dead from the concussion.

It took several minutes before dazed people were brave enough to venture out to find out what happened, but once outside, it was obvious. The house that was nestled in the cul-de-sac, or what was left of it, blazed and cracked as the fire absorbed what little remained. The two closest homes were now on fire and people scrambled to see if anyone was home.

The chaos that day in that small little neighborhood drew news reporters from all over the world. Film crews trampled through neat little flowerbeds destroying what vegetation remained before the winter storms arrived.

"We're standing in front of what's left of Senator Bangle's house," the reporter said with a concerned face. "We are trying to find out if anyone was home at the time of the explosion, but the local police are not talking. We did find out that two secret service men were killed as they sat in their cars..."

Cameramen zoomed in on the roofs of the two houses still on fire. Water from the firefighters' hoses seemed to be feeding the fire more than putting it out. Police officers tried diligently to push back the crowd that was growing larger every minute. First aid was being rendered to those who needed it from the back of ambulances. The scene was anything but organized and the newscasters loved every minute of it.

Louise sat stunned in front of the television set. She didn't know whether to cry or scream. She fumbled with her cell phone trying to call her husband. It was eleven in the morning so the chance of either of them being home was slim to none. Tears fell from her eyes as she watched the commotion that was being filmed just feet from what used to be her front room.

Carrie also watched in horror. What started out as being a trip to comfort her friend, soon turned out to be much more. Nothing seemed to be making any sense. Whoever killed Nadia wouldn't dare try to blow up Nidra. That would be too bold of a move; no, whoever did this was definitely not a small-time rookie.

This was much, much more. She took a seat next to Nidra Louise and tried to comfort her. "I'm so sorry," Carrie said. "I don't know what's going on, but I will find out."

"Why?" Nidra cried. "Why?"

"I don't know," Carrie answered.

"Don't know what?" Damara asked, as she and her uncle entered the room.

"Someone blew up your aunt's house," Carrie replied.

"What? You're kidding, right?" But when she saw Nidra's face, Damara knew it was no joke.

"My God, Aunt Nidra, what is going on?" Damara cried out.

"We don't know," Carrie answered. "But I'm going to go make some calls."

* * * * *

Lewis and Greghardt sat silently in Lewis' office privately contemplating what to do next. With their confidence at an all time low, each was drowning deep within their own self-doubt. With the sudden and unexpected death of young Danny Davison came the need of recognizing and accepting their own failures. Each had to accept both their actions and non-actions. The Agency had excessive unlimited power and wealth, but unless that power or wealth was used appropriately and without biasness, nothing of any significance could or would be accomplished.

"So, do we just sit here and drink ourselves into oblivion?" Lewis asked, swallowing another large mouthful of bourbon.

Greghardt stared into his glass and frowned. "I used to think I had all the answers, but now I know I don't."

"Damn," Lewis yelled and threw his glass across the room.

"That was stupid. Now you'll have to get another glass," Greghardt added with a flinch.

"No, I don't," Lewis exclaimed. "I'll just drink from the fucking bottle!"

The two remained in Lewis' office long into the early hours of the morning, both desperately trying to forget what was haunting them;

the make-believe death of Maddie Edwards and the real death of little Danny Davison.

* * * * *

As he slept, he dreamt about how he would do it. It would be slow... it would be painful... it would be wonderful! But how to do it? Now that was the question. However he did it, it had to be done delicately and without malice, for he was purifying the blood... that was all, just cleansing the soul for his family's legacy... righting a wrong.

In his dream, he approached his niece with the tools of their trade. The tools he had used several times in the past. The tools of their father's trade; the tools of a taxidermist. He kept them clean of course, but there was never any reason to sterilize them. He laughed in his sleep.

He approached her and it felt good; it felt right. She was smiling at him, she was accepting of him because he was a family member she loved, but he loathed her. It was because of their bloodline that he had lost his mother at such an early age, and oh, how he missed her so.

"Mom!" he yelled. "Mommy, I'm here. Where are you, Mommy?"

She was shaking him and telling him to behave, but he was behaving. "Mommy, I am being a good boy," he repeated over and over again. "Mommy?"

"Uncle Aaron? Are you all right?"

"What?" Aaron jolted straight up in his bed. "Who's there?"

"I am," Nidra said, trying to comfort him. "You were crying out in your sleep."

"I was?" Aaron was confused and disoriented. "I must have been dreaming."

"You were screaming out and saying something about the dirty blood."

"I don't remember," he lied, rubbing his eyes. "Let's just go back to sleep."

"Okay, Uncle Aaron, as long as you're all right."

"I'm fine," he answered with his deep French accent. "Good night, Nidra."

"Good night, Uncle."

As Nidra headed back to her bedroom, something nagged at her thoughts. *Why would her uncle have a dream about dirty blood?*

* * * * *

Patricia had to reach Damara but she didn't know how to approach her with this strange news. It made her sick to think about what Professor Van Brunt must have endured just before her death. If it bothered her to just think about it, she could just imagine what Damara would feel. She had spoken to Parker and he gave her Carrie's cell number, but she already had that number. Patricia just didn't want to have to use it. She read over the report again as tears stung her eyes. It didn't make her physically sick anymore, but the emotions were still very much alive. As she picked up the phone to dial Carrie's number, Officer Ted knocked on the frame of her open office door. He smiled and his tall figure completely blocked out all the light that was emitting from the hall just beyond. They stared at each other for a few minutes before either spoke.

"How's the old death doctor doing these days?" Officer Ted asked with a slight grin. "Nothing personal; I'm sure I'll be one of your patients one day too."

"Very funny, Ted. The only reason I like my job much is that I can actually help those who've lost their loved ones. Sometimes I can make it easier for them. Especially for those who need to understand why they've had to leave this planet so soon. Or leave at all." Patricia lowered her head and a tear rolled down her cheek.

Ted took a seat next to Patricia and sighed. "What's the matter, Doc? I can tell you're upset. More bad news?"

"Yes, more bad news, Ted."

"Want to talk about it?" Ted coached.

"No, but I have to. Stick around and listen to my conversation; you might learn something."

* * * * *

"You stay here. I'm going to see if I can get closer," Mark told his wife. "I'll be right back."

Gail sipped her coffee and remained at the café table. The small restaurant had several tables outside and it was such a wonderful day that she just had to stay. It was a cool morning and there had been a light frost the night before, but the sun was now shining and all was wonderful. It was like a second honeymoon. Gail was happy and content. Along the streets, the merchants had their goods outside for sale. This was the way of doing business every Saturday and Sunday. *At least as long as the weather holds out*, the waitress had told them. Across the street, Carrie, Damara, and Louise were browsing through the wares and laughing. They were having a wonderful time just being together.

As she watched the girls shop, Gail noticed the clothes moving by themselves. A rack of dresses was slowly approaching the girls from behind. Gail's coffee dribbled from her lips as she realized it was Mark. He was scrunched down amongst the garments using his feet to scoot the rack closer and closer to the browsing girls. Then he jumped from the rack and slammed himself against the window of a store. The window shook and Gail watched in horror just wondering when Mark would go crashing through into a crowd of surprised shoppers. Mark inched his way along the window glancing back and forth as he went.

"What in the world?" Gail said, as she watched her husband. "What an idiot!"

Mark almost fell through the open door as he continued to hug the window. He dropped to his knees and crawled toward the girls. A woman almost fell over him as she exited the store. Mark glanced up at the woman who suddenly turned on him and began aggressively batting him with her large handbag. Mark quickly scampered away trying earnestly to protect his balding head. Gail began to laugh hysterically.

A table that was full of knick-knacks was only a few feet away from the crawling Mark Lumer... the new secret agent man. Mark crawled under the skirt of the table and Gail froze in terror as all the knick-knacks began to shake and fall over.

Louise turned around and tried to steady the table. She mush have thought she had bumped into it because she began to right each of the fallen glass figurines. Gail could see that Mark's feet were sticking out from under the cloth and just knew that Louise would see him. She scrunched up her face and leaned forward. As she did, her coffee tipped and soaked the tablecloth.

"What is he doing?" she whispered to herself.

Gail continued to watch her husband in utter disbelief. As the girls left the store for the next one, Mark crawled out from under the table, but he didn't quite get out from under it before he tried to stand up. The table and all the glass figurines fell to the ground with a large crash. Mark was half-standing, half-squatting when several people, including the girls, turned to see what all the commotion was about.

The owner of the store came running out screaming at Mark in French. It was obvious that Mark had no idea what the man was yelling about; but whatever it was, the owner of the store was furious. Louise approached the man on the floor offering him her hand. It was obvious that she thought that Mark had fallen.

"Oh, sweetheart," Gail yelped in glee. "Look, you found my earring! Oh thank you... thank you!"

"Oh, yeah..." Mark added, trying to find a hole to crawl into.

The owner continued to yell at Mark as Gail tried to position herself between Mark and the girls.

"Look," Gail exclaimed to Louise holding out her hand. "He found my earring. I had lost it here yesterday. It was my mother's. I would have died if I had lost it!"

Louise nodded her head and smiled. As Louise walked back to her party, Gail turned her attention back to her husband. A policeman was quickly approaching from the street. Mark was still on the sidewalk sitting amongst the scattered pieces of glass. He was pulling money out of his pocket. Gail glanced down at her husband shaking her head.

"If they lock you up, I'm not going to bail you out!" she scolded him.

Mark sighed and remained quiet as he continued to count his money.

* * * * *

Aaron counted out the old tools and spread them out onto the table. The memories these tools brought with them was just too sickening and revolting to dwell on. He remembered his father working diligently to make dead animals look as realistic as possible and some of his father's work was still on display at the local hotels and resorts. Then there were the memories of how they used these tools to drain the animal's blood. The dirty blood always had to be removed or it would ruin the carcass… he had always been the one to clean out the animals and he had hated it. Cleanup was a nasty, smelly job that always fell on Aaron. His stomach always turned as he walked deep into the woods with his shovel to bury the blood with the discarded internal organs.

"Hi, Unc," a voice echoed from behind.

Startled, Aaron turned to see Damara smiling from the shed door. "Hi!" He took her arm and together they both walked out into the fresh air. "You don't want to go into that dirty shed. Nothing of interest in there, just gardening junk and some old tools."

"I was just enjoying the garden. This place is awesome. I am slowly remembering more and more. I noticed that my old swing is still here. Do you think the ropes are still good?"

"I wouldn't trust them," he suggested. "Perhaps one day I will get around to replacing those old ropes. So, tell me. Are you still driving to your grandparent's today?"

"Yep, we're going to leave in a few minutes. Are you sure you don't want to come with us?"

"Nah," Aaron said with his deep French accent. "I'm not related to them, you are. You go and have a great time."

"Thanks, Unc," she said, kissing him on the cheek.

As she walked back toward the house, Aaron rubbed his face. No one had ever kissed him before. It felt both disgusting and wonderful at the same time. He shook his head and told himself that it would be her turn someday to be old and alone.

* * * * *

Carrie's cell phone rang, but as hard as she tried, she couldn't unhook it from her belt. She flipped the phone open and yelled out, "Hang in there, please… I'm trying to get to you."

Damara and Louise laughed. It was the funniest thing they had ever had the pleasure to watch.

"Carrie, you're a nut!" Damara giggled.

"Hello?" Carrie said embarrassingly into her phone at last.

"Carrie? It's Dr. Worthington… Patricia Worthington from Bozeman, Montana."

"Yes, ma'am, what can I do for you?" Carrie replied, not wanting either Damara or Louise to know who she was speaking to – just in case it wasn't good news.

"Can you talk to me privately right now?" Patricia asked.

"Not really. What's this about?"

"I have the lab results on Professor Van Brunt. I really do need to discuss the findings with you. Can you call me back soon?"

"Just talk." Carrie decided that since no one else could hear what the doctor had to say except her that it would do no harm if she took the call. All she had to do was not show any emotion no matter what she learned.

Carrie pulled her notepad from her case while listening to the doctor. Worthington described slowly what she had found inside the professor's womb and what it turned out to be. Carrie was shocked, but it was important that she didn't show her true feelings, so she just smiled and nodded her head. After several minutes, her notepad was full of scribbled writings, and her imagination was running wild. As she hooked her phone back onto her belt, both women questioned her about the call.

"Oh, it was work," Carrie lied. "I had asked for some investigative work on another case and that was my partner letting me know the results." Carrie knew it was a bad story, but it was the best she could come up with at such short notice. She stared out the window wondering how a tip of a rusty old taxidermy tool could end up inside the professor's body.

"Did you hear Aaron yelling out last night in his dreams?" Nidra asked from the driver's seat.

"No," Damara answered, looking up from the magazine she was glancing through on the backseat.

Carrie, still staring out the window asked, "Nightmare?"

"I guess it was. He was yelling about bad blood and other weird things. It was kind of eerie," Nidra Louise said while paying attention to the other cars.

"Bad blood?" Carrie repeated. Now her mind was focusing on Aaron. Tip of a taxidermist tool... bad blood... dead professor... something just wasn't adding up.

"Tell me about your Uncle Aaron," Carrie said to Louise.

"Like what?" Damara replied.

"Yeah, like what?" Louise added.

"Well, like exactly how much do you know about him?"

"I'd say you know more than I do. I didn't know that my grandparents were related; you told me that. I did know about his siblings because we met them once or twice when they'd come to see us or we'd go to visit them, but that's about it. Why?"

Carrie pulled out the sheet where she had sketched out the family chart and studied it.

"We're going to Thomas and Mary Van Brunt's home, correct?" Carrie asked.

"That's right," Damara yelped from the backseat. "My grandparents from my dad's side."

"Okay, so then... where do the LeBoisne family live?" Carrie asked.

Both Nidra and Louise were quiet for a few seconds before Nidra Louise answered. "I guess they still live in Quebec. Wait, I know that Aaron's parents are both dead, but some of his brothers and sisters might still be around. Why?"

"I think we should go to Quebec so we can meet them," Carrie answered, still studying the family tree.

"Well, I'm up for it, but why the interest?" Damara asked, now curious as to what peaked Carrie's sudden curiosity.

Carrie shook her head and replied, "Not sure, I just think we should, that's all."

Louise pulled the car into a driveway of a typical suburban home.

"How long have you been away from here?" Damara asked Louise.

"Long time, but you never forget," Louise answered. "Are you ready, Damara?"

"You bet!" Damara said, jumping from the car.

As the three walked up the deep red brick walkway, an elderly woman stood patiently on the steps.

Louise smiled and waved. "Eileen, long time no see."

"Oui, long time," the elderly woman said, smiling back.

Louise hugged the woman and whispered in her ear. A large grin and a tear appeared on the old woman's face.

"Oh my, Damara? Is it really you?" the elderly woman asked with a lot of love emanating from her eyes. "Please, come give your ol' granny a big hug."

Damara didn't walk, she ran into her grandmother's arms and it felt wonderful. "Grandma... Grandma!" Damara cried.

"I can see your father through your eyes. You are such a beautiful woman."

As they hugged, Damara asked through her tears, "Is my grandfather here?"

"Oh, yes, he's inside. Please, please, come in, do come in."

The women followed them into the house. Tom was sitting comfortably in an overstuffed armchair comfortably watching the television.

"Grandfather!" Damara hollered.

The elderly man glanced up at Damara and smiled. "Well, if it isn't my little ladybug. Come here, my sweet."

Damara knelt next to her grandfather and gave him a hug and kiss. "I can't believe I am here, Grandfather. This is more than I ever could have wished for. I had forgotten so much, but... it's strange, it's as if I've never left. I remember everything now."

"Where's baby Parker?" he asked.

"He's home in Montana, Granddad. I came with Aunt Nidra and my friend Carrie."

He nodded to them but then immediately focused his attention back on Damara. "It has been too long, ladybug; too, too long."

"Yes, it has... too long." Damara smiled at him with tears in her eyes.

"Your sisters and brother should be here soon," Eileen said with a smile.

"My sisters and brother?" Damara repeated, all excited. "I don't... wait, I do... I do remember them. I do!"

The minutes passed all too quickly and it wasn't long before her whole family was chatting away sharing stories of their successes and failures. Damara was finally reunited with her three half-siblings; Haden, thirty-four, was a successful lawyer and married with four children. Then there was Fauna, thirty-two, single, and a doctor at a local hospital. The one Damara seemed to connect with immediately was little Yanka. Yanka was thirty and the editor of the local newspaper. She seemed to have the same goals and ambitions as Damara, and both girls were close in age.

Louise was curious to see how much everyone had grown and changed. The last time she had been with any of them was about twenty years ago. Although she was not blood related to them, it was still wonderful to see them all together again.

Carrie, on the other hand, spent her time talking about Aaron. How much did they remember about him or what were his likes and dislikes. Haden seemed to have the most memories of Aaron for he was the eldest and was a teenager when Nadia and Nidra moved away.

"He was a strange character, I can tell you that much," Haden remarked.

"I guess you will want to get back in time for the holidays?" Eileen asked.

"Well, yes, my husband and son will want me home soon," Nidra replied. "Home... well, anyway, we'll be living in a hotel now for a while until our house is rebuilt."

Carrie frowned and quickly focused her attention back to Haden as the others heard about Nidra's recent excitement. "So you were talking about Aaron's father practicing the art of taxidermy? Strange hobby isn't it?"

Haden laughed. "Yes, I guess it is, but up here, a taxidermist can make some good easy cash. Aaron's father owned a general store in town and sold his animals there. I understand he was quite good at it. In fact, some of the locals would pay a hefty price to have him stuff their dearly departed pets!"

"How disgusting can you be?" Yanka added in.

Haden continued to laugh. "Sorry, but it's true."

"How did Aaron get along with the girls?" Carrie interrupted, hoping she hadn't stepped out of bounds.

"Carrie!" Damara glared at Carrie wondering where in the world she was going with these questions.

"He hated them from what I remember." Haden winked at Damara. "He was much older than all of us. In his forties if I remember correctly. I thought it was cool to hang around with him, but my parents didn't like that much."

"Much of what?" Eileen asked, entering the room with a tray of sandwiches.

"Aaron... you and Grandad didn't approve of him either, did you?" Haden asked his grandmother.

Eileen scrunched up her face and added, "Nasty boy that Aaron. Nasty."

"Oh, Eileen... was he really that bad?" Nidra Louise asked.

"Yes, he was," Eileen stated firmly. "He was a nasty young fellow. Is he still alive?"

"Yes, he's still around," Louise answered.

"Well, you watch your back around that one; I tell you. I never did trust that boy," Eileen said with such confidence and conviction that Carrie knew she had to get Eileen to join her and Haden's conversation. "One day he would be one way and the next time you saw him he'd act like a completely different person. Weird one that boy."

"Mrs. Van Brunt..." Carrie started.

"Oh no, please call me Eileen or Granny."

"Granny... um, what did Aaron do to make you dislike him?"

"Why are we suddenly so interested in Aaron?" Louise added in.

"Just curious," Carrie answered, not sure if she was going to get an answer or not, but Aaron was a subject that Eileen loved to talk about.

"That man should have been living on his own, but no... he had to stay with Damara's mother and father. He was in his forties; he had no business living there. He'd torture and kill animals just for fun, then he'd stuff and mount them. He was a nasty boy... nasty I tell you."

Louise was shocked. "He did not kill animals for fun!"

"Then who did?" Eileen asked. "Your mother used to tell me about all the mutilated animals she'd find around the property. It had to be Aaron, who else? He's as sick as one could get."

"Did Nadia object when you wanted to have the kids stay here to live?" Carrie asked.

"Not really, she had her hands full with her two little ones. It was Yanka who really wanted to stay with Nadia," Eileen said, glancing over at Yanka.

"I did love her," Yanka added. "You have to remember that my mother died when I was born. So when my dad married Nadia, I was ready for a mother. I must have bonded with her right away. Nadia had been our babysitter ever since my mother died. She was very young, but she was the only mother I ever knew."

Louise jumped into the conversation at this point. "My sister would rush home from school just so she could take care of you kids. Tom was a lot older than my sister was, but they were so much in love. My mother, Maria, wasn't too happy about their relationship at first, but there really wasn't much she could do about it. When Nadia made up her mind that was it. Tom was the only person who could ever tell Nadia and me apart. No matter what we did, we couldn't fool him. He always knew which one was Nadia."

"She was a beautiful bride," Eileen said, looking up at the ceiling as she remembered. "Oh, I have a picture of their wedding. I'll go get it."

Carrie sat silently listening as everyone compared stories of the days long past. Without saying a word, Carrie learned more about Aaron than if she had asked specific questions to each person. She discovered that when Byron and Bella died, they left their estate to Aaron and Maria. Both remained in the house but Maria brought with her a small family: a husband, Peter, and twin girls Nadia and Nidra. Soon after, Nadia married Thomas Van Brunt and left the home, but Nidra remained. When Peter died of cancer at age thirty-seven, that left Aaron, Maria, and Nidra at the old house. Neither Maria nor Aaron wanted to leave the beautiful home; they were both very stubborn so they shared it. Maria died eight years after her husband Peter from unknown causes, but it wasn't until Thomas died unexpectedly in a car crash a year later that Nadia moved back home with her two young babies and the three older step-children. From what Carrie could gather, everyone was pretty happy and content except for Aaron. Although he was in his forties, Aaron acted more as if he was in his teens. He would constantly complain about the children and the excessive noise. Haden talked about all the times Aaron spent in his garage tinkering around. With what he was tinkering with, no one ever knew, but the garage was off-limits to everyone except Aaron.

It was getting late and was soon time to leave. Damara cried as she said her goodbyes, but she promised to return soon and they all promised to keep in touch. Louise and Damara shared talk on the way home, but Carrie remained silent in the backseat. Her thoughts were running and she was slowly putting together the pieces of the puzzle.

* * * * *

The snow blanketed the landscape and created a peaceful and beautiful winter wonderland. Crystal-clear icicles hung precariously from the trees and roof edges. As they twinkled in the morning sunlight, birds chirped announcing the early hour. Small critters rustled through the dried leaves of the underbrush in search of food. Every breath Arvol took gave him a sense of wanting more, of wanting to be a part of the world... to merge with his environment.

"Beautiful morning, isn't it, Chad?" Arvol asked, as he took in another huge breath of fresh air.

"If you say so, sir." Chad pulled the collar of his coat closer around his neck. He shivered in the brisk cold air. "What's the temperature out here? It has to be below zero."

"It is wonderful out here."

As Devon Arvol took in another breath of fresh air, Chad shook his head and shivered again. *This man is a nut!* Chad thought, as he followed Arvol up the walk toward the large old house.

Aaron was quick to open the door, which he only allowed to open a few inches. "What do you want?" he asked in his deep French accent.

"I would like to see Ms. Clarke and Ms. Van Brunt if you please?" Devon asked in French. He knew he didn't say it exactly correct, but he was sure it was close enough for the meaning to get through.

"I speak French, you do not. They left early this morning, they are not here," Aaron replied. He was perturbed by being bothered so early in the morning.

Devon took a step back and rubbed his fingers through his hair. He glanced over at Chad then back at the slightly opened door. Now he was confused. Where would they go so early in the morning?

"You must be Aaron. Let me introduce myself. I am Devon Arvol. I'm Carrie's friend. Do you know when they will return?" he asked the old man.

"Not today!" and the old man shut the door.

"Well, I guess that ends this session," Chad chuckled.

"I guess so." Devon pulled out his cell phone and found Carrie's number. As it rang, he walked around the yard and admired the beauty. "Carrie? Where are you?"

"In Canada, why?" she asked.

"Well, I'm here at the house and you're not," Devon replied.

Carrie's voice came over loud and clear. "What are you doing here? Are you following me?"

"Carrie, now... before you..."

"Before I what?" she yelled into the phone. "Now answer me, why are you here?"

There was never an explanation that would satisfy Carrie if one went around her wishes and Devon Arvol was just about as circular as it got at this particular moment.

"Carrie, I..."

"Don't Carrie me!" she yelled. "I'll be back in about a week or so. I'll call you when I return!"

His cell phone was dead. Carrie had hung up.

"Well, I guess that ends session two," Chad smirked.

Arvol huffed and headed for the car leaving Chad standing in the snow alone. Chad started to laugh. He just realized that Devon Arvol was not the big monster he thought he was; Arvol was human just like everyone one else... just human.

"Would you just get in the damn car!" Devon yelled out.

"Coming," Chad yelled back. "Coming."

Chad continued to laugh all the way back to the hotel, as Arvol fumed about hating a stupid tablecloth.

"When I get home it's going in the trash," Devon whispered.

"What's that, sir? What's going in the trash?"

* * * * *

Gail studied the map with intent then chose her words carefully. "I have no idea where they're going," she finally said.

Mark didn't say a word, but continued to follow the car that was about a half mile ahead of them. The snow banks were quickly getting higher and the temperature was dropping. Although he wasn't afraid to drive in the snow, Mark was concerned as to what the roads would be like if the temperature dropped any further.

"Well, we'll just keep following them, okay?" he asked his wife.

"Sounds like a plan to me since we don't have anything else to do," Gail replied.

Gail puckered her lips then smiled. She licked her lips then puckered them again. Gail was repeating this little ritual until Mark finally asked her what she was doing.

"I'm *thinking*," she replied sarcastically.

Mark glanced over at her and smiled. "Thinking of what?"

Gail took in a deep breath and let it out slowly before answering. "I'm wondering if..."

"If what?" Mark asked.

"Nothing, just a hunch." Gail reached into the backseat and grabbed Mark's computer. She started it up, and then asked him for his password.

"That's a company computer, I can't..."

"Give me the dog-gone password and don't be a dweeb!" Gail demanded.

She typed in the letters and numbers exactly as Mark said, and the computer came to life.

"Now I need the code to get into The Agency's mainframe," Gail said.

"Now that I can't do," Mark said.

"Look, I need to see if my hunch is right and remember... I'm not the enemy. Now give me the code."

Mark finally relented and The Agency's welcome screen flashed up.

"You don't know what you're doing," Mark said, trying to watch Gail and the road at the same time.

"Look, Mark," Gail said, getting upset. "You just watch the road and don't lose sight of them. I'll take care of this."

Gail was sure her hunch was correct; it just had to be. It was during indoctrination that she had heard how powerful The Agency's computer system was, and now she wanted to test her theory.

Gail followed the maze of links through the mainframe until she finally stumbled onto what she was looking for. "Found it!"

"Found what?" Mark asked.

"Nothing."

Gail was concentrating hard on the pages that flashed before her eyes. She couldn't lose focus now, not now that she was so close. The link was small, but she was sure that was it. She clicked on it and the little computer worked away. The screen popped up and Gail typed in the requested information to the best of her knowledge. Then she clicked on the submit button.

"Now we wait," she said, glancing out at the beautiful landscape. "It is absolutely beautiful here."

"Yes, it is, very serene and peaceful," Mark answered. "Now will you tell me..."

"Not until..." Gail started to say, but the results were coming in. "Wow, it worked. I know where they're going!" she announced proudly.

"How did you find out?"

"Easy, I remember being told about the computer system and how all the large computers of the world are connected to it or... that The Agency's computers can get information from them or something like that. So, I found the page and typed in all the information I knew about Damara and her aunt. Then I told it in what direction they were headed. It came back and told me that the most logical conclusion was Quebec where her family originated. It was easy actually."

"Does it jive with the map?" Mark asked.

Gail picked up the map and smiled. She nodded her head then went back to the computer.

"Now what are you looking for?" he asked.

"Nothing, just snooping," she replied.

* * * * *

Montgomery, Quebec was a bustling city just as any other city in any other town. People were busy going about their daily routine by car or on foot. The roads had been cleared of snow and were relatively dry. Carrie had long ago calmed down from her heated discussion with Devon and had joined in on the conversation coming from the front seat. She wasn't sure what she was expecting once arriving, but for some strange reason, Carrie just felt something would be different... something would be enlightening; almost as if something would be revealed.

They drove through the city before stopping for lunch. It had taken a couple of days to get to Quebec by car. Carrie had not realized how far away it actually was in miles, but the drive had been relaxing and enjoyable; all except for those few miles she was steaming about Devon.

Carrie enjoyed her privacy; she thrived in it. Her privacy was the one thing that bothered her about her relationship with Devon. Although she loved him, Carrie had to have her own space... her own life. A part of her had to exist without Devon, but that was the one thing Devon could not understand. That was the one thing that kept their relationship from going any further. Her commitment stopped at the edge of her privacy. It just was the way Carrie was; in fact, it was a part of Carrie's existence.

"We don't have forever on this, Carrie," Louise said from out of the blue. "I do have to get back to work... and with Christmas coming, I do need to get home soon."

"I know, but I feel this is important," Carrie replied.

They stopped for lunch at a small out of the way restaurant then headed for the outskirts of town to visit the old homestead.

"Now remember, I do not know if anyone lives in the old house or not," Louise said, turning down a quaint little street.

"Well, we can ask Lewis when we meet with him. Perhaps we can find out who owns the old house now," Damara suggested.

The house of Lewis John LeBoisne was small, but sat on a rather large wooded lot. Although little, the home looked wonderful to Damara.

"So how am I related to this guy?" Damara asked.

"He's your aunt's uncle, just like Aaron. In fact, he is Aaron's full brother. Remember that Nidra and your mother are only half-sisters to Aaron. Lewis John is a full brother to him. So Lewis would be your great uncle." Carrie smiled at Damara.

Although her mother had died when she was very young and although she despised her father, Carrie's life was full of grandparents, aunts, uncles, and cousins. She didn't have any brothers or sisters, but her cousins had made up for being an only child long ago.

"I'll go ring the bell," Damara said, jumping from the car and almost running to the door.

The Agency

"I do believe she is enjoying this," Carrie surmised from the backseat.

Louise laughed. "You think?"

A somewhat elderly but physically fit man answered the door. Damara smiled. He didn't smile back but glanced back and forth from the car to the young lady standing on his doorstep.

"Oui?" he asked.

"Oh my, I hadn't realized you may not speak English," Damara said quickly.

"I do all right with it," he answered her. "Now, may I ask what it is I can do for you?"

"Yes, you may." Damara was relieved that she didn't need an interpreter. "I want a huge hug, Uncle Lewis."

Surprised, the man again glanced between the car and Damara. She realized that she had surprised him, but this is what she had intended.

"I am Nadia Louise Kundick's daughter. Her mother was your half-sister." Damara stood back to watch his reaction, and she was excited when she saw a large smile on his rather handsome face.

"Oh, what a surprise. You must be... oh, don't say... Damara! That's it, you are little sweet ladybug Damara." He glanced over at the car and added, "So who are your friends?"

"Oh, I'm sorry." Damara turned and waved for the others to join her. "I have Nidra Louise with me and a friend from the States, Carrie Clarke."

He reached out, hugged Damara, and kissed her forehead. When the others reached the porch, he reached out and hugged Louise.

"What a wonderful surprise, please come in, come in. May I offer you something to drink?"

It wasn't long before they were all in front of the fire drinking hot tea. They talked about old times and Lewis was quite upset to hear about Nadia's sudden death.

"I must say, I am so very sorry to hear about my niece. Like you, Damara, I, too, lost my mother at an early age."

"We were hoping you could tell us about your mother; my great-grandmother Bella," Damara said, hoping she had not hit a sore spot.

"That was a long time ago," he said. "Long time. I have some pictures if you'd like them. I have no one else to give them to."

"You never married, Uncle Lewis?" Louise asked.

"Oh, call me LJ, please. Yes, I have a daughter. But she already has copies of these." LJ stood and left the room. When he returned, he had a small box in his hands. "Here are the pictures I have. I never put them in a book or anything. Never had any reason to do so."

Carrie glanced through the pictures, but most of them were the same ones they already had.

"What can you tell us, Uncle LJ, about Sheila and Bella?" Louise asked this time.

"Well, I hope you already know this, but Byron, my father, and Bella were cousins. That is why we stayed here. We hated her... my sister, brother, and I. We refused to go with them." LJ lowered his head. "We loved our father and it was hard to say goodbye, but we also hated him."

"Do you remember your mother?" Carrie asked.

"Oh yes, very much. She was a wonderful woman but very frail. She loved my father more than life itself. More than us kids. And when..." he stopped talking when Carrie found a picture of his father and mother.

Carrie handed him the photo that got him talking again. "She was beautiful. My father had an affair with his cousin for years. We all knew it. I'm sure my mother knew it. It made us all sick, but there was nothing we could do. My grandfather was so angry he never spoke to either of them again. He even turned his back on us kids. We moved in with my mother's parents here in Montgomery and tried to forget about him. We did all right I guess."

"Can you tell me how your mother..." Carrie started.

"Died? She killed herself. It was their wedding anniversary..." His eyes were fixated on a time that had long since passed and his face had a look of sorrow written across it as if he was reliving the moment. "...my mother was fixing my father his favorite meal. My grandfather came over and told my father that his niece was pregnant by my father again. She didn't want to believe it. I remember her crying and crying. When my father finally returned, well, of course, the dinner wasn't prepared. My mother spent the time crying and tearing through my father's things. Anyway, there was a fight, my parents never fought... never. They had lived through burying several children and raising the

The Agency

others. They always had more important things to do than fighting, but this night they fought. My mother yelled at him, cursed him and his cousin. She said how much she hated him and wished she had never married him. He yelled back and eventually he left angrier than I had ever seen him before. My sister Sarah was about seventeen at the time and she tried to calm my mother down, but nothing she said or did helped. Therefore, Sarah started to work on dinner so we kids could eat. My eldest brother, Jacob, ran after my father, but he didn't return until early the next morning."

The three sat stunned and quiet. They had read of this story, but this was the first time they heard it from someone who had actually *lived* it. This man was explaining what happened in his life many years ago. Damara and Louise both were starting to feel guilty because they were related to the person who destroyed his mother. Somehow, they felt it was their fault, their responsibility.

"My mother ran to her room and locked herself in. My sister put dinner on the table. We all sat down to eat, but none of us was very hungry. It was after we had put the dishes away that the knock came. It was our neighbor, seems his wife had seen it happen..."

"What happened, Uncle LJ?" Louise asked, taking his hand into hers.

"My mother had gone to the attic and jumped from the window. She fell three stories to her death. The neighbor had run the whole way to our house somehow praying she would still be alive. You see, my mother was seven months pregnant."

"Oh, my God!" Louise exclaimed.

Damara began to cry. Carrie sat quietly in shock.

"It was a terrible time... terrible," he said with his head hung low.

"I am so very sorry," Louise said.

"Why?" he asked. "It wasn't *your* fault, it wasn't *your* mother's fault. It was *my* father's demise. Only he could accept the responsibility. He knew better than to have fought with my pregnant mother. Not when she was so vulnerable; so weak."

Damara stood and walked around the room. She had to do something, anything, but there was nothing to do. They all remained quiet for what seemed like forever before Carrie spoke up.

"What about their house?" Carrie asked.

"Oh, it's still there," LJ answered. "Why?"

"We wish to go see it. Who owns it now?" Carrie added.

"We do... the family," he said.

Carrie looked puzzled. "You mean Aaron and..."

However, before she could finish her sentence he interrupted her. "We do not speak about the boys. Not now, not ever. I'll arrange for you to visit the house. I believe it's time for you to leave." LJ stood and faced his nieces. "Drive safely. Here's the address and directions. I'll make the call. You can probably go straight there if you'd like. It will take you some time to get there, especially in this weather."

They said their goodbyes and left quietly. During their ride to the house, nothing was said, no words spoken. The trip had been spoiled. It was no longer an adventure, but had somehow changed to become a memorial service for a woman they never met... a woman they were not related to; but a woman they were now connected to.

Damara thought about Sheila and what must have gone through her mind. She was pregnant... her baby would have moved around inside her by then. How could she kill her child and leave the others alone with that monster? She must have been in so much pain that it was all she could think of. Pain so strong, so deep that she had to stop it in any way she could... and only in death would the pain go away. They drove the rest of the afternoon to their destination deep in their own thoughts.

The old home of my family, Damara said to herself. *This is where I come from?* Bozeman was not her home after all; it was nothing but an illusion.

"We're here." Louise's voice woke the others from their dreams, their feelings, their thoughts.

"Already?" Carrie asked.

"We've only been driving about two hours," Louise said sarcastically.

"Didn't seem that long," Damara said.

"You weren't driving," Louise added.

The three gasped together as they stared at the house before them.

"Oh, my God!" Damara exclaimed.

"Did we accidentally take a wrong turn?" Carrie asked. "Are we back at the lake?"

* * * * *

Gail and Mark stood speechless at the edge of the snow-covered forest. The knew they didn't have any place to hide, so they stood there as if they were tourists, which in a way they were. Gail had found a bed and breakfast only a few miles away from the *ol' homestead* in Quebec. They could go on long walks in the snow and people would just think they were strange Americans, but when they reached the edge of the forest that sat next to the LeBoisne house, they were taken aback by what they saw.

Before them was an identical house to the one that had been built in Falcon Lake. Each brick, every window, each door looked exactly the same. The landscape was identical, down to the very last tree. Although there were no leaves, Gail was sure that each tree was identical to the one in Manitoba. The only difference was the garages. This house had a large two-story garage that resembled the façade of the large house. In Falcon Lake, the garage was small and was built of wood and painted white. It didn't resemble the house at all.

"I wonder if the garage burned down in Falcon Lake and was rebuilt later?" Gail asked, still staring at the house.

"Maybe," Mark added, not removing his eyes from the house.

"This is nuts!" Gail said, now walking toward the house.

"What are you doing?" Mark asked.

Gail shrugged away from her husband. "I don't know, but I have to get closer."

Mark pulled out his cell phone as Gail approached the house. It was still a long ways away from her, but she had to get closer. This was an unbelievable sight. Two beautiful large and intricately built houses stood thousands of miles apart, but were identical in every detail. Gail knew at that instant that they were not here to watch Carrie, but they had been hired to track down some lunatic... some crazy person.

Gail stopped when she saw the girls standing in front of the house. They looked as shocked as she did. She pulled out her binoculars and watched as they slowly approached the old home. From the corner of her eye, Gail noticed a man sitting on a horse. When she looked closer at him, she almost screamed. She knew that the girls were in serious trouble.

* * * * *

The papers were scattered all over her desk with no rhyme or reason to their placement. Tears rolled down her eyes as she continued to read. Aside from the sorrow she felt, anger rose from deep within. "I'm the goddamn president for Christ's sake!" Vivian yelled out. "I'm the *fucking president!*"

Anger, stronger than she had ever felt before, rose from within. She wanted to... she wanted... she didn't know what she wanted, but she was angry. The question was - who was she more angry at? This was the second time she had been used... the second time she had been stupid enough to fall for a man's trick.

"Damn it," Vivian said repeatedly.

The knock at the door had brought her back to her senses. "Come in," she said, trying to compose herself.

"You asked to see me, Madame President?" Stan asked, as he entered the room wearing his pristine pinstriped suit.

Vivian didn't answer. She walked boldly up to Stanly Hartman and slapped him as hard as she could across the face. His glasses flew from his nose as his head snapped back. The strike took him by surprise and he lost his balance. As he fell back he grabbed onto nothing, but his arm slammed against the bookcase and it fell forward. The edge of the bookcase barely missed Vivian's shoulder as it smashed against the floor. The glass figurines shattered and the books scattered across the room, but she didn't flinch; Vivian stood firm and strong.

"What the hell?" Stan yelled from the floor.

"Get up, you fucking bastard... get up!" Vivian yelled at the top of her lungs.

"What in the hell is the matter with you?" Stan screamed, as he tried to sit up.

"Get the fuck up, you coward!" Vivian yelled at him again.

"Are you crazy?" he asked, rubbing the side of his now bruised face.

"Not exactly, Stan. In fact, I'm more sane today than yesterday... and probably a little bit wiser. As I said... get up, you fucking bastard!"

"I'm not moving until the secret service gets here, you're crazy!" he ordered from the floor.

"I'm crazy? *I'm crazy?*" Vivian shrieked. "Who accepted the money to kill the senator? Hmm? Would you like to answer that one? Would you, Stan?"

Now Stan was suddenly very quiet. How in the world did she find out? There was no way, no way possible she could know that for sure.

"I don't know what you are talking about," he stated.

"Don't know?" Vivian started to laugh, she laughed harder than she had ever laughed before. It was a hysterical wild laugh, an uncontrollable laugh. "You don't know shit, Stan. You don't know shit."

Stan stared into Vivian's eyes. Terror gripped at his stomach. He didn't know what to do. Where was the damn secret service? They had to have heard the noise.

"Praying that help will arrive soon, Stan? Feeling helpless are we?" Vivian continued to laugh. "I know who you were mad at a while back. It was the man you hired. He missed his mark didn't he! He didn't succeed in killing her so you didn't get the rest of the money did you? That is what you were mad about. I know all about you and your stupid little plans. I know more than I ever wanted to know about you! You're a real piece of cake, Stan Hartman. But your game is over... all over, my dear friend."

Vivian continued to laugh as she headed to the door on the other side of the room. As she opened it, several armed men rushed in and took Stan into custody. As they read him his rights, she smiled at him.

"You can't prove shit!" he yelled out over the armed men's voices. "You can't prove shit!"

"I don't have to," Vivian said, her smile now gone.

Stan's face went white with fear, the blood draining down into his feet. His heart pounded begging to be released from his chest. As they escorted him from the room, Vivian waved goodbye and smiled, but Stan wasn't smiling anymore.

When the door closed, Dr. Greghardt entered the room from behind Vivian. "Are you all right?" he asked her.

"Yeah, I'm okay," she answered. "I just wish my damn hands would quit sweating."

* * * * *

The house gave the girls an eerie feeling as they stood in the living room. The furniture was exactly the same as in the house in Falcon Lake. It was even placed in the same spot. There were only a few minor differences. It was an amazing sight and must have taken great care and money to duplicate to this extent, but what frightened Carrie was how the two houses had remained the same to this day. Surely, someone would have changed the furniture or moved a picture or two. Perhaps painted a room a different color, but no, each house was an exact copy of the other.

"This is too creepy," Louise said, walking from room to room.

"Who lives here?" Damara asked.

"I don't know," Louise said.

They walked from room to room, examining everything they could. Even the dishes in the dining room were the same.

"What the hell was going on all those years ago?" Carrie asked. "This is impossible! What kind of relatives do you have anyway?"

"Weird ones," Damara surmised.

They walked through the rooms on the first floor. Everything was the same, the rugs, the pictures on the walls, the paint, and even the wallpaper. It was uncanny. None of them had ever seen anything like this before.

"He must have wanted to give Bella the same home," Damara said. "Maybe he loved her so much..."

"No, not Bella," Carrie said. "Aaron, he wanted his son to live in the same house. Little Aaron... he would have been about five years old. This was for Aaron, not Bella."

They continued to walk through the rooms in amazement. When they ascended the stairs, they were amazed that everything was the same on this floor too.

"Oh, come on," Carrie stated firmly. "Something has to be different somewhere. Or we've been drugged and this is just my dream."

"Well, then we're all having the same dream," Louise surmised.

"Yeah, me too," Damara added.

The Agency

As they started to head back downstairs, something crawled up Carrie's back and startled her. She yelled and tried to grab whatever it was.

"What's the matter?" Damara asked.

"If feels like something went down my blouse," Carrie said, squirming and trying to reach it.

"Here," Louise said, looking down the back of Carrie's blouse. "There's nothing here."

Carrie stopped and looked around nervously. "Did you hear that?" she asked.

"Hear what?" Damara asked.

"I could have sworn…" Carrie stopped talking. "That room."

"What room?" Damara asked.

Carrie ran down the hall and up a flight of stairs. When she reached the attic, she ran through the room searching, searching for something.

"What is it?" Damara asked.

"It's here… somewhere!" Carrie screamed.

Louise was now starting to get scared. "What is?"

"I don't know, but Nadia wants me to find it," Carrie screamed, searching around boxes and covered furniture.

Louise and Damara began to search too, but they were not sure what they were looking for exactly. Damara reached over a large desk and yanked a sheet off what she thought would be a mirror, but discovered a large old oil painting on canvas.

"Oh my," Louise said. "I believe that Damara has found what you are searching for."

"How do you know?" Carrie yelled from across the attic.

"The same as you know," Damara answered.

The three stood silently in front of a painting of twin boys at the age of about three or four. They stood silently… speechless.

"My God," Carrie finally said. "Aaron's a twin too. It said nothing in the paperwork about Aaron being a twin!"

* * * * *

Devon was beside himself. He couldn't stop pacing the floor in his office. He had rushed off to Canada to save someone who didn't need saving, and now he felt like a complete idiot. Why was he always so impatient when it came to Carrie? Every time he tried to act like her superhero, he only ended up making matters worse or making a complete fool of himself. Not to mention how long it took him to get back into her good graces. He loved that woman more than life itself. In fact, it was more than love... he was obsessed with her every move. However, she wasn't obsessed with him.

"Devon?" Chad stood meekly in the doorway. "I'm sorry about the last few days, sir. I gave you a hard time."

"No, Chad, it's me who should be apologizing, not you," Devon said and he wasn't smiling. "It was stupid for me to drag you up there in the first place. Carrie is just fine and she'll be back soon."

"Yes, sir, I'm sure she will." Chad turned away feeling sorry for this big strong man who wasn't so strong any longer. It seemed funny to Chad how a small little woman such as Carrie could crush such a large tough man as Devon. Chad shook his head as he walked away.

Devon decided it was time to start working again to get his mind off Carrie. He clicked on his e-mail and skimmed through all the notices. One in particular caught his attention immediately. It was from Mark Lumer. As he read the e-mail, once again, Devon's flags raised and his heart started to pound. He was right damn it, he was right. The more he read the more angry at himself he got. Now that she was angry with him, Carrie would not be taking his calls, but this was an emergency.

Her cell phone rang and rang, so all Devon could do was to leave a message, but what kind of a message would he be leaving.

"Watch out, sweetheart because according to Mark Lumer, the man who is trailing you that you don't know about, said that the two houses are identical and so are the boys?"

Now that would go over just great wouldn't it? When her voice came on asking to leave a message Devon spoke clearly and without hesitation. "Carrie, I love you. Be safe my love... and I am so very sorry. Please call me when you get a chance."

It was all he could do at this point other than to discuss it with Dr. Lewis. There was really nothing else he could do.

* * * * *

The room was ice cold and the lights were dim. He glanced around and no matter how hard he tried to remember where he was or how he had gotten there, Stan remembered nothing. Nothing except being slapped by that crazy woman who called herself the president of the United States and then being carted off by the police. Aside from that, he had no memories. He stood but his head ached relentlessly and the room began to spin uncontrollably. He felt sick to his stomach and his heart pounded.

"Damn," Stan whispered, as he fell back down to the cot. "Those fucking idiots must have slipped me something."

The door opened and someone entered, but Stan's head hurt too much to move. Footsteps echoed through the room and he heard the screeching of a chair being dragged across the floor. The louder the noise; the more his head hurt.

"Good day to you, sir," a gentle voice spoke.

"It's not too good to me, my fucking head hurts," Stan complained, holding his head with both hands. "What in the hell did you guys give me anyway."

"Nothing you won't recover from," the soft voice answered.

"Who in the hell are you?"

The voice answered softly, "My name is Maddie, but most people call me Mad. It's so very nice to meet you."

Stan lay still for a few seconds wondering who this idiot was and prayed it wasn't another crazy woman.

"Okay, Mad, I give up, what do you want?"

"I want answers, that's all, and we have all the time in the world to talk," she said softly. "All the time in the world."

Now Stan was curious. He used all his remaining strength and lifted himself onto his elbows. He turned his head to gaze into the face of the most beautiful woman he had ever seen in his whole life. She wasn't young but middle-aged, probably in her late fifties or so, but damn if she wasn't something nice to look at. He groaned as he dropped back down onto the pillow.

"I'll get you something for your head. It should make you feel better. Then I'll bring you something to eat."

As the woman left, Stan asked himself, "Room... where the hell am I?"

* * * * *

The drive back to Falcon Lake seemed to take longer than the trip to Quebec. A storm had settled across the area and was pelting them with ice and snow. Although it was in the middle of the day, it almost seemed like night. The three were nervous wrecks and none of them were enjoying the ride.

"Well, that was almost a waste," Louise said from the driver's seat.

Damara was shaking and was trying to concentrate on the road. She just knew that at any minute they would skid off the road and end up dead. Instead of screaming, Damara simply stated, "Oh, I don't think so. After all, we got to meet Uncle LJ."

"Yeah, but all we're figuring out is that our relatives are and were completely nuts," Louise added.

"It is kind of strange that he wasn't there when we got back. Or maybe he knew it was us knocking and he just didn't answer the door," Carrie surmised.

"I don't know," Louise said. "But when I see Aaron, I think I'll kill him! I don't understand why he didn't tell us about his twin."

The girls kept their minds off the bad weather by trying to figure out what was going on with their family and what other secrets they held. It wasn't long before Louise was pulling the car into the driveway and they all exhaled with relief.

"Thank God," Carrie yelped.

"About time," Damara said with a huge smile.

"I'm going to attack my uncle!" Louise stated, jumping from the car.

They all ran to the house slipping through the snow and ice. When they entered, they immediately noticed some mugs of hot liquid were sitting on a small table in the living room.

"What's this?" Louise asked, picking up a mug and smelling the contents. "Hot cocoa?"

"Really?" Damara asked, taking a sip. "Mm, It's good, too!"

"Thank you," came a reply from the kitchen. "I tried."

"Uncle Aaron," Louise demanded. "Why didn't you tell us you're a twin? Did you think we wouldn't find out?"

"I'm no damn twin," he said firmly with a frown. "Where did you get such a crazy idea?"

"We saw a painting," Damara added quickly.

"You were at the house?" he asked. "Is it still the same?"

"What's going on, Aaron?" Carrie jumped in. "Why are there two houses exactly the same? Why is there a painting of you with another little boy... and who is that little boy if it isn't your twin. You two look identical."

"I don't know, but I can tell you what I do know," he said, limping to the couch. "You probably should not have gone up there alone."

"Are you all right?" Louise asked.

"Yeah, it's just my gout acting up again, I'll be fine," Aaron said, lifting his leg onto the footstool. "Please sit down, we should talk."

* * * * *

Mark and Gail almost kissed the ground when they arrived at the lodge. Gail had never been so happy to be out of a car before in her whole life.

"Some ride, huh?" Mark chuckled.

"If you like *ice* skating!" Gail almost cried. "When can we go home? I'm tired."

"Soon, sweetheart, real soon... I hope."

After eating and bathing, Mark settled down in front of his computer. He had a reply back from Devon Arvol. He was anxious to hear what he had to say. As he read the e-mail, he smiled. Although the information was intriguing, Mark's e-mail must not have meant much to Devon... other than the senator's family must be a little off their rocker.

Mark clicked off the computer and lay down next to his wife. "I love you, Gail."

She stopped reading her book and smiled at him. "I love you, too, Mark... and thanks for not killing us out on the highway today."

"You are quite welcome," he replied.

* * * * *

Maddie smiled down at her shaking visitor. He was afraid and it showed in his eyes.

"Where in the hell am I?" he demanded.

Maddie smiled. "We're all alone."

As he tried to sit up in bed, Stan realized that he had been tied down.

"What in the hell is going on here?" he demanded again. "...and where in the hell am I?"

"Such language for such an important man," Maddie giggled.

Stan tried to remember, but as hard as he tried, he could remember nothing except being escorted from the oval office.

"Don't try to think," Maddie giggled again. "It's hazardous for your health."

She sat the tray of food at the end of his bed, then began to untie his ankles. When she finished unbinding his feet, she loosened the straps around his wrists. Stan kept glancing over at the door as he shook his hands.

"Go ahead and run, but I don't believe you'd get very far," she smiled.

"Why... guards?"

"I told you..." Maddie laughed. "We're all alone. Now sit up so you can eat. How's your head?"

"My head?" Stan asked.

"Yes, do you still have a headache?"

The man looked confused. All he remembered was being escorted from Vivian's office.

"I see, you don't remember. Well, let me refresh your memory. When you first woke, you had a headache. I gave you some medicine. I guess it's gone because you are not complaining and holding your head. Great."

Maddie placed his tray on his lap. She smiled at him. "After you've eaten, perhaps a nice shower? Your bathroom is through that door... and I just put some clean towels on the shelf. You'll be quite comfortable here, I'm sure."

Maddie closed the door as she left. Stan was starving. He poked around at his food and decided that if it had been poisoned that it didn't really matter. If he refused to eat, he would only starve to death.

He wanted to see what was outside, but it was too dark... he surmised that he had slept through the day. The only scene was his reflection in the window. As he ate, Stan tried again to remember, but he had no memories.

* * * * *

Carrie watched Aaron closely as he spoke. She knew he had to be the murderer, but how could she prove it? He hated his family,

The Agency

which was only too obvious by his evil gaze at Damara and Louise. She had sent a text message to Devon asking him to run a check on Aaron, but she hadn't heard back from him yet. It was his eyes that gave him away... and that dream he had where he kept yelling about the *bad blood*. He had to be the one... and she would be the one to prove it.

"Uncle, who was that other boy in the painting?" Louise asked.

"As you probably now know, my father and step-mother were cousins. So obviously he wasn't all there to begin with." Aaron used his finger to circle his ear... the universal sign for *crazy*.

"We know," Damara added.

"My father built the house in Quebec for my *real* mother. He built the other one here for my step-mother."

"Why?" Louise asked.

"My step-mother loved the house in Quebec, and she didn't want to leave because of that house. It was the only way my father could get her to move here."

"So they could pretend they were married?" Damara asked.

"Well, I doubt the family would have allowed them to live in peace if they had stayed. They really didn't have a choice," Aaron added.

Damara scooted closer to her uncle on the couch. "How old were you then?"

"When we moved here?" he asked. "Oh, about five or so I guess."

"You were young," Damara surmised.

"Yes and too young to understand what was really going on." Aaron frowned.

"Who's that other child?" Louise asked.

"I do not know of the painting you speak of," Aaron added quickly. "I've never seen it. Perhaps a cousin?"

"Did you have any younger sisters or brothers other than my mother?" Louise asked.

"No," he answered.

Carrie studied the old man as he spoke. She felt he was lying... it was almost as though he was trying to hide something.

"What are you not telling us?" Carrie asked firmly.

"Now what would I have to hide?" he asked scowling as he spoke.

To Carrie, his eyes were evil... she did not trust this man.

Louise gave Carrie the *eye* and added, "We're leaving for home tomorrow, Uncle. I'll miss you."

"I will too!" Damara exclaimed while leaning over and kissing him on his cheek.

Carrie watched his reaction. It was obvious that he didn't like closeness or this type of close affection. If fact, he almost looked repulsed by it.

"Well, I'm going to bed," Carrie said standing up and stretching. "It's been a long day."

"Yes, it has," Louise added. "I think we all should go to bed."

Aaron stood and walked with his family to the stairs. "You have a good sleep and I will see you in the morning."

Both Louise and Damara kissed him before heading off for bed. Carrie stood back and watched. To her, actions were always louder than words.

Part 7

As her eyes opened, the sunlit room materialized slowly from her foggy dreams. Carrie smiled as she realized where she was and rolled over to stare into Devon's sleeping face.

"Good morning," he smiled. "It's good to have you home."

Happily surprised that he was awake, she gave him a kiss. "I love you," she whispered. It felt so wonderful to finally be in her own bed, but at the same time, she was worried about her friend Damara.

"She'll be safe at her aunt's house," Devon said softly, seeing the concern in her eyes. "It's where she should be over the holidays; with her family."

Carrie sighed and stretched before getting out of bed. "I guess you're right and Parker's flying out to be with her, so everything will be just fine... just fine."

"Give her a call in a day or two and you'll see. Now come back to bed."

Carrie walked sleepily into the bathroom and studied the face in the mirror. She didn't feel like the same person she used to be. She felt different somehow. *A shower would feel good about now*, she told herself, as she turned on the hot water in the tub.

"What's wrong, sweetheart?" Devon asked from behind.

Startled, Carrie turned toward him and sighed. "I don't know."

He knew he loved her more than life itself, but Devon also knew he couldn't help her right now. As always, he understood that right now she was feeling as though she had failed her friends. Carrie had told him of the fight she and Damara had over the Canadian uncle just before she came home.

"Everything will turn out okay, Carrie. So don't be so hard on yourself." Devon took Carrie into his arms and held her tight. He wanted her more than ever right now, but she didn't need sex. What Carrie needed now was simply to just be understood.

"I know," Carrie replied, then turned and dropped her robe onto the bathmat.

As she stepped into the sprinkles of hot water, it took all of Devon's strength not to grab her and make love to her. Instead, he left the room to go downstairs and start on breakfast.

The hot water felt wonderful and gave her a cleansing sensation, not on the outside, but on the inside. She didn't have any proof, but Carrie just knew that old Uncle Aaron had to be the family murderer. It all fit, his age, his motive. Carrie knew he hated his two nieces. It showed in how bothered he was that they had gone home for a visit. After all, who'd want to be reminded every day about a past such as his? It was so obvious to Carrie why Uncle Aaron would want them all dead. Not to mention that he was obviously hiding something in that old shed. That was one thing that Carrie knew for a fact.

Damara loved him and wouldn't listen to her though. They had argued and neither said goodbye when Carrie left for the airport. It seemed that only Paulie was upset about her leaving. Carrie cried on the plane never once remembering how much she hated to fly.

* * * * *

"Happy?" Mark asked Gail, as they ate breakfast for the first time in months in their own kitchen.

"No," Gail answered sternly, reading over the report again for about the hundredth time.

Now he was puzzled. All she had wanted for weeks was to come home... and now that they were home, she wasn't happy.

"Okay, I give. What's wrong now?"

As she swallowed her bite of eggs, Gail used her fork to point at the papers in front of her. "Your report..."

"What's wrong with my report?" Mark asked defensively.

"Nothing I can point my finger at... it's all in here but there's something missing."

"Such as?" he asked.

"I don't know, but something," Gail whispered, knowing that a vague reply was not a good one to toss at Mark. Therefore, she quickly added, "...such as how did Aaron get to Quebec so fast and who murdered Nadia?"

As he rose from the table, Mark replied, "Put it away, Gail, the case is closed." He shrugged his shoulders and added, "Who cares?"

* * * * *

The holidays had passed quickly and before she knew it, Damara was standing alone in her mother's house staring out the kitchen window. The snow-covered lawn and trees gave her a sense of safety, innocence, but something was missing from her heart. Was it her mother, or was it something else?

The old grandfather clock announced it was ten o'clock and woke Damara from her waking dreams. Ted was picking her up at eleven sharp for lunch and she didn't want to keep him waiting. As she headed for the stairs, the kitchen phone rang.

"Hello?" Damara answered.

"Hi," Carrie replied meekly.

Damara started to cry. "Carrie, I miss you! I wish you were here."

"Me, too," Carrie replied back. "Can I come home?"

"Yes, yes, come home!" Damara yelled.

Both girls had felt empty inside since their argument, and both needed the other more than they ever knew. The days they had spent together searching for the truth that never revealed itself had bonded them into one soul... their hearts beating to the same rhythm.

"I need to go by my office and do a few things, but I have a flight for home tomorrow."

"Oh, Carrie, I'm so sorry," Damara cried.

"Me, too!"

They cried and apologized for what seemed like hours, but were actually only a few minutes before Damara realized the time. When Damara told Carrie about her date, Carrie was more than willing to hang up. Their laughter made them feel much better... almost back to normal. Now Damara pranced happily up the stairs anxious to see Ted. She hummed as she pulled on her jeans and sweatshirt. Housie raised his head from the bed and winked. It was wonderful to be home...

to feel home. The doorbell rang and Damara's heart jumped into her throat.

"He's here, Housie!" she giggled. She was so excited she almost tripped jaunting down the stairs.

"Well, hello there," Ted smiled, as she opened the door.

"Well, hello to you, too. Ready?" she asked.

The ride to the restaurant was quiet as they both remained silent. Damara was anxious and didn't know what to say. Ted was mesmerized by her beauty and his plain dumb luck to her saying yes to the date. As he opened her car door for her, Damara gazed into Ted's beautiful green eyes. They stared at each other for the longest time before Ted gained enough courage to kiss her. It felt wonderful and both their stomachs flip-flopped inside their bodies. Damara never wanted a kiss more than at that moment and Ted didn't want it to ever stop.

"I'm in love with you, Damara Louise Van Brunt," Ted finally whispered. "I've always loved you."

Damara stood quietly staring into Ted's beautiful eyes. She didn't know what to say or do. A man had never told her such a thing before. In fact, a man had never even kissed her before. Damara had always been so busy trying desperately to either just make it through school or get her career started that dating or love was never an option.

"I... I..." Damara stuttered.

Ted smiled and took her arm. "Shall we go? Our food is waiting."

* * * * *

Maddie laid on the beach as the sun warmed her body and the rhythm of the waves lulled her to sleep. Birds chirped overhead as if welcoming her back. It was very relaxing and peaceful. This island had saved her sanity once and she owed it everything. Therefore, she bought it to protect and enjoy it. Life was peaceful here. Life was...

"Excuse me," a voice said, disturbing her paradise.

Maddie sat up and used her hand to shade her eyes from the sun. The man resembled more of a shadow than a face as the bright sun gleamed from behind his head. She smiled at him.

"About time you left your room," she stated, lying back down on her blanket. "Ready to talk yet?"

The Agency

Stan dropped onto the sand a few feet from Maddie's blanket. He blinked several times in the bright sunlight.

"Afraid of a few rays?" she mocked him. The man was whiter than a sheet.

"May I ask you a question?"

"Shoot," Maddie replied, enjoying the warm sun.

"Where the hell are we?" he asked.

Maddie tossed a bottle of suntan lotion at him and said with a smirk, "Here... you might need this."

He sighed as he looked at the small bottle of suntan lotion with no sun block. "Thanks, I think."

"So you ready to talk?" Maddie asked again. "If not, no problem... I have *all* the time in the world."

* * * * *

Carrie dropped her suitcases on the floor and ran up the stairs. She yelled out, but Damara and Parker were not home. Only Housie who had been sleeping on Damara's bed came downstairs to investigate. He answered her with a meow. Although now alone, Carrie felt relieved. It was better being here than to be with Devon right now because here, she was home. Devon had been very upset about her decision to leave so soon... but as usual, he had to accept her decision. As she stood in the quiet house petting Housie, she figured that Parker was probably in class, but where in the world was Damara?

"Answering machine," Carrie said to Housie.

During college, the girls left each other messages on the answering machine. She ran down the stairs and hit the play button on the old machine... and sure enough, Damara had left a short message. She was having lunch with Ted... again!

"Good," Carrie smiled. "She needs him right now."

The light continued to blink, which meant there was another message. Carrie hit the play button. It was a message from Damara's grandmother in Quebec. It was urgent that she call her as soon as possible.

"Oh great..." Carrie said, as she looked up the grandmother's number in the small black address book that was always on the desk. "...now what?"

179

"Hello? Mary Eileen? This is Carrie Clarke. What's up?"

"Oh... I am so glad it is you, Carrie," Mary said softly. "Poor Damara has been through so much already."

"I hope it's not anything..." Carrie started to say, but Mary cut her off.

"I'm afraid it is, Carrie. We've had another tragedy I'm sorry to say."

Carrie's heart sank fast believing that it was Damara's grandfather. "What's happened?"

"Carrie..." the old woman paused then slowly said, "...there's been another murder."

"Murder!" Carrie screeched. "Who?"

Mary sighed before answering. "Her Uncle LJ... Lewis John."

Carrie's mind searched through all the new faces she had recently met over the last few months and the old uncle's face from Quebec suddenly appeared in her mind.

"Oh no," Carrie sighed. "Not LJ."

"I'm afraid so. It seems that someone broke into his house and stabbed him."

"Was anything stolen?" Carrie asked.

"No, no. It was as if they didn't want poor LJ in this crazy world any longer. Nothing was stolen... nothing was moved," Mary reported.

They spoke for a few more minutes before hanging up with Carrie promising to have Damara call as soon as she returned home.

Murdered? *What in the world was going on*, Carrie thought to herself. Why would Uncle Aaron kill Uncle LJ? She ran to the attic and studied the papers that were still plastered on the walls. There had to be an answer here, but where was it?

* * * * *

Mark had gone off to take a nap, and Gail remained at the kitchen table studying the words on the paper. Something just didn't add up and was driving her crazy.

"Woman killed... twin sister almost killed?"

Gail was talking to herself when Mark surprised her from the hall. "What in the world are you doing?"

The Agency

"Mark, something isn't right," Gail said, staring up at him.

"The case is closed. Put it to rest, Gail! Let's go get some dinner."

"Someone tried to kill the senator and someone did kill Nadia. How can you eat?" she demanded.

"I did my job and the case is finished. There's nothing more to do. Now let's go, okay?"

Gail's anger was starting to brew. How could her husband be so cold? This just wasn't like him.

"You go eat, I wish to read," Gail said, turning her attention back to the report.

"Honey, there's nothing more you can do," Mark said, putting his hands on her shoulders. "Come with me, please?"

It was hard, but Gail relented to his pleas and followed Mark outside to the car, but the report was still in her hand.

* * * * *

"Nothing," Carrie said, as she sat the papers back on the computer stand. "Absolutely nothing!"

Housie meowed from the stairs letting her know it was time to eat.

"Okay, Housie, I'm coming."

As she entered the living room, Carrie noticed the mailman leaving the porch.

"Let me get the mail first, Housie... just a second, sweetie."

The door creaked as she pushed the screen open and the mailman turned, startled by the noise. When he saw Carrie, he waved to say hello; Carrie waved back. With a small stack of mail, she headed for the kitchen to feed Housie and make a cup of tea. After throwing the empty can of cat food into the trash, she glanced over at the mail on kitchen table. One envelope stood out among the bills. The postmark was from Quebec, Canada.

"Now what?" Carrie asked, as she pulled the envelope out of the small stack.

Her heart froze during a single beat when she noticed the return address... Lewis John LeBoisne. The dead man was reaching out from his grave.

"Oh shit!" Carrie almost screamed, as she tore open the envelope that was addressed to Damara. At that moment though, Carrie was Damara.

As Carrie read the letter, fear tore through her body and singed her soul. It was as if she was standing over the doors of hell about ready to fall in. The more she read, the more she trembled. Never before in her life had fear, nor the idea of being alive, frightened her more than at that very moment in time.

"Damn!" Carrie yelled. "Why didn't I see this before?"

* * * * *

Gail waited until Mark had headed upstairs to take a shower before pulling the report from her purse.

Maybe The Agency's computers have some answers, she said to herself.

Mark's computer was in his bag, but if he caught her using it, he'd be angry.

What to do... what to do, she asked herself.

The hallway closet door was slightly ajar, which gave her a brilliant idea. It was a little difficult to get settled amongst the winter coats, but after folding a few blankets that were on the floor, she had made a rather comfortable chair. As she settled in nicely, Gail realized it was too dark to find the computer's *on* switch... she couldn't remember where it was located on the laptop computer.

"Darn," she said, fumbling in the dark, now searching for the doorknob.

With the door slightly open, the light from the hall was enough for her to find the on/off switch for the computer. Now with computer screen on, Gail had all the light she needed. She pulled the door shut and settled in the best she could. The login prompt flashed on the screen and her fingers typed in the username and password as though it was her normal routine to do so. She was thankful now that Mark had asked her to submit his work for him during their trip. At least it gave her the chance to remember his codes if nothing else.

Now, where to go in the system?

Anything and everything a person needed or wanted could be found on The Agency's computers. The only stumbling block was that one had to be smart enough to know where to find it.

The steps creaked above her head; Mark was coming down the stairs. Gail's heart pounded as she heard his footsteps pass the closet door. Surprisingly, this both excited and frightened her. It was childish, but it was also fun.

"Gail!" Mark hollered from the kitchen.

She did not answer. Her heart raced as she wondered what she would do if he opened the closet door, but why would he?

"Gail?" he yelled again. When she didn't respond, he headed back up the stairs.

It wasn't unusual for her to go on walks around the neighborhood without telling him; even during the cold winter months. *Good*, she thought to herself. *He probably thinks I'm out walking.*

Now it was back to the work in her lap. Her fingers flew over the keys as the computer flipped from one screen to the next. It wasn't until she came to the census reports that she felt she was finally getting somewhere. Going through the years, Gail decided to stop and look at the 1940s census of Quebec. She typed in the name LeBoisne and waited. Several names popped up, but it wasn't until she found the name of Bella LeBoisne that Gail froze.

"This can't be," she said. "This just can't be right."

Gail used the light from the computer screen to read over Mark's report again. Then she used her fingers to help her count. Her blood sped through her veins as her heart pounded faster and faster. The adrenaline released by her sudden terror wasn't helping much right now either, but now everything made complete sense to her… everything.

"Oh, my God!" she yelled aloud, as she slapped her hand over her mouth.

* * * * *

Damara and Parker arrived home at about the same time, but the house was dark and empty.

"I thought you said Carrie was coming back today?" Parker asked.

"I thought she was too."

They entered the house and Damara ran upstairs to look for Carrie while Parker searched the downstairs. When they didn't find her they tried calling her cell, but there was no answer.

"Damara, did you see this note on the fridge from Carrie?" Parker asked, handing the note to Damara.

"This is weird," she said, looking up at her brother. "It just says she'll be in touch."

"I wonder where she went," Parker asked.

Damara shook her head. "I have no idea."

* * * * *

The aroma from the meat sizzling on the hot grill woke Stan from a deep sleep. He rubbed his eyes and remembered he had fallen asleep in the hammock. He sat up but felt dizzy. His stomach churned and his jaws prickled from the vomit trying to rise. Without the strength to stand, he fell to the grass and rolled onto his back. As he gazed into the sky, Maddie's face hovered menacingly from above.

"Hi there," she said with an eerie grin.

"I don't feel so well," he moaned, his arms pushing down on his stomach, trying to quench the pain.

"I wouldn't think you would with all that junk in your system," Maddie giggled. "Otherwise, it would be rather weird."

Stan blinked his eyes and tried to remember what had happened. Lunch was the only thing that came to mind... and it was a wonderful lunch too. Chicken salad and a strawberry mousse that was out of this world, but as he thought about it now, Maddie was way too curious about how much he ate and kept offering him more.

"What did you give me, you fucking bitch?"

"Oh, nothing much," Maddie giggled. "At least nothing you'd be able to pronounce. Especially now anyway," Maddie laughed out hysterically. "Oops, wouldn't want the steaks to burn now would I?"

As she pranced back to the grill to flip the steaks, Stan knew he had to release the contents of his stomach. He lost what little was left of his noontime meal, but the waves of nausea wouldn't stop. The pain and dizziness were unbearable.

"Well, would you like to talk now?" she asked with a little more firmness in her voice. "That sure doesn't look like a very pleasant experience if you ask me."

"What?" he asked, heaving uncontrollably.

The Agency

Maddie sighed. "You silly, silly boy. Without the antidote soon, you'll have very little to talk about at all. I highly recommend that you agree to talk... at least just a little."

His stomach muscles relaxed a little and he took the brief opportunity to breathe in a much needed lungful of air. With little to no strength, he rested back on his knees. His face was hot and his stomach was ripping apart from the inside. *This crazy bitch poisoned me!* he told himself.

"Mm, doesn't dinner smell wonderful?" Maddie asked, walking slowly back over to the steaming grill.

Stan screamed in agony as he fell to the earth. His stomach tightened again and he braced himself for another onslaught of the heaves. It felt as if he weighed a million tons. Even his fingers were too heavy to move. He looked up at Maddie and tried to talk, but no words escaped his mouth.

"I'll tell you what," Maddie said with a giggle. "Blink once for yes that you'll talk to me or twice for not a chance in hell, okay?"

As he blinked once, he felt a sharp prick in his left shoulder and his private world of hell became dark, very, very dark.

* * * * *

Gail looked at her sleeping husband and smiled. She loved him so very much, but at the moment was also so very angry with him. Why couldn't he ever trust her judgment? Why did he always have to question her, why? Was it a man thing or was this something every woman had to endure? Since Mark had been the only man in her life, Gail had nothing to compare her situation to. After she laid her note on her pillow, Gail quietly exited the room. The taxi was waiting patiently outside. She slowly hauled her heavy suitcase down the stairs trying not to make any noise. It was important not to wake him. Otherwise, he'd spoil everything. She opened the front door and stared solemnly back into the dark house before closing it.

"Home..." she said out loud. "I'll miss you." Then she quickly locked the door and walked solemnly to the waiting taxi.

As the taxi sped off, a tear fell from her eye. She was terrified, but this was something she had to do. Gail had to prove to herself and to her husband that her hunches were right. She just knew they were, and if she was right, a lot of lives were in danger. Gail had to stop what was about to happen, and she had to stop it now.

* * * * *

Two planes landed about the same time in Manitoba. The snow on the ground was thick and the cold arctic air froze any water that dared to touch an exposed surface. Gail headed for the taxies as soon as she grabbed her luggage from the turnstile. Carrie was already standing by the glass doors not sure if she dared to venture out. The cold air hit her hard every time someone entered or exited the airport.

"Damn," Carrie whispered. "I hate the cold!" She turned to head back inside when she suddenly collided with another woman. Their luggage flew from their hands and they fell to the floor.

"Oh my," Gail gasped, not recognizing Carrie. "I am so sorry."

"No, no," Carrie said. "It's my fault..."

Carrie recognized her at once and didn't even try to hide it. "What in the world are you doing here?" Carrie asked.

Gail looked into Carrie's eyes and almost panicked. "You?"

"Yes, it's me, now where's your husband?" Carrie looked around expecting to see Mark, but there was no one that even resembled him close by.

"I left him at home," Gail answered meekly, gathering her luggage.

"You came here alone?"

Gail smiled. "Yes... and you?"

"Alone."

They both laughed as they picked up their things.

"Where are you staying?" Carrie asked.

"You probably won't believe this, but I hadn't thought that far in advance," Gail replied, now feeling a little stupid. "I've never done anything this rash before."

"Come on, I'll share my hotel room with you. We probably have a lot to talk about anyway. Besides, Dr. Lewis would kill me if I left you alone in Canada."

They hailed a taxi and headed off for the Fort Garry Hotel. Carrie had reserved a special room before leaving Montana... she had reserved room 202.

The Agency

Carrie suddenly laughed as they walked out into the cold arctic air together.

* * * * *

Mark rose early with a splitting headache. He tried to move slowly so as not to wake his wife. When he entered the bathroom, he even closed the door before flipping on the light. After relieving himself and turning off the light, he headed for the kitchen. It wasn't until a few hours later that he found her note lying on her pillow.

* * * * *

Gail and Carrie sat in the dining room of the Fort Garry Hotel enjoying a wonderful breakfast. They were so tired the night before that they fell straight to sleep. The next morning after a hot shower and fresh clean clothes, they headed downstairs to compare their notes and eat a hearty Canadian-style breakfast.

"So tell me, why did you come here alone?" Gail asked. "Assignment?"

"You go first," Carrie said, sipping on her juice.

"Well," Gail started, "I just didn't feel that the case was closed. I mean, one person died and…"

"Two," Carrie interjected, taking a bite of her bacon.

"Two?" Gail asked. "Who's the other one?"

"Sorry for interrupting, go ahead and say what you were going to say. I'll explain later."

"Oh," Gail said, now confused. "Anyway, I was reading over Mark's notes and just had this weird feeling that there was more to it. I mean… I just knew that the uncle you stayed with just had to be the murderer."

"I know… me too," Carrie said, chewing on her muffin. "He's a pretty strange dude."

"But when we got home I started to think… two houses exactly the same… and someone had tried to shoot the senator during Halloween… and…"

Carrie passed her the cream when Gail poured more coffee into her cup.

"So…" Gail continued, "I used Mark's computer and searched the census database for Damara's family and there's more kids listed in the household than what's on that family tree."

"Well, I've got some other good crap for you..." Carrie said, taking a sip of juice again.

They continued to talk and share facts and ideas until way after ten in the morning. Both were turning each other's ideas and findings repeatedly in their minds.

"We seem to think alike." Carrie smiled.

"I like you, Carrie." Gail smiled back. "I really do."

"Come on," Carrie said, standing up to stretch. "Let's go see if we can find a ghost before leaving."

"A what?" Gail asked, tossing her napkin onto the table.

* * * * *

"Calm down, Mark. She couldn't have gone far," Devon said, trying to comfort his new friend.

"Not far!" Mark yelled into the phone. "With a plane ticket she can go practically anywhere."

"I have people working on it right now... hold on. I think this is it. Yes?" Devon asked Chad as he entered the office.

"Sir, I found that Mrs. Lumer landed in Manitoba late last night, but, sir..." Chad stuttered with a frown. "So did someone else."

"I give up, Chad, who else landed in Manitoba?" Devon asked sarcastically.

"Carrie, sir," Chad replied very carefully. This was an answer that would wake up the devil inside Devon Arvol.

"Carrie?" he screamed. *"My Carrie?"*

"Yes, sir, that's the one," Chad answered, backing slowly out of the room.

Devon's face flared red with anger, which was a signal for Chad to run.

"Oh, fuck me!" Devon yelled, which made the walls vibrate.

"What?" Mark demanded into the phone. "What?"

* * * * *

"We can't stay long because they'll come looking for us," Carrie said, standing rigidity in the middle of room 202.

"How will they know where we are?" Gail asked, smoothing out the bed so she could sit down.

The Agency

"Because of the plane tickets, silly. Devon and Mark will probably be here sometime today. I can practically guarantee it."

Gail watched as Carrie closed her eyes and remained motionless between the two queen-sized beds. Not sure what else to do, Gail simply watched.

"Nadia?" Carrie whispered. "Are you here, Nadia?" Of course, there was no reply.

Carrie continued to stand silently for a few more seconds before Gail gasped loudly.

"What!" Carrie demanded, turning around to stare blankly at Gail.

With a face as white as freshly fallen snow, Gail shivered as she pointed nervously to the large mirror on the wall.

"Look!" Gail whispered. "I see..."

Carrie turned slowly toward the mirror and almost wet her pants when she saw what appeared to be a woman with dark hair staring back at her from the mirror. Tears instantly fell from Carrie's eyes as she faced Nadia for the first time in years.

"Mom?" Carrie whispered.

However, as quickly as it was there, whatever it was, was gone.

"What in the world?" Gail shrieked, jumping from the bed. "Did we just see what I think we saw?"

"Let's go," Carrie bellowed out, heading for the door.

"I'm right behind you," Gail yelled, as she ran after Carrie. "But what was that?"

* * * * *

"I'm sorry, sir, but they're not here," the desk clerk told Mark and Devon again for about the fifth time. "As I said, they checked out just before lunch."

"Any idea where they were headed?" Mark asked.

"No, sir."

"Thanks for nothing," Devon moaned, pulling Mark away from the counter. "We'll find no answers here. Tell me, where exactly did you and Gail go next?"

"Falcon Lake," Mark answered.

"Then we go there, too," Devon replied.

"But..." Mark started to object, but Devon finished for him. "We have nothing else."

* * * * *

The rental car was small but big enough for the two of them.

"Do you remember the way?" Gail asked.

"I'll never forget," Carrie replied.

"Do you think we threw them off track by hopping on the plane to Quebec instead of driving?" Gail asked.

"I hope so. I'm really praying that the rental car we left at the airport won't be found for a few days, but I'm sure they'll figure it out sooner or later. We may have only gained a day's lead. We'll go straight to Uncle LJ's first. From the police report I downloaded from The Agency's computers yesterday, it wasn't a simple killing."

"Oh?" Gail had been feeling safe being with Carrie, but suddenly her courage melted down between her knees.

"Yes, from what the report said, the only thing left behind was his torso."

"Excuse me?" Gail wheezed.

"If there's one thing I've learned from my investigations is that there's a lot of sick puppies in this world."

"You mean..." Gail asked, now wondering why she ever left the safety of her home in the first place. "Someone cut off his head... arms... and legs!"

The drive was very noisy as the chains around the tires tore through the icy roads. By the time they reached LJ's small house, their ears rang with the imprint of the crushing sound. As expected, they found that the yellow police tape was still hugging the parameters. They walked together toward the front steps, as a police detective pulled into the driveway.

"Thank you for meeting us here, Lieutenant," Carrie said, flashing him her FBI badge.

"No problem," he replied with a smile. "But what possible interest could the United States FBI have with this nasty little case?"

"Not sure just yet, sir," Carrie answered, following him into the house.

Gail almost fell over from the stench that hit her nose. Dried blood and severed skin were scattered around the room. The blood was so thick in one area that it had soaked up the skirts on the bottom of the sofa.

"Damn," Gail said, before she realized what she had spoken.

"It takes some getting used to," Carrie remarked, looking around the room to find a point of reference.

"As you can see," the police lieutenant said, "nothing was disturbed."

Ignoring his comments, Carrie asked, "Where exactly was the body found?"

"Here," the man answered, pointing to a spot on the carpet where the blood had gathered into a dark red pool.

After examining the spot, Carrie stood and walked into the kitchen then she entered the bedroom, but there was no sign of blood or trauma anywhere else.

"Witnesses?" Carrie asked, picking up various items to study.

"No one heard or saw a thing," he replied.

"Well, thank you. I don't see..." But Carrie stopped talking when she noticed a torn piece of paper on the floor. "What's this?"

"Let's see," he said.

Carrie studied it closer and recognized it immediately, but didn't say a word to the man.

"Here," she said, handing it to the lieutenant. "We'll be leaving now."

As the girls drove away, Gail asked, "What did you find?"

"Someone tore up a picture of Damara. We had left Uncle LJ some pictures. I recognized the color as that of Damara's blouse. Whoever killed LJ also tore up his family photos."

"Seems to match our conclusions," Gail surmised.

"I believe you are right."

"Onto the old house?" Gail asked.

"Yep," Carrie answered, trying to keep the car on the road.

"Then what do we do?"

"We call the police once we've found him," Carrie said, as the car suddenly skidded over a piece of ice.

* * * * *

"Aunt Nidra, it's not like her to just disappear!" Damara cried.

"Didn't she leave a note?" Nidra Louise asked.

"Yes, but it only said she'd be in touch." Damara continued to cry. This was all her fault. If only she had listened to Carrie instead of arguing with her. The thought of losing Carrie at this time was too hard for her to imagine or accept.

"I'll make some calls and call you right back. Now calm down," Louise demanded of her niece.

* * * * *

Maddie sat nervously in a small office on her private island and pondered over what she had just been told. A man from Canada hired him to kill the senator, but he had no idea as to why. Cash... the man paid in cash. Also, the man was old... very old. She punched in Dr. Lewis' office number and waited. He picked up after the first ring.

"Lewis, it's the strangest thing I've ever heard. He said he didn't know the man's name, and he had paid him a small fortune... in advance and in cash!" Maddie almost screamed. "And... he was told that if he did a good job that there were a couple of other ones for him."

"Believe it or not," Jeff began, "Devon has just run off to Canada to find Carrie and Gail. Seems they both went up there for a reason no one knows about except for them."

"You can't let them go!" Maddie yelled. "It's not safe."

"Well, you're a little late. They're already there. But we're right on top of it, Mad," Lewis defended. "I'm sending agents that way right now even as we speak."

"This man, whoever he is, is insane. You've got to stop them before he kills them! It seems he is hell-bent on ending the bloodline of his family."

* * * * *

The house was dark as Carrie parked the car behind some barren trees and snow-covered brush. They glanced at each other then pulled their coats up around their necks before exiting the car. The January air was frigid and cut through their parkas as if they were wearing light sweaters. Both were freezing as they walked down the snow-covered dirt road. The crunching of the snow beneath their feet and the cold air made them both wish they had at least waited until the spring thaw to investigate and try to prove their claims.

"Do you think he's here?" Gail asked, rubbing her gloved hands together to stay warm. "It's freezing out here."

"I believe he's here, yes."

They came to the shed, which mimicked the shed back in Falcon Lake and Carrie giggled.

"What?" Gail asked, wiping her nose.

"I was just wondering if the junk in this shed is in the exact same place as the other shed."

"You mean the houses were identical on the inside, too?" Gail asked.

"Yep..." Carrie stopped talking and pulled Gail close to the side of the shed. "Listen, it didn't dawn on me until you just asked that I realized there has to be a connection between these two houses. A current connection!"

Gail's body suddenly became even colder as she realized what Carrie was trying to say.

"How else would they have known if either of the houses had changed or not?" Carrie continued.

Gail's eyes widened in horror. "Do you think they're both in on it?"

"I don't know," Carrie answered, now believing they were both in grave danger.

"We can go back," Gail surmised, peeping around the corner of the shed to view the front of the house. "All's still quiet here."

"Let me look around first... you stay put. Got it?" Carrie asked, leaving Gail's side and walking up toward the house.

"She's either crazy or has lots of guts," Gail said to no one.

"She's crazy!" a deep French accent echoed from behind Gail.

But before she could react, Gail's head felt strange. Almost as if it had been squeezed into some kind of a helmet... then all went dark.

* * * * *

The first thing Carrie noticed after leaving the shadows of the shed was that the snow had not been disturbed on the front stairs. No footprints anywhere. She slowly climbed the stairs, being careful to push the snow aside with her foot as she stepped. The porch was loaded with pristine snowdrifts. She turned around first to make sure Gail hadn't followed then peeked through a large window. A fire was glowing in the hearth and a mug sat idly on a small table. Carrie couldn't see anybody. She walked along the front porch that wrapped around both sides of the huge house. As she came to a corner, Carrie peeked around cautiously first. Fear gripped at her sanity as she saw footprints everywhere along the back of the house heading from the shed.

"Ah, shit!" Carrie whispered, as she pulled her gun from her shoulder holster, which wasn't an easy feat. Because of the cold, she had to unbundle herself from all the heavy clothing first. Carrie pulled off her glove from her right hand to give her more control. *My hand will just have to freeze,* Carrie said to herself, as she held the gun firmly between her fingers.

As she studied the footprints, a deep pain hit her stomach. "Damn, Gail..."

Carrie turned and ran down the stairs slipping all the way. When she reached the side of the shed where Gail was supposed to have been, she found no one.

"Gail?" Carrie said softly, but there was no answer. "Shit!"

Immediately, she noticed the double set of footprints heading toward the back of the shed. As she inched herself toward the back of the shed, Carrie held her gun close to her head ready to fire. When she reached the clearing, she slowly peered around the corner... no one.

"Damn," she said again.

Before following the prints toward the house, she glanced back over her shoulder. All was quiet. Slowly, she walked toward the house. The snow crunched loudly with each step. Following the footprints, Carrie just knew that Gail was dead and it was all her fault. She should never have left her alone. After all, Carrie was the agent, not Gail. When she had run into her at the airport, she should have immediately thrown Gail back on a plane straight for home. As she reached the back steps, Carrie noticed that the footprints led straight to the basement doors at the side of the house. Suddenly, Alfred Hitchcock's movie *Psycho* played before her eyes.

"Damn," Carrie whispered as she hesitated.

With no other choice, Carrie slowly followed the prints looking all around so as not to miss a thing... a thing such as a psycho running at her with a knife. The basement doors were closed and locked from the outside, which was something she had not expected.

"Damn," she said aloud again.

"Byron?" Carrie yelled. "Come on out, Byron. I know you're here!"

But all was quiet. Not even the birds were chirping.

"Byron? I want to play."

Still, no answer. The snow was almost gone now from the back of the house. It had been walked on too many times and now it was just a muddy slush. She had to get into the basement and find Gail, but how? Was the only way in was to go through the house? Carrie edged toward the far side of the large structure, careful to examine each bush... each tree that could hide a crazed person. She carefully peered around... again no one.

Again, she looked all about her before proceeding. The snow was much thicker on this far side of the house. It was obvious she was the only person to have walked this way in days. When she reached the front of the huge house, Carrie climbed the brick steps as her feet slipped on the ice. As she slid into the screen door, she tried the knob. It was unlocked. The large sculptured door creaked as it swung open.

"Is this an invite, Byron?" Carrie asked, as she stepped into the foyer. "Hello? Anybody home?"

Still, all was quiet... too quiet.

The fire in the living room was now blazing hot. It was obvious that the logs had just been turned. A mug sitting on the small table was empty, but there was still some liquid on the bottom. She used her finger and felt the brown fluid; it was still warm. Carrie now knew that Byron, or someone, had just left this room. In the other house at Falcon Lake, the basement door was located just off the kitchen. Knowing that both houses were identical, she walked through the living room into the kitchen and... there was the basement door. It had been left ajar as if inviting her to enter.

"Okay, Byron, we'll play your little game," Carrie said, as she peered through the door.

No light was on in the basement. She reached inside and felt for a light switch, but when she flipped it, no light came on.

"Terrific," she sighed. "Just my luck... Gail? Are you down there, Gail?"

When no one answered, she slowly started down the stairs, but Carrie couldn't see a thing. Her eyes had become accustomed to the bright snow-reflected light from outside. She now had two choices facing her. She could either hold onto her gun or she could be safe and use the handrail. Carrie decided on the gun. When she reached the third step, the kitchen door slammed shut behind her. Immediately, she turned and climbed back up the stairs. When she tried the door... it was locked.

"Oh, this is just wonderful!" Carrie said, feeling like a total idiot. "How do I get myself into these messes?"

Not sure as to what to do next, Carrie turned and continued down the stairs, but when she reached the fifth or sixth step, her left foot fell through where a stair should have been and she lunged forward. As the weight of her body fell out of control, her leg remained lodged deep into the space of the missing step. As her head aimed for the lower steps, she heard the shinbone in her lower leg snap... it was either the bone or her knee that was now in two pieces. The pain was excruciating and tore like lightning through her body to her brain. Sparks of tense agony attacked every raw nerve cell she owned. Carrie let out a scream and instinctively reached out with her arms to cushion the fall. Her gun flew from her hand and hit the floor somewhere far below. When her head smashed into the lower stairs, Carrie didn't see or feel a thing. The hard impact made everything go even blacker than it was, and all the pain was pleasantly gone.

* * * * *

When Devon briefed him on the whereabouts of Carrie, Lewis didn't think twice about sending other agents to Canada. He couldn't allow another innocent life to be smothered out during his watch. Therefore, when Louise called, Lewis didn't think nor did he care of the consequences when he told her everything he knew. Louise calmly thanked him and called Damara. Together, they agreed to meet at the airport in Quebec the next day.

The Agency

* * * * *

Mark felt a rush of relief when he saw Devon at the airport. There were several other men with him and although he didn't recognize any of them except Devon, Mark was still relieved.

"Thank God you're here," Mark said, shaking Devon's hand.

"Nice to see you, too," Devon replied. "We need to find someplace private to talk. I have to brief you immediately."

Mark's heart and stomach raced toward his throat at the same time. It felt like he was having a heart attack and was going to be sick all at once.

"Is it Gail, is it my wife?" Mark whispered.

"Not really, but we need to talk."

* * * * *

Maddie had called Lewis on his private line and had briefed him on the additional information she had obtained from her guest, but her hands shook and tears welled in her eyes as Lewis again explained where Carrie had gone.

"My God, Jeff!" Maddie cried into the phone.

"I have... I have sent help," Lewis kept repeating into the phone.

Greghardt patted Lewis' shoulder from behind trying to reassure him as he spoke to Maddie. For the first time in a long time, Greghardt knew why he had been so depressed lately. It was because of what he had ordered when Maddie needed him the most. He had sold her out when she relied on him... trusted him.

When Jeff hung up the phone, he turned and stared at Allen. "This case makes me sick... and to top it off, it didn't even start out as a case."

Greghardt shook his head and said, "Do they ever?"

* * * * *

Louise and Damara arrived at the house only a day behind Carrie and Gail. An early morning snow shower blanketed the landscape with a shiny new crust of pristine innocence. Only a deer stood between the two women and the old house. The crunching of wheels against the earth announced the presence of a car pulling in behind them.

Louise sighed and yanked her coat tighter around her neck. "I had forgotten how damn cold it could get up here."

"Not me," Damara replied, shivering as the old man limped toward them.

"Okay, you got me up here," Aaron said when he reached them. "So what's going on?"

Louise wasted no time and said, "You're going to introduce us to Uncle Byron, that's what going on."

With a very deep accent and fear in his eyes, he said, "Who told you about him?"

"That isn't what's important..." Louise started to say, but Damara cut her off in mid-sentence.

"He has Carrie that's why!"

"Carrie?" Aaron asked. "What would Carrie be doing here?"

"She must've found out about him and came back to investigate," Louise surmised, taking a strong grip of Aaron's arm.

"This isn't good," he added solemnly.

"No, it isn't," Damara added. "Now tell us about Byron."

"Now, Uncle!" Louise hollered into his face.

Aaron lowered his eyes and stared blankly into the recently fallen snow. Harsh breathing and shaking hands told the women that he was actually frightened. Louise had to shake him violently before he would finally look at her.

"Aaron, are you all right?" Louise asked. After glancing around and taking a deep breath of fresh air, Louise suggested they sit in their car to talk.

Aaron shook his head and whispered, "Oui."

Snowflakes drifted through the sky as the sun's filtered rays danced off their edges, but as beautiful and calming as the scene should have been, the three sat nervously in the warming car.

"Okay," Louise said sternly. "I think you owe us an explanation."

"There's nothing to explain," he said slowly, staring into his hands.

"Excuse me?" Louise almost screamed at him. "You obviously have a twin brother, which you failed to tell us about. You lived in two identical houses your whole life, which..."

Damara interrupted her aunt by suggesting, "Start at the beginning, Uncle Aaron. We're listening." Damara reached out, took her uncle's hand, and rubbed it gently. "I'll always love you, Uncle Aaron. No matter what."

Louise gave her niece a glaring stare, but Damara ignored her. She had to hear the truth, and her uncle was not responding to the harshness of her aunt's demands. So maybe he would react to love. They all remained quiet for a few moments before Aaron spoke.

"The beginning... there is no beginning," he said with tears in his eyes.

"What do you mean there's no beginning?" Louise asked.

Once again, Damara jumped headfirst into the conversation. "How about if *I* ask you a few questions, Uncle Aaron?"

It took a few seconds before he responded, but Aaron finally nodded his head in agreement. Louise and Damara glanced at each other before Louise nodded to Damara, which was a signal for her to start. Louise knew that Aaron and Damara had bonded over the last several months, and in a strange sort of way, she knew he trusted her.

After a deep breath, Damara began. "We'll go slowly. Okay, Uncle Aaron?"

Aaron nodded his head to answer yes. Damara took in a deep breath and let it out slowly before asking any questions. Louise sat back to listen and learn.

"Where were you born?" Damara asked.

"In this house." He coughed, clearing his throat.

Damara smiled. "Okay, that wasn't so hard. Now, who's your father?"

He nodded again and said, "Byron LeBoisne."

"Good. Who's your mother?"

No answer.

"Uncle Aaron, you promised," Louise scolded, but Damara immediately raised her hand to stop her aunt from continuing. Louise backed down.

"Uncle Aaron?" Damara coached softly. "Who was your mother?"

Tears dropped from his eyes as he replied meekly, "Sheila raised me... she took care of me... she loved me." Aaron began to cry. His body trembled and Damara started to worry about his health. She had to continue though; she had to know what had happened all those years ago.

"So Sheila was your birth mother, right?" Damara added.

Aaron shook his head and whispered something they couldn't quite hear.

"What did you say?" Louise asked.

Once again, Damara and Louise studied each other before Damara frowned.

"Uncle Aaron," Damara whispered. "You loved your mother didn't you?"

Aaron shook his head yes.

"You wanted your mother to love you didn't you?" Again, Aaron nodded. "You were jealous of your siblings weren't you?"

Aaron sat quietly as the tears rolled down his cheeks.

Louise looked over at Damara with a *where are you going with this kind of questioning* stare, when Damara suddenly asked, "You know who gave birth to you don't you, and you hate her... don't you, Uncle Aaron?"

Suddenly, a high-pitched squeal left Aaron's lips and he started to rock back and forth in the backseat. He was talking to himself, but they couldn't tell what he was saying.

"Uncle Aaron, answer me!" Damara screamed.

"We're not allowed to say," he cried.

"Why?"

"It's the blood," he cried out. "The blood is bad!"

* * * * *

Mark sat silently in the van as they drove along the snow-packed roads. Even though there had been an earlier snowstorm, Quebec was still busy with people going about their busy lives. Mark had to chuckle to himself. If this had been Washington, DC, a snow shower of this magnitude would have shut the city down. Here it was as if there was no snow at all.

It seemed like hours since they left the airport, but it had only been several minutes. Devon had been right; flying into Quebec instead of Manitoba had saved them many hours of travel time. Even though Carrie had rented a car in Manitoba, Devon knew where she was headed... he had no doubt. He was praying they would get there before her and Gail.

The Agency

Mark thought of his wife and tears flooded his eyes. If he lost her, he would lose his world. Why hadn't *he* listened to her? Why did *he* always have to be so stubborn? She knew from the beginning that there was more going on than what was showing on the surface, but he just *had* to argue the point. He couldn't just let things drop and follow her hunch. Gail had been so patient and understanding with him, and he had treated her this way throughout their whole marriage. He had always been told that women were too emotional to be able to make a logical conclusion on their own. After all, it was a proven fact that women thought with their hearts and not their minds as men did. Mark wanted nothing more than to trade places with his wife right now. He should be in trouble... not her. When this was all over, he would promise her that never again would he ever doubt her intuition. No matter what the situation, Mark would listen to his wife completely.

* * * * *

Stan's head was pounding and his vision was blurred as Maddie entered his room. He hated this woman... he didn't know who she was or how he had gotten here, but he knew one thing for certain... he hated her.

"You fucking bitch!" he yelled as she entered. The voice echoing through his head make it pound even more. As he pressed his palms against his temples, Maddie bellowed out a hysterical, scornful laugh.

"You're no prize yourself. Besides, I've been called worse," she mocked. "So tell me. How could you bring yourself to agree to help such a creep?"

Stan sighed as he continued to rub his temples.

"Want something for the pain?" she asked.

"Fuck no, I don't trust you. You'd probably give me some cyanide or rat poison."

"It's just pain medicine, silly. Besides, you're going to be pretty miserable until that stuff I gave you wears off. Are you drinking lots of water?"

"As much as I can without puking it back up! What was that shit you gave me anyway?"

Maddie shook her head and grinned. "Nothing you'd recognize." They sat in silence for a few seconds before she added, "What else can you tell me?"

"Nothing, I told you everything I know. My life is now in your hands. Why would I lie?"

"Because people like you do, that's why." Maddie smirked at him.

Stan had a look of utter defeat splayed across his face. "I guess you're right. No, I told you everything I know."

* * * * *

It was hard to breathe, but there was no pain, just darkness. Her eyes darted all around, but there was no light of any kind. It was the blackest evil Gail ever had the unpleasantness to experience. She reached out to her legs and was happy to find that her body was still intact. No pain or anything damaged that she could tell. As she took in a deep breath, her mind raced to remember what had happened. The shed... she had been standing by the shed in the snow waiting for Carrie to return.

"Carrie?" Gail whispered, but there was no reply.

Gail wondered if she was alone or if Carrie was with her. If she was here, where was she? Gail raised her arm above her head and couldn't feel anything. Reaching out to her sides didn't help either... no walls.

At least I'm not buried alive, Gail surmised.

She tried to get on her knees but began to feel dizzy and nauseated. It was important that she knew where she was.

"Carrie?" Gail said a little louder, this time hoping for some kind of a response.

She felt around on the floor and knew she was on cold dry dirt, but where? It was too dark and too quiet for her situation to be good. Any sound she made was muffled and stamped out. This wasn't good.

"Carrie!" Gail yelled this time.

A moan came from somewhere, but Gail couldn't tell in what direction.

"Carrie?" Gail yelled louder this time.

It almost sounded like someone said, *here.*

With what little strength she had left, Gail pushed herself onto her knees and hands. Her body immediately began to spin uncontrollably in all directions at once, and her head felt like it weighed a hundred pounds. The lower she dropped her head, the less the spinning, so with her head almost dragging on the ground, Gail crawled around the dirt-covered room in search of the moan. It seemed to take hours to only crawl a short distance, but then her left hand felt something hard. The more she touched the object, the clearer it became in her mind. It was a boot... a man's boot, but was it Carrie's boot? No, it was too large to be Carrie's. Gail continued feeling her way along the boot to the leg. It was a large leg... a man's leg... a cold man's leg.

"Oh, my God." Gail almost screamed when she realized that the person she was sitting next to was dead.

"Calm down, Gail," she said aloud to herself. "Calm down... a dead person can't hurt you."

After a couple of seconds, she regained her composure and continued to feel along the body. The pants ended with a belt around the waist and the shirt was partially tucked in. Some of the buttons had been ripped off the shirt and the man's chest hair was protruding out. Gail stopped and took in another deep breath before continuing. Now she felt embarrassed, as though she was molesting this poor deceased soul. The shirt felt stiff... hard, as though something had dried and encrusted between the threads of the material.

"Blood," Gail whispered. It was obvious that the man had bled profusely.

Her knee struck the man's arm and she stopped crawling.

"Sorry," she whispered. But then she giggled nervously. "Great, now I'm talking to a dead person. I'm losing my mind."

Her hand continued to feel along the man's arm to his upper torso... his shoulders... but then where his head should have been...

Gail screamed. She screamed louder than she had ever screamed in her whole life. As she slowly pulled her hand away from the bloodied encrusted severed neck, Gail laid her head on his chest and continued to scream. She screamed until her voice grew hoarse and her throat ached. She didn't know who this person had been, but what horrified Gail even more than finding the dead body was the realization that she was being introduced to her own destiny.

* * * * *

"Uncle Aaron," Damara coached softly. "I know you're afraid, but there's really nothing to be scared of. We're here and no one..."

Aaron cut her off when he said, "Please, Daddy, please don't spank me. I won't tell... I won't tell..."

"You won't tell what?" Damara asked.

"I won't tell..." and then Aaron began to cry out in his native tongue.

Louise searched her purse and pulled out a small container. "Here."

"What is it?" Damara asked.

As Louise opened a small bottle of drinking water, she replied, "Valium. Maybe it'll calm him down enough to answer our questions."

"Good idea," Damara said, taking the small blue pill and placing it in Aaron's mouth. "Here, drink this," she said, taking the bottle from Louise and putting it up to Aaron's lips.

Aaron did as he was instructed and as they waited for the pill to take some effect, the two women glanced out the car windows. Nothing seemed out of place, other than the simple fact that they were hundreds of miles from home, drugging their uncle and trying to coach him to reveal his... their heritage. As Aaron began to calm down, Damara started asking her questions again.

"Why did your father want to hide Byron from everyone?" she asked.

"I was born first," he admitted softly. "My brother was in the wrong position in the womb and it took the doctor quite some time to get him out. He didn't have enough oxygen..."

"Brain damage?" Damara asked and Aaron nodded his head.

"Autism," he replied.

"But why hide him?" Louise asked. "Autism is something that can be worked with..."

"He hid all of us except..."

"All?" Louise asked.

"Except... me," he stated firmly, as a tear dropped down his cheek. "He told us that *Sheila* was our mother."

"But Bella was your true mother, wasn't she?" Damara added.

"Yes," he answered through his tears.

"How many others were there?" Damara asked and Louise looked up with terror in her eyes.

"Many," he cried. "And... and..."

"And Byron killed them didn't he? Your father gave those babies to Sheila to raise, but Byron killed them. He killed them all until..."

The Agency

"Bella said no more! She wanted her babies back that Byron took from her." Aaron looked up at his two nieces and screamed out, "*No, it wasn't Byron who killed those babies. My father loved all his babies. It was... Sheila! It was Sheila. She never wanted those babies in her house... in her perfect life.*"

"So that's why Sheila killed herself," Louise concluded.

Aaron shook his head. "I don't think she did. I believe it was Bella or my father who pushed her off that balcony. She was pregnant with their child and Bella was jealous. My father almost went mad when he found her body. He loved Sheila."

"But why hide Byron?" Damara asked.

"Because... he wasn't right... my father didn't want anyone to know that Bella was the real mother. She was only twelve when she gave birth to us." Aaron dropped his head into his hands and cried. "Maria could call her mama, but we were never allowed. My father was too *proud* of a man. He had been with Bella almost her whole life. I don't know if you know this or not, but he raised her after her father died. Bella was only nine when my uncle died. My father and Sheila raised her as their own! Sheila was told to care for her and her children."

"But your father and Sheila had other..." Louise started to say, but was cut off by Aaron.

"You don't understand..." Aaron cried into his hands.

"Try us!" Louise demanded.

Aaron looked up into Louise's eyes but his stare showed an ugliness that made Louise sick. "I guess you have a right to know the truth." He paused as he rocked himself in the backseat. "My father and Sheila had six children. My father and Bella had many more... it started with Byron and me. Bella hated my Sheila... I mean mom. There were others born between Maria and me, but Sheila killed them as soon as she got the chance. She'd drown them or put a pillow over their face, and then she'd put them in their crib and tell my father that they just died. We used to watch her. We'd hide and watch her kill those babies. Byron and I would lie awake at night wondering when it would be our turn. It wasn't until Bella was pregnant with Maria that Bella finally put her foot down... things changed after that. She threatened my father and said she'd go to the authorities if he didn't do as she demanded. When my mother, Sheila, died, my father died too. He became a zombie and did whatever Bella wanted... whatever Bella said."

Aaron's cries were taking over his body. Damara and Louise sat in the front seat more confused than ever watching an old man rock back and forth in his seat. What they had just heard completely changed everything.

"Bella was my mother and we couldn't have her," he cried. "We couldn't love her. We couldn't tell anyone. Sheila reminded us every day that we were nasty and that our bodies held the dirty blood. That we had to help cleanse the blood!"

* * * * *

Gail sat up and rubbed the back of her head. Dried blood was caked all through her hair. Her head ached terribly, but at least the dizziness had subsided. At least now, she was able to pick up her head and not feel sick to her stomach. As she leaned back, her hand pushed down on the man's leg. The realization of where she was came flooding back as if being struck by a speeding train, but all Gail knew for sure was that she was in a pitch-black room that had a dirt floor. Exactly where that dirt floor was, she had no idea.

Gail patted the man's leg and said, "Well, at least your head doesn't hurt." Gail laughed aloud. It wasn't a fun laugh, but a morbid hysterical laugh. Then she began to cry.

"Carrie?" Gail yelled out again. Still, no one answered.

Gail sighed and tried to stand. Her legs were weak, but she believed they could hold her weight. With her arms stretched out in front, through the darkness, Gail inched her way to the wall. Feeling dreadful, her fingers searched through the emptiness until they made contact with some wooden shelves that were filled with miscellaneous items, but there must have been more dirt than items; a layer of a powered substance laid thick on the planks that Gail decided was old dirt and dust. Not the thick dirt that was found in flowerbeds, but a superfine powder of dead earth that is found only after years of dust had settled. The thought of spiders and other crawly insects crossed her mind, but she was determined to find a way out. Gail could not give up now; she had to find Carrie.

Paint cans, or what felt like paint cans were stacked everywhere. Brushes, saws, and other once handy things, but now discarded, were scattered along the shelves. Her leg smacked into something hard and as she leaned over to feel what it was, her head hit against something that was hanging from a rope. As she clasped her hands around the dangling object, Gail instinctively knew she had found a flashlight.

"Please, God, let it work," Gail whispered.

Hope and dread ran through her body as she closed her eyes and shook the object. Something rattled inside. *It has to be batteries*, she prayed silently to herself. As she pushed the rubber button with her thumb, pinkness flashed before her closed eyes. Gail sighed with relief, but now she had to find the courage to open her eyes.

The room was filthy. She had been right; the shelves had several inches of dirt and dust with large piles in the corners. Objects new and old lined the shelves. As she flashed the light to the right and left, Gail discovered she was standing in a corner with shelves on both sides. As she slowly turned around, Gail kept the light pointed to the floor. Terrified, the first thing the light grabbed a hold of was the legs of the dead man. With a deep breath, Gail allowed the light to follow the man's body to where his head should have been.

As long as his head isn't rolling around here somewhere, I should be all right.

It was obvious that the body had been lying there a while. As she had requested, the head was nowhere in sight. A strong feeling of trepidation loomed over her as she scanned the room. It was small with shelves along each wall; a kind of a storeroom, but she wasn't cold; in fact, she felt warm and comfortable. Therefore, Gail surmised she could not be in the outside shed. A wooden door was at the end of the room. With fear grabbing at her heart, she slowly walked toward it. Before pushing it open, Gail picked up a large hammer off a shelf and was ready to use it if necessary. A loud ringing in her ears reminded her that she had already been hit on the head once, and she wasn't going to allow that to happen again.

"Carrie?" Gail softly hollered. Not a sound came back.

Dust fell from the top of the door as it creaked open. The room beyond was just as dark and doom ridden as the room she had awoken in. Not to mention that this room wasn't any cleaner than the room with the dead man. As the light scanned the dark hidden spaces, Gail's heart dropped lower than ever before when she saw Carrie lying in a pool of blood in a dark corner. It was as if the woman had been broken then thrown away not to be thought of again.

"Oh, God... *No!*" Gail yelled, as she ran to her. Tears fell from her eyes as she tried desperately to find a pulse. "Carrie, please be alive," she cried out. "Don't leave me here alone."

* * * * *

"Uncle Aaron," Louise said slowly. "You're not responsible for what your parents did or didn't do, but you can be responsible for what happens to Carrie and Gail if you don't help us. You have to get a grip on yourself."

"She's right," Damara added.

Aaron rubbed his eyes and glanced up at them. "You don't hate me for what I am? For *who* I am?"

Damara shrugged her shoulders and added with a large loving smile, "In case you have forgotten, just who do you think we are?"

"But the blood?" he asked with swollen red eyes.

"That blood runs in our veins too, Uncle," Louise replied.

"That's right, same blood... same DNA." Damara smiled.

"What they did to you and Byron was incomprehensible... unforgivable. What kind of parents make their children ashamed of who they are? As babies, we do nothing except come into this world. How can a baby do something wrong? And that's what you need to concentrate on. You were an innocent child; how could you have been their sins? If anything... you were their redemption," Louise stated firmly while lovingly rubbing his knee. As a small smile crossed his face, Louise added, "Now, let's go rescue our friends."

* * * * *

Worried that her new friend was too injured to survive, Gail was about ready to panic. She carefully looked over each of Carrie's wounds; she had a huge knot on her forehead with a nasty gash that would eventually require stitches, but it was Carrie's leg that worried Gail.

Something had to be done and it wouldn't wait. Gail stood up and glanced around the dark room. She needed wood and rope, but it was hard to see with just the shallow dim beam of the flashlight. Carrie's leg required to be set immediately. The bone had broken through the skin, and had to be put back into place. Otherwise, an infection would set in and Carrie would lose her leg. Gail knew it was important to keep the wound clean, but there wasn't much she could do about that right now. She would have to chance it and set Carrie's leg anyway. As Gail gathered what she could find, Carrie moaned softly and Gail rushed to her side.

"I'm here... I'm here," Gail whispered.

"Wha...t," Carrie tried to say.

"Shh, just lay still. I must tend to your leg. Then I'll find some water or something for you to drink. Please, don't try to talk."

With Carrie quiet again, Gail went to work searching for the needed supplies. After sifting through the old discarded junk in both rooms, she finally found a small strand of twine and a short strip of plywood. When Gail stepped on the plywood to snap it into two pieces, Carrie flinched as if knowing what was to come. Gail gently placed the wood on both sides of Carrie's damaged leg. She wound the twine around the boards and pulled gently on both strands. Carrie moaned a little louder this time. Gail placed a small but strong piece of wood gently between Carrie's teeth.

"Okay, my friend," Gail said, not sure who would feel it more, Carrie or herself. "Now listen up. I have to pull on your leg to set the bone, and it's going to hurt like hell. Do you understand?"

Carrie nodded her head as tears rolled down her face. The streaks left a clean trail on both her cheeks. Gail wanted to run and hide, but knew she had to find the courage to help her friend. Gail took in a deep breath and tried to gather all the courage she could, but it just didn't feel like she had any left.

"Ready, Carrie?" Gail asked with trembling hands. She was ready to pull, but with her hands shaking as much as they were, Gail wondered if she had the strength and control needed to reset the bone properly. "Okay, on three. One... two..."

Gail began to cry and her voice cracked as she yelled as loud as she could, *"Three!"*

At the same time, she shoved her foot into Carrie's crotch and pulled on her foot as hard as she could, but it seemed that nothing was moving. The bone was still poking through the skin and what was worse; the bleeding had started up again. Carrie was moaning and Gail knew she was hurting her. Tears rolled down her cheeks as she continued to pull.

"God, help me!" Gail yelled.

Suddenly, Carrie's whole body shuddered violently and the bone surprisingly snapped back into place. As the pain tore through Carrie's small frame, it fried each nerve cell instantaneously. Carrie let out a horrifying scream that froze Gail's heart between beats. Knowing there was nothing else to do but continue; Gail placed a knee on each side of Carrie's leg to hold it in place. With all her remaining strength and courage, she pulled hard on the twine and tied the ends together. Another small piece of wood was used to twist the knot even tighter. It also allowed Gail to loosen the pressure on the leg from time to time to ensure the blood was flowing throughout the leg. After what seemed like hours, but were only a few minutes, Gail fell back and released her grip on Carrie's leg. Carrie continued to scream as Gail continued to pant.

"I'm so sorry, Carrie," Gail wept. "Please, forgive me. I'm so sorry."

* * * * *

Standing in front of the car, they heard the loud cry of agony. Their hearts stopped as they realized it had to be either Gail or Carrie.

"Carrie!" Louise shrieked, as they all rushed toward the house. "Gail!"

Damara was the one to try the front door first... it was unlocked. Rushing in all at once, they were completely unaware of the man's shadow in the hall only a few feet away. The house was warm and a fire blazed in the hearth.

"Carrie," Damara yelled. "Carrie, where are you?"

"Byron?" Aaron whispered with fear emanating from his eyes. "Byron, come to me now! Check out the basement, girls... hurry!" Aaron yelled. "I'll look for Byron."

"How nuts is he exactly?" Damara asked, pausing for an answer.

"Depends on your definition of nuts," Aaron replied with a smile.

As the women ran through the living room and into the kitchen, Damara was still amazed as to how identical the two houses actually were. Until this very moment, the likeness was not something wicked but an oddity. However, now she realized that her ancestors were not only crazy, but also very evil and immoral. How could anyone have done such terrible things to their own babies? Didn't people realize that such a terrible deed only made matters worse? Why couldn't they have seen that how they treated their children actually took their sins to a higher level? Their malevolent actions were magnified many times over in their own children!

"This is crazy," Damara said, staring down into the dark basement with dread.

"Tell me about it," Louise replied, pushing the basement door open a little further. "Carrie? Are you down there?"

"Answer me this, Aunt Nidra, why is it that whenever someone's been kidnapped, they always end up in a dark and creepy basement?"

"You know what... you're right, but this isn't a movie, Damara. She could actually be anyplace." Louise looked over at Damara with apprehension in her eyes. "Is this where we get whacked to death by our crazy uncle?"

"I hope not," Damara answered with a weird grin. "Carrie, would you answer us, please!"

* * * * *

The men pulled up outside the house and immediately saw the two cars. They knew one was a rental, but the other had Quebec license plates. As they ran toward the house, Mark knew something was wrong when he saw that the front door was wide open. He froze in his tracks.

"Something's wrong!" he yelled out.

Devon stopped and turned toward Mark. "Why? What do you see?"

"No one keeps a front door open in these temperatures!" Mark screamed. "Something's wrong I tell you."

The deep red rose began to pulsate in Devon's mind. Knowing that blood would soon be spilled made his stomach crawl. Even though he was a large strong man, the feeling of helplessness ran though his veins. Life was too precious to Devon Arvol to be taken lightly. And now... his Carrie's life was in jeopardy. He was so frightened, Devon's mind refused to work. He didn't know what to do.

"What do you recommend?" Devon asked Mark, not being able to think.

"Who gives a damn? Let's go." Mark ran up the stairs and the others followed.

"Mark!" Devon screamed. "Don't be hasty."

Chad was running so fast and he was so excited that he lost his balance and fell through the entrance knocking over Mark and another agent. He finally skidded to a stop at the bottom of the stairs, but not before kicking over a potted plant and pulling a chair across the floor with him. When the noise finally subsided, Arvol shook his head in utter disbelief.

"Well, any surprise attack is now off. The whole world knows we're here. Carrie!" Devon yelled.

"Gail!" Mark screamed out. "Gail, where are you?"

The men searched the first floor but there were no signs of a struggle nor were there any women. Devon had ordered Stan and the other agent to search the upper floors. As Devon ran through the kitchen, Mark followed so closely that they almost tripped over each other near the kitchen table.

"Damn it, Mark, watch it," Devon whispered.

"What about you!" Mark stated sternly. It was his wife in trouble, a wife of forty-five years.

As he pulled open the basement door, Devon almost crapped in his pants, as he stood face-to-face with Louise.

"Shit!" he yelled. "What are you two doing here and where's Carrie and Gail?"

"They're not down there," Louise answered, just as surprised to see him. "What are you doing here?"

"Agency sent us," Mark answered, feeling suddenly more lost and alone not having found Gail.

"What do you mean they're not down there?" Devon asked.

"First you say it then you do it. But I don't smell a thing," Damara answered, coming up from behind Louise. "No one is down there. It's empty; just as she said."

"Anyplace to hide?" Mark asked.

"Nope... nothing," Damara said, tossing the flashlight onto the kitchen table. "Just a big empty basement with a washer and dryer."

"Where the hell are they?" Devon screamed out.

"Sir," one of the agents said from the kitchen door. "Sir, there's a dead man upstairs."

* * * * *

With the pain slowly subsiding, Carrie was finally able to pull herself up to a sitting position.

"Are you sure you should be doing that?" Gail asked, trying to help Carrie get comfortable.

"I don't know. God, how could I have been so stupid!" Carrie complained. "I should have known better than to fall through a missing stair! I can be such an airhead sometimes."

"Stair?" Gail asked. "What stairs?"

"Basement stairs; I was going down into the basement to look for you, but one of the steps had been removed and I fell in."

"Yow!" Gail said, rubbing her own leg. "That must have hurt."

"Not really; what hurt was the waking up," Carrie giggled nervously. "I'll need something to use as a crutch."

"Wait a minute, young lady, you're not going..."

Carrie cut her off. "We don't have time to sit around and wait for a rescue. I don't know about you, but I want to live. Whoever tossed me down here obviously wasn't counting on me waking up."

"I'll be right back. You stay here and I'll run to a drugstore and get you some," Gail sneered at Carrie. "Now where am I to find crutches?"

"Have you seen anything I could use?"

"Not really. I could try and support you."

"Yeah, but..." Carrie said, rubbing her head. "The hopping will be hell on my head."

"Fine, let me see what I can find."

"Gail?" Carrie asked. "How did he get you?"

With that question, Gail realized that she hadn't given it much thought. "I'm not sure exactly," she replied. "I remember watching you go up the steps to the house and the next thing I knew I was waking up next to that dead guy."

"Dead guy? What dead guy?"

Realizing how odd it was not to have mentioned it before, Gail laughed nervously. Although she had attended a few funerals during her life, she had never actually touched a corpse before. Not to mention that the dead guy was missing a head and was already starting to decompose.

"Long story... later perhaps. I've got to find something for you to use as a crutch."

"Gail?" Carrie whispered. "I want to see that dead guy."

"Right... I'll make you an appointment."

"And Gail?"

"Yes?" Gail asked as she began to rise.

A tear fell from Carrie's face. "Don't be long?" She had never felt so helpless before.

"I won't." Gail smiled.

* * * * *

"Poor old bloke probably never had a chance," Arvol said, staring at the severed head that was staring back at him from the dresser. "Any idea where the rest of his body is or for that matter who he is... um was?"

"No, sir," Chad answered, as fear tore through his body from the inside out. Chad had never seen a dead person before, let alone a severed head.

"Sir," the other agent yelled from the other room. "There's another one in here."

"Chad, call the police," Arvol demanded. "Two heads? Are they running a special or something? And keep those girls out of here!"

Mark couldn't remove his eyes from the severed head. It was obvious the kill was a few days old because the head was starting to decompose. Whoever this had been, it had been a while since he had taken his last breath, but before he could examine it further, Devon yelled for him from the other room.

The Agency

"Coming," Mark answered.

As Mark entered the other room, sirens wailed down the driveway.

"That was quick," Devon Arvol stated, wondering how in the world they could have responded so quickly. "Where's Chad anyway."

"Here, sir, and I hadn't called them yet," Chad answered with a strange look on his face.

"Mark, you and Chad go meet the local police," Arvol ordered with concern shining from his eyes. "We don't need them arresting us… and don't forget to flash your FBI badges!"

As the two men hurried off, Devon and the other agent stared ominously at the second severed head.

"This one's fresh," Arvol surmised with a deadened tone.

"How do you know?" the agent asked.

"It's still dripping with blood," Arvol replied.

* * * * *

Gail had found an old push broom and shouted out excitedly, "Hey, I think I found something!"

"Has the bleeding stopped yet?" Carrie asked, taking in several large deep breaths.

Gail bent down to get a closer look. The beam from the flashlight was weakening so she couldn't see much, but it was important to keep Carrie's spirits up, so she lied. "Yes, I believe so."

"Good, help me up," Carrie said sternly.

"I really don't think this is such a good idea."

"We've got to get out of here," Carrie demanded.

The broom was taller than Carrie was. Gail sighed and took the broom from Carrie's hand. As Carrie wobbled on one leg, Gail shoved the broom handle between the back of the old wooden door close to a hinge. With all her weight, Gail pushed on the handle until the end snapped off.

"A little lopsided but it should work." Gail smiled.

"Thanks," Carrie replied. "Sorry I'm so short."

"No shorter than me." Gail laughed.

There was only one door that Gail had not yet opened. Together they pushed on it and were discouraged when they saw a dark tunnel before them.

"This is just great!" Carrie sighed. "The light's dying and we've got nothing but more darkness! Just what we need... more darkness."

"I like dark," Gail said and Carrie just looked at her.

* * * * *

"Who called you?" Devon asked when the sheriff entered the bedroom.

"Well, actually, we received several calls," the sheriff replied, glancing around the room and pulling out a notepad. Reading from his notes he said, "First, a Bob Bangle called from New York... then a Parker Van Brunt from Montana... and finally an officer Ted Grafton; same place. Having received three calls from the United States all within an hour, I decided I'd better take a ride." The sheriff was an older man, probably in his seventies. Devon was relieved that at least he had the wisdom to bring a few younger deputies with him. As Devon filled him in with what he could say, the sheriff listened but never flinched; he didn't even look concerned.

"I see," the sheriff said. "But I find it hard to believe that Byron would harm anyone. He's autistic and stays pretty much to himself. There's an old woman in town that comes to care for him almost on a daily basis. She's never had any problems; never."

"There are *two* missing women, Sheriff; we need to find them. Are you going to help or not?" Mark screamed from the doorway.

"Yes, I see." The sheriff called over his two deputies and instructed them to thoroughly search the house and grounds. "I'm going to wait downstairs for the coroner to arrive. There's nothing more we can do here."

"No investigation?" Chad asked. "No pictures?"

"I doubt if the heads are going anywhere, sir," Arvol said to Chad, but his anger toward the sheriff was growing. What kind of a game was this man playing? Why didn't he have more concern for the missing women? "I've got a few calls to make. Make yourself busy... both of you!" Devon snapped at Mark and Chad. "Damn it... search the grounds!"

"Yes, sir," Chad replied, giving Mark a long, strange look.

As Chad hesitantly left the room, Mark shook his head. "Where are they, Devon?"

"I don't know," he answered. "I don't fucking know."

* * * * *

Their pace was slow. Carrie had to make use of her makeshift crutch to hold her weight as she limped down the dark long tunnel. It was painful trying to keep her knee slightly bent and she could feel something warm running down her leg. Exhaustion was pulling her down, but Carrie also knew that to stop now was a death sentence. The flashlight was almost dead and only gave them the ability to see a few inches past Gail's hand.

"Perhaps you should turn it off," Carrie suggested. "Save it. We're not walking fast enough to fall or trip over anything anyway."

As Gail turned off the light, the darkness engulfed them in a smothering embrace. Carrie groaned and Gail took hold of her arm. Their movement was slow but methodical.

After what seemed like an eternity, Carrie finally said, "I have got to sit down."

"Me too," Gail answered, helping Carrie to the ground. "I wonder where we are."

"In a hole." Carrie sighed. "Gail? Did you see who hit you?"

"No... did you?"

"Well, no one actually hit me. I kind of knocked myself out, gave the guy a break. But whoever it was slammed the basement door shut behind me so I couldn't see where I was going."

"I bet Mark is going crazy by now. Do you think they're looking for us? I mean, things didn't actually go as we had planned."

Carrie laughed. "Really? Oh, you think so? So tell me, what was your first clue, Gail?"

They both laughed until they could laugh no more. Their minds could no longer handle the stress and they released it through their laughter.

"Oh, they're looking for us all right." Carrie laughed. "But the question is where *are* we?"

"I thought we were in the basement of the old house." Gail laughed. "But now I'm not so sure."

They started laughing all over again. Both were wondering if this is what it felt like to lose one's mind, but it felt wonderful to them to release all of their pent-up emotions.

"This is no basement, this is a tunnel." Carrie began to settle down and to get serious again. "I've been in one other tunnel before and it was just as creepy." Carrie rubbed the top of her leg and added, "I think it's bleeding again."

As Gail flipped on the light to adjust Carrie's makeshift bandages, Gail asked, "Oh? Where?"

Carrie told her the story of Maddie and the old tunnel in Ohio. It passed the time and put their minds on something else other than their troubles at hand. It also seemed to ease the pain a little too. Carrie was thirsty and felt lightheaded, which could only mean trouble. It was important for her not to lose consciousness. So she continued to tell her story and as she did, Carrie missed Toby and Maddie more than ever.

* * * * *

Devon watched as the coroner and another technician placed the heads in body bags. He wanted to laugh thinking about the wasted space, but thought better of it. The full search of the house and grounds did not produce any missing women, but it did produce two severed arms and two severed legs. Altogether, the two heads were missing one complete body and one torso.

"Well, Sheriff, do you *still* believe Byron is an innocent man?" Devon asked sarcastically.

"Agent, we do not go into your country and tell *you* what to believe. So why must you come here to subject us to..." the sheriff began but was cut off in mid-sentence by Devon's angry response.

"Because two of our people are missing and are probably dead because of one of you. That's why!"

As Devon said the word *dead*, Mark's heart stopped beating. His world would cease to exist without his wife. Life with no Gail would mean a life with no purpose. It was something he would not survive. He sat on the front steps and cried harder than he had ever cried before.

Sounds of crunching snow in the distance announced the arrival of another vehicle. Devon turned around just in time to see a black van come to a complete stop only a few feet away. Several men and one woman jumped from the van wearing a black zip-up work suit with black boots. They also wore dark sunglasses to cover their eyes.

The sheriff looked sternly at Devon and said, "These must belong to you?"

Devon shook his head and replied, "No, I thought they belonged to you."

As the dark group approached Devon and the sheriff, they stopped just a few inches away. One man, who must have been in charge, had an earpiece attached to his head. A microphone stopped just halfway down his face. He didn't smile, but he didn't frown either.

"Who are you and what are you doing here?" Devon demanded.

"Agent Arvol, I presume?" the man asked.

"And who wants to know?"

Without moving a muscle, the man replied, "We are here on behalf of the US and the Canadian government. We'll take over from here."

At that moment, another black vehicle arrived that looked more like a bus without windows. Even before it came to a complete stop, several people emerged with gurneys and black suitcases. They took custody of the body parts from the coroner and quickly stored them in the black bus-like vehicle.

"Now wait just a minute," the sheriff demanded. "I'm in charge here!"

"Not anymore, sir," the man in black answered.

As the strange man gave orders to his men, the sheriff used his cell phone to call his office. He had an odd look on his face as he listened. After the call ended, he turned to Devon, smiled, and shook his head.

"Seems that we've been called off the case. Good luck to you." The sheriff turned and yelled out to his deputies.

As the sheriff's tires crackled against the ice, Chad stood quietly next to Devon scratching his head. "This case is getting a little too weird for me, sir."

* * * * *

"I need water," Carrie whispered, as they continued their journey down the long dark tunnel.

"Me too," Gail said, not realizing how thirsty she had been. "How long do you think we've been walking?"

"I don't know," Carrie answered, stopping suddenly. "What was that?"

"What was what?" Gail fumbled for her flashlight just knowing that it had to be one of the crazy twins.

"Stop... listen," Carrie whispered.

A deathly silence hung over their heads. The only sounds were from the beating of their frightened hearts.

"I don't hear anything," Gail whispered.

"Shh!"

A faint, almost inaudible sound of a woman's whisper vibrated through their ears.

"I heard that!" Gail whispered. Not believing her own ears, Gail searched the darkness for any signs of another presence.

"It sounded like..." Carrie started but Gail finished.

"What way?" Gail whispered.

"Say it again," Carrie stated firmly.

Again, the faint whisper of a woman's voice floated through the wind and past their ears.

"Which way, Nadia?" Carrie yelled. "Which way!"

A cold but pulsating breeze hit their faces as gentle as a powder puff. The two stood silently holding each other's hands. Gail was shaking uncontrollably.

"Nadia? Is that you?" Carrie screamed and her voice echoed back from both directions of the cave at the same time.

"An echo in stereo, now that's something you don't hear every day," Gail giggled nervously.

Through the darkness, only a few feet in front of them, a misty figure appeared. Gail gasped and Carrie cried. It could only be one person and no matter how afraid she was, Carrie had to trust her.

"Let's go," Carrie said, as she leaned on her broom for support.

"Go where?" Gail cried.

"Nadia will take care of us," Carrie answered, limping toward the misty figure.

* * * * *

Mark and Arvol stood alone in the front yard feeling helpless. Neither knew what to do. Mark glanced around the vast property and noticed a rot iron fence off in the distance.

"I wonder what that is," Mark questioned, pointing toward the horizon.

"Hmm, never noticed that fence before. Maybe the property line?" Devon surmised.

"Can't be," Mark said, as he took a few steps in that direction. "The property for both of the homes is many acres. That fence cannot be on this property, it's too close."

Devon followed Mark but remained a few paces behind. His heart was breaking and he felt useless. Never before had he felt like such a loser. Why did he agree to let Carrie run off to Montana? He knew she was upset and when Carrie got upset, it only lead to trouble.

"It's a graveyard!" Mark yelled out.

Devon hurried to meet up with Mark and they stood silently by the old rusty gate that led into a small family plot. The iron above the gate was shaped into the name LeBoisne. The largest headstone that greeted you as you entered was in the shape of a man and a woman holding hands with the name of LeBoisne in large block letters. Two smaller names were underneath but written in script, Byron and Sheila. The death dates were 1973 and 1949.

"So where's Bella?" Damara asked from behind, startling the men who almost pissed in their pants.

"Damn it..." Devon shouted. "Will you stop that, please?"

"Stop what?" Louise asked.

"Every time I... oh, fuck... never mind. Who's Bella?" Devon asked. "And where have you two been?"

"Uncle Aaron and Byron's mother," Damara answered, searching the headstones for Bella's name. "We were searching the house and were about to search the grounds when we saw you two heading up here. Does anyone have a notepad?"

"I do," Mark answered, still shaking from the shock of the two visitors. He pulled a small pad of paper and a pen from the inside of his jacket and handed them to Damara.

Damara sketched out a family tree and jotted down the names. She had gazed at her family tree that Carrie had drawn out for her for so many hours that it was now permanently imprinted in her memory.

"Here," Damara said, shoving the handwritten tree to Devon. "Help me move away the snow. Let's see who's really buried here."

With warm leather gloves protecting their hands, they each took turns brushing the snow from a headstone and yelling out the name.

"Here's Sarah Mary and her husband!" Louise hollered and Devon checked it off.

Mark wiped away the snow and yelled, "Here's a Peter and Maria."

"I remember her funeral, but I don't remember it being up here," Louise stated, walking over to Mark. "That's weird."

"Found Thomas Howard," Damara announced from the front gate.

"There are more LeBoisne's over here. A Mortimer and his wife and a Sinjon and his wife," Devon screamed out from the top of the graveyard.

"We're missing some people," Damara yelled. "Where's Jacob Lee?"

"Maybe covered up with snow," Louise said, staring down at her mother and father's grave.

"Keep searching!" Damara yelled.

More names from deceased family members were being hollered out from all sides of the fenced-in graveyard, but Jacob Lee was not there.

"When did he die?" Devon asked.

"Supposedly several years ago," Louise answered.

"Maybe he's buried someplace else," Mark interjected. "Not every family member is always buried in a family plot."

"Perhaps you're right," Damara stated not concerned.

"Lots of babies are buried up here," Devon interjected with a strange expression on his face. "No names, they just have the dates."

Louise explained the morbid past of their family's legacy as they jotted down the dates.

"My God, the woman was only ten years old when she had the twins!" Devon declared. "How many babies did she have before your mother?"

"We're not sure, but we've found five graves so far," Louise said sorrowfully.

A whistle and a waving hand was gesturing them back to the house.

"Maybe they found something," Damara yelled, as she ran through the gate.

* * * * *

The apparition faded into the darkness, but as the two allowed their eyes to adjust, a faint line of light was in the distance.

"The end?" Gail asked.

"God, I hope so," Carrie replied.

Gail did not want to believe that they were being escorted out by a ghost. That just wasn't possible. She was born and raised in the Jewish religion, and proud of her heritage. There just wasn't any room for ghosts. Oh, she believed in a god, and she loved that god, but there just wasn't any room in her religion for a spirit.

When they finally reached the light, two paths confronted them: one straight ahead with a door and the other to the left that led down into a dark abyss. As she reached out to push on the door, Gail felt a slap on her wrist.

"Ouch," Gail whispered. "Why did you slap me?"

"I didn't," Carrie said, clinging to Gail's shoulder. "I'm holding onto the boom and your shoulder, try the knob again."

Gail knew Carrie could not release the broom and stand up by herself, and her other hand was on her shoulder. Once again, Gail reached out to touch the wooden door and was slapped on the wrist by an unknown presence.

"Oh, my," Gail sighed. "I'm not liking this."

"Did it happen again?" Carrie asked.

"Oh, yes."

Before Carrie could speak, the low whisper of a woman's voice passed their ears. *Other way...*

"Did you hear that?" Carrie asked.

"Yes, but I don't want to go down there," Gail cried.

"Me neither," Carrie whined.

"So what do we do?"

"I don't know," Carrie sighed.

"You stay here and sit on the step. If anyone comes through that door, you can scoot down into the dark. I'll go down and check it out."

"I don't know about…"

"It's all we can do. Now you stay here," Gail ordered sternly.

As she flipped on the flashlight, Gail slowly descended the dirt stairs that circled into the unknown. After a few steps, she could no longer see Carrie who was sitting on the upper stair, but the further down she went, the warmer it got. Then she realized that neither of them had been too cold or too hot throughout their whole ordeal. It didn't take long before she was on the bottom. Instead of dirt, she was standing on solid rock. The flashlight was about useless now and as she felt her way around, Gail soon bumped into a table. Fortunately, the light was enough to see a candle and matches. Did she dare light the candle? After she thought about it, if anyone was in the room with her, they would have known of her presence long ago.

Gail climbed the stairs and slowly helped Carrie down into the small room that was lit by only a candle. A cot was against one wall and Carrie thanked Nadia as she lay down. Bottles of water were on a shelf and the two immediately gulped down a bottle each.

"There's some food here too," Gail said happily. "Some breakfast bars and other things like that. You can eat and rest and regain your strength."

"How's my leg?" Carrie asked.

"Swollen as I expected it would be. At least the bone is staying in place. Does it hurt?"

"Yes, it's throbbing," Carrie complained.

"Good, means there's blood flow. Now rest," Gail ordered.

"Thank you," Carrie whispered before she fell into a deep sleep.

She found some blankets and after making a bed for herself on the floor, Gail blew out the light.

* * * * *

"We've identified one of the heads and we've found another body. We need someone to identify it." The agent was cold and factual in his voice and mannerisms.

Louise suddenly spoke up. "Uncle Aaron?"

"Yes, where's Uncle Aaron?" Damara yelled out. "We haven't seen him since we got here. Where's the body?"

"In the shed," he answered.

The girls ran as fast as they could through the trampled snow and mush. Devon and Mark ran after them realizing no one had asked if it was a male or female body. When they reached the shed, two other men were zipping up the body bag.

"Let them see," the man in charge stated and the other agents backed up to give the family some time alone.

Damara let out a yell as Louise knelt down next to the body. "Uncle Aaron," she cried out. "Uncle Aaron, what happened! Who did this?"

"No! That can't be, not Uncle Aaron," Damara cried. "But it has to be. Uncle Aaron... oh, my God, no!" Damara screamed. "Uncle Aaron, I'm so sorry."

* * * * *

Carrie woke up in a pitch-dark room. She was shivering and her skin felt like she was lying on a bed of nails. Her whole body ached and she felt dizzy even though she was lying down.

"Gail," Carrie whispered. "Gail?"

"I'm here," Gail answered sleepily. "Do you need some water?"

"I'm sick."

As Gail felt Carrie's forehead, panic filled her soul. "Oh no, you have a fever."

With the candle lit, Gail examined Carrie's leg. It was swollen three times the normal size and was a dark purple in color.

"Damn, your leg's infected. I have to find help."

"You can't..." Carrie ordered.

"Look, you're in no condition to be giving any orders. Now you lay here and rest. I'm going to check things out."

Gail blew out the candle after getting Carrie some water and another blanket. As long as she could reach her drink, she'd at least not get dehydrated. Crawling up the stairs, Gail's heart was beating fast. She was terrified as to who she'd run into at the top, but at the same time, she was also afraid of Carrie's poor health to simply wait for help to arrive. Besides, if they didn't know where they were, how could help find them in time? When she reached the top, Gail noticed that the light was still on behind the door, but this time, slap or no slap, she had to go through. Gail couldn't see under the door so she had no choice but to open it. As she pushed softly on the wooden door, it creaked as it swung open. Gail froze in place waiting for someone to jump at her, but all remained quiet and calm.

A little braver this time, Gail pushed harder on the wood that kept her in this nightmare and away from reality. The door swung completely open this time. The next room was well lit with a light hanging from the ceiling. A small table and chair sat in the middle of the room. No one was there. With a huge sigh of relief, Gail entered the small room. A crossword puzzle and a cup of something resembling coffee sat on the table. She felt the cup and it was still warm. Someone had just left. If they had not gone down below, they probably would have been caught. But caught by whom?

The other door was in much better condition and almost looked new. Staring at the silver doorknob, Gail's heart continued to flutter and beat wildly.

"Please give me strength," Gail prayed.

As her hand touched the knob, two hands gripped tightly on her shoulders. As she swung around to confront her attacker, Gail realized she was still alone.

"Nadia," Gail sighed. "Next time... how about a little warning."

Instead of fear, Gail felt a sudden rush of boldness and security. All her anxieties were gone, and a strong sense of encouragement filled her with an intense bravery she had never experienced before.

"Why thank you, Nadia," Gail whispered.

She turned the knob and pulled the door toward her expecting to have to fight. Instead, a brightly lit world welcomed her with a blast of cold mountain air. A fresh layer of snow blanketed the trees and ground with a false sense of peacefulness. There were fresh footprints in the snow leading down a small path. Being careful to keep everything the same, Gail closed the door behind her and placed her feet exactly in the same place as whoever just left them. She was freezing and pulled her jacket closer around her neck. As she did, she was thankful that their kidnappers didn't think to take their jackets away from them. Her hands were chilled and she jammed them into her pockets where she unexpectedly found her gloves.

"This is just too good. I know nothing bad will happen now," she said softly to no one.

Following the footsteps down the path was not easy and she almost lost her balance a couple of times. After several minutes, which seemed like hours, Gail finally knew where she was.

"This is impossible!"

* * * * *

"Who are you guys anyway?" Devon asked the man in the black outfit when he they finally reached the house.

"We're from The Agency, sir. We're here to support you."

"Well, why didn't you say that in the first place?" Devon asked, shaking his head.

The man in the black suit only smiled and replied, "We couldn't say much with the law enforcement here, sir."

"Well, they're gone. So what did you want? You waved for us to return," Devon replied, more agitated than excited. Devon briefly glanced over at the others when they finally caught up.

"We've made a positive identification on one of the..." The man coughed. "Heads."

"And..." Damara asked, butting into the conversation.

Devon glanced over at her and wondered how it always seemed that he was riddled with women on his missions that would interrupt and make ridiculous suggestions. It was just his dumb luck that did this to him time after time. And when a woman was around it was almost impossible to conduct a real investigation, for they were always asking the wrong questions.

"The latest kill upstairs was a Lewis John, male... 75 years of age..." the agent started, but was cut off by Louise.

"No, that wasn't Uncle LJ!" Louise stated firmly.

Now Devon Arvol was starting to get angry and tried to say, "Okay, now would you let me..." but he was cut off again by Damara.

"No, it wasn't," she added, ignoring Arvol.

"According to dental records and a quick DNA match, I'm sorry to say it is," the agent tried to explain.

"But we were just with him last month," Louise defended. "And that *isn't* the man we visited."

"If that's Uncle LJ in that body bag, then who did we spend an afternoon with last month?" Damara asked, looking puzzled and afraid.

* * * * *

The teapot whistled as LJ dropped his teabag into the cup. As the hot liquid hissed, he glanced out the kitchen window - all was peaceful and serene. He grabbed the package of lemon cookies from off the shelf and tore it open. The scent sent him reeling back in time and he thought of Nadia and how much she resisted to his cause. Suddenly, he felt an urgent need to complete his work.

"Dirty blood must be cleaned... before it's too late," he moaned in French to himself, as he carried his snack into the den to sit next to the warm, blazing fire.

As he dunked his cookies to enjoy a soggy sweet and tart treat, LJ paused to rub his leg. Although finally healed, the gash he received from the razor sharp fence in Bowman, Montana still ached, which made him limp.

"Damn fence," he said, as he took another sip of hot tea.

The pictures on the piano and the large portrait of Maria over the fireplace stared at him... almost mocking.

"You think you've got the upper hand?" he yelled out in French. "Well, you're wrong! As always you are wrong!" he yelled. "I'm almost finished... and then *my* mother can finally rest in peace."

LJ laughed at the silent pictures and portrait. He finished off his snack with a snarled grin and keeping one eye on his relatives. After flipping on the television, LJ settled in for a little nap. He knew the two women were either dead or close to it. The first one was hit hard on the head and went down quietly. The other one... he had to laugh. She did it to herself! All he had to do was clean up the mess. As he fell asleep, LJ dreamt of his dear departed brothers and wished they could have been spared, but they were all devoted to stopping him. They were always trying to stop him... even stupid Byron. He couldn't blame Byron, after all, Byron had always been a little slow to catch on. Now Sheila, his mother, was standing at the sink... she was crying and holding her belly. LJ was nineteen again and felt helpless. As he slept, he also cried.

The Agency

* * * * *

"So who's the dead guy in the shed?" Mark asked, deciding that another person butting in and asking questions couldn't hurt. "Is it their other uncle?"

"That was Aaron, yes. We finally got a positive match." He glanced over at the two women who were crying. "I'm sorry."

Damara and Louise nodded as tears fell from their eyes. Both felt it was their fault. If they hadn't asked him to come, then he would still be alive.

"Where is Byron?" Louise asked between sobs.

"Who's Byron?" Devon asked.

"He's Aaron's twin brother," Damara sobbed.

"You mean there's two of them?" Mark asked.

The women nodded their heads and walked away to console each other.

"Sir," the agent said. "There's no one else on the property. We'll search again, but I can personally guarantee you that there's no one here but us."

"Carrie?" Devon whispered. "Where in the *hell* are you, sweetheart?"

* * * * *

"Oh, no... oh, no... you can't go... you can't..."

The voice of a man who resembled Aaron LeBoisne startled Gail as she tried desperately to step where the other person had left the imprints in the snow. He looked like Aaron but was a little chubbier and wore glasses... and he had more hair, but was holding his hands in front of his face.

"Hello," Gail said, realizing at once that she was meeting Byron LeBoisne for the first time.

"Oh, no... oh, no," he kept saying. "Trouble... trouble... need to go back... need to go back."

Byron was rocking in place and moving his fingers in front of his face as if trying to figure out how he could fix the problem. He was obviously upset and nervous.

"Oh, it's okay, Byron," Gail lied. "He said I could go."

"Oh, no... oh no..." Byron continued to chant.

"Hey, Byron, want to play?" Gail asked.

Byron continued to rock back and forth as though contemplating what Gail had just asked him. He remained silent but looked up into the cloudy sky as if expecting to find the answer somewhere above.

"Byron, come on," Gail urged.

"LJ be mad... LJ be mad," he chanted.

Gail knew she had to think quickly or her chance would be lost. She was miles away from the town Falcon Lake and knew she'd never make it on foot. Gail had to get to a phone and the only phone was in the house, the house where LJ was sleeping.

"Byron," Gail said softly. "I want to be your friend."

"Byron has no friends... no friends."

"I'll be your friend, Byron," Gail coached.

* * * * *

"So who owns the other head?" Mark asked.

"Have some sympathy will ya?" Damara yelled out from the porch.

Mark rolled his eyes and whispered to Devon, "Do they hear everything no matter where they are?"

"Yes!" Louise yelled out.

"We're not sure about that," the agent replied. "Once we've got a match with the DNA, we'll let you know."

"Thank you," Devon said, pulling Chad and Mark to one side. "Look, guys, I have no idea where the girls are and that's not good. We need to regroup and strategize our next move. I'll get the other agent to go back to Falcon Lake and check out the other house. Chad, I need you to hit the Internet. There has to be something we've missed. Mark, we'll go check out LJ's house. Everybody in the family is dead except those two, and I don't think they're our..." Devon stopped in the middle of his sentence.

"No way," Mark defended. "One was teaching a class and the other was across the country. They are *not* your murderer. It has to be Byron."

"Byron has to be the other severed head!" Devon wanted to scream but whispered instead. "I just don't know who to believe or what to believe anymore, Mark."

Devon turned around and stared at the two women standing on the porch shivering. *Why don't they go inside where it's warm?* he asked himself.

* * * * *

Lewis paced the floor. It had been hours since he last spoke with any of his agents in Canada and now he was worried. When the phone on his desk rang, he almost tripped over himself trying to get to it.

"Hello!" he screamed into the phone.

"Having a bad day?" Maddie asked.

"Sorry," he answered. "What's up?"

Lewis knew that Maddie would not call his direct line unless it was important. It was just too risky.

"I received all the paperwork you sent me and I was reviewing the LeBoisne family history. I asked Nate to do some extra snooping and what he found really bothers me."

"And what's that?" Lewis asked, now bothered himself. Maddie had been one of his best agents before she had to go into hiding. Now he assigned her to only highly covert operations such as the one she's doing now. If anyone could get to the bottom of things, it would be Maddie. The only other agent that even comes close to matching Maddie's cunning abilities is Carrie, and she was missing.

"The funds in this jerk's bank account came from the LeBoisne's account... that we already knew. And we also knew that the money was transferred by LJ."

"Okay, and..." Lewis wanted her to get to the point.

"We all thought that LJ was Lewis John, right?" Maddie asked.

"Well, we thought it was, but someone killed him," Lewis added. "It doesn't add up."

"Right, it doesn't make any sense. A killer wouldn't kill himself. To shut himself up, that is. So only the real murderer would kill LJ... and since he was taken apart piece by piece, then we must assume that the murderer is personally involved somehow. He *had* a reason to take that guy apart. It felt good!"

"Get to the point, Mad."

"On this chart, there's another brother with the same initials... a Lee Jacob. He was older than LJ, but all the records state he's deceased,"

Maddie explained. "Supposedly in 2000, but I can't find his grave listed anywhere."

"So you think what... that he could still be alive?" Lewis asked.

"I'm grasping at straws here, but just think about it, Jeff. He would have been about 19 when his mother killed herself. That's more than old enough to know about things. He probably would have been aware of what his father was doing; he *had* to know. You can't bring a baby into a house and keep it a secret, especially to an older child."

Lewis listened and wished she were here in his office instead of miles away on that island. Why did life always have to change? Why couldn't it stay the same forever? He was happy back then, but he wasn't happy anymore.

"Go on," Lewis encouraged.

"I also had Nate check out some old doctor reports. Lee Jacob also went by the name LJ. Both boys used the initials instead of their actual names. On all the paperwork, Lewis John actually went by the name *Little LJ*, not LJ. The medical reports said that LJ had been on medication his whole life for a bi-polar disorder. He was on all kinds of stuff. It also states that he had a terrible temper that he could not control. After his mother died, he went to shrink after shrink, but nothing they prescribed or did seemed to help. In the summer of 2000, it's reported that LJ drowned during a fishing trip... but I have a sneaking suspicion that he didn't really die."

"Perhaps they never recovered the body," Lewis suggested.

"Perhaps, but you still file a death report. There's no death report filed anywhere on the older LJ!"

* * * * *

Gail followed Byron down the snowy slope toward the old house. It was cold and she was tired and hungry. Her thoughts kept flashing back to Carrie, which was the only thing that kept her moving.

"Byron? Can I ask you a question?"

Byron stopped and waited for her to catch up. "Byron says yes... you ask. Byron says yes," he chanted.

"Who's LJ?"

"LJ big brother... yes... LJ be mad..."

The Agency

Gail wished he would stop chanting so she could get some straight answers, but she knew that sometimes with autism comes the chanting.

"Byron," she asked cautiously. "Does LJ like dead animals?"

Suddenly, Gail realized that she hit a sore nerve. Byron turned on her and instinctively, she had an urge to run. Instead, she stood in place, holding her ground.

"LJ bad... LJ hurt Byron's friends... LJ bad," he chanted, now running toward the shed. "LJ bad..."

This wasn't good. The shed was too much in the open. Anyone standing in the kitchen would be able to see her and know that she had escaped her tunnel grave.

"Byron, no," Gail whispered, but it was too late.

Byron had already entered the shed and was chanting, "LJ bad... LJ hurt..."

Gail ran to the back of the shed and moved cautiously around to the other side. She kept looking all about to ensure that no one would ever hit her on the head again. When she reached the far side, she peered through a dirty window into the shabby old structure and could see a shadowy figure rocking back and forth.

"Great! Just great... he's chanting to himself now," she complained to herself.

"Byron!" a voice from the back door yelled out with a deep French accent. He screamed some words in French, but Gail couldn't understand. She knew that this guy was angry.

Byron left the small shed and slowly walked toward the back steps. He had obviously forgotten all about Gail and was now more concerned about the caller. As the back door slammed shut, Gail quickly darted into the dark shed. Dead animals that had been stuffed many years ago were mounted and placed everywhere. The shelves now resembled some kind of a freak show to her and gave her the creeps. Odd-looking sharp tools were scattered about. Feeling curious, Gail carefully picked up one and examined it closely. It resembled something her dentist used to clean her teeth recently. Feeling dirty inside by just touching it, Gail immediately tossed it back on the wooden table.

"Hmm," she said. "I wonder who did all this work?"

"Moi," came a reply from behind her.

* * * * *

Carrie opened her eyes and took in a deep breath. She ached all over and was terribly dizzy. Her leg was killing her and she wanted nothing more than to fall back to sleep. Wishing she was home with Devon and knowing that focusing on her emotions didn't help, Carrie slowly pushed herself up into a sitting position. After another deep painful breath, she slowly stood and maintained her balance. Not knowing how long it had been since Gail left to find help, Carrie knew she couldn't wait any longer.

Sitting on the bottom stair, Carrie started the long task of hauling herself up. She was exhausted and hungry, but had to go on. When she finally made it to the outer door, the bright afternoon sunlight burned her eyes.

"Damn," she said, shielding her eyes. "This sucks."

The air felt cool against her hot face and the fresh mountain air was a wonderful pleasure after being cooped up under the damp earth. It didn't take her long before she realized she was not in Quebec, but back at the house at Falcon Lake.

"Now if this isn't something," she remarked.

Following and limping down the trail, Carrie was cautious so as not to be seen. When she got close to the house, she hid under the trees in order to sneak even closer. The sun was now setting over the mountain ridge and the shadows were becoming deeper and darker, which was great for her... more cover, but also not good... it was getting colder. When she reached the back of the house, she could hear voices coming from the kitchen.

Damn, Carrie said to herself. There was no way she could enter from back here. They would see her immediately.

Cautiously, she limped and hopped to the front of the house. Using the sitting position again and balancing the old broken broom handle, she slowly made it to the front door. Carrie turned the knob very slowly and ever so lightly pushed on the door. As the door opened wider, she peered in. There were two men standing in the kitchen and Gail was sitting at the table with a saddened face.

Knowing of no other way, Carrie sickened at the thought of having to put pressure on her wounded leg. Gathering all her strength and preparing for the pain, she stepped into the house leaning on the broom handle for support. She wanted to scream when her sore leg took the weight, but held it in. Once the door was closed, she headed straight for the stairs to use the sit and scoot method again. After a short while, she finally made it to the guest bedroom where the door had been closed. Since this room was directly above the kitchen, she moved slowly so the floor would not squeak and give her position away. The phone was on the desk by the bed only a few short feet away, but to her, it was more like miles. She sighed and closed the door behind her. As she sat next to the bed, she cried before trying to reach the phone.

As she pushed herself up to reach the phone, her leg bone snapped and broke through the already swollen and sore tissue. The pain radiated throughout her body. Carrie wanted to vomit and faint at the same time. As the darkness started to overwhelm her, a voice whispered softly in her ear.

"I'm here, Carrie, my love. I'll take your pain..."

It was Nadia and as wonderful as it was to hear her voice, it was just as wonderful to feel and see nothing. Suddenly, it was as if her leg had never been injured. Carrie was able to stand up and put pressure on her leg, but looking down at her injured leg, she could see it was still bleeding... there was no pain though.

Am I dreaming? Carrie wondered.

"Get onto the bed," Nadia coached in a soft whisper.

Carrie lay down on the soft blankets and it was a wonderful relief. She settled in on the propped up pillows and reached for the phone. Dialing the well-memorized number was a strange comfort.

* * * * *

Dr. Lewis was staring at Dr. Greghardt and wanting nothing more than to tear the man's head off.

"How many years have we worked together?" Lewis asked.

"Too many," Greghardt answered. "And I sometimes wonder why I stay."

"I've wondered the same thing," Jeff Lewis replied.

"Jeff," Greghardt said, as he poured himself a drink. "We had no idea what Carrie was getting herself into when she first called. I wish we had done more..."

"I'm changing a few things around here, Allen," Lewis interrupted. "From now on, when an agent asks for help, they're going to get it. No questions asked."

"That's probably not a bad idea," Greghardt replied.

Lewis wondered if Allen really meant that or if he was just trying to get back into his good graces. As he pondered over Allen Greghardt's motives, Jeff's phone rang loudly from his desk.

"Lewis," he answered.

After a short pause, Lewis smiled and grabbed his cell phone. As he dialed Devon's number, he glanced over to Greghardt and replied, "Let's see if you're as good as your word."

* * * * *

The unmarked helicopter hovered only a few seconds before landing in front of the huge old house. Devon and the others climbed aboard and buckled themselves in for the short but harried flight. Damara was both angry and excited. She glanced over at her aunt and smiled. Nidra Louise smiled back and rolled her eyes. Mark remained silent; he was worried about his wife. Lewis never did say whether Gail was still alive. Devon Arvol stared hopelessly out into the setting sun praying silently to his god that his world wasn't about to change.

* * * * *

As the sheriff's car hummed outside, the old man grabbed Gail by her arm and shoved her down the basement stairs. She didn't know whether it would be wise to object, so when he told her to stay quiet if she wanted to live, she did. He locked the kitchen door after slamming it shut, but Gail climbed back up the stairs anyway to listen where the floor and door separated.

"Good evening, Byron, how are you doing?" a man's voice said.

"Good, Byron is good..." Byron chanted.

"I'm glad to hear that," a man's voice said.

"What do you want, Ben?" the old man's voice said.

"I got a call that you were housing some guests," a man's voice said. "I came to meet them."

The Agency

The old man began speaking in French, but the other reply was in English. From then on, Gail could only understand half of the conversation.

As she waited, the men's voices got louder as they began to argue.

* * * * *

Carrie was sleeping peacefully with Nadia at her side. It was a heavenly sensation. She was lying in a bed of fragrant flower petals and the sweet aroma was soothing. There was no pain, and she wanted to sleep forever... there would be no regrets. Carrie could hear Nadia talking somewhere in the distance. What was she saying?

"No, I don't want to wake up," Carrie whined. "Please don't make me get up."

* * * * *

Gail was about to give up when she realized she was watching the moonlight fill the basement with a dim beam.

"Moonlight?" she asked herself with a sudden realization. "A window?"

Now all she needed was a way to reach it.

* * * * *

The unmarked black helicopter landed only a mile away from the old house at Falcon Lake. It was now pitch-dark and after the copter departed, the only light that guided them was the dim moonlight.

"If only there weren't any clouds," Damara complained, feeling her away along behind Nidra.

"Be thankful we've got this much," Mark added.

"Ouch," Damara cried, as she tripped over a broken branch.

Devon suddenly stopped and confronted them. "You must be quiet," he whispered. "Or you're going to get us killed."

"Sorry," they all whispered in unison.

Devon shook his head and turned to continue the short trek to the house, but came face to face with a man who stood boldly in front of them.

"What the hell..." Devon gasped in shock.

The others stood paralyzed in their tracks behind him.

"Help Byron? Byron needs help... yes, he does..." The man was rambling and not making any sense.

Damara and Louise knew immediately who the man was blocking their way and ran to his side.

"Byron? Hi, I'm Damara, your niece," Damara said, smiling. "And this is Louise... I mean Nidra, your other niece... or one of them... or..."

The two women smiled while waiting for the axe to tear into their flesh, but Byron only rocked himself in place as he chanted, "Byron needs help... yes he does..."

* * * * *

The blunt thud of a body hitting the wood floor echoed, threatening into Gail's ear through the basement door. As she jumped back, she almost lost her balance and to tumble down the stairs now would surely mean a death sentence. As she leaned forward again to listen, a pool of blood floated under the door. Not knowing whether it was the local sheriff or the crazy old man that was bleeding and probably already dead, Gail decided to back down the stairs. With her heart pounding as fast as it was, her mind continued to race through unthinkable thoughts.

What to do... what to do, she asked herself nervously.

Now the sound of furniture being dragged across the floor was even louder above her head. It wasn't until the old man yelled out for his younger brother that Gail realized who was still alive. She wanted to cry, but her mind wouldn't let her. Frantically, she searched for something to stand on. She had to get out of the basement of that house, and she had to get out now.

* * * * *

"What's wrong?" Damara demanded from Byron. "What are you scared of?"

"Byron needs help," he continued to chant.

Mark pulled out his binoculars and stared at the house. When he saw the sheriff's empty car, he wasn't sure if he should be afraid or happy. As he slowly lowered the binoculars, he asked, "The sheriff's there?"

All eyes were not on Mark because Byron was chanting and wildly flinging his arms through the air. "Brother is mad... brother is bad!"

"Byron," Damara asked. "Where *is* your brother?"

"House... house... LJ in house..." Byron stuttered.

Damara stared deep into Byron's eyes and asked slowly, "Did you see any strangers here today?"

Byron immediately stopped dancing and chanting and looked Damara straight in the face and said as seriously as he could, "LJ will kill the pretty lady... LJ bad... LJ kill the pretty lady... help the lady... Byron help the pretty lady... yes, Byron help." As tears welled in his eyes, Damara gave him a hug and turned to her aunt.

"Get him someplace safe! I'm going in," yelled Chad.

"Oh no you are not!" Arvol ordered. "If anyone is going in, it'll be me."

As the two continued to argue, Mark took his cue. He ran to the back of the huge old house and silently situated himself on the back stairs. It wasn't until he entered the back door that anyone noticed that he was gone.

"Where's Mark?" Arvol asked.

"He was just here," Damara stammered. She was angry with this man and couldn't understand why he was being so controlling. These were *her* relatives not his!

The others stared at each other and shrugged their shoulders.

"Damn!" Arvol screeched.

* * * * *

LJ was angry. He hated it when he had to clean up a mess; blood wasn't an easy thing to clean up and what was worse, if you didn't get it all, the smell could kill you after a few days. Even in below zero temperature, the odor from the blood that remained hidden in the cracks of the floor was pure torture. After tying a rope around the sheriff who was now neatly wrapped in plastic trash bags, LJ was ready to dump him in the basement. It took all his strength to just get the body ready, so now he wasn't sure if he had enough strength to finish the job or not. Yesteryear, LJ was able to do everything he needed to do in order to cleanse the family blood... but now he just didn't have the energy like he used to.

Huffing and puffing, LJ heaved one last time and the sheriff's limp body slowly bounced down the stairs to the basement floor. He had forgotten all about the woman who he had shoved in earlier and hadn't thought twice about her until he felt the cold breeze from the open basement window. Then everything came flooding back and his anger rose.

"Damn bitch!" he yelled in French.

He limped back up the stairs and yelled for his brother Byron, but there was still no answer. "Where in the hell is that stupid imp anyway?" LJ asked aloud.

When he reached the kitchen, LJ stood face to face with a man he did not know. The shock took him back a step and he stared at the man with a strange angry smile.

* * * * *

He was now gawking straight into the eyes of the cold-blooded killer and for the first time in his life, Mark felt a strong sense of hatred. It wouldn't take much for him to kill this man right where he stood.

"Where is my wife?" Mark demanded. "Bring her to me at once you... you... heathen!"

After a few simple words in French, LJ added, "She has left already."

Not expecting this answer, Mark became silent, befuddled. He had rushed in to save his wife, but now she wasn't there to be saved. This was an awkward moment and he didn't quite know what to do. He glanced around half-hoping that Arvol would rush in to save him, but Arvol was nowhere in sight. It now occurred to Mark that perhaps he was a bit too hasty.

LJ had to laugh. "You Americans watch too much television. There is no one here to save you."

At that precise moment, Mark felt a fiery burning sensation below his left ribcage. At first, it was only awareness; but all of a sudden, he was having difficultly breathing. The more he tried to catch his breath, the harder it became to breathe. Then the pain hit. It was such a fierce and deep burning pain that Mark doubled over and fell to the floor.

LJ continued to laugh as he stepped over Mark and walked nonchalantly out the back door. The room began to spin and his stomach wanted to heave. Mark closed his eyes as a peaceful calmness began to engulf him. It was the most wonderful sensation he had ever experienced, and there was nothing more he wanted at that moment than to continue in his wonderful painless existence.

* * * * *

After brushing off the snow and ice from her pants and jacket, Gail looked around to get her bearings. As soon as her eyes caught hold of Damara and Louise, she ran as fast as she could toward them. She was never as happy to see anyone before in her life.

"Damara!" she yelled out. "It's me, Gail! I was with Carrie... do you remember me?"

Arvol grabbed Gail by both arms and shook her violently. He demanded that she take them to Carrie at once, but before Gail could say a word, Byron started his chanting again. This time, Byron was looking Devon Arvol directly in the eyes.

"LJ mad... he kill... Byron help... yes, yes... Byron help."

Arvol was now furious. He wanted nothing more than to find Carrie, but the more he tried to shut up Byron, the louder Byron chanted.

"Damn it, you fool... shut up!" Arvol yelled.

"No, Byron help!"

"Damn moron, get out of my way or I'll shoot you!"

With a gun now pointing directly at Byron's head, Damara screamed, *"No!* Leave him alone!"

Louise and Chad could not believe what they were watching. It was crazy the way Arvol was acting.

"Oh, Byron not helping, Byron help..." Byron's chants were getting louder and stronger.

"He is trying to tell us something!" Damara demanded. "Listen to him."

"He isn't saying shit!" Arvol yelled. "I need to find Carrie."

"Blonde not in cave... Byron help..."

"What?" Damara asked. "Where is the blonde girl, Byron?"

Louise had had just about enough of this foolishness, but she didn't know how to stop it. Someone was going to be killed if everyone didn't calm down and take control of their own actions.

"This is ridiculous!" Louise yelled out.

"Shut the fuck up!" Arvol yelled, trying to maneuver around Byron, but Byron was too strong and too big. Byron stood his ground.

"He's trying to tell us something!" Damara yelled out again.

As they continued to argue, they were completely unaware of the old man lurking in the shadows with a gun.

* * * * *

The haze of a blaring light was penetrating deep into his eyes and the pain would be unforgiving if he gave in. His side was throbbing and no matter how hard he tried, Mark refused to wake up. The more he wanted to sleep and forget about the pain, the more focused Gail's face became.

"Gail!" Mark yelled out, as he tried to sit up. "Sweet Jesus!" he screamed, as the pain tore through his chest. He yearned for a strong deep breath, but with the air, his body also demanded a cough. As he pulled his hand away from his mouth, Mark panicked when he saw all the blood.

"Shit!" Mark whispered. "Shit, shit, shit."

* * * * *

"Shouldn't we look for Mark?" Louise asked. "He's been gone a while now."

"Mark?" Gail asked excitedly while looking around for him. "My husband's here?"

"He was," Arvol yelled out angrily. "That is until he ran inside to save your damn ass!"

"But that crazy man is in there!"

"Byron's mad... Byron's mad..." Byron chanted.

Damara stared over at Byron who now had a look of terror on his face. As she followed his gaze toward a line of shadowed trees, Damara screamed.

"No, the crazy man is here!" LJ slowly walked out from the shadows pointing a shotgun directly at them. "Let us go into the house where it is warm..." he said in English with his deep French accent.

The Agency

* * * * *

The head agent sat nervously in the back of the helicopter waiting for his signal from Devon Arvol, but something was bothering him. It had been quite some time since they had dropped the small group off, and they should have contacted him way before this. He pulled out his beeper to make sure the batteries were still good then slipped it back into his pocket.

"How long do we wait, sir?" the young agent asked.

The head agent smiled and replied, "As long as it takes."

As they admired the view from the open helicopter door, the agent's phone rang.

"Smitty here," he answered.

"Agent Smith, this is Dr. Lewis. I need your position."

"Sir, yes. We are about five miles from the house, sir. I am waiting for Agent Arvol's signal, sir."

"I just got a call from another agent and I'm not happy," Lewis stated sternly. "I gave you a mission and I'm not sure it is being carried out."

"Sir?" the agent was surprised at the doctor's actuations. He had followed Devon's orders explicitly.

"Now, this is what I want you to do..."

* * * * *

Mark lay on the floor trying not to scream as he breathed. The pain was almost unbearable now, but he knew he had to act fast if he was to survive. There was no way he could get off the floor and he knew there was no way he could crawl. As he lay helplessly on the cold linoleum floor, Mark watched the minute hand of the wall clock tick down to the moment of his death.

"What a way to go," he said to no one but the walls.

* * * * *

Carrie opened her eyes and looked around the room. It was dark and she didn't know what time it was or how long she had been asleep. A dark figure stood quietly in the middle of the room. The longer Carrie stared at it, the more it seemed to fade away.

"Nadia?" Carrie whispered. "Is that you?"

A strong urge of needing to be downstairs hit Carrie like a ton of bricks. Without thinking, she almost jumped off the bed and headed for the door. It wasn't until she was standing in the foyer that she remember her injured leg. The blood was pooling around her on the floor, but there was no pain.

I've gotten this far! she said to herself. At the same time, Carrie wondered if she was dreaming.

The urge pulled her toward the kitchen and when she saw Mark on the floor, her heart skipped several beats.

"Mark?" Carrie whispered, not daring to speak out. "Are you all right?"

As he watched the blood flowing freely from Carrie's pants, Mark stated, "I think I'm doing better than you. Are *you* all right?"

"I think we've both been better," she answered, searching for something to use on his wound. "We've got to get you out of here."

"And where do you suggest we go?" he asked sarcastically. "We don't have a car and there's a crazy guy running around with a shotgun."

"Yeah, I know. He got me too." Carrie wrapped an old tablecloth around Mark's chest and pulled on it tightly. He moaned but didn't object. "I need you to stand up."

He laughed slightly and tried to roll over. "Damn!" he almost screamed.

"Come on, Mark," Carrie urged. "Ignore the pain!"

Mark took in a deep breath and held it as he got up onto his hands and knees. Then he let it out slowly before taking in another deep breath. When he was on his feet, the room began to spin and he thought he would be sick.

"Come on, we don't have much time," Carrie demanded, as she guided him through the living room.

"Um, Carrie?" Mark asked.

"What?"

"You're leaving a trail," Mark said with a worried look.

As Carrie glanced over her shoulder, she said, "Crap! I'll clean it up once I get you upstairs."

It seemed like hours, but it was only a few minutes before she was able to get Mark into the spare bedroom and onto a bed. In the bathroom, Carrie found an old sheet that she used as a bandage to wrap her leg. With the bleeding under control, she was able to wipe up her blood from the stairs and foyer. She was feeling weak, but aside from that, there was still no pain. When she was finished, Carrie quickly searched the kitchen for drinks and food. Although she had no idea where anyone else was, her number one concern was staying alive. When she met back up with Mark, her arms were shielding two glasses of milk and two sandwiches, and her face had a big, warm smile.

* * * * *

The snow was falling now and the sun had completely left the horizon. The only light was from the kitchen window several yards away. The small group stared oddly at the old Frenchman who was pointing a loaded shotgun at them.

"And what do you hope to accomplish with that?" Arvol asked him. When the old man gave him an evil glare, Arvol continued. "There are five of us and only one of you!"

"Five?" the old man asked.

As Arvol glanced around, he counted the three women and himself, but Byron was nowhere in sight.

"Okay, four," Devon Arvol corrected himself. "So what do you plan on doing... killing us all."

"Perhaps," he replied.

"This is nuts!" Louise stated. "Uncle, you can't keep killing everyone."

"Uncle? I am no one's uncle."

"Oh, I beg your pardon," Damara shouted out. "You are very much an uncle."

"And whose uncle would I be now?"

As Louise and Damara glanced at each other they said together with their arms folded, "Ours!"

"Who are you?" he asked with his head cocked to one side.

* * * * *

As they ate, they talked. Although he wasn't hungry, Mark felt the least he could do for Carrie was to at least give it a try.

"So, are you not concerned that there is no pain in your leg?" he asked.

"Sort of," Carrie answered while chewing on her food and drinking her milk.

"I mean, that isn't normal!" Mark said, pointing to her injured leg.

"I know," Carrie answered.

Mark shook his head. "Carrie, your leg is broken in two and you're walking on it. That is impossible!"

"I know," she answered.

"And?"

"And what?" Carrie asked, finishing off her food and using the back of her hand to wipe her mouth. "I'm going to go and see if I can find out what's going on. You stay here."

Mark didn't reply. He could not believe his own eyes. It was physically impossible for Carrie to be able to walk on that leg, yet she was able to. Either he was hallucinating, or something very unnatural was going on in this house.

* * * * *

"Uncle LJ, don't you recognize us?" Louise asked.

"Actually, for a dead man he looks quite good," Damara stated sarcastically.

"How do you know my name?" LJ demanded.

"But to kill your own brothers. Now that's pretty bad," Louise squealed, not taking her eyes off him.

LJ remained silent and stared at them, his eyes darting between Louise and Damara.

"And to think that I was eager to meet *all* of my family," Damara laughed.

"You are lying!" he shouted.

"*We* don't lie," Louise shouted back. "My mother was Maria Lee LeBoisne. I'm Nidra Louise... LJ."

LJ took a step back and froze in place. His face was full of terror and his eyes emanated his shock. Devon didn't like the look on the old man's face and gripped his gun firmly behind his back. Both Louise and Damara were ready to challenge this guy and he knew there was probably nothing he could do to stop them.

"And *my* mother was Nadia Louise!" Damara yelled out proudly.

As the two women stood firmly in front of the stunned LJ, Devon slowly inched his way in the direction of the house.

"What's the matter, Uncle," Damara mocked. "Did the cat get your tongue?"

LJ began to laugh. Before long, the laughter was echoing between the surrounding hillsides. A wild and eerie laughter bounced amongst the group and chilled them to the bone.

"This is wonderful!" LJ shouted out. "The blood came to me! Finally, I get a break."

* * * * *

The men in black jumpsuits picked their places on the far side of the old house. From their stations, they could not see the small group shivering in the clearing just beyond the old shed. Unfortunately, they had no way of knowing the fate that awaited the small group. The head agent slowly crept toward the front porch and peered around the corner. To his surprise, he came face to face with a woman wearing a light bathrobe.

Not knowing what to say or do, the head agent removed his sunglasses and smiled. The woman smiled back.

"Um," he coughed. "Do you live here, ma'am? Is this your house?"

The woman stared at him as though she didn't understand. She continued to smile.

"Ma'am, we're here to help our friends. We received a call and..." he stopped in mid-sentence realizing that something was very wrong. "Ma'am?"

The woman turned and slowly descended the steps into the newly fallen snow. She was barefoot. He watched her, mesmerized, as she headed for the other side of the house completely unaffected by the cold. Once she was out of sight, he quickly ran back to the other agents.

"You guys will not believe what's walking around," he panted.

"A crazy person?" one of the men asked.

"There's a lady out here in only her bathrobe!" he declared.

The other three agents gave him a weird look and glanced around. "Sir, it's got to be almost freezing out here, are you sure?"

* * * * *

Carrie had made it as far as the back steps before she had to stop and rest. The pain in her leg was slowly returning and it was now too painful for her to put her full weight on it. She tried to rub her leg, but that only made it worse. Tears formed in her eyes and she wasn't sure if she could go on. She was just about ready to give up when something caught her eye. Something was moving by the shed. The harder she strained to see what or who it was, the more it looked like...

"Agent Clarke?"

The sound of a human voice jolted Carrie back to the real world. When she twisted to see who was talking to her, she almost lost her balance but not before knocking over a pail that was on the step next to her. After crashing to the ground, she quickly glanced over to the shed, but the person was gone.

"Yes, who are you?"

"Agent Clarington, ma'am," he answered. "We need to know where the others are."

"Well," Carrie answered sarcastically, "I'm here, there's an injured agent upstairs in the first bedroom, and I have no idea where in the hell the others are right now."

"Ma'am?" he replied.

* * * * *

Gail stood frozen in her tracks. The last few days had been not only the most terrifying, but also the most invigorating days of her life. Never before had she felt so alive, so important, but as she stood frozen in time from both the terror and the cold, Gail noticed a solemnly figure approaching from the small trail that wound behind the old shed. The person was wearing what appeared to be a pink bathrobe. As the person got closer, Gail immediately recognized her. She knew that the woman approaching was the same woman she saw in the mirror back at the hotel with Carrie.

"Oh, my God!" Gail whispered.

Damara and Louise were hesitant to remove their gaze from LJ, but as they followed her stare, they both gasped when they saw the woman.

"Mom?" Damara mouthed.

LJ continued his demands to know who they were and what they wanted, but as each set of eyes slowly moved away from him, he, too, eventually turned to face the woman in the pink bathrobe.

A sudden eerie quiet blanketed the forest and not a word was spoken. All eyes were now on this mysterious creature that stood only a few yards away.

"What in the name of hell is going on here?" LJ demanded.

"Pretty woman help... pretty woman... yes, yes..." Byron chanted, rocking in place.

"Is this the woman you were taking about?" LJ asked. "I thought you were talking about her." LJ pointed at Gail as he said *her*. "Don't move or I will strike you where you stand!" he yelled at Devon.

LJ backed down toward the woman not taking his eyes or the shotgun off the small group who stood shivering on the snowy mountain slope. The closer he got to the woman, the further away she seemed.

"What in the..." The more LJ tried to see her, the more the woman faded away. "What kind of game are you playing?"

LJ turned and fired the shotgun directly into the woman wearing the pink robe. She didn't fall nor did she flinch. He turned back to the mesmerized group with total confusion written all over his face. It was obvious that LJ did not know what to do. Suddenly, a warm breeze touched his face and he jumped back. When he turned to see what she was doing now, the woman in the pink robe was gone. Dazed from both confusion and terror, LJ turned his full angry attention back on the small group that was huddling close together for warmth.

"You'll have to kill us all, Uncle LJ!" Damara yelled.

Louise grabbed her arm and said sternly, "Damara, don't!"

Damara was beyond stopping. "Uncle LJ, did you hear me! I said you'll have to kill us all!"

LJ wasn't sure if he should be happy or afraid.

Damara screamed, "I am Damara Louise Van Brunt. My mother was Nadia Louise Kundick and her sister is standing right here! I am *your* niece!"

"No, quiet!" Louise yelled at her.

"We know everything, Uncle LJ!" Damara screamed. *"Everything!* Give up, Uncle LJ, give up!"

LJ laughed hysterically. "I will now avenge my mother!" LJ lifted his shotgun and pointed it directly at Louise. "If you are who you say you are, then my job is done. The blood will be clean!"

As he pulled the trigger, LJ stepped back from the shockwave. Louise closed her eyes and thought only of her sister and mother. Gail prayed that death would come quickly and Arvol wondered how many shots it would take before everyone was taken down.

As the blast headed toward them, their ears popped as a pressure forced them closer together. The small round bullets hissed past them faster than their eyes could focus. Gail gasped and Louise screamed, but Damara stood firm.

"It won't work, Uncle!" she yelled. "She won't let you kill us!"

LJ looked down the shaft of his shotgun and shook his head. As he cocked the barrel to shoot again, two hands gripped the shaft and ripped it from his grip. Terror filled LJ's eyes as he stood face to face with his younger brother Byron.

"No!" Byron said defiantly. "I will not let you hurt them! They are family."

"You stupid moron; get out of my way!" LJ yelled.

"No!" Byron shouted.

Part 8

Carrie stretched and shifted her hips. Her mouth was dry and she wanted a drink of water. When she tried to roll over, the pain shot through her body as a shockwave flows through the ground. With her eyes wide open, the realization of where she was came flooding back.

"Good morning," Arvol said, taking a sip of hot coffee. "How are you feeling?"

"Ugh!" Carrie groaned.

"That good!" Devon Arvol chuckled. "I'm glad to see my old Carrie is back."

The nurse entered the room with a small silver tray. "Time for her medication," she announced. "It's better if she has her pain medication before her breakfast is brought in."

After the nurse left, Carrie smiled at Devon. "What a trip!"

"Yep, you seemed to have solved it again, Ms. Clarke," a voice from the door stated.

"Jeff!" Carrie yelled and held out her arms.

After a rather long embrace, Jeff nodded over at Arvol and sat next to Carrie on her bed.

"How's Mark and Gail?" Carrie asked.

"They are just fine... just fine," he replied.

After breakfast, Damara entered the room with Louise. "Hey, you," Damara said, kissing Carrie on the forehead. "How's the leg?"

"Okay, I guess," Carrie answered, staring at her leg that was hanging in traction. "I can't move or anything, but I guess it's okay."

"Does it hurt?" Louise asked.

"Only when I laugh," Carrie laughed and groaned.

As they all laughed and released their held up anxieties, Gail entered.

"Sounds like you're having way too much fun in here!"

"Hi," Carrie said, as they hugged. "How's Mark?"

"Oh, he'll be here a while," Gail said. "But he'll be just fine."

"Good, I was really worried about him," Carrie confessed.

Gail glanced over at Damara and Louise and asked, "So, would you like to tell her what happened?"

"What happened?" Carrie asked with a worried look.

"Oh, nothing much," Damara smiled.

"I read the reports," Jeff interjected. "I didn't read anything unusual. The younger brother took the shotgun and handed it to Devon, right?"

"Well, sorta," Louise smiled.

"What do you mean sorta?" Dr. Jeffery Lewis asked. "The report... are you saying the report is not accurate?"

"Oh, it's accurate. We just didn't put everything in it that's all," Devon added.

"What are you guys talking about?" Carrie asked. "What didn't you report, Devon?"

"The little part about my mother," Damara giggled.

"Your mom? Nadia?" Carrie asked, trying to sit up in bed.

"Ah, yep, that's the one!" Damara replied.

Carrie and Lewis stared at each other but both having different thoughts. Carrie was excited realizing that she wasn't the only one to see Nadia, and Lewis feeling confused not understanding what in the world they were talking about.

"Really!" Carrie stated, now highly interested.

"Here, let me help you," Damara volunteered, sliding another pillow under Carrie's head.

"It was very exciting," Louise added. "She actually saved us!"

"No," Carrie exclaimed. "Really?"

"Yes, really," Damara added in.

"Would someone please tell me what is going on?"

Damara ignored Lewis and continued to talk. "And I'm going back with Aunt Nidra and we're going to collect the family pictures. I even found some old diaries. I can't wait to get back there and read them."

"What about Byron," Carrie asked.

"Well," Damara started to say but was cut off.

"As I said, would someone tell me what is going on?" Lewis demanded again.

Devon calmly took Lewis by the arm and led him to the door. "Come with me and I'll explain..."

The women continued to explain to Carrie what happened and how Byron saved them. She listened to every little detail, especially the stories about Nadia and how she showed up to save everyone.

* * * * *

The hours had led into days, and the days had led into months. Before she knew it, Damara's life was heading into summer. The roses were in full bloom and the landscape was beautiful. She waved as Byron hollered at her from the shed. Louise handed her a glass of lemonade and they both sat on the porch swing to enjoy the wonderful aroma and sights.

"So, what do we do now?" Louise asked.

"I don't know," Damara said. "We've gone through all the pictures and read all the diaries. We've found old family records and now understand everything. It's not so bad actually."

"No, it's not and what is great is that these people are *our* family. I'm proud of them even if they were a little off."

"Me, too," Damara added, resting her head on her aunt's shoulder. "What I just can't figure out is why."

"What do you mean, sweetie?"

"Well, here I thought it was only Parker and me. We would have done anything to have a family. I mean more than each other and our mother. And here they had a huge family and each other and they threw it all away... why?"

"Well," Louise tried to explain. "I guess that when you have it every day, you just don't know what you've got. Since you live it, you get used to it. So I guess you get to where you don't really want it... or you think you don't really want it."

Damara laughed. "I think I get what you're trying to say."

"I hope so because I'm not so sure if I really get it or not and I may need you to explain it to me!"

They both laughed.

"Well, I'm glad I have my family now," Damara added.

"Me, too," Nidra Louise said. As she stood up she added, "Bob and the others should be back anytime now."

"Yeah, I'm glad that Parker and Paulie have hit it off. They're good for each other."

"I'm going to go see what Byron is doing," Louise said, as she descended the old front porch.

The cell phone lying next to Damara rang and she knew right away who it was. "Hi, Carrie!"

"Hey, what's up?"

"Nothing," Damara replied. "Just enjoying being home."

"So which home are you enjoying right now?"

"Does it really matter?" Damara asked.

"No, not really," Carrie surmised.

They continued to talk as Louise entered the small shed.

"What ya doing, Byron?" she asked.

"Byron clean... Byron clean," he answered.

"What are these?" Louise asked, picking up the strange instruments that resembled the tools her dentist used.

Byron looked at her and then looked at the shiny slender tools in her hands. A worried look appeared on his face. At first, Louise wasn't sure what he was feeling, but then Byron smiled and took the tools from her hands.

"LJ's," he said, tossing them into a trashcan. "You don't worry, Nidra, Byron clean... Byron clean good..."

"Yes," Louise said smiling and leaning over to give him a big hug. "I love you, Uncle Byron." Then she kissed him on the cheek.

"Byron loves you, too... Byron clean... yes, Byron clean..."

"Yes," Louise said, as she left the shed. "Byron clean."

* * * * *

Mark and Gail stood calmly at the edge of the water and held hands. Gail used her binoculars to view the couple in the boat.

"Now don't let them see you," Mark whispered.

Gail sighed. "Why are you whispering? It's not like they can hear you!"

"You never know," Mark answered.

The Agency

"They have to be a mile out, Mark. There's no way they can hear you!"

"Look, just because Jeff gave you this assignment doesn't mean you're a full agent yet," he replied.

Gail took in a long deep breath and resisted the urge to smack the binoculars over Mark's head.

"Well, this *is* my assignment and I say we don't have to whisper."

"And I'm saying you still have to be careful."

The two continued to argue as the couple in the boat proceeded to dump a small packet into the lake.

"Look, Mark," Gail stated firmly. "You promised you'd follow my intuitions from now on... remember?"

"Yes, but all I'm saying is..." Mark stated firmly, as Gail removed her cell phone from her purse. "What are you doing?"

"Making the call."

"What call?" he asked.

"The call I'm supposed to make once they drop the package."

"But they haven't dropped it yet," he said, rolling his eyes.

All Gail did was sigh again and entered the memorized code into her cell phone. After clicking the phone off, she turned and headed for their car.

"Gail!" Mark whined. "We're not done here."

"I am," she replied, opening the car door.

"We have to wait..."

But before Mark could finished his sentence a police helicopter flew overhead and headed straight for the couple in the boat.

"...Gail, you should not have made that call!"

Gail watched in her binoculars as two men in scuba gear surfaced. One was holding the small package. As they approached the car, Mark's jaw almost hit the concrete that the car was resting on.

"How did you know?" he asked her.

Gail accepted the package and laid it on the backseat. She nodded to the two dripping agents then closed her car door.

"Are we leaving or are we going stay for a while longer to enjoy the view," she asked.

Mark shook his head and tried to remember. Did he see them drop the package? *No...*

Special Recognition and Thank You's

Mr. and Mrs. Mark J. Lumer *"Mark and Gail"* are long time friends of mine and I would like to thank them personally for being a special addition of The Agency Series. Mark and Gail have been married for over 35 years. They have three grown children and have been blessed with two grandchildren.

Mark is currently the Principal Assistant responsible for Contracting for the U.S. Army Space and Missile Defense Command (SMDC) in Washington, D.C., Huntsville, AL., Colorado Springs, CO., Frederick, MD, and Kwajalein Missile Range in the Marshall Islands.

Gail works for the U.S. Army Contracting Agency which is a Field Operating Agency reporting to the Assistant Secretary of the Army for Acquisition, Logistics, and Technology.

Perhaps when they get to the retirement age, they will find themselves as Secret Agents for The Agency in Oklahoma. After all, once touched by The Agency, your life is forever changed.

Please visit The Agency website at: www.TheAgencySeries.com and urge Mark and Gail to take on another assignment in the near future so we can all enjoy their adventures.